FEATURING SHADWELL RAFFERTY

A PENGUIN
Mystery

The
Disappearance
OF
Sherlock
Holmes

LARRY MILLETT

Author of
*Sherlock Holmes and the
Secret Alliance*

ISBN 0-14-200340-9

9 780142 003404

50699>

EAN

A PENGUIN MYSTERY

THE DISAPPEARANCE OF SHERLOCK HOLMES

A former columnist for the *St. Paul Pioneer Press*, Larry Millett is also the author of *Sherlock Holmes and the Red Demon*, *Sherlock Holmes and the Ice Palace Murders*, *Sherlock Holmes and the Rune Stone Mystery*, and *Sherlock Holmes and the Secret Alliance*, all available from Penguin. He lives in St. Paul, Minnesota.

The Disappearance of Sherlock Holmes

*A Mystery Featuring
Shadwell Rafferty*

LARRY MILLETT

PENGUIN BOOKS

PENGUIN BOOKS

Published by the Penguin Group

Penguin Group (USA) Inc., 375 Hudson Street, New York, New York 10014, U.S.A.
Penguin Books Ltd, 80 Strand, London WC2R 0RL, England
Penguin Books Australia Ltd, 250 Camberwell Road,
Camberwell, Victoria 3124, Australia
Penguin Books Canada Ltd, 10 Alcorn Avenue, Toronto, Ontario, Canada M4V 3B2
Penguin Books India (P) Ltd, 11 Community Centre,
Panchsheel Park, New Delhi—110 017, India
Penguin Books (N.Z.) Ltd, Cnr Rosedale and Airborne Roads,
Albany, Auckland, New Zealand
Penguin Books (South Africa) (Pty) Ltd, 24 Sturdee Avenue,
Rosebank, Johannesburg 2196, South Africa

Penguin Books Ltd, Registered Offices: 80 Strand, London WC2R 0RL, England

First published in the United States of America by Viking Penguin,
a member of Penguin Putnam Inc. 2002
Published in Penguin Books 2003

1 3 5 7 9 10 8 6 4 2

PUBLISHER'S NOTE
This is a work of fiction. Names, characters, places, and incidents either
are the product of the author's imagination or are used fictitiously, and any
resemblance to actual persons, living or dead, business establishments,
events, or locales is entirely coincidental.

THE LIBRARY OF CONGRESS HAS CATALOGED THE HARDCOVER EDITION AS FOLLOWS:
Millett, Larry, 1947–
The disappearance of Sherlock Holmes : a mystery
featuring Shadwell Rafferty / Larry Millett.
p. cm.
ISBN 0-670-03140-2 (hc.)
ISBN 0 14 20.0340 9 (pbk.)
1. Holmes, Sherlock (Fictitious character)—Fiction.
2. Private investigators—England—Fiction. I. Title.

PS3563.I42193 D57 2002
813'.54—dc21   2002025886

Printed in the United States of America
Set in Cochin   Designed by Erin Benach

To Al Eisele and Al Silverman,
who got me started

ACKNOWLEDGMENTS

A number of people helped me as I wrote this book. My agents, Al Eisele and Bob Barnett, provided expert advice and encouragement. At Viking Penguin, Carolyn Carlson did her usual fine job of editing. Thanks also go to Lucia Watson for her help along the way. And, as always, I owe a debt of gratitude to my wife, Stacey, and my youngest children, Alexandra and Corey, for putting up with a writer in the family.

The Disappearance of
Sherlock Holmes

Prologue

§ ξ

"You Do Know Who I Am, Don't You?"

NEW YORK CITY, MONDAY, JULY 16, 1900

Well past midnight, in fog so thick that it seemed to have swallowed up all of Manhattan, Sherlock Holmes stood beneath the portico of St. Paul's Chapel on Broadway, waiting for a ghost from his past. Holmes, of course, put no more credence in otherworldly specters than he did in fairies or leprechauns, and the elusive figure he hoped to capture was, he knew, as dangerously made of flesh and blood as anyone could be. Yet there had been times over the past fortnight when his adversary had indeed appeared to possess almost superhuman powers.[1]

Time and again, Holmes had been put on the defensive, kept off balance by a wild proliferation of clues—as well as several stunning surprises—that threatened to make a mockery of his legendary deductive prowess. He had been impersonated, embarrassed, misled, even framed, and worst of all he was still searching for the woman whose abduction had touched off these bizarre events. In Holmes's mind, the case had come to resemble a particularly vivid and outrageous dream, only he knew there was as yet no waking from it. Even so, he was not deceived by the case's fantastic qualities. Behind all that had happened, he knew, lay at least one criminal mind of extraordinary calculation and malice.

Holmes had been led to believe that his adversary and tormentor was none other than the notorious Chicago gangster, Abe Slaney. Two years earlier, in England, Holmes had captured Slaney after solving the mysterious code of the dancing men. It was a case that had added much to Holmes's luster, both in England and America. Slaney had later been sent to prison for murder, only to perish during an escape attempt. Or so it was thought.[2]

Now, he seemed to have come back from the dead, although Holmes was by no means convinced that Slaney had in fact managed his own resurrection. Until he saw Slaney—he of the bristling black beard and dark glowering eyes—in the flesh, Holmes would remain a skeptic. What he did know for certain was that someone—if not Slaney, then an accomplice or sympathizer—had masterminded an elaborate criminal scheme. Indeed, so many questions remained as to the true identity of his nemesis that Holmes had by now decided to refer to him simply as the Conspirator.

Holmes had already pursued this shadowy figure, along with the woman he and his confederates had kidnapped, all the way from England to New York. It had been a long and frustrating chase for Holmes, with many setbacks, but that was all about to change. Holmes had finally managed to set a trap for the Conspirator, and he planned to spring it this very night.

The trap was a complicated business, but everything had gone smoothly until the fog began rolling in from the East River after midnight. Settling over the city like a bowl of warm, watery porridge, it left Holmes—and the watchers all around, Watson among them—effectively blind. Even so, it was too late to back off. Holmes knew this might be his best chance to capture his enemy and free the kidnapped woman, and he did not intend to miss it.

Why the Conspirator had chosen St. Paul's Chapel to exchange his hostage for money was only one of many mysteries associated with the case. Dominated by an English-style steeple more than two hundred feet high, the small stone church—where George Washington had once worshipped—lay in the busy heart of Lower Manhattan. The chapel's tall portico, supported by four massive Ionic columns, was particularly exposed, since it nestled right up to the sidewalk on Broadway.[3]

If secrecy was the Conspirator's goal, Holmes thought, he certainly could have chosen any number of less visible places. Even the other end of the chapel, set well back from Church Street behind a leafy yard sown with crooked tombstones and guarded by a high iron fence, would have afforded far more privacy. The ransom instructions had been very specific, however. The exchange was to take place in the portico, and nowhere else.

On any other night, Holmes's vantage point would have afforded him a magnificent view up Park Row past the bulbous-roofed post office toward city hall and the cluster of tall buildings occupied by New York's major newspapers, which jostled for a place on the skyline as fiercely as they competed for stories. In the other direction, to the south and east along Broadway, rose the mighty business temples of the financial district, including the recently completed Park Row Building, then the tallest in the world.[4]

This magnificent urban tapestry might have been on the other side of the world as far as Holmes was concerned, for in the fog and darkness he could see little beyond the tip of his long nose. The suffocating fog, however, had not dampened the usual sounds of the night. Standing as close as he was to Broadway, Holmes could clearly hear the early morning life of the city—draymen rattling uptown with their carts, the occasional creak of carriage wheels, the fast-moving footsteps of late night pedestrians, drunkards breaking out in song as they wandered down from one of the Bowery's dreary gin mills.

Holmes, who had arrived hours in advance of the purported hostage exchange, welcomed these sounds, for otherwise there would have been nothing to occupy his senses except the rhythmic cadence of his own quiet breathing. Between breaths, Holmes sometimes encountered moments of astonishing silence—the one commodity thought unobtainable in the ceaseless din of Manhattan. In these eerie silences, amid the impenetrable fog, Holmes almost felt as though he were floating in a cloud, untethered from the earth and its mortal destinies.

Still, Holmes knew better than to trust such ethereal sensations. His nemesis, somewhere in the murk out beyond the circling tombstones, was very much of this world, and matters of life and death were at stake. At any moment, the Conspirator would arrive at St. Paul's, supposedly to receive his illicit payment of ten thousand dollars in cash, after which he was to turn over the woman whose kidnapping had electrified England. Holmes knew better, however, for the Conspirator almost certainly planned a murderous double cross. Abetted by the forces of law and order, Holmes would be ready for him.

Watson was but a short distance away in the graveyard along Vesey Street on the north side of the chapel. Inspector Wilson Hargreave of the New York Police Department was also on hand, along with half a dozen of his best men. Hargreave, who had been of great help to Holmes in his earlier capture of Slaney, was confident no one could slip through his protective cordon, regardless of the fog. At the sound of a police whistle—which Holmes, Watson and all the policemen carried—everyone would converge on the portico, and the Conspirator would be caught in a perfect trap. It all seemed foolproof.

Watson, who had arrived on the scene less than half an hour earlier following a night filled with strange adventures, was not quite so confident, however. Upon reaching the chapel, he had talked briefly with Holmes, who insisted that save for the fog everything was going exactly as planned. Yet as Watson waited nervously in the grave-yard, he found himself assailed by terrible premonitions, which had gathered at the back of his mind like ravenous wolves drawn to the scent of disaster. Watson had experi-enced such intense premonitions only once before, on that fateful day nine years earlier when he and Holmes had hiked toward the haunted chasm of the Reichenbach River in Switzerland. Watson's fears had been well-founded then. This time, he prayed he would be wrong.[5]

While Watson fretted, Holmes continued his calm wait in the blank stillness, his acute senses alive to every possi-bility of the night. Despite his careful preparations, Holmes knew that the Conspirator would not be easily captured. In anticipation of trouble, Holmes had armed himself with a heavy pistol and was fully prepared to use it.

Holmes was trying to stare through the fog, a futile ef-fort despite his unusually acute vision, when he felt a gust of wind—the first he had noticed all night—blow in from the east. The breeze quickly accelerated and before long the fog began to part. Broadway and its tall buildings came into view. So, too, did the dark mass of the old Astor House hotel directly across Vesey Street to the north. As Holmes scanned this newly revealed scene, searching for some sign of the Conspirator or his confederates, he heard, from behind him, a voice that whispered, "Come in this in-stant, alone, or she dies."

Holmes turned around and was startled to see a faint light glowing through the big Palladian window between the chapel's entrance doors. He also noted that one of the window's small panes, just above the sill, had been neatly punched out. The voice must have come from inside the chapel, yet Holmes did not see how this could be. He and Hargreave had thoroughly searched the chapel before they took up their positions. Moreover, they had taken great care to turn off the lights and secure the doors.

Yet it was now obvious that the Conspirator, perhaps with his kidnapped victim, had somehow gotten inside. Holmes's first thought was to blow his whistle and bring in Hargreave's men to storm the chapel, capturing the Conspirator before he could escape as mysteriously as he had arrived. Further thought, however, revealed the flaw in this approach. Holmes had hoped to take the Conspirator by surprise, but that opportunity was now lost. This meant that the Conspirator—whether Slaney or someone else—might well have time to carry out his threat and kill the hostage before she could be freed.

Holmes finally decided to keep his whistle in his pocket, at least for the time being, and enter the chapel alone. He was well aware how risky this would be. Yet he also knew that he was still alive only because the Conspirator had chosen not to kill him. Standing with his back to the window only a few feet away, Holmes had presented an easy target to the man inside. The man had not taken the shot, however, and Holmes thought he knew why. More importantly, Holmes believed it was still possible to snap shut the jaws of his trap, for he doubted that the Conspirator knew how many policemen lay in wait just outside the chapel.

Holmes checked his pistol one last time, returned it to his coat pocket and then went to the nearest of the tall, pedimented doors within the portico. Originally, these had been rear doors—the chapel had been designed to face Church Street rather than Broadway—but they were now the most commonly used entrances. The last time Holmes had checked this door, it had been tightly secured like all the others. He tried it again. It was unlocked.

As Holmes prepared to open the door, he wondered whether the woman really was inside. He couldn't be sure. But he did know that Slaney—a man of dark passion and fierce will, and a convicted killer—was entirely capable of carrying out his threat to kill the woman. And if the Conspirator were someone else—well, the result might be the same. Holmes could not let that happen, for he had grown very fond of the beautiful young woman whose life now lay in his hands. Taking a deep breath, he pushed open the door and stepped into the chapel.

Because what was now the front of the church had originally been its back, the door led through a small vestibule directly to one side of the sanctuary. Holmes stopped at the vestibule's inner door and peered out into the long, narrow chapel, which had galleries on either side overlooking rows of pews separated by a central aisle. The light was so dim that Holmes could make out no more than a dozen rows of pews before the chapel dissolved into darkness.

"Up here," a man's voice said as Holmes stepped through the doorway. The man was standing in the chapel's ornate pulpit, immediately to Holmes's left behind the communion rail. Illuminated by a small overhead lamp, the man—whose hands rested in plain view on the pulpit's small lectern, as though to show he was not armed—looked down upon Holmes with a kind of malevolent amusement. Compactly built with a swarthy complexion, he had a thick black beard, a broad nose and small, crafty eyes. He wore dirty overalls—a detail Holmes noted with considerable interest—and when he spoke, his voice was disturbingly familiar.

"Welcome, Mr. Holmes," the man said. "You do know who I am, don't you?"

"Yes," said Holmes. "I know. I must salute you, sir, on your enterprise and daring. It is quite a little game you have been playing. Now, however, it is time for the game to end, so I think it best that we get down at once to the business at hand. I suggest you begin by producing the woman."

"In due time, Mr. Holmes, in due time. I suggest you begin by producing the money. You've brought it, haven't you?"

"I have," Holmes lied, for the money had been with Watson all along.

"Show it to me."

"First, the woman. Where is she?"

"She is safe, so long as all those policemen outside don't try anything foolish. Oh yes, I know all about your plans with Inspector Hargreave. He's not bad as coppers go, but still a little slow, don't you think?"

"I believe he will prove quick enough for you."

"We'll see about that. Now, I must ask you once again, Mr. Holmes, to show me the money."

"No, I must see the woman first," Holmes repeated. "It is the only way you will receive payment."

The man, whose face was crisscrossed by shadows, stared down at Holmes and said, "You disappoint me, sir. Do you really think it is the money I want?"

"What more could a greedy criminal such as yourself desire?" Holmes asked contemptuously, although he had understood from the very beginning that the case wasn't really about money.

"You are what I want, Mr. Holmes," the man replied, his voice as cold and dry as dust, "and now, it would seem, I have you."

"I rather think it is the other way around," said Holmes, who reached for his whistle and blew a shrill warning out into the night.

On the following afternoon, the New York *World*, whose offices were only a few blocks from St. Paul's Chapel, broke a story that was destined to create a sensation on at least two continents. The story's headline — SHERLOCK HOLMES DISAPPEARS — was certainly eye-catching. However, a subhead below was even more shocking, for it announced: POLICE SUSPECT FAMED DETECTIVE IN KID-NAPPING AND MURDER.[6]

Book One

England

Chapter One

§ ₹

"The Message Is Quite Clear"

FROM THE NARRATIVE OF DR. JOHN WATSON:[1]

The beginning of what I do not hesitate to call the most challenging case ever to present itself to Sherlock Holmes may be dated to the afternoon of July 3, 1900, when a most curious letter arrived at our flat on Baker Street. We had spent the morning uneventfully—a not uncommon occurrence, or so it seemed, since the conclusion of the affair of the Napoleons in early June. Despite the drought of new cases, Holmes was in a surprisingly agreeable mood, for he had been hard at work on his latest monograph. It was devoted to a namesake, Henry H. Holmes, the notorious Chicago murderer of women. Sherlock Holmes believed that Henry Holmes and others like him represented a distinct species of murderer because of the serial nature of their crimes, and that certain characteristics might be common to all such killers.[2]

Holmes was descanting at some length and with much enthusiasm upon his theory when Mrs. Hudson brought up the mail. Like a hungry tiger pouncing upon its prey, Holmes quickly tore through the pile of letters, tossing aside those that appeared to offer no hope of satisfying his endless appetite for adventure. He had nearly completed this ritual when an envelope suddenly caught his attention. Holmes stared down at it, a look close to shock on his face, and then, without a word, handed it to me.

I saw at once why the envelope had produced such an electric reaction in Holmes, for in lieu of the usual return address was an inscription in the cipher of the "dancing men," as Holmes had dubbed it. We had first encountered this secret code two years earlier in the case of the Chicago criminal, Abe Slaney, who murdered Hilton Cubitt of Ridling Thorpe Manor. Holmes had easily broken the cipher, which employed a system of stick figures to signify letters of the alphabet. He then captured Slaney, who was in love with Cubitt's wife, Elsie. Slaney later admitted to his crime and was sent to Dartmoor prison, but he died not long thereafter while attempting to escape. There the case had ended, or so I had assumed.

"Well, my dear Watson, what are we to make of this?" Holmes asked as I handed back the envelope. "It would seem the dancing men are up to their old tricks."

"Perhaps it is from Elsie Cubitt herself," I noted. "After all, your relationship with her —"

"Is not a matter we shall discuss at the moment," Holmes said curtly. "Now, let us see who has written this singular missive."

Holmes slit open the envelope and found a sheet of common paper bearing a brief message written in the cipher. It did not take Holmes long to translate the chilling message, which he read aloud: "You are not finished with me, nor I with Elsie. Catch me if you can. I will be waiting. Abe Slaney." Holmes also translated the brief inscription on the envelope, which said simply: "Greetings from Chicago."

Holmes picked up his favorite pipe, lit it and said, "Well, Watson, do you still believe Mrs. Cubitt is the author of this letter?"

"Of course not, but it must certainly be someone's idea of a bad joke. Abe Slaney is dead, as is well known."

"Perhaps," said Holmes. "Yet if it is a joke, it is a very clever one, Watson, for who except Slaney — or one of his associates—would know of the dancing men? As you may remember, Slaney pleaded guilty to his crime, and the specifics of the cipher were never entered into the public record. Nor have you as yet committed the case to paper. I am therefore left to wonder how the cipher became a matter of general public knowledge."[3]

"I am sure I do not know, but I must remind you again that Slaney is dead."

"No, he is presumed to be dead, Watson, or have you forgotten?"

Before I could answer, Holmes began rummaging through one of the several stacks of yellowing newspapers that littered our quarters. He soon found—how I cannot say—the story he was looking for.

"Ah, here it is in the *Daily Telegraph*, from last March 15. I will read you the first few paragraphs: 'Authorities in Devon have abandoned their search for Abe Slaney, the Chicago criminal serving a long term at Princetown Prison for the murder in 1898 of Mr. Hilton Cubitt in Norfolk. It is now believed that Slaney, who escaped from the prison two days ago, was drowned in Plymouth Sound, which he apparently attempted to navigate in a small rowboat stolen from a local fisherman. The search for Slaney had concentrated in Plymouth following the discovery of several articles of prison clothing in a trash barrel near a small inlet where the boat was kept. Inspector Barrington of the Devon constabulary said Slaney "could not have survived" the storm, even though his body has never been found.'"[4]

"So you believe Slaney might still be alive?"

"I believe nothing, Watson, as I have insufficient evidence to form an opinion one way or the other. Slaney could indeed be dead, though I would point out to you that, insofar as can be gleaned from the newspapers, his body remains unrecovered to this day. Or, he could be very much alive and the author of the letter we have just received. Or—"

"Someone else could have written the letter," I said. "But why?"

"Perhaps to attract my attention, Watson. If so, the writer's strategy must be accounted a success. I would also point out that the postmark on the letter is in many ways as intriguing as the letter itself."

I looked at the envelope again and saw that it had been sent from North Walsham, a small Norfolk village seven miles from Ridling Thorpe Manor, where Elsie Cubitt— who had attempted suicide after her husband's death but ultimately recovered—now lived as a wealthy widow.

I knew at once what Holmes intended to do. "I will begin packing," I said, "since I imagine we shall be gone for several days."

"Be quick about it," Holmes said, "for we have not one moment to spare. It is entirely possible that Elsie Cubitt's life may again be in great danger. Now, if memory serves me correctly, there is a train at five o'clock, which will take us to North Walsham. We should just have time to catch it."

We reached North Walsham just before dusk and hired the first carriage we found. Once we had settled into our seats, Holmes instructed the driver to proceed "with all due speed" to Ridling Thorpe Manor. Our driver, a stout young fellow with a firm grip on the reins, was happy to comply, and we went tearing off through the broad green countryside of East Anglia just as the sun slid beneath the horizon. We had hardly gotten clear of town when the driver aroused our curiosity by asking if we were with the police.

"What leads you to believe that might be the case?" Holmes asked.

"You haven't heard then," said the driver.

"Heard what?"

"Well, it's all the talk around here. Mrs. Hilton Cubitt is missing and there are some what think she was snatched. Others aren't so sure. Most of the Norfolk constabulary is out at the manor as we speak."

"I see," said Holmes, his face going pale. "Tell me everything, sir, and there will be a handsome reward in it for you."

The driver now related a most singular story, which he had heard from a servant at Ridling Thorpe:

Early that morning, an upstairs maid at the manor had gone to Mrs. Cubitt's bedroom to offer breakfast. The maid found the door open and went in. She found a note by the bed. Written in what appeared to be Mrs. Cubitt's hand, the note stated that she had awakened early to go riding. This was unusual as she was not an early riser by habit and generally rode her horse in the evening. Still, the maid saw no cause for alarm and went about her normal business, as did other members of the household. By early afternoon, however, Mrs. Cubitt had not returned and her absence began to be troubling, as she was supposed to meet at two o'clock with a friend. A check of the stables revealed that Mrs. Cubitt's mare and saddle were indeed gone but turned up no other evidence.

"Do you know if Mrs. Cubitt was accustomed to saddling the horse on her own?" Holmes asked the driver.

"No, I'm sure that job was left to one of the stable hands, but I expect she could do it in a pinch if she had to."

"Very well. Pray, continue."

The driver now related that two stable boys and the manor's chief groom decided to search for Mrs. Cubitt, fearing she might have fallen from her horse or suffered some other mishap. Soon thereafter, the groom made a disturbing discovery. Just outside the manor's main gate, along a road coming up from North Walsham, he found Mrs. Cubitt's mare, idly grazing in a field. The horse was still saddled. There was no sign of Mrs. Cubitt, however, although the groom carefully searched the area.

"A most curious situation," said Holmes. "What happened next?"

"Well, as you can imagine, the folks at the manor started to get very worried. As they have no telephone as yet, they sent a lad out to the village to fetch Inspector Martin."

"Ah, and is the inspector at the house now?"

"Last I heard, he is."

"Good. I shall want to talk to him at once."

Holmes then questioned the driver closely regarding other details of Mrs. Cubitt's disappearance but learned little else of interest.

Night was about to fall as the margin of the German Ocean suddenly appeared like a broad dim stripe on the eastern horizon. Moments later, the manor house came into view. Tucked within a small island of trees, the house displayed two exceptionally high, steep gables of half-timbering and brick, but was otherwise unremarkable. In the deepening darkness, as wind clattered through gnarled old trees, the house presented a somber and melancholy aspect, just as it had in August of 1898 when we first visited it to unravel the deadly mystery of the dancing men.[5]

We went inside and found Inspector Thomas Martin sitting in an overstuffed chair in a large, oak-paneled hall at the center of the house. Martin was the same police officer who had investigated Hilton Cubitt's murder, earning Holmes's respect in the process. A tidy little man with a meticulously maintained black mustache and quick brown eyes, Martin was quite astonished to see us. He rose at once from his chair and shook our hands with great enthusiasm.[6]

"My God, this is an unexpected pleasure," said the inspector. "How on earth did the two of you get here so quickly?"

"You might say, inspector, that we were invited," Holmes replied.

Holmes now showed the inspector the letter we had received purporting to be from Slaney.

After examining the document, Martin said, "It is not a thing I wish to believe, Mr. Holmes, and yet I am beginning to think that I must. The authorities at Dartmoor were very certain that Slaney drowned, but without a body—"

"Without a body, we must leave open all possibilities. You are absolutely right, inspector. Now then, I should be interested to hear what you have learned to this point."

Martin gladly complied with Holmes's request. Upon arriving at Ridling Thorpe late in the afternoon, the inspector had begun by organizing a team of constables and locals to search "every square inch" of the manor, including the house itself, for some sign of Mrs. Cubitt. Thus far, they had found nothing. Martin had already talked at length with the servants, who noted that Mrs. Cubitt had been somewhat distracted over the past week but had given no indication why this was so. The servants also stated that no suspicious visitors had been seen recently at the house or in the vicinity of the manor.

"As far as I can tell, the lady's disappearance came out of the blue," Martin told us. "Nobody in the house seems to have thought anything was seriously wrong."

"You have, I presume, inquired as to whether she received an unusual letter or other type of message recently?" Holmes asked.

"Of course. It was my first thought, given what happened here two years ago when Slaney sent those messages. The butler, who takes the mail to Mrs. Cubitt every day, was here at that time and would certainly have recognized a new letter using the dancing men, as you call them. He saw no such letter, nor have I found one in the library or elsewhere in the house."

"You are to be commended for your thoroughness, inspector," said Holmes. "I also imagine you have sent men to check nearby villages and railroad stations to learn if anyone saw Mrs. Cubitt today."

"Yes, and I have just received a most curious piece of information from one of my men, who spoke earlier with a banker in North Walsham. It seems that yesterday Mrs. Cubitt withdrew five thousand pounds, in cash, from her account."

Not even Holmes, I think, anticipated this development. "Did she say why she was withdrawing such a large sum?" he asked.

"No, she said nothing to the banker," said the inspector. "Naturally, we are looking for the money here but I have a suspicion we won't find it."

"I fear you are correct," Holmes said.

"Still, we will keep searching, both for the money and the lady," said Martin. "I've already wired Scotland Yard, and more officers will be coming up in the morning."

"Good. They will be needed. Now, I should like to see Mrs. Cubitt's bedroom."

"By all means. I have only had time to take a cursory look at it and saw nothing amiss. However, I shall be happy to avail myself of your practiced eye, Mr. Holmes."

Mrs. Cubitt's bedroom was at the rear of a long hall on the second floor. The room was large, airy, well-lit by two casement windows and handsomely furnished with a canopied bed, two tall oak chests, a vanity and a pair of side chairs. What I took to be family photographs adorned the walls. One picture in particular—of a grim-faced old man in a plain shirt and suspenders who stared with unnerving directness at the camera—seized my attention. The picture seemed almost alive, so powerful was the man's gaze.

Holmes came up behind me and said, "Ah, I see the late Eban Patrick has caught your eye, Watson. He was not only Elsie's father but also led one of the most vicious gangs in Chicago. As you may recall, Mr. Slaney told us that it was Patrick who invented the code of the dancing men. He must have been quite a clever fellow."[7]

We now continued our inspection of the bedroom, which was orderly in every respect and showed no signs of a struggle or other unusual activity. A door at the far end of the room led into a large closet in which numerous dresses, skirts, blouses and other items of apparel hung with military precision. The closet also contained a long shelf where dozens of pairs of shoes were arrayed in an equally fastidious manner. Holmes seemed particularly interested in the closet and examined it closely before returning to the bedroom.

"I note that the bed is made," he said to Martin. "Was that the way the upstairs maid found it this morning?"

"No, she says she made it up after finding that Mrs. Cubitt was already gone."

"I see. I would like to speak briefly with the maid, if you don't mind."

The maid, named Agnes, was quickly ushered in. She was perhaps eighteen, short, with a broad peasant build and a doughy face most notable for its shrewd, close-set black eyes.

"Agnes, I am working with Inspector Martin and would like to ask you a few questions about your mistress," Holmes began.

"Certainly, sir," said the girl. "She's a very fine lady, she is, and I am very worried about her."

"As are we all. Let me start by asking you about Mrs. Cubitt's bed. It was unmade when you came in this morning, is that correct?"

"Yes, though I guess you could say it was neatly unmade, as far as such things go."

"Explain yourself please."

"Well, what I mean is, sir, the sheet and blanket were turned down and the pillows moved about a bit but it didn't really look like anybody had slept in the bed. At least that was how it appeared to me."

Holmes smiled and said, "Ah, I can see you are a most observant young lady, Agnes. Now, tell me this: Do you normally take care of Mrs. Cubitt's wardrobe?"

"Well, I put things out for her, if that's what you mean. The laundry's done by someone else, of course, and as for any mending—"

"Thank you. That is what I wanted to know. Since you put out Mrs. Cubitt's clothes, and presumably hang them up as well, I imagine you are as familiar as anyone with the various elements of her wardrobe."

"I am, sir. Mrs. Cubitt will even ask me sometimes if I like a certain dress or if such and such a blouse looks nice with this or that skirt. I've a very good eye for such things."

"I have no doubt that you do. Now, since I am told you did not see Mrs. Cubitt before she disappeared this morning, I suppose there is no way you could tell what she might have been wearing, is there?"

This was an odd question, I thought, but its brilliance soon became apparent, for Holmes had in effect issued a challenge which the clever maid was more than ready to meet.

"Oh, there might be a way, sir, if you want to know the truth."

"And what might that be?"

"Well sir, I could look and see what's missing. I know everything Mrs. Cubitt has got. I've even organized her clothes by color to help find things more quickly."

"Agnes, I knew you would be a splendid help to us," said Holmes, whose talents included the skillful use of flattery. "Very well, go to it! We shall patiently await your findings."

The maid went at first to the two chests, opening every drawer and carefully examining the contents. Then she disappeared into the closet. She emerged some minutes later with a quizzical expression.

"Well, what have you discovered, Agnes?" Holmes asked.

"There are two outfits missing, some underthings and two pairs of shoes," the maid replied.

"Describe these items if you would."

"Well, there's a set of riding clothes gone, which is to be expected. Her best riding boots are missing, too. What's queer is that she also took along a very nice gray and white dress she sometimes wears and a pair of matching dress shoes."

"Is anything else missing?" Holmes inquired. "A suitcase, perhaps, or a small bag?"

"Come to think of it, there is a small canvas bag she usually keeps. Let me look again."

She returned to the closet, made a brief search, and came back shaking her head. "It's gone all right," she said. "Why, if you don't mind me saying so, sir, it's almost like Mrs. Cubitt decided to take a short trip."

"I think you are right, Agnes, although I fear the lady's trip may prove much longer than she expected. Now then, I have but one more question: Who was Mrs. Cubitt's closest friend here, the person she would go to first if she were in trouble and needed help?"

The girl thought for a bit and said, "Well, if you'd asked me a month ago, I would have said Mrs. Allenby over at Whitefield Manor just down the road. Lately, though, Mrs. Cubitt spent a lot of time in the village with that crazy French woman—the one who calls herself Mme. DuBois."

"Who is this woman?"

"Why, she claims to be one of those spiritualists, she does. Says she can see into the future. All nonsense if you ask me. Mrs. Cubitt didn't see it that way, though. She was going into North Walsham two or three times a week to have 'readings'—that's what she called them—with the madame."

"Did Mrs. Cubitt ever say what she hoped to learn from these readings?"

"No. You'd best ask the madame herself."

Holmes smiled again, handed the girl a gold piece and said, "Thank you for your help, Agnes, and be assured that I will talk to Mme. DuBois as soon as possible."

Holmes was as good as his word, and less than an hour later we were in a carriage, riding across the dark plains under a sparkling canopy of stars toward the village of North Walsham. Martin came along and there was much animated discussion, during which Holmes made a surprising observation regarding Mrs. Cubitt's mysterious disappearance.

"I think it entirely possible," he said, "that Mrs. Cubitt left Ridling Thorpe of her own accord, to meet someone nearby, and that she is already some distance away."

"What leads you to that conclusion?" I asked.

"Her clothes, Watson. The riding apparel missing from her closet was to be expected, but as the observant Agnes noted, why did she take along a dress and shoes as well unless she knew she would be traveling somewhere?"

"I see what you're getting at, Mr. Holmes," said Martin. "The outfit was to be her change of clothes once she met up with her confederate outside the manor. And, of course, there's the money, which also suggests she was preparing for a trip—perhaps even a very long one— though if that were the case, you'd think she would have brought along more clothes."

I was still not convinced that Mrs. Cubitt would have left of her own free will. "But why would she decide to take a trip without notifying anyone here?" I asked.

"Ah, my dear Watson, that is indeed the question," said Holmes. "Perhaps Mme. DuBois will have an answer for us."

We were informed by our driver, one of the manor's groomsmen, that Mme. DuBois maintained a small parlor at an establishment called Smythe's Inn, where she also lived. We arrived at the inn at eleven o'clock, engaged rooms and rang at once for Mme. DuBois, despite the lateness of the hour.[8]

She appeared within minutes, descending the inn's narrow staircase rather like a very large rubber ball bouncing downhill. She was wide and fleshy—nearly two hundred pounds, I judged—and quite short, with no neck to speak of, so that her huge round head seemed to sprout directly out of her shoulders. Coal black eyes, sly and observant, lay in deep wells above her cheeks. Her long, equally black hair was flecked with gray and adorned with pink and white flowers. She wore a tentlike dress of dark silk, cut low enough to reveal her formidable bosom. Silver chains dangled from her plump wrists and jeweled rings adorned her fingers. I guessed her to be perhaps sixty years of age, although ten years more or less would not have surprised me.

Her appearance, I thought, was altogether remarkable, made more so by two small tattoos—a sun and a crescent moon—on her puffy cheeks, which were heavily rouged. Oblivious to my stares, she approached, looked us over with her piercing eyes and asked in a heavily accented contralto, "You are interested in a reading, gentlemen?"

"You might say that, madame," replied Holmes, "although we are not inclined to look to the stars for answers. We are seeking information about Elsie Cubitt."

Martin now introduced himself. At Holmes's request, he went on to present us merely as "assistants in the investigation."

"I have heard the strange news from Ridling Thorpe," Mme. DuBois said. "I knew this would be a day of evil. The heavens, they are unsettled and even the stars, I fear, are wobbling with doubt. Now, you will tell me please what has happened to Elsie?"

"That is what we are hoping to find out from you, madame," Holmes said, "since it is our understanding that you possess powers of foresight beyond those of mere mortals."

Casting a cold eye upon Holmes, she said, "So, you are one of the doubters, I see. Oh yes, there are many like you who do not feel flowing through them the hidden currents of the world. Well, about that I can do nothing, but come anyway. We will talk in the parlor."

As she led us toward a small room off the lobby, Holmes whispered to me, "She is no more French than you are, Watson. Indeed, her painfully fake accent cannot hide the fact that she is an American."

As Holmes had always possessed a superb ear for the nuances of language, I did not doubt him, even though Mme. DuBois had not sounded at all "American" to me.

At the parlor a sign over the door read: MME. SIMONE DUBOIS: READINGS AND CONSULTATIONS. YOUR FUTURE IN THE STARS. Unlocking the door, she directed us to sit at a round table in the center of room, which was painted dark red and displayed signs of the zodiac in a stenciled frieze around the walls. A large painted sun and moon, identical to those on Mme. DuBois's cheeks, looked down upon us from the midnight blue ceiling.

"I will help you, of course, in any way that I can but you must not expect too much of me, as I am but a humble servant of fate," Mme. DuBois said. "It is my gift to see the broad shape of the future but not its every detail. I am a listener and a watcher, a student of the heavens, but the heavens, they are wary of giving up too many of their deepest secrets. Now, I must ask you again what has happened to Elsie."

Martin obliged her with a brief recounting of Mrs. Cubitt's disappearance, ending with a question of his own: "We are told, madame, that she visited you frequently in recent weeks. What did the two of you talk about?"

"Why, we talked about her future, of course. She was, you see, having—what is the word?—ah yes, premonitions, that something terrible was about to happen. Naturally she sought my assistance."

"When did these premonitions begin?" Holmes inquired.

"Perhaps two weeks ago. She told me she was having dreams about a certain man with whom she had once been in love. She was worried that this man, who was very powerful and demanding, might do her great harm if she continued to spurn him."

"Did she say who this man was?"

"No, that is a thing she chose not to reveal to me."

"How unfortunate," said Holmes. "As to her frightening dreams, did she tell you what had prompted them?"

Mme. DuBois said with an air of resignation, "Who can say what it is that brings to our heads dreams in the middle of the long dark night? They are messages from the other side and they come when they wish to come. It is that simple."

"Please spare us talk of the 'other side,' madame, as it will be of no use in finding Mrs. Cubitt," Holmes said with some aspersion. "What will be of use is hard evidence. Therefore, I should like to know if Mrs. Cubitt stated a specific reason for her anxiety. Did she, for example, receive a letter or some other communication which alarmed her?"

Mme. DuBois shook her head slowly, as though preparing to correct an especially dense student, "Ah, I see that you, sir, are one of those people—so common among the English—who worship the facts. Myself, I have always found that the facts, they are useful for everything except the real truth of the world. But if it is the facts you want, I will give them to you."

She then stood up, went over to a small desk behind the table, withdrew a document from one of the drawers and returned to her seat. She pushed the document toward Holmes and said, "Here is one of your beloved facts. It is a copy, made by me, of a letter Elsie received yesterday. You will agree, I think, that it is a strange thing, which is why I copied it. Of course, I could not read its secrets but Elsie, she knew the meaning at once and told me."

Holmes carefully examined the letter, which I could see was a brief message written in the code of the dancing men.

"What does it say?" I asked.

Holmes, in a curiously flat voice, replied, "It says, 'You are in grave danger. Tomorrow morning, five o'clock, meet at front gate as per previous instructions. My man will pick you up. Tell no one and come alone.'"

"Now we are getting somewhere," said Martin. "I don't suppose it says who sent the message?"

Holmes offered a weak smile and said, "On the contrary, the message is quite clear in that regard, for it purports to be signed by the well-known detective Sherlock Holmes. Perhaps, inspector, you have heard of him."

Chapter Two

❦ ❦

"Money Won't Do You No Good"

Inside what she had come to think of as her wooden prison—the curious enclosed wagon that had been used to abduct her from the road outside Ridling Thorpe Manor—Elsie Cubitt was feeling more foolish than frightened. She realized in painful hindsight how incredibly gullible she had been in her dealings with Mme. DuBois. The woman, Elsie saw clearly now, was a fraud through and through and had undoubtedly been part of the conspiracy to kidnap her. But she had played on Elsie's biggest fear—the possibility that Abe Slaney might still be alive and want vengeance—and Elsie had taken the bait like some naive girl being talked into bed by a crafty seducer.

If only she had confided in Holmes from the start! But Mme. DuBois had insisted on secrecy, saying that the "arrangement," as she called it, would fall through if Slaney discovered that Holmes or the police were trying to thwart his scheme. Elsie, confident as always in her ability to handle any situation and reluctant to drag Holmes once again into her troubled past, had agreed. She had taken out the five thousand pounds—supposedly to pay off Slaney once and for all—although in her mind it was purely for show, since she had no intention of giving it to the man who had murdered her husband. Instead, her plan had been to confront Slaney and to make sure, by one means or another, that he would never bother her again.

Then the letter had come, supposedly from Holmes, in the secret language only he (or Abe Slaney) could have known, and she had jumped headlong into the trap. The letter, in which Holmes promised to help her deal with Slaney's latest threats, had not really come as a surprise. After all, Holmes was a man who seemed to know everything, and she had been both moved and comforted by his willingness to intervene on her behalf.

Now, of course, she realized that the letter had been a fake—and one she should have spotted. To begin with, the wording of it hadn't been quite right, for Holmes had a very particular way of expressing himself that was not easily duplicated. There had also been the odd request, for which no explanation was proffered, that she "bring along a fine dress" to their meeting. This, too, should have set off alarm bells, since the real Holmes—proper gentleman that he was—would never have made such an unusual request without giving his precise reason for doing so.

But Elsie had overlooked these obvious incongruities in her rush to see Holmes, and so had ridden into the trap that lay waiting for her outside the gates of Ridling Thorpe Manor. It had been cleverly set—the men's attire, as well as the wagon they used had put her off guard, and they had pulled her off her horse before she could use her pistol to defend herself. Even so, she had put up a desperate fight—one of her abductors had a swollen eye and was feeling great pain in an especially sensitive place—but in the end they had simply been too powerful for her.

Although she was quietly furious about her own stupidity, Elsie Cubitt knew that dwelling on past mistakes would do her no good. As she sat in the wagon, her hands tied and a gag pulled tightly across her mouth, she turned her attention to her present circumstances and considered how she might make her escape.

Like Sherlock Holmes, the man she adored, Elsie Cubitt possessed a quick and highly observant mind, and she had already made several deductions about her situation. She knew, for example, that she would be taken from the wagon at some point and put aboard a train to London. She had deduced this from bits and pieces of overheard conversation, since her two captors seemed to spend much of their time arguing over one thing or another. And even though curtains were drawn across the wagon's two small windows, Elsie could tell by the angle of the sun shining through them that she was traveling more or less to the south.

She had also concluded that her captors—one a large and rough-looking fellow, the other much smaller but seemingly more intelligent—were hired help and nothing more. Someone else, it was clear, had ordered her kidnapping, and she assumed it must have been Abe Slaney himself, if for no other reason than both of her captors had distinctive accents that linked them to the American Middle West, where Elsie herself had been born and raised.

Although she was reasonably confident Abe had arranged the kidnapping, she was far less certain about what he intended to do with her. However, she doubted that Abe, who had been obsessed with her since they were children in Chicago, would have abducted her simply to obtain a ransom. Her guard—a repulsive character with rotting, tobacco-stained teeth—had said as much when she had offered him a thousand pounds to let her go.

"Money won't do you no good," he had told her. "That's not what they'll be wanting from you."

Elsie had then asked who he was talking about, but the man's only response had been to gag her after enumerating various unpleasant things he would do to her if she "tried anything funny."

Her guard, however, had said something of great interest after delivering this warning. "Not even the great Sherlock Holmes himself can save you now," the man stated. "Fact is, he's got a big surprise coming himself, he has, and I only wish I could be there to see it."

Elsie had been pained to hear this, because it led her to wonder whether her kidnapping was itself a trap—for Holmes. She prayed this wasn't so, for Holmes had showed her such kindness and even affection that she could not bear the thought that she might be the cause of great trouble for him.

Now, in the heat of the afternoon, as the wagon swayed and lurched over Norfolk's rough roads, Elsie thought back to her first meeting with Holmes, nearly two years earlier at 221B Baker Street. After recovering from her self-inflicted bullet wound, she had paid a visit to London to thank Holmes for bringing Abe Slaney to justice. Before the meeting, she had reread Dr. Watson's tales and, like everyone else who followed the great detective's adventures, she had formed a complete idea as to what he must be like.

In some ways, she was to discover, he was just as depicted in the stories—a lightning quick thinker, impossibly observant, spectacularly impatient, tenacious in pursuit of his ends and a firm believer in the power of logic to illuminate the manifold mysteries of life. Yet as she grew to know him better, she had also found him to be in some ways quite endearing, even if he became almost awkwardly juvenile when their conversation turned to the decidedly irrational topic of the human heart.

At their first meeting, however, Holmes had been rather distant and formal—Dr. Watson had been much warmer and more welcoming. Holmes, who did not bother with the usual preamble of small pleasantries, began the conversation by inquiring why she had failed to tell her late husband about the source of the messages in the dancing men code.

"It is a point which has always bothered me," he said. "Was it fear, Mrs. Cubitt, or simply a desire to shield your husband from your past?"

As she looked into Holmes's steely eyes, she imagined that he expected her to burst into tears and offer some nonsense about how she had indeed wished to spare dear Hilton the pain of knowing about her earlier life. But that had not been the case at all, she informed Holmes. Instead, she stated that she had fully intended to deal with Slaney on her own, with a pistol if necessary, so as not to entangle Hilton in troubles that were properly none of his concern.

She went on to say that she would have killed Slaney herself that fateful night at Ridling Thorpe had not Hilton suddenly rushed into the study, grabbed her pistol and then been shot dead in an exchange of fire with Slaney. As she held her husband's lifeless body, she realized that she was responsible for his death by failing to warn him of the danger posed by Slaney.

"I then decided," she said matter-of-factly to Holmes, "that I had no choice but to atone for my sin by forfeiting my own life."

She would always remember Holmes's response: "And yet you have now decided to live, Mrs. Cubitt. Why is that, may I ask?"

"A fair question, Mr. Holmes. The only answer I can give you is that I have finally come to understand that suicide is the way of the coward, and I do not wish to be known as such."

The rest of their conversation had been more routine — Holmes seemed primarily interested in clearing up "cer-

tain minor points" in connection with Hilton's murder—
and that night she had returned to Ridling Thorpe.
Holmes, she assumed, would have no need to talk to her
again. But the next day, she had been surprised to receive
a letter from Holmes in which he complimented her on
her courage and forthrightness, among other things. She
had sent back a note of her own, and so began a correspondence that would over time blossom into a much
deeper relationship.

His letters—followed by a series of visits to Ridling
Thorpe—had convinced her that beneath his supremely
confident demeanor, Holmes was a man groping toward
self-awareness of his own suppressed instincts. Indeed,
like most men who professed to need nothing, he needed
almost everything, only he didn't know it. Still, she had no
doubt that he was attracted to her, as she was to him, although she thought it unlikely he had ever entertained the
possibility of falling in love. Of course, he had never discussed this delicate subject with her. Perhaps it wasn't in
his power to do so, she thought, and suddenly wondered
if she would ever see Holmes again.

Her reveries came to an abrupt end as her captor
spoke up: "We'll be stopping for the night, and you can
have the wagon to yourself—them's the orders. But remember what I said about trying anything foolish."

To underscore his point, the man took out a knife and
slowly ran the blade across Elsie's throat. "I'll cut and fillet
you if I have to, and there'll be no one the wiser. So be a
good girl. Understand?"

Elsie nodded that she did. The man then removed her
gag and untied her hands. "Sleep tight," he said, and as he
went out the door at the rear of the wagon, Elsie caught a
glimpse of purple twilight and a few early stars already
twinkling overhead. In Chicago, where the sky was a
soiled thing, she could hardly remember seeing stars, and

one of the glories of her new life in England had been the glittering night skies over the great flatlands of East Anglia. Now, as the wagon door slammed shut, she made a wish upon the vanished stars—for freedom and for the courage she would need to win it.

That same night, in the quiet of his room at Smythe's Inn in North Walsham, Holmes lay in bed, absorbed in thought, his long fingers curled behind his head, his eyes fixed on a small chandelier that provided the only light. During the course of his career, Holmes had tracked down many of the great criminals of the age, including the most notorious of all, Professor James Moriarty. The professor had left a kind of signature on all of his cases— the dark mark of criminal genius, as Holmes had remarked more than once.[1]

Now, Holmes believed he was in the presence of an equally dangerous and sinister mind. The use of his own name on the message to Mme. DuBois had been the convincing clue in this regard. Only a supremely confident adversary would have taunted Holmes so boldly. Moreover, the details of Elsie Cubitt's disappearance—the message in the dancing men cipher, the withdrawn money, the missing clothes—all pointed toward a carefully crafted scheme whose every feature was as perfectly polished as the facets of a fine diamond.

It was also clear to Holmes that the crime was directed as much at him as at Elsie Cubitt. Whoever had spirited her away—and Holmes had no doubt that she was the victim of a kidnapping—knew that Holmes would not rest until he found her. Indeed, he had literally been invited, in the coded message sent to Baker Street, to enter the case.

Abe Slaney, supposedly back from the dead, had proclaimed himself to be behind the crime. In some respects,

Slaney was the perfect suspect. He was a hardened criminal, he was obsessed with Elsie Cubitt, he had good reason to hate Holmes and he was the kind of man who just might have survived an ocean storm in a rowboat. But did he possess a subtle enough mind to have orchestrated Elsie Cubitt's kidnapping and all the planning that had gone into it? On this score, Holmes continued to have his doubts, which was why he had decided to think of his adversary simply as the Conspirator—a criminal mastermind whose identity had yet to be firmly established.

Of one thing, however, Holmes was very certain. Regardless of why Elsie Cubitt had been kidnapped or who had committed the crime, he would do all in his power to find her—even if that meant walking, eyes wide open, into a trap.

Chapter Three

§ ‰

"We Are in the Hands of a Magician"

FROM THE NARRATIVE OF DR. JOHN WATSON:

The next day was to prove as anxious and trying as any I had experienced in a long while. As one troubling revelation followed another, Holmes became convinced that we had stumbled upon a "vast conspiracy" in the matter of Elsie Cubitt's disappearance. Indeed, not since the day of the Hinckley fire had I seen him so agitated in mind and spirit, although in this instance it was one person's fate, as opposed to thousands, which was the cause of all his anxiousness. Fearing Mrs. Cubitt would come to great harm if not found quickly, Holmes at one point even suggested—facetiously, I am sure—that we appeal to the Good Sword of Winfarthing in hopes its supposedly magical powers might lead us to her. . . .[1]

I knew, of course, that Holmes was very much taken with Mrs. Cubitt. Indeed, I still recall vividly their first encounter, when she visited us at Baker Street some weeks after the arrest of Abe Slaney. Although still in mourning and clothed somberly in black, she was nonetheless vibrantly beautiful, with shimmering auburn hair, deep blue eyes and a kind of dense, voluptuous presence which seemed to charge the very air around her. She was then no more than thirty-five years of age, and in the full bloom of her womanhood. It became evident from our conversation that she was also a woman of rare intelligence and wit, and unusually strong-willed. Holmes stated after she left that he "finally understood" why Slaney had crossed an ocean and "risked all" to regain her favor.

Holmes made no other comment then, but within days, letters began to fly back and forth between Baker Street and Ridling Thorpe Manor. Holmes did not share these letters with me, and I therefore assumed they must be of a highly personal nature. The most recent of Mrs. Cubitt's missives, in her characteristically bold handwriting, had arrived only a week before her disappearance. But like all the others, its contents remained unknown to me, for Holmes—despite the apparent kidnapping—continued to volunteer no information about his relationship with the lady.

All of which is by way of prelude to a most curious incident which occurred Wednesday morning when we came down for breakfast at Smythe's Inn. As we took our seats, the inn's proprietor—whom we had not seen the night before—came up and said to Holmes, "Why, Mr. Baker, how nice to see you again. I trust you had a good night's sleep."

Holmes stared icily at the man and replied, "I fear you are mistaken, sir, as I am not Mr. Baker, nor have ever been in this establishment before now."

The proprietor, a portly and balding man who introduced himself as Peter Smythe, took on a look of utter bewilderment and said, "My apologies, sir, but there was a gentleman here last week by the name of John Baker who must be your twin, for the two of you look exactly alike."

As Holmes sometimes used the name of John Baker when traveling incognito, Smythe's statement was quite mystifying, though Holmes gave no hint of surprise.

"You intrigue me, sir," he said. "When exactly was it that this Mr. Baker stayed here?"

"Why, just a week ago today," the innkeeper said. "You—I mean, he—arrived in the early evening, spent the night and left early the next morning. Do you remember now?"

"No, but perhaps you can enlighten me. What did Mr. Baker do during his visit?"

"I can't really say, sir, other than that you—ah, sorry sir, he—made inquiries about sending a message to Mrs. Cubitt at Ridling Thorpe Manor."

"Ah, why am I not surprised to hear that? Was a message in fact delivered to the lady?"

"Why, yes, one of the local livery men agreed to take it and was paid most handsomely for the job, I might add. Indeed, it was not long after the man came back that Mrs. Cubitt herself arrived."

"You mean here at the inn?" Holmes asked.

"Yes. She went upstairs at once, to visit Mme. DuBois, or so she said." Smythe delivered this last phrase with a slight smirk.

"But you think that she actually went to Mr. Baker's room. Is that it?"

"I am sure I could not say, sir," Smythe replied unctuously. "I certainly make every effort to run a clean and respectable business, as I'm sure you understand."

"Of course," said Holmes. "The innkeepers of England are renowned for their elevated moral standards and I am sure you are a splendid example of this vaunted incorruptibility, Mr. Smythe. Now then, what time did the lady leave?"

"As I said, sir, I do not make it my business—"

Holmes reached into pocket, took out a sovereign, pressed it into Smythe's hand and asked, "What time?"[2]

"Half past three. My night clerk saw Mrs. Cubitt leave."

"Did she say anything?"

"No. My clerk informs me that she simply came down the stairs and calmly walked out."

"I see. Do you or your night clerk know for a fact which room Mrs. Cubitt actually visited that night?"

"No, I cannot say that we do. You must understand that I have never made it a habit to pry into the personal affairs of my guests."

"How admirable of you. Now, let us return to Mr. Baker for a moment. Other than sending a message to Ridling Thorpe, did he do anything of note during his visit?"

"Not that I am aware of, sir."

"One more question. Had you seen Mr. Baker here at any time prior to his visit last week?"

The innkeeper shook his head and said, "No, I do not recall seeing him before."

"All right, that will be all, Mr. Smythe," Holmes said and waved the innkeeper away.

After eating our breakfast, we stepped outside to smoke. The day was clear and mild, unlike Holmes's frame of mind.

"I trust you see what is happening here, Watson," he said.

"Obviously, someone has been impersonating you."

"Indeed, and by the look of it, he is doing an excellent job."

"But what might be the purpose of such a charade?"

"I am not certain. It is a dark business, Watson, a dark business. Still, I would note one suggestive fact, which can be no coincidence. Do you remember where I was last Thursday night?"

I thought for a moment before recalling that Holmes had been gone all of that night, after receiving an urgent message promising crucial new information regarding the theft of the Chesterfield ruby.

Said I, "So you now think the message was a trick, I take it."

"What else could it have been, Watson? As you recall, I traveled up to Norwich, where I was to meet a man at an old farmstead not far from town. When I finally arrived, however, the farmstead proved to be empty. I waited several hours to no avail and finally caught an early morning train back to London. It was all what our American friends call a wild goose chase. Meanwhile, someone pretending to be me was checking into the inn here."

"I must ask again, Holmes, why would anyone go to such trouble?"

"I imagine we shall find out soon enough. There is a purpose behind everything that has been happening here, and unless I am mistaken, it is a large and strategic purpose. We have become pawns, Watson, in someone's game. Very well then, we shall act the part."

"What do you mean?"

"We shall keep moving, Watson, until we can see the man who would be king."

With that in mind, we went for a stroll through town, which was pleasant in the grand old English manner with its sturdy brick and stucco buildings and winding streets. At market cross, newly renovated, a large clock chimed ten o'clock as we entered the telegrapher's office, where Holmes made arrangements—at no small expense—to send a coded cable to Detective Clifton Wooldridge in Chicago. The message sought the "latest word," as Holmes put it, regarding Abe Slaney and the activities of his old gang.[3]

Back at the inn, we hired a carriage to return us to Ridling Thorpe Manor, where Inspector Martin had already gone.

Said Holmes, "I fear the good, gray detectives of Scotland Yard will be on the scene by now, swarming like barn sparrows and no doubt making as big a mess. Unfortunately, there is no avoiding it, as I need to know whether any additional evidence has been discovered at the manor."

Although Holmes held Inspector Martin in high esteem, he had long been on rather mixed terms with the Yard, whose detectives he considered to be for the most part lacking in imagination. Moreover, his relationship with the Yard had deteriorated notably in recent months because of what happened after the theft of the ruby. The Chesterfield stone had been taken in broad daylight, despite being under police guard, and the Yard's subsequent handling of the investigation proved so inept that Holmes was finally compelled to speak out in the *Daily Telegraph*. Naturally, his public enumeration of the Yard's shortcomings did not endear him to the superintendent or the home secretary.[4]

Holmes chose not to dwell on his troubles with the Yard, however, and our ride out to Ridling Thorpe was uncommonly delightful as the rich Norfolk plains spread before us in sunlit abundance. Our conversation soon turned to Mme. DuBois, whom Holmes pronounced "a most fascinating character," adding, "It would be instructive, I think, to know more about how she and Mrs. Cubitt met."

He noted that during our interview the previous night, Mme. DuBois had described her first encounter with Mrs. Cubitt as "accidental." Her story was that they had met at the market in town while "comparing some vegetables" and struck up an immediate friendship. According to Mme. DuBois, their subsequent conversations focused on Mrs. Cubitt's desire to "expand her realm of consciousness" and made no mention of her previous involvement with Abe Slaney or her roots in the Chicago underworld. Nor did they discuss other details of Mrs. Cubitt's personal life. So, at least, Mme. DuBois claimed.

"What did you make of her account?" Holmes asked.

"I cannot say that I made much of it one way or the other."

"I fear that is not the sort of answer a good detective likes to hear, Watson. Every interview conducted in the course of an investigation has value, no matter how seemingly innocuous the subject, either because of what is said, or what is not. In the case of Mme. DuBois, I must say I found her story to be peculiar."

"How so?"

Holmes rubbed his chin and said, "Do you remember our meeting with Mrs. Cubitt, in September of 1898?"

"How could I forget?" I said. "She was quite enchanting, as I am sure you would agree."

"'Enchanting' is not a word I have heard you use before, Watson," Holmes replied, raising an eyebrow. "Still, I will admit that in Mrs. Cubitt's case, it is the right one. Yes, she was enchanting but I think you will acknowledge that she also demonstrated superior intelligence and great strength of character. I must therefore wonder why a woman possessing such commendable qualities would suddenly adopt as her dearest friend an itinerant fortune-teller of the likes of Mme. DuBois. The woman is obviously a charlatan, as indeed are all the spiritualists of her ilk, and I find it highly unlikely that Mrs. Cubitt would have relied upon such a person for advice of any kind."

"What are you getting at, Holmes?"

"I am suggesting that Mme. DuBois almost surely initiated the relationship and probably did so by passing along certain intriguing bits of information to Mrs. Cubitt."

"What sort of information?"

"I imagine it had to do with Abe Slaney. We shall find out soon enough, however, for I intend to have another talk with the mysterious madame before the day is done."

We reached the gate of Ridling Thorpe Manor at eleven o'clock, but to my surprise, we did not enter the estate. Instead, Holmes ordered our driver to stop by the entrance. Holmes stepped down from the carriage and began walking along the side of the road—a picturesque lane that ultimately led down to the sea some ten miles distant. I followed Holmes, although the purpose of his endeavor was obscure to me. Holmes went about thirty paces in one direction, then doubled back and went in the other, using a long stick to poke at tall grass and ragged hedges bordering the road.

"May I ask what you are looking for, Holmes?"

"Anything, Watson, anything at all."

Holmes had not gone far from our carriage when he stopped, bent down on one knee and retrieved from a clump of grass what at first appeared to be a book of some kind. His discovery was actually a stack of pamphlets bound in twine. The heading in large type on the topmost pamphlet said: THE CHURCH ARMY CALLS ON YOU. BEHOLD NOW IS THE DAY OF SALVATION.[5]

"Someone must have accidentally dropped the pamphlets here," I noted. "I don't see—"

Holmes broke in, "You don't see why they are of any importance. Perhaps you are right, Watson. They may be utterly insignificant. Then again, I would note that the Church Army, like other evangelical groups, usually goes about its business of saving souls in a large van of some kind. I would also note that these pamphlets appear to be in perfect order. I wonder—"

Not bothering to finish his thought, Holmes turned and strode back to the carriage to speak to our driver, a dour man of middle age with large, extremely crooked teeth and a harelip.

"Tell me, when did it last rain here?" Holmes asked the man.

"Why, it would have been two days ago, sir, on Monday."

"Was it a heavy rain?"

"Cats and dogs, sir, as they say."

"When did it stop?"

"'Twould have been in the evening, sir, just as darkness was settling in."

"I see. Now, let me ask you something else. Is the Church Army active in this area?"

"Oh yes, sir, I see their van quite often."

"What sort of van is it?"

"'Tis quite a big one, sir, almost like a train carriage, and there's a little platform in front where the preachers do their work. You can't miss it, what with all the religious messages painted on the sides. Not for me, mind you, as I do not countenance selling God like cheese or tinware."

Holmes bestowed a generous tip on the driver, then said to me, "Well, we now know that these pamphlets were dropped here within the last two days, since they show no evidence of ever being wet."

"I have generally found that there is some method to your apparent madness, Holmes, but in this instance—"

Holmes laughed and said, "The word 'generally' does not qualify as a ringing endorsement, my dear Watson, but I understand your confusion. You see, I am trying to solve a vexing little problem and the pamphlets may shed some light on it."

"The problem being?"

"The problem being: Where did Mrs. Cubitt change her clothes? I presume she must have done so, for why else would she have brought along that dress when she left the manor house? I also presume that she changed her clothes not long after leaving here, since her riding attire would hardly be suitable for travel except on a horse. Indeed, riding gear would only have called attention to her. A van waiting by the front gate would have provided just the place for her to put on a different outfit, which is what her kidnappers undoubtedly demanded."

"But surely you do not think the Church Army was somehow part of the plot?" I said.

"I rather doubt it, as kidnapping is not generally accounted part of the Lord's work. In any case, I should be interested to hear what the crack investigators of Scotland Yard have concluded from yesterday's events."

We climbed back into our carriage and told the driver to take us to the manor house, where we found half a dozen other vehicles parked in the turnaround. A constable stood guard at the front door and would not let us pass until Inspector Martin was summoned to vouch for us.

"I knew you'd be back," Martin said. "Well, come right in. You've arrived at a critical moment, gentlemen. We've just within the past hour received a ransom note for Mrs. Cubitt."

This was obviously news Holmes had not expected to hear. "How very strange! I must see it at once."

Martin nodded and said, "I'm sure that can be arranged. But it'll have to be cleared by Deputy Chief Inspector Butler. He's in charge of the case."

"I do not know the man," Holmes said.

"Count yourself lucky," Martin replied. "David Butler fancies himself the meanest bulldog in the Yard and acts accordingly. Come along then, but don't expect a warm greeting. You are not the most popular person among the brass right now."

As we followed Martin through the house, Holmes asked him whether any vans, wagons, carriages or other vehicles were known to have been stolen recently in the vicinity.

Martin stopped and stared into Holmes's inscrutable eyes. Then he said, "A funny question, Mr. Holmes. Is there something you know that I don't?"

"No, I am merely curious how Mrs. Cubitt left the area, since we know she did not ride far on her horse."

"Ah, I see what you're getting at, Mr. Holmes. A good question indeed! However, the answer is no—there have been no such thefts reported to us and we are always the first to hear of such things."

We found Deputy Chief Inspector Butler sitting at a writing table in the study—a small room with bookcases built into three walls and a single window overlooking the garden. As I stepped into the room, I was instantly flooded with memories of the tragic events of two years earlier, when Abe Slaney had stood outside the window and fired the bullet which killed Hilton Cubitt. The study was also where Elsie Cubitt, believing she had caused her husband's death, tried to take her own life. The deadly odor of gunpowder had still lingered in the room when Holmes and I arrived, and I could almost smell it again now, although I knew this was merely a trick of memory.

Butler looked up as we entered and said curtly, "Who are these men, Martin? I have no time for visitors."

"Perhaps, sir, you would have time for Mr. Sherlock Holmes and his friend, Dr. John Watson," said Martin.

Butler stared up at Holmes and me, and he did not sound impressed when he said, "Is that a fact? Well, it must be my lucky day."

He now rose slowly from his chair and presented an imposing appearance as he stood before us. Tall and solidly built, he had alert blue eyes, ruddy cheeks, a square jaw and bright red hair, cut short and already receding at the brow. I put his age at about forty All in all, he looked rather like a prizefighter past his prime but formidable nonetheless, as his pugnacious manner was soon to demonstrate.

"It is a pleasure to meet you," said Holmes, showing no sign that he was offended by our chilly greeting. "As Dr.

Watson and I have some familiarity with events both past and present here, I believe we may be of some assistance to you."

"I'll be the judge of that, Mr. Holmes," said Butler. "Besides, judging by what I read in the newspapers, you don't think too highly of the Yard, so I'm surprised you now want to help us, poor ignorant fools that we are. Still, your arrival is convenient, for I was about to have Inspector Martin fetch you in any case. I'm curious about that message sent to Mrs. Cubitt in your name."

"What is it you are curious about?" Holmes asked. "It is patently obvious that an impersonator sent the message."

"That would be the same impersonator, I suppose, who spent the night at Smythe's Inn a week ago—a night that, as it so happens, Mrs. Cubitt was seen visiting someone there."

"Ah, I see you have already spoken with that paragon of innkeeping virtue, Mr. Peter Smythe," said Holmes. "I would be as interested as you are to find out whom Mrs. Cubitt saw that night, but as I have no evidence as to which room she visited, I can draw no conclusions. One possibility, of course, is that she went to see her friend Mme. DuBois."

"Mme. DuBois denies it," Butler said. "Perhaps you have some other explanation."

"The only explanation required, deputy chief inspector, is that someone has been going about pretending to be Sherlock Holmes. The reason for this charade is not yet known to me, but you may be certain I will find out. In the meantime, I should like to have a look at the ransom note received this morning."

Butler glared at Martin, who stood next to Holmes, and said, "I expect discretion from my men, inspector. It would seem to be a quality you do not possess."

"I'm sorry, sir, but Mr. Holmes—"

"Can speak for himself. Inspector Martin merely showed common professional courtesy in apprising me of the ransom note. Now then, I must ask once again to see the note."

"I'm afraid you have no standing in this matter, Mr. Holmes, other than perhaps as a witness to certain crimes," Butler said, as though Holmes were some underling who had exceeded his authority. "I therefore see no reason for you to inspect the note. I'm sure you understand."

I wanted to cuff the insufferable fellow, who clearly lacked appreciation for Holmes's many services to the cause of justice, but Holmes found a superior way to deal with the problem.

"I understand perfectly," Holmes replied smoothly, "although I am not sure the home secretary, for whom I recently performed an especially valuable service, will be equally tolerant of your boorish behavior. Come along, Watson, I have a telegram to send. We will return this afternoon, as the inspector will by that time be posted elsewhere, assuming of course that he is still employed by Scotland Yard."

Martin now turned to Butler and addressed him with uncharacteristic bluntness: "If you value you position, sir, you had best show that letter to Mr. Holmes, since I know for fact that he has the secretary's ear. You sir, I must hasten to add, do not."

Butler responded at first with an exclamation of disbelief, then glanced up at Holmes, whose gaze was as obdurate as Scottish granite. I could see, in Butler's subtle change of expression, the instant when he realized Holmes would indeed carry out his threat.

Martin saw the same thing and skillfully intervened, telling Butler, "Since I know how busy you are, sir, I will be happy to brief Mr. Holmes and Dr. Watson on the latest developments in the case, including the ransom note. Would that be all right?"

Butler looked down at some papers on the table and said, "Very well, but be quick about it."

"Certainly, sir," said Martin as he picked up an envelope—containing the ransom note, I presumed—from the table. We then left without another word and went into the dining room, where we took seats at a massive oak table almost as long as the room itself.

"Well, I must say that Deputy Chief Inspector Butler is a singularly unpleasant individual," said Holmes as he gazed up at the fine stapwork on the ceiling. "Given the state of Scotland Yard these days, I imagine he will go far." Holmes then turned his sharp eyes toward Martin and said, "Now, if you don't mind, let us see the ransom note."

Martin passed the envelope to Holmes, who studied it with his usual thoroughness, noting that it was "in every respect unremarkable and therefore not an item that might be readily traced to its purchaser." He also noted that the letter, addressed in crude block letters, bore a postmark from the city of Lincoln, over one hundred miles to the northeast. The ransom note itself, on common stationery and written in block letters, read as follows: £5,000 FOR MRS. CUBITT'S SAFE RETURN. DELIVERY TO BE MADE FRIDAY IN GLASGOW. DETAILED INSTRUCTIONS TO FOLLOW. DO NOT BRING POLICE OR SHE WILL DIE. ABE SLANEY.

"A most peculiar letter, I must say," Holmes observed.

"Why do you say that?" Martin asked.

Holmes leaned back in his chair and said, "Kidnappers in my experience do not provide two days' notice as to where they intend to collect their ransom. Indeed, the trick is just the opposite—the wise kidnapper will keep the location secret until the last possible moment in order to stay one step ahead of the police. But the greatest curiosity presented by this note is its very existence. As you well recall, inspector, Abe Slaney came to England two years ago because he was desperately in love with Mrs. Cubitt. I can understand why he would abduct her, but why does he now demand a ransom for her return and even threaten to kill her? And why does he want a mere five thousand pounds, not to mention all the risk entailed in a ransom drop, when it is likely he already has the five thousand pounds withdrawn by Mrs. Cubitt from the bank?"

"Perhaps he holds her responsible for his imprisonment and is therefore seeking revenge," I offered.

"That is a possibility," Holmes acknowledged, "but I do not think it a very likely one."

"You are right, Mr. Holmes," Martin said. "Unfortunately, your friend the deputy chief inspector does not see matters that way. Butler has already sent men up to Lincoln and he's put the police in Glasgow on alert as well. He's convinced the lady is being taken to Scotland."

"Then the inspector is an even bigger fool than I thought," Holmes said. "Very well, we shall have to go ahead on our own."

Holmes thanked Martin for his help and promised to keep him posted as to the progress of our investigation. We then returned to North Walsham in our carriage. Along the way, as we enjoyed the drowsy late afternoon sun, I asked Holmes what he intended to do next.

He said, "Scotland Yard is going north, Watson. Therefore, I anticipate that we shall go south. First, however, I should like to find out more about the Church Army."

"I see. Incidentally, I was not aware you had recently assisted the home secretary in some 'sensitive matter.' Indeed, I had heard he was hopping mad after your comments in the *Telegraph*."

"Ah, my dear Watson, that was a little tale I told for the benefit of Deputy Chief Inspector Butler. I must say I was impressed with how quickly our friend Martin waded in to support my fiction. He is that rarity among the constabulary—a man who can think on his feet."

Once back in town, we ate a quick lunch at the inn, then began making inquiries about the Church Army. After several false starts, we were finally put in contact with the rector at a local church who informed us that the army's two preachers in Norfolk had been called to London two days earlier and had not yet returned. We learned from this same source that when not in use, the army's van was stored in a large shed at the west end of town, not far from the railroad station. After receiving directions, we went to look at the van.

Holmes easily picked the padlock on the shed's door and we found the van inside. It was just as our carriage driver had described it—a large enclosed wagon, with small double windows on one side, a transomed roof and a door at the front beneath an arched canopy on which was stenciled in bold letters: GOD IS LOVE. Other messages adorned the sides of the van. HOW SHALL WE ESCAPE IF WE NEGLECT SO GREAT SALVATION?, read one. Another assured potential converts that NO ONE IS LOST TO THE EYES OF GOD.

Holmes stepped up on the platform and tried the door, noting, "I did not know God required so much advertising, Watson, but perhaps even His message can benefit from a good sales pitch. Ah, the door has conveniently been left open."

I followed Holmes up into the van, which was a veritable church on wheels, lacking only pews. Bibles, pamphlets (identical to the ones we had found earlier by the roadside), hymn sheets and other materials were stored neatly on built-in shelves along one side. On the other side was a small closet in which we found robes and other vestments. There was a harmonium next to the closet and

Holmes idly played out a tune with one finger as his eager eyes swept in the scene, committing every detail to memory. He soon spotted something beneath the bench along the back wall and went over to pick it up.

"What have you found, Holmes?"

"A wedding ring, Watson, and a rather expensive one at that, judging by the size of the diamond."

He held up the ring to the window, turned it over several times, then handed it to me. I was able to make out an inscription inside the gold band. It said: HDC TO EMP 8-13-97.

"Unless an amazing coincidence is at work, it would appear we have found Mrs. Cubitt's wedding ring," said Holmes. "As I recall, Mr. Cubitt's middle name was Donald. Elsie's is Marie. The initials therefore match perfectly, as does the date of the wedding."

"But if Mrs. Cubitt was taken here in this van, where is she now?" I asked.

"If only I knew, Watson, if only I knew," Holmes said, sitting down on the bench. "I trust, as the message outside proclaims, that she remains within sight of God. However, she is for the moment most certainly lost to us, and she will not be easy to find. Just think, Watson, of the planning that has already gone into this affair. Mrs. Cubitt's abductors 'borrowed' this van to spirit her away from the manor house, then returned it without its owners even knowing it had been stolen. Indeed, I should not be at all surprised to learn that the preachers who normally use this vehicle were in fact called away to London on some pretext."

"But wouldn't it have been easier just to rent or steal a coach in town?"

"Perhaps, yet if you think about it, using this van was a clever touch. It is, after all, a vehicle well known in every corner of the county and its presence near Ridling Thorpe would not have occasioned any suspicion."

"I have been thinking, Holmes. The railroad station is but a few blocks from here. Is it not possible that she was put on a train to Glasgow, as Scotland Yard believes?"

Holmes said, "When it comes to this matter, I am beginning to think that anything is possible. We are in the hands of a magician, Watson, and I suspect he has many more tricks planned for us. Still, I would be willing to wager any amount you please that Mrs. Cubitt is not in Glasgow, or on her way there. Our magician would not be so clumsy, and that is why I am more convinced than ever that the ransom note is a ruse."

"That is all well and good," I said, "but where are we to go next, if not to Glasgow?"

"There is one person who may know the truth," Holmes replied. "It is time, I think, for another talk with Mme. DuBois."

Half an hour later, upon returning to Smythe's Inn, we discovered—much to Holmes's regret—that Mme. DuBois was gone, having decamped around noon after settling her account. According to Smythe, she stated that a "dire family emergency" required her to leave immediately and that she would return later to close up her business. Smythe said she had then taken a cab to the railroad station but did not reveal her ultimate destination.

"I should like to see her room," Holmes said.

Smythe, looking very apologetic, replied, "Oh, I am sorry Mr. Holmes, but I could not permit—"

With a sigh, Holmes reached into his pants pocket, found a five-pound note and passed it over the counter to Smythe without comment.

"I'll open the door for you," Smythe volunteered as he slipped the note into his shirt pocket.

Mme. DuBois's room, which we searched thoroughly, proved to be a disappointment. We found only clothes, the usual furnishings, toilet items, two crystal balls (neither of which seemed to offer a view into the future), plus a scattering of knickknacks, figurines and the like. The only item out of the ordinary was a white hand towel folded over the sink that bore the initials SPH. Obviously, these initials did not conform to Mme. DuBois's name. There was nothing, however, that seemed to offer any clue as to her whereabouts.

After finishing our search, we came back downstairs and ate supper. Holmes looked quite dejected, blaming himself for failing to keep better watch on Mme. DuBois.

As he picked at his kidney pie, he said, "She was our best hope, Watson."

"Well, perhaps we can trace her movements from the railroad station."

"Oh, that will be easy enough. Mme. DuBois would stand out in any crowd and I have no doubt the ticketing agent will remember her. I fear, however, that she has gone to the one place in England where tracking even a woman of her decidedly unorthodox appearance will be difficult."

I mulled Holmes's comments for some time before it occurred to me what he meant.

"Ah, so you believe she has gone to London."

"Yes, Watson, and it will be the devil's business to find her—or Mrs. Cubitt—for I think it likely both women are there now, in one of the greatest hiding places on earth."

Chapter Four

§ ℥

"Where Are You Taking Me?"

The Fourth of July was a great celebration of independence in Elsie Cubitt's homeland, but she knew no freedom in England. Instead, she spent the morning tied up in the wagon, her guard as sullen as ever. He amused himself by openly leering at her, and she was certain that he must have been under strict orders not to touch "the goods," or else he would already have tried to have his way with her.

The guard, however, was to prove the least of her troubles, for sometime after noon, the wagon finally came to a stop. Elsie had no idea where she was, but she was pleased when her guard removed her gag, after admonishing her not to scream unless she wanted her "pretty face cut all to pieces." She therefore sat in silence for several minutes until the rear door of the wagon swung open and she was startled to see a tall, slender, well-dressed man who might easily have been mistaken for Sherlock Holmes.

The man's features—a thin hawkish nose, piercing gray eyes, a strong square chin—which gave evidence of stage makeup, were certainly Holmesian. Even so, the resemblance was not entirely convincing to Elsie's practiced eye. She noticed that the man was a good inch or two shorter than Holmes, and he also carried himself differently. Holmes, whom Elsie had studied very closely the first time they met, had a particular way of holding his head that the impostor hadn't got quite right. Nor did she see on his hands the faint chemical stains so common to the real Sherlock Holmes. On the whole, however, the figure presented a good likeness, right down to his tweed coat.[1]

"Ah, Elsie my dear, how are you?" the man asked, in a voice that mimicked Holmes's distinct way of speaking with uncanny accuracy.

"I have been better," she replied coldly. "And who are you, sir, may I ask?"

"Why, don't you recognize me, Elsie? I am your ardent lover, Sherlock Holmes."

"You are a fraud, sir, and not a very good one in my estimation."

"I shall be good enough," the man said with a kind of theatrical swagger that led Elsie to believe he might well be an actor hired to play the role of his life. "Most people, Mrs. Cubitt, are not as observant as you are. I think I will make a very convincing Sherlock Holmes, if I do say so myself."

To Elsie's mind, there was something almost comic about the man's absurd display of self-confidence. No one, she thought—wrongly, as it turned out—could possibly be fooled by his performance. Still, Elsie recognized at once that the attempt to masquerade as Holmes was no laughing matter. The mere fact that the man had taken on the role suggested some sinister purpose, although Elsie was not certain just what it might be.

She had little time to ponder the matter, however, for her second captor—the short man whose name was Pete—now entered the wagon. He was carrying a small case, which he opened to reveal a set of hypodermic needles and syringes.

"What is that?" Elsie asked, suddenly feeling very frightened.

"It's just a little something to make your journey more pleasant," Pete said, preparing an injection.

"Where are you taking me?" she demanded as Pete jabbed the needle into her arm.

"On a very long trip," he replied, "only you won't be awake to see the scenery."

In what would be his last night at Smythe's Inn in North Walsham, Sherlock Holmes was too restless to sleep, and so he let his mind wander through the growing labyrinth of Elsie Cubitt's disappearance. Holmes had over the years developed a theory that criminal cases were in some sense organic, growing and sending out shoots in the manner of a seed. Some grew quickly, some slowly. Some produced small and simple plants, while others developed into mighty trees with limbs extending out in all directions.

Part of a great detective's skill, Holmes believed, lay in his ability to know, at a very early stage, what sort of criminal seed had been sown and what it might grow into. Now, in the long silence of the night, Holmes began to envision the dark seed that had already been planted in the case of Elsie Cubitt. And the more he thought about it, the more certain he became that unless he could find a way to cut it down very soon, it would grow into a thing of monstrous proportions.

Chapter Five

"Do You Dream About Her?"

The next day, a cool and dreary Thursday with a sharp wind blowing in from the east, was one which seemed only to add to the fantastic aura surrounding Elsie Cubitt's disappearance. It also became more apparent than ever how deeply Holmes cared about Mrs. Cubitt, for he displayed furious energy in the search for her. The only other time I had observed such passion in Holmes was during his long and rather mysterious entanglement with Irene Adler, which demonstrated that despite his supreme rationalism, not even he was impervious to the unpredictable effects a woman can have upon a man.[1]

We began the day by checking out of Smythe's Inn and going with our luggage to the North Walsham station. There, as Holmes had predicted, we readily learned that Mme. DuBois had taken a train to London the day before. We also inquired whether Mrs. Cubitt or anyone resembling her had been observed at the station in the past two days. The agent told us no one recalled seeing her, noting that Scotland Yard detectives had already asked the same question.

I assumed we would now go to London ourselves but Holmes instead purchased two tickets for the next stop down the line—the sturdy old wool town of Worstead.

"What do you hope to find there?" I asked.

"Confirmation of a certain theory, Watson. I only pray it is correct."

The Midland and Great Northern local came within an hour and we boarded for the brief ride to Worstead. Along the way, Holmes explained his theory, which was that Mrs. Cubitt's abductors would not have risked boarding a train with her at North Walsham, since she would be instantly recognized there. It was thus possible that they had gone to Worstead, or some other nearby stop, where Mrs. Cubitt was hardly known.[2]

Upon arriving at Worstead's small brick depot, we went to the office of the stationmaster, a burly man with a twirled black mustache and twinkling brown eyes. His name was Walter Pashley, and he looked astonished to see us, especially after Holmes introduced himself. We soon learned why.

"Ah, so you're on the job here again, Mr. Holmes, and this time you've brought Dr. Watson along!" said Pashley.

Holmes, looking uncharacteristically puzzled, said, "May I ask what you mean by 'again,' Mr. Pashley?"

"Ah, you're joshing me, aren't you? Why you were here just yesterday, Mr. Holmes, at half past seven in the morning, with a lady. Of course, I realize now that you were operating in disguise."

Holmes, who to my knowledge had been in bed at Smythe's Inn at that hour, replied calmly, "Of course. You are a most observant man, Mr. Pashley, most observant. Let me see just how keen your skills are. Tell me all about my visit yesterday and the lady I was with. To begin, what sort of dress was she wearing?"

"Why it was gray, with a small collar of white lace. I must say the dress looked very handsome on the lady, at least in my humble opinion. She was a most striking woman, though I never caught her name. May I ask who she is? I only do so because I read the paper this morning and saw a drawing of that woman missing up in North Walsham. I was just telling my wife at breakfast that the woman I saw yesterday with Mr. Holmes—I guess that would be you, wouldn't it now—looked a bit like the one in the paper."

"Yes, there is some resemblance," Holmes admitted. "Could you describe her in more detail?"

Pashley, who obviously had an admiring eye for the fair sex, readily provided a description that certainly fit Elsie Cubitt.

"What about my attire?" Holmes asked. "What was I wearing yesterday?"

Pashley grinned and said, "Well now, sir, you looked very godly, you did. You were dressed all in black, with the usual churchman's collar. You were even carrying a Bible. I must confess, Mr. Holmes, that if I were escorting a lady such as the one you were with, my thoughts wouldn't necessarily be turning to heaven, if you catch my meaning."

"I understand you perfectly, Mr. Pashley. Now, if you do not mind, I should like to hear more about my religious disguise. Could you tell, for example, what sort of churchman I was supposed to be?"

"That's an easy one, sir. You were posing as a preacher for the Church Army."

"Mr. Pashley, you continue to impress me. Pray tell, how did you know I was pretending to be with that organization?"

Pashley gave Holmes a conspiratorial wink and said, "Close observation, Mr. Holmes. You see, not long after I spotted you and the lady I happened to look out my window and noticed one of those big wagons the Church Army has. It was just leaving and so I put two and two together, as it were. The two of you must have come in the wagon, don't you see?"

Holmes, who had long since mastered the art of outlandish flattery as required, said, "A most splendid deduction, sir! I do not suppose you saw the wagon's driver?"

"Sorry, Mr. Holmes, but I can't say that I did."

Holmes asked numerous other questions, many of which dealt with how Mrs. Cubitt and her companion had acted while at the station. The gist of Pashley's response was that she and Holmes's look-alike had sat quietly in the waiting room, showing no signs of agitation or worry. There was also no indication that Mrs. Cubitt was under any sort of duress.

"A final question, Mr. Pashley, and then I shall let you return to your important business," said Holmes. "Where were the woman and I supposedly going?"

"To London, Mr. Holmes. The two of you left on the express that goes out every morning at eight. But I guess you've come back, haven't you?"

"So it would appear," Holmes said. "However, I must tell you, Mr. Pashley, that I was not here yesterday, with the woman in question or anyone else."

Pashley peered intently at Holmes, as though scrutinizing his face for some subtle sign of mendacity, and said, "Oh no, you can't fool me. It was you all right."

Holmes let out a long sigh and asked, "Did you talk at all with the man who was here yesterday?"

"No."

"Well, if you had, then you would know he was an impostor. Is that clear, Mr. Pashley?"

"If you say so, Mr. Holmes, I must agree. But why—"

Holmes, growing irritated, cut him off: "That will be explained in due time, Mr. Pashley. For the present, you need only know that a criminal conspiracy is at work and that all is not what it seems. Now then, when will the next express to London arrive?"

After glancing up at the station clock, Pashley said, "In forty-five minutes."

"Then Dr. Watson and I had best be on it," said Holmes. "Good day, sir, and thank you for your help."

As we sat down to wait for the train, Holmes was still fuming over the news that he once again had been impersonated.

He said, "Our adversary's humor is growing stale, Watson, and I do not find myself inclined to laugh. Nonetheless, I am forced to admit that my impersonator must be regarded an actr51or of consummate skill, since he has managed to fool everyone with whom he has come in contact."

"Even Mrs. Cubitt?" I asked.

"A good question, Watson. I cannot say, though I am doubtful in that regard. Very doubtful."

Holmes would not expand upon this answer, which left many questions in my mind, given that Elsie Cubitt had apparently made no attempt to escape from the man pretending to be Holmes. Hoping he would address my questions later, I changed the subject: "Tell me more about your impersonator, Holmes. Do you suppose his purpose is simply to mock you?"

"That is part of it, I am sure, but only a small part. You see, I am growing more certain by the minute that Mrs. Cubitt is not at the center of this affair. She is merely a necessary attraction—bait, as it were—to catch a bigger fish."

I looked into Holmes's eyes and saw at once what he meant.

"Good Lord, Holmes, if that is the case, then you are in the gravest danger. You will be stepping into a trap."

"Indeed I will, Watson. You might even say that is my plan."

Despite my concerns, Holmes refused to discuss the matter further. Instead, the talk turned toward Scotland Yard, and I asked Holmes whether he intended to inform

Deputy Chief Inspector Butler of Mrs. Cubitt's true destination.

Holmes replied, "Do you suppose he would inform us, if the situation were reversed?"

"I hardly think that likely."

"Nor do I. Therefore, I do not propose to hand out any favors to Scotland Yard. Besides, I understand the weather in Glasgow can be quite delightful this time of year."

The express arrived on schedule and we were soon on our way back to London. Holmes, who could be a morose traveling companion, was in an unusually talkative mood. As the level East Anglian countryside rolled by under leaden skies, he discussed at some length the problem before us.

"As you well know, Watson," he began, "the city of London has many a sinkhole into which the darker elements of society may readily disappear. Finding Mrs. Cubitt amid the broad fields of Norfolk is one thing; finding her in the dense tangle of London is quite another. Nor can we be entirely certain that she is even in London."

"But we know she and your impersonator took the train from here," I protested.

"Do we? Could an impersonator, however skillful, fool you, Watson?"

"Of course not. I know you far too well, Holmes."

"Might not the same be said of Elsie Cubitt?"

I now had the answer to my earlier question about Mrs. Cubitt, for I saw at once what Holmes was driving at. "So you do not think that was Elsie Cubitt at the station yesterday with your impersonator?"

"Let us just say, my dear Watson, that I would be very surprised if it was. Even so, I still believe we are heading in the right direction, especially in view of the fact that Mme. DuBois, who is undoubtedly allied with the kidnappers, has already gone to London. That is where we must concentrate our search."

"But as you said, Holmes, London holds many hiding places. Where do we start?"

"We shall start where our trip ends—at St. Pancras Station."

"With all the trains that go through there every day, do you really think someone might remember seeing Mrs. Cubitt or someone impersonating her?"

"An excellent question, Watson. As I have said, our search will be very difficult. However, I have a question for you. Which would be easier to find in a haystack: a simple, straw-colored object or one that is large and garish?"

"Why, the garish one, of course."

"Precisely. Do you see my point?"

I did. We would be looking not for Elsie Cubitt but for the flamboyant Mme. Simone DuBois.

We reached St. Pancras Station before noon, pulling into the huge iron and glass train shed exactly on schedule. The scene was filled with the usual commotion— passengers rushing to and fro, red-hatted baggage men pushing carts piled high with luggage, conductors urging travelers to board quickly, all amid the excited din of voices and hissing of steam from idling locomotives.[3]

After making arrangements to have our luggage sent on to Baker Street, we established that Mme. DuBois's train would have arrived on the same track as ours and then began making inquiries as to who might have seen her. A dozen or so porters were in evidence along the platform, so Holmes and I split up in hopes of finding one who might have assisted Mme. DuBois. Our task proved far easier than anticipated, for within half an hour I found a man who had indeed carried Mme. DuBois's luggage and who, not surprisingly, remembered her very well. Better yet, he recalled her asking him how long the cab ride would be to a certain address—the man could not remember it—on Baker Street.

Holmes, who had come over to join me, now interrogated the porter at some length but was unable to elicit additional information. He thanked the man and gave him a crown for his trouble.

"I suppose it cannot be a coincidence that Mme. DuBois asked about an address on Baker Street," I noted.

"No, but I would not account it a valuable clue, either," said Holmes. "Indeed, I suspect the madame was simply having a little amusement at our expense on the chance we might be following her."

We left the train shed and went through the main concourse to the adjoining hotel, which was nearly as busy as the station itself. As we passed by the front desk, Holmes suddenly stopped and stared at something on the wall behind the clerks. I looked up and saw what had caught his eye: a large panel on which the letters SPH (for St. Pancras Hotel) were emblazoned. Those letters, in identical script, were sewn into the towel we had noted in Mme. DuBois's room at Smythe's Inn.[4]

Holmes approached the first available desk clerk and said in a most ingratiating manner, "I am to meet Mme. Simone DuBois today for a consultation but I seem to have misplaced her room number. As I recall, it is 414, but I am not certain. Could you look it up for me?"

The clerk did so and told Holmes that she had actually been in room 316 but had checked out several hours earlier.

Looking very distraught, Holmes said, "Oh dear, there must be some mistake. We were to meet at half past one. Did Mme. DuBois say where she would be going?"

The clerk said she had not, although he believed she had left in a hansom. I now knew what would happen next and I did not look forward to it.

I said, "I imagine we shall be going up to room 316."

"You know me too well, Watson. Yes, there is no avoiding it. We must have a look."

We climbed the stairs to the third floor and found room 316 near the end of a long, gaslit hallway. Holmes knocked on the door three times—there was no answer—and then bent over to inspect the lock while I kept watch.

Holmes straightened up and removed a set of picks from his jacket pocket. He said, "The lock is a standard item. It will present no problem."

It took Holmes only seconds to open the lock and we slipped inside the room, which was actually a suite with two chambers. The bed was unmade, indicating the maids had not yet done their work. Holmes took this as a positive sign, since anything left behind by Mme. DuBois would not have been taken or discarded.

We began a methodical search of the suite—by this time I was beginning to feel rather like a scavenger picking at the remains of Mme. DuBois—but we found no personal items which might have belonged to her. Even the wastebaskets were clean except for a folded copy of the *Times*. Holmes viewed clues in the manner of a starving man coming upon food—that is to say, no morsel was too small to be digested—and he therefore examined the newspaper carefully, page by page. When he had reached the next-to-last page, his infallible eye caught something.

Handing me the paper, he said, "Look at this page, Watson, and tell me what you see."

I did so, noting that the page contained a miscellany of information, including a schedule of passenger ship sailings from London, Southampton, Liverpool and other ports. I ran down the list and noted a small pencil mark, little more than a dot, beside the *Campania*, a Cunard liner leaving Liverpool at noon Saturday and bound for New York.[5]

"I presume it is the dot next to the *Campania*'s name which interests you," I said.

"It is," Holmes replied, "and I fear the kidnapper's plan is to take Mrs. Cubitt to America."

"You are reading a great deal into a single pencil mark, it seems to me."

"Yes, but at the moment it is all I have to read. Come along, Watson, I need to use the telephone."

Back in the lobby, Holmes placed a call to the ticket office of the Cunard Line. Identifying himself as Inspector David Butler of Scotland Yard, he asked whether a certain Simone DuBois had booked passage for Saturday's sailing of the *Campania*. She had. Holmes then inquired whether passengers by the name of Mr. and Mrs. Cubitt, Mr. and Mrs. Slaney or Mr. and Mrs. Patrick were also ticketed for the trip. They were not. Holmes thought for a moment and then, to my surprise, asked about a Mr. and Mrs. John Baker or a Mr. and Mrs. S. Holmes! I could not tell what the answer was, for Holmes's only response was to say, "I see." He made several more inquiries, mostly relating to the purchase of tickets, and hung up.

"Well, Watson, the charade continues," he finally said. "Not only has Mme. DuBois booked passage on the *Campania*, but so have a certain Mr. and Mrs. John Baker, who, I might add, gave their address as Watson Lane in London."

"I have never heard of it," I said.

"That is because it does not exist," said Holmes. "Still, you should be pleased to know that our adversary has included you in one of his little jokes. Now we face something of a conundrum. Should we go to Liverpool, or do we assume a false, if subtle, clue has been planted and that Mrs. Cubitt and her kidnappers remain in London?"

"We go to Liverpool," I said at once.

"Why?"

"Because we have no choice. If Mrs. Cubitt is in London, we have, by your own admission, absolutely no idea where she might be. On the other hand, we do know that she could be in Liverpool, or traveling there, to take passage on the *Campania*."

Holmes slapped me on the shoulder and said, "Watson, you grow better as a detective by the year. I can find no fault in your analysis. Liverpool it shall be."

Chapter Six

ჰ ჩ

"I Fear Great Trouble Is Coming Your Way"

That night at Baker Street, as Watson faithfully attended to his journal, Sherlock Holmes once again found sleep impossible, his mind a racing locomotive stoked on the infinite fuel of ideas. As he pondered Elsie Cubitt's abduction, and the curious array of clues that had led him inexorably to London, he found his thoughts wandering back to a time long ago, in the green English countryside where he had been raised.

He recalled how, as a child, his parents would always celebrate his birthday by devising a special treasure hunt for his amusement. His mother, with a bit of help from his father, would write clues on small slips of paper and then hide them all about the house. The first clue, which his mother would give him to start the hunt, always began with the same simple rhyme: "Young Sherlock here's a clue/That's made just for you/Use your brains and your eyes/And you'll be sure to find the prize."

His mother was very clever—far more so, Holmes thought, than his father—as her scandalous and long-secret affair with a local don was later to demonstrate with tragic consequences. But she had a certain genius for devising games, and as Holmes grew older, the clues for his annual treasure hunt grew ever more abstruse and subtle.

By the time he was twelve, however, he had become so adept at finding the treasure—usually a book but in one case a prized model ship and in another a chemistry set—that his mother finally decided she no longer had any hope of fooling him.

Now, Holmes wondered whether he was on a similar sort of hunt. The clues he had discovered—the Church Army pamphlets, the wedding ring and the newspaper found at the St. Pancras Hotel, among others—all felt far too pat, as though carefully placed for his convenience. Holmes could not be sure that he was being manipulated, however, for he had learned over the years never to underestimate the stupidity of even supposedly brilliant criminals (Professor Moriarty being the singular exception).

Still, the abduction of Elsie Cubitt gave every indication of being a meticulously planned crime, and Holmes found it difficult to believe that the perpetrators could have made so many careless mistakes. If the clues had indeed been planted, then Holmes was—for the time being, at least—a reluctant player in a game not of his own devising, and he knew he could never win until he seized control of the board.

The question was whether he could do so in time to rescue Elsie Cubitt, who had became an invaluable, and irreplaceable,. pawn in the game. He was certain, however, that she had not been on the train from Worstead the day before. The Elsie Cubitt Holmes knew was a keen-eyed observer of the world and far too astute to have been taken in by an impostor, no matter how skillful he might be. She would have seen through the masquerade at once, Holmes thought, and she would never have cooperated with Abe Slaney, if he was indeed the mastermind behind the abduction.

Unfortunately, Holmes had no idea where Elsie might be at the moment, and he was very worried. Already, he found himself missing the wise and witty letters she sent to him at least twice a week, not to mention their frequent visits at Ridling Thorpe Manor and elsewhere. He could not bear the thought that she might come to harm. His life, he knew, would not be the same until he found her, and he would turn the world on end if that was what it took to bring her home.

Holmes, his long feet dangling over the edge of the couch where he lay, took out his watch and saw that it was nearly midnight. Tomorrow, he and Watson would go off to Liverpool on what Holmes feared would be a fool's errand. The fact that Mme. DuBois and the impersonators traveling as Mr. and Mrs. Baker had all booked passage on the *Campania* did not strike Holmes as any great cause for optimism, since he very much doubted they would actually board the famous Cunard liner.

There were at least three other liners, as well as several smaller vessels catering to the immigrant trade, scheduled to leave either Southampton or Liverpool for New York on Saturday. Elsie Cubitt and her kidnappers might be on any one of these, or they might, for all Holmes knew, be somewhere else entirely. Still, Watson had been right. Since the clues pointed to Liverpool, there was no point staying in London absent some compelling reason to do so.

Although Holmes remained in the dark as to Elsie Cubitt's whereabouts, he had at least learned something useful about her background in Chicago. This was a topic she had absolutely refused to discuss with him, for as she had written in one letter, "Chicago was the Dark Ages for me, Mr. Holmes, and I see no reason to go back to that period of my life by dredging up old and painful memories. I am a new woman here in England and I intend to stay that way."

Now, however, Holmes had in his possession a cable from Detective Wooldridge in Chicago that had arrived late in the afternoon. It revealed, among other things, that

Eban Patrick—Elsie's father and a legendary Chicago hoodlum—had been shot dead only two months earlier while leaving his saloon late one night. Wooldridge went on to report that the assassin had yet to be identified, although suspicion had fallen on a rival crime lord. With Eban Patrick dead, his gang had been taken over by one of its most prominent members, Jake Slaney, Abe's younger brother and the operator of a dozen brothels on Chicago's notorious South Side. As for Abe Slaney, Wooldridge reported that he had not been seen in Chicago for more than two years and was "presumed dead."

In all their correspondence, Elsie Cubitt had never talked about her father—to her, he was perhaps just another rejected piece of her past—so Holmes was not surprised that she had never mentioned his violent end. Yet Holmes could not help but wonder whether Eban Patrick's recent death was somehow related to his daughter's disappearance. With that in mind, he had already sent another cable to Wooldridge requesting more information about Eban Patrick's demise and about Jake Slaney.

It was well past three o'clock in the morning by the time Holmes fell at last into a fitful sleep. He was soon to be awakened, however, in order to receive a startling piece of news.

"It is Inspector Martin on the telephone," a voice said out of the darkness.

Holmes opened his eyes and saw the familiar face of Watson, hovering over him like a pale, distracting moon.

"Very well," Holmes said, unbending himself from the confining contours of the couch and taking out his watch. It was just after six o'clock. "The inspector is up terribly early, don't you think, Watson?"

"He says it is urgent. And in any event, we must be ready shortly. The Liverpool train leaves at half past seven."

"So it does," said Holmes as he walked into the sitting room and picked up the phone, which sat atop a desk next to one of his prized possessions—a photograph, taken at Ridling Thorpe Manor, of Elsie Cubitt.

"Good morning, inspector," Holmes said. "You must have news of great importance to call at such an early hour."

"I do, and must say I am happy to have reached you, Mr. Holmes, as I was by no means certain where you might be found. Now, before I begin, I must ask you to treat this call as strictly confidential. Butler in particular must never know about it. Indeed, it would be best, Mr. Holmes, if you were to regard this call as never having taken place. Otherwise, I could be in great trouble."

"You may rely absolutely upon my discretion, Inspector Martin. Now, what is it you have to tell me?"

There was a long pause before Martin said, "It is about some letters, Mr. Holmes, which were discovered last night in the study at Ridling Thorpe. They were in a hollowed-out book. The letters, Mr. Holmes, are from you to Mrs. Cubitt."

Holmes had expected that the letters would be found, and while the thought hardly pleased him, he also knew that there was nothing in them that should be of interest to the authorities.

"I have had a long correspondence with Mrs. Cubitt," Holmes said, "but I fail to see of what interest that would be to Scotland Yard or anyone else."

After another long pause, Martin said, "Well, sir, there is one letter which is—I am not sure how to put this—very explicit in its language."

"Explicit in what way?"

"In the way a man might talk about making love to a woman, sir."

"I wrote no such letter," Holmes said at once.

"Well, sir, the problem is, the handwriting looks just like all the other letters from you. There is something else you should know, Mr. Holmes. The letter speaks of you wanting to go away with Mrs. Cubitt, only it seems she was not willing to do so. At least, that is what the letter suggests, sir."

"Read me the letter," Holmes said. "I wish to hear the great lie."

"Very well, but as I said, you will not like it one bit."

As Holmes listened with appalled disbelief, Martin read the letter, which was dated June 23, 1900, and went as follows:

My dearest Elsie:

It is time to come to a decision, my love, regarding our fate together. I have for many months now felt the powerful stirrings of a passion only you can invoke in me. Indeed, I had long thought I could never have feelings for a woman such as those I have for you. Late at night, playing some lonely melody upon my violin, I find that you are the true music of my soul and that only by becoming one with you—in every sense—can I ever hope to satisfy the desire which threatens to overwhelm me. To feel your warm body against mine, in the sacred union of the flesh, is now the highest hope I dare aspire to. In this you must not deny me or I fear for both of us.

I know you are reluctant to leave Ridling Thorpe Manor, as you would somehow regard this as an insult to your late husband. Yet I do not believe that Hilton would want his memory to stand in the way of your happiness. I also know I could never hope to live the dull and regular life of a country squire. I require the stimulation which only London, or some other great city, can provide. Surely you must understand this. Indeed, your moving to London, or even New York if that is your preference, does not seem too high a price to pay if it is the only way for us to be together.

We have already talked much about this, perhaps too much, and now you have said your mind is made up. I refuse to believe that! When I hold your alabaster hand in mine, when I behold the intoxicating swell of your gentle bosom, when I gaze into your limpid eyes and see there all that any man could ever want, I refuse to entertain the dread thought that you might never be mine.

If you do not consent to join me soon, I shall be as a man condemned to a dungeon and lost forever to the light of the world. Please, Elsie, do not abandon me, or I shall not be responsible for what might happen, since I will do everything—and anything—to keep you.

Yours in the Greatest Love and Affection,
Sherlock Holmes

When Martin finished, Holmes felt a primal anger rising from deep inside, and it was only with the utmost effort that he maintained a level voice. He said, "How could anyone possibly believe I would ever write such tripe? It is the stuff of some cheap novel for the lovelorn, and it is most certainly part of a crude scheme to discredit me. I am sure you must be aware of that, Inspector Martin."

"I am happy to believe every word you say, sir, but Deputy Chief Inspector Butler, well, he has other ideas. That is why I called you, Mr. Holmes. He now regards you as a suspect in the lady's disappearance. You see, we have heard nothing as yet from the supposed kidnapper about claiming his ransom. Butler is beginning to think the whole business is a charade and that you may have been involved in kidnapping Mrs. Cubitt. The idea is ridiculous, of course, but I thought you would want to know what is happening up here. I fear great trouble is coming your way, Mr. Holmes, and I can only hope you will be ready for it."

Chapter Seven

§ ₹

"Now We Must Do a Bit of Heavy Lifting"

FROM THE NARRATIVE OF DR. JOHN WATSON:

The telephone call from Inspector Martin on Friday morning was but the beginning of a series of events so startling that even Holmes was hard-pressed to keep up with them. These developments brought home to us in the starkest manner imaginable that we were confronting villainy at once brilliant and remorseless. Indeed, I had the sense that we had been plunged headlong into an abyss and must now find our way through a dark and uncharted realm of criminal manipulation.

The letter read to Holmes over the telephone was but one example of how our world had been made as topsy-turvy as the plot of a Gilbert and Sullivan opera, but without the humor or song. Although Holmes described the letter to me only in general terms, I knew from the few phrases he quoted that he could not possibly have written it, even if he was in love with Elsie Cubitt. Holmes's writing was always precise and scientific, and he abhorred the sloppy sentiment found in popular literature (of which, however, he read a great deal). And yet Scotland Yard now seemed ready to believe in the genuineness of a letter which was an obvious forgery!

Said Holmes, "I am all but dumbstruck, my dear Watson, by the Yard's handling of this matter. It would ap-

pear that my article in the *Daily Telegraph* not only
touched a nerve but inflamed it to the point that the patient has gone mad!"

"Perhaps you should call the superintendent of the
Yard, or even the home secretary, and make your outrage
known."

"Under normal circumstances I would agree with you,
Watson, but I somehow doubt either gentleman would be
interested in hearing from me at the moment. I would ask
Mycroft to intercede on my behalf but he is not due back
from the continent for another week. Besides, there is no
time to waste in such petty arguments when we have a
train to catch in an hour."[1]

We left London at half past seven for the trip to Liverpool, and as I feared would be the case, Holmes was silent
during much of the train ride. The forged letter clearly
preyed upon his mind and was the topic of what little discussion we had. Even so, he refused to reveal anything
about his genuine letters to Mrs. Cubitt, or of her letters
to him, despite what I confess to be intense curiosity on
my part. However, I knew well enough not to press
Holmes on the matter, since he has long proved immune
to my limited tools of persuasion.

At one point, Holmes emerged from a long silence to
observe, with a tinge of bitterness I rarely heard in his
voice, that Deputy Chief Inspector Butler "would have to
be a perfect idiot to consider the letter as anything other
than a hoax."

"Perhaps you should have telephoned him before we
left, to explain the situation," I suggested.

"You may be certain, Watson, that I very much wished
to do so," he replied. "However, I might then have put our
friend Inspector Martin in jeopardy, since Butler would
wonder how I had learned of the supposed love letter."

Holmes's explanation made perfect sense, yet I now

began to fear that our trip to Liverpool could leave the impression we were fleeing the authorities. I put this concern to Holmes, but he dismissed the notion as "absurd" and said the hunt for Mrs. Cubitt must take precedence over all else.

"I care not one whit for what the authorities at Scotland Yard think about me," he added sourly, "since they have thus far demonstrated a remarkable inability to think intelligently about anything at all having to do with this case."

We arrived on schedule at the Lime Street Station in Liverpool, which looked as dreary as ever under a deck of low clouds. Holmes bought a newspaper with the latest shipping news and we then went by cab to the Trials Hotel. As we rode toward the hotel, Holmes—who was becoming ever more wary and watchful—thought a man in another hansom might be following us. Holmes directed our driver to make several turns until the pursuer, if indeed he was one, fell out of view.

At the hotel we signed in under new aliases—Holmes as John Hudson ("a salute to our landlady at Baker Street," he told me), and I as Peter Stamford (after the man who had introduced me to Sherlock Holmes years ago). We then went upstairs to our rooms on the third floor. Without bothering to unpack, Holmes sat down on the bed in his room and pored over the schedule of ship departures.[2]

"I see the *Campania* is still scheduled to depart tomorrow for New York, while the White Star's new *Oceania* will leave this evening," he said. "A number of smaller ships will set sail later today or tomorrow. Ah, what have we here?"[3]

"I take it you've found something of interest," I said.

"Perhaps. It seems that one ship has already left today for New York. The ship, as it so happens, is called the *St.*

Paul. I wonder if our friend Mr. Rafferty knows there is an ocean liner named after his fair city?"[4]

"We shall have to ask him the next time we see him, although I doubt that will be soon."

Said Holmes, "When it comes to Mr. Rafferty, I have found that expectations have a way of being capsized, as it were. In any case, we have our work cut out for us today, Watson, and we had best be at it immediately."

Our first stop turned out to be the busy dockside offices of the Cunard Line, operators of the *Campania.* The offices, in an old stone building on Strand Street not far from the vast, forbidding warehouses of Albert Dock, were crowded with passengers of every conceivable nationality and class. As we made our way toward the ticket counters I heard a sufficient number of exotic languages to convince me that we had arrived in the new Babel.[5]

After a wait of some minutes, we finally reached the window of one of the ticket agents—a moon-faced man with lugubrious brown eyes and a double chin which drooped almost to the collar of his crisply starched uniform. Holmes presented himself as an acquaintance of Mr. and Mrs. Baker, the names under which the conspirators— or perhaps even Elsie Cubitt and a companion—were thought to be traveling.

"I trust you can help me, sir," Holmes began earnestly. "I am trying to locate a certain Mr. and Mrs. John Baker of London, who are to travel on the *Campania* tomorrow. There has been an emergency at home—their little boy, Jack, has been taken fearfully ill—and I must reach them immediately. Unfortunately, I do not know which hotel they are staying at, or even whether they have reached Liverpool as yet. It occurred to me, however, that they might already have checked in here, in which case you might be able to tell me where they are staying."

The agent, in a voice that fairly oozed indifference, replied, "It is company policy not to provide information about passengers to unknown parties."

Holmes directed a withering stare at the agent and said, "I see. Is it also Cunard Line policy that two first-class passengers should be allowed to depart for America without being told that their only son is deathly ill? If it is, then I would think such a policy would be of great interest to the newspapers of Liverpool and even London, as would be the cruel-hearted agent who enforced it. In fact, I know my acquaintance, Mr. Lanier at the *Daily Telegraph*, would be particularly happy to learn of such a story."[6]

The agent's dead eyes came to life as he scrutinized Holmes and realized that he was just the sort of man who would indeed make trouble. "Well, sir, I do not think you need take matters to that degree," the agent said. "Perhaps I could be of some assistance to you after all. Just let me check the bookings. Ah, yes, here they are, Mr. and Mrs. Baker. I am afraid they left only a London address, sir, but I can tell you that they have not yet checked in today."

"I see. How long do they have to do so?"

"We close at five o'clock, sir."

Holmes turned as if to leave but then spun back around to face the agent. He said, "I have just thought of one more possibility. A dear friend of the Bakers, Mme. Simone DuBois, is sailing with them tomorrow. Has she perchance checked in or left an address here in Liverpool where we could reach her?"

Again, the agent went through the passenger list and informed us that Mme. DuBois had indeed checked in earlier and could be reached at the North Western Hotel next to the Lime Street Station.[7]

We proceeded at once to the hotel, a mammoth stone pile with arched windows, towering pavilions and a look of shabby gentility. Holmes used one of his usual subterfuges with the front desk clerk to learn that Mme. DuBois had taken room 224 on the second floor.

"Would you see if she is in?" Holmes asked the clerk.

After signaling her room through an enunciator system and receiving no response, the clerk said, "It would appear she is out, sir."

"I presume, then, that you would not know where she has gone."

"She left no information in that regard, sir."

"Thank you," Holmes said. "We will try to reach her later."

We went back outside and I knew, of course, what Holmes had in mind.

I said, "It is to be yet more breaking and entering, I assume."

"I prefer to think of it as routine investigative work, Watson. Besides, I do not plan to break anything."

We found an open door on the alley side of the hotel and walked up the back steps to the second floor. Once at Mme. DuBois's room, Holmes knocked several times as a precaution. Receiving no answer, he took out his set of lock picks and put them to use. The lock yielded readily under his expert touch. After taking one last look up and down the hallway, Holmes pushed open the door.

The room was large, handsomely furnished and gave no evidence of recent occupation except for a brown leather suitcase on a small stand beside the bed. Holmes made a swift tour of the room, noting that the bed was neatly made and that no toiletries or other personal items were to be seen.

"It would appear Mme. DuBois has not yet taken the time to unpack," he said. "Well, Watson, I shall have to have a look at the suitcase. In the meantime, I think you'd best go back outside and stand guard by the stairway. If Mme. DuBois should happen to return, find a way to delay her and be noisy about it so that I may leave without being seen. Rest assured, I will not be here for very long."

I went out to wait in the hallway but saw no one during my vigil. Holmes joined me ten minutes later and we left the hotel by the same route we had entered. Safely outside, Holmes reported yet another intriguing find.

"The lady's suitcase contained all the usual items of travel and one that was quite extraordinary—a necklace with an attached locket," Holmes said. "I naturally opened the locket and inside I found a photograph of Hilton Cubitt. Now, unless Mme. DuBois had some sentimental attachment to the late Mr. Cubitt, which I doubt, then we must assume that the locket belongs to his wife."

"Was the locket of itself a valuable piece of jewelry?" I asked.

"I see your line of thinking, Watson, and it is a very good one. To answer your question, the necklace and locket are of quite ordinary quality."

"Then I must wonder why Mme. DuBois bothered to take it with her."

"As must I, Watson. It suggests, as you have previously noted, that our adversary is deliberately leaving a trail of clues behind in order to lead us into a trap of some kind."

"Well, if that is to happen," I said, spotting a restaurant across the street, "I do not propose to be ambushed on an empty stomach. I am starving, Holmes, and we have had no lunch. I suggest we avail ourselves of the restaurant over there."

Holmes glanced at the restaurant, which was called the Criterion, and said, "Yes, it will do, Watson, so long as we take a table by the window. If Mme. DuBois returns to the hotel, we shall spot her, although I suspect she has already gone elsewhere."

"But her baggage is in the hotel," I noted.

"So it is. However, it may already have served its purpose, in which case she has no intention of reclaiming it. Well then, let us see what the Criterion has to offer."

Lunch, however, proved disappointing in every respect. The food was dry and overcooked and there was no sign of Mme. DuBois. At three o'clock, Holmes announced that we should return to our hotel, since he held no hope we would catch sight of the elusive madame. As I began to slide back in my chair, Holmes reached across the table and grabbed me firmly by the wrist.

"We shall not be leaving by the front door, Watson," he said very quietly. "There is a gentleman sitting at the other end of the restaurant who came in not long after we did. He is perhaps forty years old, has brown hair and eyes, is of average height and build, possesses conventional features and is wearing very ordinary clothes. He is, in other words, a perfectly unremarkable fellow, except for one thing: he is the same man who, I am now certain, followed us from the train station to our hotel. Presumably, he has been observing us ever since, although I would note that he is quite proficient at his craft, for this is only the second time I have spotted him."

I said, "It could be a mere coincidence, Holmes. He may be staying at the North Western or some other hotel and simply came in for a quiet lunch."

"Perhaps, but I very much doubt it," Holmes replied. "Indeed, what is most peculiar about this week is that absolutely nothing appears coincidental." This remark was followed by an odd question: "You went to the water closet earlier, Watson. What did you see? Tell me everything you can remember."

As this was far from the strangest query ever put to me by Holmes, I did not hesitate to answer it. I soon learned why he was so interested in the water closet, for after pronouncing himself satisfied with my response, Holmes sketched out a plan we were to follow.

I sipped the last of my tea, arose from the table, and then went toward the water closet, located past a sharp turn in a hall that led to the back door of the restaurant. Once inside the water closet, I opened the door just enough to see into the hall and then waited. A short time later, Holmes—who had stayed behind to pay the bill—came down the hall and went past me toward the back door.

Holmes had predicted that the "unremarkable" man would follow. He did. Looking to be in a great hurry, the man fairly sprinted past me but when he reached the back door he found he could not push it open. Again following Holmes's instructions, I came up quietly behind the man and, using the butt of my pistol, delivered a blow sufficient to knock him senseless. Assault had now been added to the day's roster of crimes.

Holmes, who had leaned against the back door to block it, stepped back inside and went through the man's clothing. He found nothing except a small amount of money.

"Perhaps we should try to question him," I said.

"There is no time, Watson, and this is hardly the place to do so in any event. Besides, I have little doubt the man is a well-paid professional. As such, he would provide us with no useful information. Now, let us be on our way before he wakes up and makes a scene."

We followed a circuitous route back to the Trials Hotel, with Holmes acting as vigilantly as a sentry on the battlefield. When we reached the hotel, Holmes insisted that we enter by the rear door to avoid any watchers in the lobby.

It was now late afternoon and I intended to take a much-needed rest. I parted with Holmes at my room, which adjoined his. However, I had barely enough time to loosen my tie and sit down before there was a knock at the door. I opened it to find Holmes, his long face pale and solemn.

"You had best come into my room at once, Watson."

I knew by Holmes's expression that something was seriously amiss. But I was hardly prepared for what happened next. I stepped into Holmes's room and saw, lying face down on his bed, a woman who was both naked and by all appearances dead. Her left arm dangled over the side of bed, while her right arm curved up toward her curly auburn hair. Her legs were spread widely apart in a provocative but unnatural way. Her clothes—a white blouse with a lace collar and puffed shoulders, a short red jacket with large shell buttons, a long dark skirt, a bustle and various other undergarments—were strewn on the floor around the bed.

"My God, is it—" I began.

Holmes said, "No, it is not Mrs. Cubitt. That was my first thought as well. You will, however, find that this woman's facial features are very close to hers. Indeed, they could almost be sisters. Now, come around, if you would, and examine her for any sign of life, although I hold no hope in that regard."

I soon confirmed that the woman had no pulse and was not breathing. Her body was still warm, however, and there were no signs of rigor mortis, indicating that she had died very recently—probably within the past hour. The cause of her death was no mystery, for I noted ligature marks around her neck. This was clear evidence that she had been strangled with a rope or cord of some kind. Her head was twisted to the left and I could see that Holmes had been right about how much she looked like Elsie Cubitt. I guessed her to be about thirty-five years old.

"Who do you suppose she is and how did she get here?" I asked.

"Watson, you have as usual cut to the heart of the matter," Holmes replied. "I can answer both questions in a general way but this is not the time for lengthy explanations. We must first make a thorough search of the room. Then we shall have to remove the corpse so that—"

"Remove the corpse? How on earth do you propose to do that, Holmes, in a large hotel such as this and at an hour when many people will be about?"

"I am sure I will find a way. The trick will be to move her just far enough to lead the police astray."

"But shouldn't we be calling the police to inform them of this murder?"

Holmes looked coolly at me and said, "What, pray tell, would be our explanation, Watson? That the body mysteriously appeared in my room while we were out? Of course, that happens to be the truth, but I should imagine even the dullest constable would have a question or two about such a tale. As a result, we would most certainly be at police headquarters for hours, by which time Mrs. Cubitt and her abductors might be long gone, assuming they are not already far away, which I fear is a distinct possibility. Besides, I see no need to call the police, since I am inclined to think they will arrive shortly as it is."

"Why do you think that?"

"Let us just say it is an educated guess, based on what we know about our adversary. Now then, why don't you look about the room while I go through this poor woman's clothes? Make sure you search well, Watson, for I should not be at all surprised to find that some piece of evidence has been planted to incriminate us in the crime."

I began my search immediately but could find nothing out of order. Holmes's suitcase was where I had seen it earlier in the room. The furniture also gave no sign of having been moved, nor could I find blood on the floor or anywhere else in the room. Indeed, the room appeared exactly as it had when we left—except, of course, for the dead woman sprawled on the bed. At Holmes's request, I also looked for anything, such as a purse or wallet, which might help us identify the victim. Again, I drew a blank.

Holmes, however, found something of great interest—a folded sheet of stationery carefully tucked under the top drawer of a dresser in the corner of the room. He opened it at once and cursed softly as he scanned the contents.

"What is it, Holmes?"

After refolding the document and putting it into his coat pocket, he said, "It is a letter I wrote some weeks ago to Mrs. Cubitt. The murderer left it here for the police to find, just as I feared. Keep looking, Watson! There may be more unpleasant surprises."

We could find nothing else of an incriminating nature, however. Holmes then sprang his latest surprise. He said, "I recall seeing a fire alarm in the hallway, Watson. I would like you to go out and pull it. Then begin shouting 'fire' at the top of your lungs. Make sure you direct everyone who responds to the alarm to leave the building immediately."

"But why—"

"Just do it, Watson. I will explain later."

I had learned through many adventures with Holmes that, like a great field marshal, he was always master of the situation and that his every action, no matter how inexplicable it might appear, was directed toward some ultimate strategic end. I therefore went out into the hall, broke the glass casing and pulled the alarm. Instantly, bells began sounding. I did my best to add to the confusion by shouting out warnings and pounding on the doors of the dozen or so rooms on the floor. Startled guests began pouring into the hall, including a woman and a man whose lack of attire was nothing short of scandalous.

Within minutes the hall was empty, all the occupants of the floor having fled downstairs in the belief their lives were in danger. Hardly had the last person left before Holmes went down to a room several doors away from his and speedily gained entry with his lock pick.

"All right, Watson, we must do a bit of heavy lifting," he announced. "Come with me."

I now understood what Holmes had in mind and was, I admit, quite stunned by the prospect before me. Never before during my many adventures with Holmes, not all of which entailed strictly legal behavior, had I felt so much like a criminal. Yet I also knew that the case of Elsie Cubitt's disappearance was different from any other in our experience, so strange and almost dreamlike in its particulars that even Holmes, I think, was thrown off his usual balance.

The task before us, however, was disturbingly real, and I had to fight off feelings of disgust and shame as I helped Holmes lift the woman's body from his bed. Holmes took her head and shoulders while I hoisted up her legs, and off we went, two gentlemen from London in the novel business of relocating a corpse. Holmes made a last check of the hallway, which was deserted, before we carried our grim cargo to the vacant room. Once inside, we laid the woman gently on the bed, in the same way we had found her. Holmes then went back to his room to fetch her clothes while I waited with the corpse. He was back moments later and tossed her clothing around on the floor, just as it had been in his room.

"I must tell you, Holmes, that I find what we have done to be extremely distasteful," I said.

"As do I," Holmes responded. "However, it is our best chance to gain some time."

"Do you really think the police will be fooled into thinking the woman was murdered in this room?"

"One should never doubt the ability of the police to reach the wrong conclusion, Watson. In any case, we have done all we can do to mislead the forces of law and order. It is time to leave."

We returned to our rooms to pick up our belongings. As neither of us had unpacked, this was quick work, although Holmes spent extra time making a last sweep of his room to be sure we had left behind no clues which might link us to the dead woman. He also left a payment for our rooms and then quickly scrawled out something on a notepad.

I asked Holmes what he was writing.

"A little clue for the police, should they care to notice it."

He tore the note from the pad and handed it to me. It said, "George Square, Glasgow, noon Sun., under Scott, red tam, folded newspaper right hand."[8]

At first, the note made no sense to me, but then I recalled that the supposed ransom exchange for Elsie Cubitt was to be in Scotland. "I imagine you hope to trick the police into searching for us in Glasgow," I said.

"That is the idea," Holmes acknowledged. "My note, I believe, will be interpreted as referring to a meeting of some kind in connection with Mrs. Cubitt's disappearance. Now then, Watson, kindly fold up the note and put it in your pocket. When the police find out I occupied this room, they should also find the impression left by my message on the notepad. The baying dogs will then, with luck, be sent toward Scotland and away from us."

The corridor was still empty by the time we left Holmes's room and went down to the alley-side door by which we had entered the hotel less than an hour earlier. Suitcases in hand, we walked down the alley and around the corner to Lord Street, where we hailed a cab. As we stepped into the hansom, three fire engines followed by a pair of police carriages raced past us toward the hotel.

Our driver remarked that there must be a fire, to which Holmes responded, "It is probably just another false alarm."

I had only the faintest idea where Holmes intended to go next, but his intentions became clear when he instructed the driver to proceed to the ticket office of the White Star Line.

Barely three hours later, after Holmes had sent a cable to Inspector Wilson Hargreave of the New York Police Department, we were aboard the *Oceania* en route to America, leaving in our wake more trouble than I cared to imagine.

Chapter Eight

ᔓ ᔓ

"We Will Be Home in Chicago Before Long"

Sherlock Holmes knew that going to America was a tremendous gamble, but as he stood late that night on the deck of the *Oceania* and gazed up at a pale crescent moon coursing through banks of clouds above the Irish Sea, he was confident he had made the right decision. Indeed, it was possible Elsie Cubitt could even be hidden away somewhere in the cabins below him, drugged and kept under lock and key by her abductors.

Yet Holmes thought this unlikely, and he thought it even less likely that she would board the *Campania* when it sailed in the morning. That would have been far too obvious. Holmes believed she was most probably aboard a small ship—a freighter, say, or even a chartered yacht. It would be far easier to transport her across the North Atlantic under that sort of arrangement than to risk discovery amid the bustle and crowds of a large liner.

As he considered how skillfully she had been kidnapped, Holmes felt grudging respect for the mind of his opponent. It was a mocking kind of mind that prized cleverness and misdirection and made meticulous plans. Yet as the murder of the unknown woman in Holmes's hotel room had demonstrated, it was also a mind capable of great ruthlessness. This latter quality certainly suggested the involvement of Abe Slaney—Chicago criminals, as Holmes knew, had a well-documented fondness for acts of barbaric brutality. Subtlety, on the other hand, had never been Slaney's strong suit, and Holmes wondered if he might have a partner, or even a superior, in crime. Of course, that assumed Slaney was alive—a fact by no means in evidence.

What Holmes did know was that he and Watson had left England under a cloud—or, at the least, one that would be forming very soon. Although the *Oceania* was the largest and newest liner afloat, it had not yet been equipped with Marconi's wireless system, and so Holmes had no way of knowing what the police had found by now in Liverpool, but he could guess.[1]

He suspected, to begin with, that either the police or firemen had had sufficient sense to look into all the rooms on the hotel's top floor following the alarm. This meant they must have found the corpse. Holmes was also fairly certain that the police had quickly learned that he and Watson had been guests on that floor. Much to his displeasure, Holmes was so widely recognized in England (thanks to Watson's stories and Sidney Paget's skillful illustrations) that traveling incognito was very difficult without full disguise. In fact, when Holmes and Watson had checked in at the Trials under their assumed names, the clerk had given them a knowing look as if to say, "You can't fool me but if you want to use a fake name, so be it."[2]

Holmes could not be certain what would happen when he and Watson reached New York but he expected the police would be on hand to greet the *Oceania* when it docked. From there, he would have to talk his way out of any trouble. This was a minor concern, however, compared to the disappearance of Elsie Cubitt. Although Holmes had no real evidence (as opposed to the manufactured variety) that she was on her way to America, he believed that had been the destination of her abductors all along.

He could not explain with his usual precise logic exactly how he knew this. However, when Watson had raised the question not long after they boarded the *Oceania*, Holmes had told him, "I know Mrs. Cubitt is going to America because the world is notable for both symmetry and chaos; indeed, the one cannot exist without the other. And as we have already had chaos aplenty in this affair, I think it is time to look for symmetry."

Watson, whose mind tended to be blessedly literal, had not thought highly of Holmes's "explanation" and pressed for a better answer. Holmes had none and Watson had gone off unfulfilled once again. To Holmes, however, the situation was simple. Elsie Cubitt had come out of the Chicago underworld, and now she was being pulled back into it, as surely as a ship being sucked into a giant whirlpool. Symmetry demanded it.

On the morning of Thursday, July 12, while the *Oceania* still plied the North Atlantic, the S.S. *St. Paul* docked at the Chelsea Piers in Lower Manhattan after a six-day crossing from Southampton. Of its eleven hundred passengers, fewer than one hundred had traveled in the first-class cabins. Among them was a black-bearded man and his feverish, bedridden wife, who had to be wheeled down the gangplank in a hired gurney. The man, said to be a prominent physician from Chicago, told other passengers that his wife had become violently ill in London and that he was taking her at once to see the finest specialists in New York.

"Do you suppose she will survive?" asked one matron with whom the doctor chatted.

"I am certain of that," he replied. "Indeed, I do not doubt that we will be home before long."

Book Two

New York

Chapter Nine

ʃ ֆ

"I Told Them to Go to Hell"

FROM THE NARRATIVE OF DR. JOHN WATSON:

As we approached New York after a smooth crossing aboard the *Oceania,* I was in a state of some apprehension. I feared that upon arrival we might be taken from the ship like common criminals on orders from Scotland Yard. Holmes himself accounted this "a distinct possibility" given the bizarre events in Liverpool and the open animosity of Chief Deputy Inspector Butler. As we strolled late at night on the deck, watching a long knife of moonlight part the waters of the North Atlantic, Holmes talked at some length about the events which had caused us to leave so suddenly for America.

"I have not been good company for the past few days, have I, Watson?" he began, rather uncharacteristically.

"No worse than usual, Holmes. I have learned that you are not a man who enjoys the sea."

"True, but at least this trip has given me time to think about our situation. What happened in Liverpool could have unfortunate consequences for us."

"Are you really so certain of that, Holmes? After all, you have many friends—not to mention your brother, Mycroft—at the highest levels of government, and I still find it difficult to believe the Yard could ever consider us to be criminals."

"So it would seem, Watson. I trust, however, that you have not forgotten our little investigation earlier this year at Ten Downing Street. The results were hardly what Lord Salisbury had in mind, and I imagine he would take some pleasure in seeing me humiliated. The prime minister could make any number of unpleasant things happen to us, if he set his devious mind to the task. He would not, for instance, be above using Scotland Yard to express his displeasure. That is one reason why the dead woman in Liverpool is so troublesome."[1]

"Do you have any idea who the woman might have been?"

"I do not know her name, of course. However, I think it safe to conclude that she served as Mrs. Cubitt's stand-in. It was she who was seen at the station in Worstead with my impersonator. For all I know, she may even have paraded around London with the fellow, to ensure additional sightings, before they moved on to Liverpool."

"But where has Mrs. Cubitt been all this time?" I asked.

"I do not know. My assumption, however, is that she was subdued and perhaps drugged not long after being taken into the Church Army van outside her estate. She was then transported in some manner to Southampton or another port—almost assuredly not Liverpool—and taken aboard a liner, a freighter or some other ship bound for America. I trust the cable we sent to Inspector Hargreave will allow him to find her before she disembarks in New York, which is where almost all the transatlantic liners from England dock. As for Mrs. Cubitt's stand-in, she was murdered because our adversary had no further use of her services. My guess is that she was a courtesan or perhaps an actress and may well have known nothing about the real reason for her engagement."

I found it difficult to accept Holmes's analysis, for the idea of someone going to such elaborate lengths to embarrass and entrap us seemed almost too incredible to contemplate. When I mentioned these doubts to Holmes, I also pointed out that if our antagonist wished to implicate Holmes in some wrongdoing regarding Mrs. Cubitt, he could have done so most dramatically by leaving *her* body in Holmes's hotel room!

"My dear Watson, the older you get the more astute you become," Holmes said with a smile. "However, you forget that Slaney—if he is indeed the great Conspirator behind all of this—has long professed his love for Elsie Cubitt and presumably would be unwilling to murder her. Besides, I am sure he reasoned that the discovery of any corpse in my room would be sufficient to provoke scandal and tie us up with the police for many days. In the meantime, of course, he intended to escape with Mrs. Cubitt to America. However, I think he will be surprised to learn that we evaded his snare and are not far behind him."

Holmes paused to light his pipe and after several satisfactory puffs continued, "As for your observation, Watson, that the elaborate scheme I have described seems too fantastic to believe, I would note that the improbable can be perfectly logical, if no other explanation fits the facts. However, if you have a better explanation . . ."[2]

I confessed that I did not, to which Holmes's only immediate response was an irritating smirk. Later, however, before I retired for the night, Holmes—while further discussing the means and possible motives of our adversary— offered what I can only describe as a chilling prophecy.

"The Conspirator has set in motion a scheme which is full of masquerades and dodges and laid everywhere with traps for the unwary. I have even likened it, more than once, to a game of sorts. Yet do not doubt for a moment, Watson, that behind it all is a cold and powerful malignity of spirit. Our adversary's sense of humor, if it can be called that, is very much of the graveyard variety, and what he wishes in the end, I am convinced, is to achieve nothing less than the ruin of our lives, and Mrs. Cubitt's as well. That is why the game we find ourselves in can end in one of only two ways: either we shall destroy our enemy or he shall destroy us. There can be no other resolution."

We steamed into New York Harbor just after nine o'clock on the morning of Friday, July 13—an inauspicious date, as subsequent events were to demonstrate. The day was clear and calm and we had a magnificent view of the Statue of Liberty, the Brooklyn Bridge and the towers of Manhattan. No other city on earth, I thought, offered a more sublime interplay between the divine hand of our Creator and the ceaseless work of human civilization. After the immigrants aboard had been taken off by ferry to the customs office, the *Oceania* was guided up the Hudson River and maneuvered by tugs into the Gansevoort pier near Twelfth Street.[3]

Now came the moment of trepidation, for as the great vessel finally settled into its berth, I looked down at the gangplank and saw a contingent of uniformed police officers. I presumed they were waiting for us and wondered whether Holmes and I would now be placed under arrest or, at the least, subjected to lengthy interrogation. When we reached the bottom of the gangplank, the officer in charge came forward and said, "Am I correct in thinking that you are Sherlock Holmes and Dr. John Watson?"

"You are, sir," said Holmes. "Is there something you want of us?"

Replied the officer, "You are to come with me immediately."

Other policemen fell in around us and we were marched to a small office in one of the pier's freight stations. Inside, we were greeted by a most delightful surprise. Standing by a file cabinet and looking perfectly at ease was a tall, heavy set man of middling age, with a thick nose, small hazel eyes beneath startling white lashes and a large round head undisturbed by any eruption of hair. A badge was attached to the breast of his finely tailored silk suit coat.

"Inspector Hargreave! What a pleasure to see you again," said Holmes.

"The feeling is entirely mutual, sir," came the reply. "Welcome to New York City."

Our first dealings with Hargreave dated to the early 1890s, when he had cabled Holmes for information about a notorious London criminal thought to be operating in New York. Holmes's timely and enlightening response had enabled Hargreave to solve the case. Since then, the two detectives had been in occasional contact across the Atlantic, and Hargreave had provided valuable information about Abe Slaney during the affair of the dancing men. However, we had not actually met Hargreave until September of 1899, while we were in New York investigating a small matter for the Astor family. Our most recent contact had been in April, when Holmes had aided in the capture of a notorious Tammany Hall embezzler who had fled to London.[4]

"I must say, inspector, I am surprised you saw fit to bring along so many policemen to escort us," Holmes remarked.

"Just part of the show, Mr. Holmes, to keep the brass happy. You see, our department received a cable Wednesday from Scotland Yard. Seems there's been something of a hullabaloo in England involving you and Dr. Watson. It's in all the newspapers over there, or so I understand. According to Scotland Yard, you and the supposed kidnap victim were last seen together holding hands at St. Paul's Cathedral in London. Now, the Yard thinks that maybe you brought her here for some nefarious purpose."

I had wondered how long it would take the sensation-alists of Fleet Street to drag Holmes into the affair of Mrs. Cubitt's abduction, not to mention the murder of the woman in Liverpool. Clearly, it had taken no time at all and I thought it possible Scotland Yard itself had impli-cated Holmes in the press.

"And what do you make of all this strange news from England?" Holmes asked Hargreave.

"I am of a mind, Mr. Holmes, that somebody across the pond is telling a fairy tale. Be that as it may, the cable from Scotland Yard said you and Dr. Watson might be ar-riving on the *Oceania* today. The Yard asked that we de-tain you pending additional instructions."

"Really. What exactly are we to be detained for?"

"Well, sir, it seems that you and Dr. Watson are 'mate-rial witnesses' in a murder case in Liverpool. Seems a London prostitute by the name of Lily Young was found strangled in the hotel where the two of you were staying. It further seems there are 'some questions'—that is how it was phrased—regarding your role, if any, in the lady's de-mise."

"I see," said Holmes. "May I ask how you responded to Scotland Yard's request?"

Hargreave answered in a booming voice, "Why, I told them to go to hell, of course, in the biggest damn hand-basket they could find. I also told them that when the day comes that Sherlock Holmes cannot be trusted to do the right thing, why that will be the same day the stars fall from heaven and the sun don't shine."

"Inspector, you have my deepest thanks," said Holmes, "and you may indeed be assured that Dr. Watson and I have, as you put it, 'done the right thing.' Still, I should be interested to know what you have heard about our recent adventures in Liverpool."

"I know damned little beyond what I've already told you. Business as usual, in other words, when it comes to

Scotland Yard. Those fine, high-fallutin' gentlemen of the Yard"—Hargreave pronounced these words with obvious contempt—"are not inclined to share information with a mere plebian such as myself. That being the case, I see no need to share anything with them, including your whereabouts, Mr. Holmes, if that's the way you want it. You should know, however, that my superiors over on Mulberry Street will not like it when they find out from the brass at Scotland Yard that I ain't cooperating with them. Once the heat gets turned on, I don't know how long I can protect you."[5]

"Then we shall broil together," said Holmes gallantly.

"Fair enough. Now, if you'll tell me why you're here, I'll be happy to help you in any way I can."

A shadow of concern now crossed Holmes's face. "It was all in the cable I sent last week," he said.

Looking very much mystified, Hargreave replied, "A cable, Mr. Holmes? I'm afraid I've received no communication from you for several months."

"How very strange," said Holmes. "I have normally found the cable service to be extremely reliable."

"I'm sorry, Mr. Holmes. I can check—"

"It is too late for that. I fear the damage has already been done."

Holmes now provided a brief account of our investigation into Elsie Cubitt's abduction, ending with our hurried departure from Liverpool. However, he did not mention how we had removed the corpse from his hotel room.

"Since you've come all the way here, I take it you believe Mrs. Cubitt was spirited off to New York," Hargreave noted.

"Yes. I had asked in my cable for you to keep a close watch on ships from England. However, I think it likely she and her abductor arrived here ahead of us and intend to go on to Chicago, if they have not already done so."

"I'll put my men at the ferry terminals and train stations on the lookout," Hargreave said. "There are only so many ways to get off the island, Mr. Holmes, and we know 'em all."

"I greatly appreciate your help, inspector. In the meantime, Dr. Watson and I will be in need of a place to stay. A comfortable but inconspicuous hotel would be ideal."

Hargreave suggested the Hotel Albert, in the old neighborhood of Greenwich Village. He said the hotel was "a bit off the beaten track and very quiet."[6]

Said Holmes, "That appears to be exactly what we need. I have one other immediate favor to ask, inspector. There is a woman by the name of Mme. Simone DuBois who may be traveling aboard the *Campania,* which is due to arrive here tomorrow. It would be helpful if your men could keep a lookout for the lady, who will not be difficult to spot."

Holmes provided a description of Mme. DuBois while cautioning that she could be arriving on a ship other than the *Campania.* He also noted that it was "remotely possible" Mrs. Cubitt and her captor might also be on board, though he was all but certain they had already come in on another vessel.

"Any idea which ship they did arrive on, if as you suspect they're already here?" Hargreave asked.

"I have an idea, inspector, although I would hesitate to call it a good one. Still, it is better than no idea at all. Where are the offices of the American Line?"

Hargreave gave us directions to a pier only a mile away. Holmes thanked him again and promised to let him know what we found out. Then, after making arrangements to have our bags forwarded to the hotel and converting our money to dollars, we set off at once in a taxi for the American Line's pier.

As we got underway, I asked Holmes what led him to believe Mrs. Cubitt and Slaney had reached New York ahead of us.

"It is, I admit, a deduction based on the flimsiest of evidence. Yet if there has been one feature of this case which separates it from all the others in our experience, it is the fact that our adversary wishes to tweak us with his very brazenness. He has therefore used an impostor to make it seem that I am somehow linked to Mrs. Cubitt's disappearance. Of course, he even attempted to implicate us in a murder. Given all of this, I am of a mind that he may have thought it amusing to undertake another little joke when the time came for him to cross back to America with Mrs. Cubitt."

"What sort of joke?"

"You will see soon enough, Watson—if I am right."

I had anticipated a quick ride to the American Line's terminal but once we entered upon the dizzying chaos of West Street I feared we might never reach our destination. Although very wide, this thoroughfare, running parallel to the river, was choked with freight vehicles of every description, from huge canvas-covered wagons to small carts, as well as a tangle of carriages, taxis and bicycles. Numerous pedestrians, peddlers and loungers were also to be seen on the street, which was notable for the fact that more traffic appeared to be going crosswise (between piers and warehouses) than lengthwise, as we were attempting to do.

"I never thought it possible to see traffic worse than London's, but I must now pronounce myself wrong," Holmes remarked.

Our driver, fortunately, was a man of the classic New York temperament, which is to say he was utterly without patience, fear or regard for his fellow human beings. With commendable ruthlessness, at least from Holmes's point of view, he fought his way through traffic amid many lurid oaths and deprecations. We reached the terminal after a harrowing ride of thirty minutes, which struck me as far more dangerous than any storm-tossed crossing of the

North Atlantic. Holmes gave the driver five dollars after remarking to me that the man "could probably drive a load of
ice through hell and frighten the devil out of Satan himself."

The American Line terminal was a long, massive brick
building hardly distinguishable from the warehouses
around it. Inside was a large waiting room equipped with
rows of hard, straight-backed benches of the type found
in churches favoring mortification of the flesh. The ticket
and baggage agents stood behind a long counter at the
rear. Fortunately, the terminal was not busy, as no ships
were scheduled to arrive or depart until much later in the
day. Holmes immediately approached the nearest clerk—
a sallow man with a long freckled face, thin red hair
combed to one side and pale blue eyes beneath thick spectacles.

"Good morning," said Holmes. "I am in need of information and trust you can accommodate me."

"We are here to serve, sir. How many I help you?"

"What kind of service would this buy?" said Holmes,
slipping a ten-dollar gold piece on the counter.

"Quite a bit," the clerk replied, expertly sliding the
coin across the counter under the palm of his hand.

"I thought so. Now, am I safe in assuming that you
were working here yesterday when the *St. Paul* arrived
from England?"

"I was."

"Good. Please tell me whether a couple—a man and
his invalid wife—disembarked from the *St. Paul.* The
woman may have been taken off on a gurney, in a wheel-
chair or even by an ambulance crew. Do you remember
such a couple?"

"Indeed I do, sir," said the clerk. "Saw the ambulance
itself when it arrived."

"Splendid! What was the couple's name?"

"Rafferty, I believe," the clerk replied. "If you can wait

a moment, I'll check the passenger manifest." After rummaging in a large file cabinet behind him, the clerk pulled out a form and said, "Yes, here it is. The man who bought the ticket was a Dr. S. W. Rafferty, of London. He had one-way tickets for himself, his wife and his brother. They all came from Southampton."

The name, I realized, could not have been a coincidence, especially given that our friend Shadwell Rafferty hailed from the city of St. Paul. I also recalled that Inspector Hargreave had mentioned a supposed sighting of Holmes and Mrs. Cubitt at St. Paul's Cathedral in London. That, too, I thought, could not have occurred by happenstance.

Holmes now asked the clerk, "Did you see this Mrs. Rafferty yesterday?"

"Not to speak of, sir. She was all swaddled up. Very sick, from what I was told."

This was chilling news indeed, for it suggested—just as Holmes had predicted—that Mrs. Cubitt had been administered some powerful drug to render her insensible.

"Yes, I imagine the lady was quite ill," said Holmes. "What about Dr. Rafferty? Did you see him?"

"Sure, he was supervising the ambulance crew. I got a look at him. Average-sized fellow, black beard, quite friendly. Funny, though, he didn't sound like you gents even though he was coming from England."

"He sounded very American, in other words?"

"Yes. I'd say so."

"What about the brother?"

"Sorry, I didn't notice him."

"Very well. Now then, where did the Rafferty clan go after the ambulance picked them up?"

"You're in luck there, sir. I remember Dr. Rafferty telling one of the porters to forward their things to the Astor House."

"I am not familiar with the establishment. It would be —"

"On lower Broadway, sir, not far from City Hall," the clerk said. "It's an older hotel, but very comfortable."[7]

Holmes now asked the clerk which ambulance service had picked up the woman we suspected must be Elsie Cubitt and her two captors.

"We only allow the Mercy Ambulance Company to assist our passengers, sir. They have an excellent reputation."

"I see. By the way, when does the *St. Paul* make its next trip to London?"

"She will be leaving tonight at eight o'clock."

"Does she have the same crew going back that she arrived with?"

"Mostly, though not all the men sign up for the round trip. Is there some particular reason why you wish to know, sir?"

Holmes smiled and said, "Idle curiosity. Thank you for all of your help."

We now retired to one of the benches in the cavernous waiting room. Holmes stoked up his favorite briar pipe and said, "Well, Watson, we can now be certain that we are but a day behind Mrs. Cubitt and whoever is traveling with her. That may be taken as positive news, I suppose. On the other hand, I am not sure what to make of the fact that our adversary made a point of visiting St. Paul's Cathedral and then traveled on the *St. Paul* using Mr. Rafferty's name. However, the mere fact that he knows of Mr. Rafferty is highly suggestive."

"Why do you say that?" I asked. "After all, our friend has earned a good deal of publicity in his own right, especially after the business of the Secret Alliance."[8]

"True, but his name has never, to my knowledge, been publicly linked with ours, except perhaps in a rather limited fashion in Minnesota. Well, let us leave it as a small mystery for the moment, since we have matters of more immediate import to occupy us."

"I presume we will be going to the Astor House."

"Yes. It may be possible to find out something useful there, although I do not hold out any great hopes."

"Perhaps the ambulance service might be a better source of information," I suggested.

"Perhaps. However, I think that is work best left to Inspector Hargreave and his men. Ah, I see a telephone against the far wall. Let us hope the inspector is back at his office by now."

He was, and over the telephone Holmes asked him to track down the ambulance crew that had taken the woman we assumed to be Mrs. Cubitt from the ship. Holmes also requested that Hargreave's men canvass the *St. Paul*'s crew to see to which of them might have come in contact with the supposed invalid and her "husband."

After hanging up, Holmes said, "Inspector Hargreave's men will set to work at once, although he cautioned that most of the *St. Paul*'s crew has probably scattered through the city already. That will make canvassing them difficult. Even so, I have no doubt his men will be up to the job. I have always found the police detectives of New York to be highly skillful, even if their honesty has frequently been called into question."[9]

"Then it would seem we have made a good start," I said.

"We have, Watson, although Inspector Hargreave also informed me, to use his words, that 'the mad dogs of the local press have started sniffing around' after hearing rumors of our arrival. I need not tell you that publicity is hardly what we need at the moment."

I was not so sure this was true. "Wouldn't it be of help if the press made the public aware that Mrs. Cubitt is here?" I asked. "The eyes of New York, millions of them, would then be on the alert."

"So they would, Watson, and under normal circumstances that might be accounted a good thing indeed. But these are not normal circumstances, simply because we do not know what the newspapers here have been told about our sudden departure from England. I fear all manner of malicious stories are already circulating and that we, as opposed to the real criminals, will become the focus of attention. I do not believe, in other words, that we can count upon the press for help of any kind."

Outside the terminal, we hailed a cab for the Astor House. I asked Holmes what he hoped to accomplish there, since it hardly seemed likely that our adversary would have given away his real destination, knowing that we might be in pursuit.

"But did he in fact know that, Watson?" Holmes responded. "Remember, he left Liverpool thinking that we would be detained there by the police after their convenient discovery of the woman murdered in my room. Therefore, he had no reason to believe, as he and Mrs. Cubitt sailed across the North Atlantic, that we—or anyone else, for that matter—would be close behind. It is just possible, in other words, that he let his guard down."

Our cab was soon underway, and before long we were plunged into the vast, noisy maw of Lower Manhattan, still looking for answers and for Elsie Cubitt.

Chapter Ten

ʃ ʔ

"Who Are You?"

As the ambulance jarred and swayed along the rough, crowded streets of Lower Manhattan, Elsie Cubitt once again began to experience the strange sensation that had haunted her for days. It was a feeling that she had been pulled out of the familiar matrix of time and space and sent hurtling through gauzy layers of twilight into some vague, faraway corner of the cosmos. Worse, her own body seemed to have been left behind, and she was conscious at times of watching it with complete disinterest, as though it could no longer be of any possible consequence to her.

All of this had begun to happen, as far she knew, on her journey across the Atlantic. Most of the weeklong voyage was already a blank. In the fog of narcotic drugs, her memories of her time aboard the *St. Paul* had faded away one by one, like ships vanishing over the horizon. What remained in her mind were a few fugitive sights and sounds—the crash of lightning near the ship one storm-tossed night, dark cliffs glimpsed through a porthole, a tenacious fly buzzing around her nose, voices as soft and indistinct as moon shadows and a man's face.

The face was by far the clearest of all her recollections, and she had done everything in her power to burn it like a fiery brand into her memory. There was, she knew, something at once familiar and, paradoxically, unfamiliar about the face, which was that of a man with a wiry black beard, dark curly hair and coal-black eyes that offered no hint of tenderness or feeling. He was, she sensed, someone out of her past, but the part of her memory that could connect names and faces seemed not to be working. Still, her reaction to the face was so visceral that she could not doubt he had once made some deep impression upon her.

"Who are you, who are you?" she murmured to herself as the ambulance pulled to a stop just before she drifted back into unconsciousness.

"Well, it looks as though we'll have to speed up the timetable a bit," said the man with the black beard as he and his assistant sat in the sparsely furnished parlor of their rented apartment in Manhattan. They had just moved in, and Elsie Cubitt lay asleep in the adjoining room, having received her latest injection.

"The two of them arrived this morning on the *Oceania*," the older man now continued. "Inspector Hargreave himself was there to meet them."

"I'm still surprised they got out of Liverpool so quickly," said the other man, who was young and clean-shaven and who was busy cleaning a handsome silver-plated pistol. "I thought for sure the coppers would hold them up for a few days while they tried to explain away the body."

"That was the plan, but Sherlock Holmes is no fool. We'll have to be very careful now, as he will turn this town upside down in search of his dear Elsie." The last words were spoken with a kind of a sardonic disgust. "Still, we have him right where we want him."

"Then when will we do it?" inquired the younger man, inspecting the barrel of his gun. "I'm ready any time you are. It'll be a turkey shoot, I guarantee it."

"I'll let you know after I've talked with Chicago," said the older man, who thought that his young hired hand, while undoubtedly as good an assassin as money could buy, had a tendency to overestimate his own prowess. It was the kind of cockiness that could get a man killed if he wasn't careful.

"What about her?" asked the young man, jerking his head toward the room where Elsie Cubitt lay. "You still plan on dragging her all the way to Chicago? If it was me, I'd—"

"You, sir, will do as you're told and leave the planning to me and to our ally in Chicago. Now, why don't you quit playing with that toy of yours and get some rest? You'll have little chance for it in the days to come."

"All right, Mr. Slaney, you're the boss," the young man said, idly twirling the pistol and thinking how his reputation among the criminal classes would soar after he had killed one of the most famous men in the world.

As the two men talked, Sherlock Holmes and Dr. John Watson were but a few miles away, in the hansom taking them to the Astor House. All around was one of the world's great urban spectacles, notable for its unprecedented agglomeration of skyscrapers, but Holmes hardly noticed any of it, for he had just been struck by a singular idea.

Although Holmes presented himself to the world as a perfect thinking machine, rigorous and unyielding in his deductions, the truth was that on occasion he relied upon inspiration. He did not like the word—it was vague and mystical—yet it was the only one he knew that described how ideas sometimes occurred to him.

Holmes was able to receive such inspiration because, like a Zen monk, he understood the incalculable value of emptiness. He approached every investigation with a blank mind, and some of his greatest moments of insight, he had found, came streaming out of the ether, unbidden and unexpected. Part of his genius lay in being able to snare these brilliant ideas before they could slip past, much as one of Marconi's new radio receivers plucked electronic signals out of the atmosphere. Of course, such ideas were always as crude as a lump of raw ore and therefore in need of heavy intellectual refinement, but more times than not they proved to be the kernel of an important theory.[1]

Now, as the cab fought its way toward Park Row through Broadway's horrendous tangle of traffic, Holmes had snagged an idea from the cosmic chaos. The idea was so startling, and so intriguing, that he could not help but play with it for awhile. Its appeal lay in the fact that it might explain what to Holmes was *the* great mystery of the case thus far: how did the Conspirator, especially if he was Abe Slaney, seem to know so much about the earlier investigations in Minnesota?

Not only did the Conspirator know about Shadwell Rafferty but he was also aware that Holmes sometimes traveled under the name of John Baker. Holmes had used this alias during only four cases—all in Minnesota. The logical conclusion, therefore, was that the Conspirator must either have been on the scene of at least one of the Minnesota cases or have been in contact with somebody who was. And if that was true, then Holmes might have to do some serious rethinking about who lay behind Elsie Cubitt's kidnapping.

Chapter Eleven

♪ ♫

"What Cheek!"

We reached the Astor House around noon after another harrowing cab ride. The hotel was surrounded by dizzying new office towers, which rose like monstrous stalks along Broadway and nearby streets. Even the steeple of old St. Paul's Chapel, across from the hotel, was easily eclipsed by these gigantic temples of commerce, which condemned the surrounding streets to a gloomy state of perpetual shadow.

The Astor House turned out to be a modest establishment of only five stories and no great architectural distinction. After paying our cabman, we went inside at once and sought information at the front desk. Holmes asked for the room of "Dr. Rafferty and his wife" but was told by the clerk—an older man with thinning gray hair and lugubrious features—that no such guests were registered at the hotel.

Holmes, looking crestfallen, said, "It is just as I feared. She must have been even more ill than we thought. So she did not arrive at all then, I take it."

"I'm sorry, sir, I don't quite understand," the clerk began. "Are you referring to—"

"Why Mrs. Rafferty, man, Mrs. Rafferty," Holmes replied impatiently. "She has been terribly ill—a bad catarrh, I believe, as well as certain problems of the female sort. Dr. Rafferty was afraid she might not tolerate the crossing, especially if the seas were rough. Perhaps she went at once to the hospital. I am certain Dr. Rafferty had reservations here. Did he cancel them? Look and see, will you?"

Murmuring his assent, the clerk began thumbing through the hotel's reservation book. "Ah yes, here it is, sir. My, this is curious."

"Why is that?"

"Well, sir, it seems Dr. Rafferty did have a reservation and was here yesterday, but then changed his mind and decided not to take a room after all."

"Did he say why?"

"I wouldn't know, sir. Perhaps you should talk to Mr. Morgan. According to the notation I have here, he was the clerk who dealt with Dr. Rafferty yesterday. Besides, he enjoys talking with private detectives such as yourself, as long as there's some money in it. I would say ten dollars—half for me, of course—would secure his complete cooperation."

Holmes smiled and said, "I see you are no stranger to inquiries such as ours."

"That would be an understatement, sir."

Holmes paid the clerk and we were directed to Morgan, who was working at the other end of the long front desk. Much younger than his fellow clerk, he had black hair cut very short, broad shoulders and sharp, aggressive features.

This time, Holmes dispensed with the preliminaries, handing Morgan five dollars and telling him we wished to know "everything about Dr. Rafferty's visit to this hotel yesterday." Just to be certain we were on the right track, Holmes described the black-bearded man who I was beginning to think might indeed be Abe Slaney.

"That sounds like Dr. Rafferty all right, though the man I saw might have been a bit younger. I can't be sure, however."

"All right, tell us what happened yesterday and do not stint with details," said Holmes.

"Well, Dr. Rafferty comes in just after noon yesterday and says he's got a room reserved," Morgan reported. "He does, so I start to get him set up. Then I see there's already a message waiting for him. I give him the message, which he opens right away, and then—just like that—he changes his mind. Says he won't need a room after all and marches right out the door. Wasn't here more than five minutes in all."

"Do you know what sort of message he received?"

"I might."

It was obvious the insolent fellow wanted more money. I would not have given it to him, nor in most circumstances would Holmes, I am sure. But Holmes was obsessed with staying as close behind our quarry as possible and had no wish to waste even a minute's time haggling. Therefore, he put another five dollars on the desk.

"This will be the last money you receive, sir," he said. "I warn you that you had best earn it or I will make great trouble for you. Now, what sort of message did Dr. Rafferty receive?"

Morgan, snapping up the second gold coin, put it into his trouser pocket and said, "It was a cable, sir, from England, I believe."

"Where in England?"

"Liverpool, as I recall."

"What a fine talent for snooping you have, Mr. Morgan. Now, when did the cable arrive?"

"I'm not certain, but it came several days before Dr. Rafferty showed up."

"What did it say?"

Morgan, doing his best to appear deeply offended, replied, "I would have no idea, sir. I do not read other people's mail."

"On the contrary, Mr. Morgan, you strike me as exactly the sort of man who would do just that," Holmes said, his voice like acid etching through metal. "Now, I must ask you again, what were the contents of the message?"

"I really don't know, sir."

"Is it more money you want?" Holmes asked impatiently, his eyes boring in on the clerk. "You will not have it, sir, but I will most certainly have the truth. Do you understand?"

Morgan, however, held his ground. He said, "I can't tell you what I don't know. I didn't read the message. I'd be fired in a minute for doing something like that."

Holmes gave the clerk another long stare and then said, "Very well, Mr. Morgan, I will take you at your word. But if you have lied to me, I promise that you will deeply regret it. Now, what did Dr. Rafferty say to you after receiving this mysterious cable?"

"All he said was that there'd been a change of plans and he wouldn't need the room after all."

"Did he say what this 'change of plans' might entail?"

"No. He wasn't what you would call the real talkative type."

"I see. Did he make any arrangements to reply to the message?"

"Not here, though we are always happy to deliver messages to Western Union for our patrons."

"Where is the company's nearest office?"

"Just two blocks down Broadway, sir, at Dey Street. Western Union's headquarters are there."[1]

After Holmes had put forth a few more questions, none of which elicited interesting answers from Morgan, we left the hotel. I assumed we would proceed to the Western Union office but Holmes was not inclined to do so. I asked why.

"The telegraph companies have strict rules regarding the privacy of messages sent through their operators," he said. "I doubt that even a substantial bribe would enable us to find out whether our adversary sent any kind of message yesterday. Inspector Hargreave, on the other hand, would have no such trouble, and so we shall have to rely on him to make inquiries."

"Then perhaps we would have time for lunch, Holmes," I said.

"Are you really that starved, Watson?"

"I merely like to eat now and then, Holmes, and would recommend a similar course to you, as it is a necessary habit you do not seem to have acquired. You cannot live entirely on tobacco."

"All right, Watson, we shall satisfy your mortal cravings. First, however, I must telephone Inspector Hargreave one more time. Then we shall sit back and see what his men can accomplish."

Hargreave's team of detectives proved to be as proficient as advertised, for by early evening the inspector had intriguing news to report on several fronts. He met us at our hotel, to which we had retreated after lunch, Holmes in the mood for solitary contemplation while I did the sensible thing and napped. Holmes called me into his room after Hargreave's arrival and we listened with great interest to his report, delivered in his usual pungent manner.

"Here's the straight dope, gentlemen," he began. "I'll start with what we learned from the crew of the *St. Paul*. There's a bunch of gin mills over in the Bowery where swabbies go to throw away their money on women, liquor and dice, so I sent a few of my men that way to see what they could find out. We got lucky right away. At a dive called Tilly's Tavern, one of my dicks found a steward from the *St. Paul* who'd seen Slaney—or the man who looks like him—and his supposed wife in their stateroom."

"Good work," Holmes said. "Pray continue."

"Well, this fellow was already several sheets to the wind, but he managed to recall that the lady—whose description, by the way, fits Mrs. Cubitt to the letter—was lying in bed, apparently asleep, the only time he got a glimpse of her. He also saw a hypodermic syringe on a table next to the bed and was told by her supposed husband that she was very sick and would have to remain sedated for the entire crossing."

"It is just as I suspected," said Holmes. "Did the steward note anything else of interest?"

"He did, though it took my detective no small effort to get anything like a coherent statement from the fellow. In any event, it seems there was a third person in the cabin—a young man—who was identified only as an 'associate' of Dr. Rafferty's."

Said Holmes, "Ah, that would be the supposed 'brother,' I imagine. Did this young man give his name?"

Hargreave grinned and said, "He did, only I'm of the opinion it was an alias. You see, he identified himself as Dr. John Watson, recently of London."

"What cheek!" I said.

"Indeed, but then that is the hallmark of our adversary," said Holmes. "Could the steward describe this 'Dr. Watson'?"

"Only vaguely," Hargreave replied. "He told my man that the young doctor was perhaps thirty, with sandy hair, blue eyes and a 'wide face,' whatever that means. As I said, the steward wasn't in the best of condition to talk. By now he's already back aboard the *St. Paul*, assuming he didn't tumble into a gutter or get rolled. I should add that aside from this fellow, we found no other crew members who recalled seeing Elsie Cubitt, though quite a few remembered 'Dr. Rafferty,' who was described as a very friendly gentleman and a handsome tipper."

"Well, please compliment your detectives for a job well done, inspector," said Holmes. "I presume your men also tracked down the attendants from the ambulance company who removed Mrs. Cubitt from the ship."

"Yes, and an interesting story it is. The attendants were instructed by Slaney, or whoever in blazes he is, to take her to a small townhouse on Gay Street in Greenwich Village. But Slaney didn't go along with her. Instead, he went directly to the Astor House, according to the hackman who took him there."

"Then who went with Mrs. Cubitt?" I asked.

"Why it was you, doctor, or I should say, the young fellow who borrowed your name. Young Dr. Watson, as I'll call him, rode with the lady in the back of the ambulance."

"Was Mrs. Cubitt still unconscious at this time?" Holmes asked.

"She was. Fact is, the attendants told my man that she appeared to be in a deep coma. In any case, they hauled her to the townhouse, then carried her up the steps inside. After that, they were promptly paid and dismissed."

"I see. Did they talk at all with 'Dr. Watson' during the ride?"

"Afraid not," Hargreave said. "He insisted that they stay up front while he ministered to the lady."

"How solicitous of him. Was anyone else at the house when the attendants arrived?"

"No. This Watson fellow had a key to the house and let everyone in. The attendants stayed inside just long enough to transfer the woman to a small bed set up in the front parlor. They did note, however, that the house appeared barely furnished—a fact 'Watson' explained by saying that the property had only recently been purchased."

"Knowing you as I do, inspector, I feel safe in assuming that your men have already visited the house in question," Holmes said.

"They have. You'll not be surprised to learn that my men found the house empty, except for the bed and a few items of linen. Nor, I imagine, will you be surprised when I tell you that the house was a rental property. But you may be surprised to find out who rented it less than a month ago."

Holmes said, "I should imagine it was rented, over the telephone, by a gentleman with an English accent named Holmes. Am I correct?"

"By God, sir, you are a wizard! It happened just as you have said. How did you know?"

"Let us just say that I would have expected nothing less. It is all a part of the great pretense our adversary has constructed, to mock and bedevil Dr. Watson and me. I do not doubt that our names will turn up in many more unlikely places before this affair is done. Now then, did anyone in the neighborhood see Mrs. Cubitt being removed from the house yesterday, as she must have been?"

"Yes. There's a grocer across the street and fortunately for us, he's a very nosy fellow. He saw the ambulance arrive. About three hours later, or so he says, a large coach pulled up in front of the house. A man got out, and judging by the grocer's description, it was our friend 'Dr. Rafferty.' Pretty soon, he and young Dr. Watson emerged from the house, carrying several large pieces of baggage, which they put on top of the coach. Then they went back inside, got the lady, brought her out on a stretcher, lifted her into the coach and signaled the driver to go. As far as we know, that's the last anybody's seen of Mrs. Cubitt, or her companions."

"What a curious series of events!" Holmes remarked. "It suggests that our adversary had a sudden change of plans and therefore had to act quickly."

"I was thinking the same thing," said Hargreave. "Otherwise, why would he go to all the trouble of hiring an ambulance to take the lady to that house, only to move her out a few hours later? Something must have spooked him."

Holmes, who had begun drumming his fingers on the side of the armchair where he sat, said, "So it did, and I think I know what it was, particularly considering the source of that cable he received at the Astor House. However, before we get into that, I should like to hear the rest of your report, inspector, beginning with the matter of Mme. DuBois. Have you found any trace of her?"

"The short answer, Mr. Holmes, is no, though it ain't for want of trying. No woman of her description was aboard the *St. Paul*, the *Campania* or any other liner docking in New York this week. Of that, I am certain, for my detectives made thorough inquiries and they can't be easily jobbed. Nor have we found any evidence that the lady hired a hack or boarded a train. In short, Mr. Holmes, I doubt this Mme. DuBois is in Manhattan. Maybe she never left Liverpool."

"Oh, I think she did. Still, she might have gone on to another port—Boston perhaps—to throw us off the scent. Do you have any friends with the Boston police, inspector?"

"Several."

"Then—"

"Say no more. I'll see to it that inquiries are begun at once."

"Thank you. That leaves us with at least one more matter of immediate interest. Did your men find out anything at Western Union headquarters?"

Hargreave looked slyly at Holmes and said, "No, but I did. You see, I went there myself since I happen to be well-acquainted with the company's regional superintendent. It took but a few minutes to learn that you were correct, Mr. Holmes. Just as you suggested to me over the telephone this morning, 'Dr. Rafferty' sent a telegram after he left the Astor House yesterday. I imagine you'd like to see a copy of it, though it doesn't make much sense as far as I can tell."

"I would indeed!"

After scanning the message, Holmes passed it on to me and I saw what Hargreave had meant. While the telegram was clearly addressed to one John Smith (presumably an alias) at 2135 South Dearborn Street in Chicago, its contents—twenty or so words—were pure gibberish. I could only assume the message was in a code of some kind, a suspicion Holmes quickly confirmed.

"It is obviously a word substitution code," he said, "but it is hardly long enough for me to have any hope of deciphering it. I would note, however, that one word—'rat'— is used four times, which is a high degree of frequency in so short a message. I would also note that the addressee, Mr. Smith, resides in the very same part of Chicago where Abe Slaney's criminal gang once flourished, for unless I am mistaken the 2100 block of South Dearborn is in the heart of the infamous Levee vice district."

"I believe you're right, Mr. Holmes," said Hargreave. "I once toured the area on a visit to Chicago. The address is probably a mail drop, however. All the smart crooks use them and I'm betting the fellow you're after ain't dumb."

"I think that would be a safe bet. Even so, I know just the man in Chicago to find out who may or may not reside at that address. Now, since we are on the topic of telegrams, inspector, I am wondering if you would be able to track down a copy of the transatlantic cable Slaney re-

ceived at the Astor House. It would have been in code, of
course, but comparing it with the message he sent to
Chicago could prove useful."

"I will get it to you as soon as possible."

"You are indeed the indispensable man, Inspector Hargreave, and I cannot thank you enough."

"It's always my pleasure to help out a fellow detective.
By the way, I'm curious about something you mentioned
earlier. You said you had an idea what might have caused
Slaney to move Mrs. Cubitt out of the house in Greenwich Village so quickly. I'd like to know just what your
theory is."

"It is, as you have said, only a theory," Holmes replied.
"Still, I think it entirely possible that the cable Slaney received at the hotel was from one of his confederates in
Liverpool. The message presumably reported that Dr.
Watson and I had evaded the trap set for us and were on
our way to New York. I think the dead woman left in my
room in Liverpool was merely a delaying action. The intent was to slow down our pursuit so that Mrs. Cubitt's
kidnappers would have plenty of time to put their plans in
place once we arrived here in America."

Said Hargreave, "I'm not sure I follow you, Mr.
Holmes. Are you saying that Slaney expected all along
that you would pursue him across the Atlantic?"

"That is exactly what I am saying. What he didn't anticipate, however, is that Dr. Watson and I would be so
close behind him—a fact he must have learned from the
cable. He therefore had to relocate Mrs. Cubitt immediately, since he knew we could trace her movements from
the *St. Paul* in short order."

"So you think he had originally planned to keep her at
the house for quite awhile."

"Yes, perhaps even for a week or longer."

"Where's the lady now?"

"Unfortunately, I have no idea, but I imagine she is still in New York, perhaps at another rented house or apartment. Perhaps your men could—"

"Make inquiries about recent rentals. We're already on that, Mr. Holmes, but it'll be no easy task in a city of this size."

"I understand, but do your best. In the meantime, I should like to take a look at the house on Gay Street, just to satisfy my curiosity."

"I'll make the arrangements," said Hargreave. "Now, is there anything else I can do to be of help to you?"

"I think not, for you have already done more than I have a right to ask of you. Besides, I expect that we shall hear shortly from our adversary. The game is far from over, inspector. Indeed, I suspect it has only begun."

Chapter Twelve

$\int\int$ ~

"Everything Is in Order"

I t was nearly midnight by the time Sherlock Holmes lay down in his spacious room at the Hotel Albert, but he had no intention of sleeping, despite the weariness lodged in every one of his angular bones. He was used to driving his body beyond normal human limits—this was both a gift and a curse—and with so many thoughts to occupy his mind sleep seemed out of the question. No, it would be a night of "wrestling," as he liked to call it, the mental tug of war by which he was able, more often than not, to pull certainty from the hard grip of doubt. The affair of Elsie Cubitt's kidnapping, however, was a contest as arduous as any he had ever engaged in, and he knew that there would be no easy triumphs of the sort the world had come to expect of him.

As Holmes saw it, the fundamental difficulty of the affair lay in establishing the true identity of his opponent. That his adversary was intelligent, powerful and ruthless was beyond question. That he was, in fact, Abe Slaney, was far less apparent. Although the bearded man posing as Elsie Cubitt's husband clearly resembled Slaney, Holmes attached no particular significance to this fact. After all, Holmes himself had an impersonator in the case, as did Elsie, and there was no reason to suppose that Slaney might not have one as well.

Several other considerations also served to feed Holmes's growing doubt that Slaney was in fact the Conspirator behind Elsie Cubitt's kidnapping. The frequent allusions to earlier investigations in Minnesota seemed to point away from Slaney, since he had no involvement in any of those cases. There was also a real question in Holmes's mind as to whether Slaney was even alive.

The official conclusion that Slaney had drowned in Plymouth Sound after escaping from Princetown Prison did not strike Holmes as at all unreasonable. As a youth, Holmes had sailed the sound's treacherous waters and knew how easily a man in a small boat there could be swept out to sea, never to be seen again. Holmes also wondered why, if Slaney was alive, there had been no word of him since his disappearance more than a year earlier. Slaney was a rough, violent and flamboyant man — not the type to melt comfortably into the background, especially in England — and Holmes believed that he would have turned up in Chicago by now had he really escaped. And if that were the case, Detective Wooldridge, among others, surely would have heard about it.

There was also the matter of Slaney's blunt and forceful personality, which did not seem to fit the nature of the case. Elaborate scheming was simply not Slaney's style, no matter what other offenses might be charged to him. Holmes had met Slaney only once, on the day almost two years earlier when he had lured him to Ridling Thorpe Manor and arrested him at gunpoint. After his capture, Slaney had impressed Holmes with his forthright admission of guilt, readily acknowledging that he had shot Hilton Cubitt. Slaney's version of events was never challenged at his trial, where he again admitted to the crime. Overall, Slaney had struck Holmes as an honest man according to his own harsh code.

Yet if not Slaney, then who was the Conspirator and

what motive drove him? Holmes hoped Wooldridge might provide some answers. Earlier that night, Holmes had tried to telephone the legendary Chicago policeman but was unable to get through because of a problem with the lines. He had then sent a telegram requesting more information about Slaney's background, about the activities of his old gang and about the address on South Dearborn Street to which Slaney (or the man posing as him) had sent the coded telegram. On a long shot, Holmes also made inquiries about a certain woman who he thought might possibly be in Chicago.

Holmes had already asked some of the same questions in his cable to Wooldridge from Liverpool. However, he had been unable to wait for an answer then due to the inconvenient matter of the naked corpse in his hotel room. This time, Holmes could only pray he would be in one place long enough to receive a reply.

As Holmes burned the midnight oil in a cloud of tobacco smoke, the man traveling as Dr. S. W. Rafferty was doing some late-night plotting of his own several miles to the north, in a suite at the posh Hotel Manhattan on Madison Avenue. With him was the suite's registered guest, Mme. Simone DuBois, who had arrived the previous evening and who now sat in a large armchair knitting a shawl. She had given up her "mystical garb," as she called it, and had also changed the color of her hair, among other cosmetic alterations. What hadn't changed was her fierce devotion to the man sitting across from her.

Dr. Rafferty, as he delighted in calling himself, had been extremely busy since his own arrival in New York. He had expected to have a week or so to lay the final groundwork for the crime that was sure to shock the world. But with Holmes and Watson in New York well ahead of schedule, everything had to be done much more quickly. This was certainly an inconvenience, but like every other conceivable contingency, it had been taken into account long ago.

"It will be tomorrow night then, I take it," said Mme. DuBois, whose French accent had disappeared along with the outlandish apparel she had worn during what she liked to refer to as her "grand performance" in England.

"Yes. Our associate will have a clear field of fire. With that rifle of his, he can't miss."

"Considering what we are paying him, he had better not," said Mme. DuBois. "And what about the police?"

"As I said, everything is in order. I have found it is actually cheaper to do business here than in Chicago. The newspapers will also be tipped off at the appropriate time. Once they get the scent of scandal, they will be after Holmes like bloodhounds."

"And what about Elsie?"

Slaney offered a grim smile. "She is resting comfortably, as they say. Our associate is taking good care of her. She will not be so comfortable when she finds out what we have planned for her."

"The little bitch deserves it," Mme. DuBois said, and went back to her knitting.

Friday night was usually a kind of scrum at Shadwell Rafferty's saloon in downtown St. Paul, and the night of July 13 was no exception. The saloon was packed with a raucous crowd of imbibers who took up every available table and chair, occupied every spot at the long mahogany bar and wedged themselves into any other parcel of real estate they could find. Rafferty, as always, was mingling among his guests, telling marvelous fibs of every size and description, while his longtime partner, George Washington Thomas, saw to the practical business of supervising the crew of six barmen, who did their best to keep up with the mob's thirst.[1]

It was therefore no surprise that it took some time before Thomas heard the telephone ringing behind the bar. Although he could barely make out the voice on the other end of the line amid all the din, Thomas knew at once that it was a call Rafferty would want to take. He got Rafferty's attention and directed him to the telephone in the saloon's office.

When Rafferty finally picked up the phone, he had no trouble recognizing the caller. James J. Hill—said by some to be one of the ten richest men in America, and certainly among the busiest—had no time for the normal formalities and asked in his usual brusque way, "Did you know, Mr. Rafferty, that our friend Holmes is in New York City, with Dr. Watson?"

"I did not," Rafferty admitted. He wondered how Hill had come upon this information but knew enough not to question its accuracy. James J. Hill—owner of the Great Northern Railroad and half the other business enterprises in the Northwest, or so it seemed—always knew everything.

"They came in on the *Oceania* this morning, my sources tell me, and are apparently trying to find a woman kidnapped in England and taken to New York. Do you know anything about that?"

Again, this was all news to Rafferty, who had to admit once again that he was in the dark—a rare circumstance in his case. Rafferty had remained in frequent contact with Holmes and Watson after their three cases together in Minnesota. Normally, Holmes kept Rafferty abreast of his latest investigations, and vice versa. Rafferty was thus surprised that Holmes and Watson had come to New York without letting him know. As it turned out, so was Hill, who in 1894 had first brought the English duo to

Minnesota to investigate a series of arsons in the logging town of Hinckley.

"Mr. Holmes is usually very good about keeping me informed," Hill said, "so it must be an emergency of some kind that brought him and Dr. Watson to New York. I was hoping you might know something about it, Mr. Rafferty."

"Sorry, Mr. Hill, but I can't help you. However, I'd be happy to do a little nosin' around to see what's goin' on. Your source in New York wouldn't happen to know, would he, where Mr. Holmes and Dr. Watson are stayin'?"

"Hotel Albert in Greenwich Village," Hill said. "Let me know what you find out, but do so quickly. I will be leaving Sunday for my fishing camp in Quebec." And with that, Hill ended the conversation as abruptly as he had begun it.

Rafferty stared down at the telephone for a minute, rubbing the thick reddish-gray beard that he had decided to grow back after going "naked" for awhile. Although there was certainly no cause for alarm, he thought it odd that he had not heard from Holmes or Watson. And who was the kidnapped woman they were supposedly chasing after? There was only one way to find out, so Rafferty picked up the telephone again and asked the operator to connect him with the Hotel Albert in New York.

Chapter Thirteen

♪ ♫

"Elsie Cubitt Shall Be Free at Last"

FROM THE NARRATIVE OF DR. JOHN WATSON:

Saturday began with unaccustomed leisure, for by late morning Holmes had yet to bestir himself from his room. As noon approached, I began to fear he had fallen into one of those deep torpors which occasionally afflict him. This was not the case, however, for when I went to his room, I found him fully alert. He informed me that as there was "nowhere to go and nothing to do which might prove immediately useful" he had been engaged all morning in "a detective's foremost obligation, which is to think whenever the opportunity presents itself."

Holmes also had some surprising news. He had heard from our friend Shadwell Rafferty in St. Paul!

"Mr. Rafferty called early this morning, Watson, while you were asleep. He had learned of our whereabouts from Mr. Hill and wished to know all the details of our case here. We had an interesting discussion, as always, and Mr. Rafferty offered some useful ideas. How I wish he were with us now, for if there is one thing we need at the moment, it is someone we can absolutely rely on."

"We have Inspector Hargreave," I noted.

"Yes," said Holmes, "though I am beginning to think he may be of less help than we think."

"What do you mean?" I asked, mystified by Holmes's remark.

My question was never answered, for the phone now rang. Holmes answered at once, muttered a few words and then hung up.

"That was Inspector Hargreave," he said. "It is time we take a little walk."

We left the hotel at once and turned west on Eleventh Street toward the Hudson River. The weather was warm but not unpleasantly so and it felt delightful to be outside. I made no inquiry as to our destination but assumed it to be the house on Gay Street, where Mrs. Cubitt had briefly been kept.[1]

To my surprise, we reached the house after a walk of less than ten minutes. It was a narrow brick structure, three stories high and of simple design. A policeman at the door admitted us with a nod, as he had been told to expect us. Once inside, Holmes took great care to inspect the premises, which were empty except for a few furnishings and bed linens. I had more than once seen Holmes find evidence where dozens of policemen had failed to do so, but in this case even he was stymied.

After we emerged from the house and turned back toward the hotel, Holmes said, "It must be accounted a remarkable piece of work, Watson. I found not a single hair, a thread, a suggestive piece of dirt, a grain of food or even a trace of tobacco ash, which might help us identify or locate Mrs. Cubitt or her kidnappers. The absence of these usual clues leaves no doubt that we are dealing with criminals of the first rank."

"What do you propose to do next, Holmes?"

"I propose to return to our hotel and await further developments, for it can be only a matter of time before our adversary announces his next move."

"You almost make it sound as if he plans to put an advertisement in the newspapers."

"I would not be surprised if he did."

There were indeed "developments" later that afternoon. At half past three Hargreave telephoned to say he had obtained a copy of the overseas cable sent to "Dr. Rafferty" at the Astor House and would forward it by messenger. He also reported some success in the hunt for Mme. DuBois. Boston police, he said, had learned that a woman resembling Mme. DuBois had come through that port two days earlier, arriving aboard the Cunard Line's *Saxonia*. She had spent one night at the Hotel Vendome in Boston and then taken a train to New York City. Hargreave said his men were attempting to establish her whereabouts by canvassing hackmen at Grand Central Station and checking hotel registrations.[2]

"With the thousands of cabs and hundreds of hotels in this city, I cannot imagine it will be easy to find the right driver," I noted.

Said Holmes, "It may be easier than you think, Watson."

"Why is that?"

"For the simple reason that Mme. DuBois, I am certain, wants us to follow her trail. That is the singular feature of this case, Watson. Most of the clues we have thus far are the ones which have been given to us. I see no reason why this trend will not continue."

Half an hour later, a messenger arrived at Holmes's room with a copy of the cable obtained by Hargreave. As Holmes had predicted, it was in a code identical to that used in the telegram to the Dearborn Street address in Chicago. Holmes noted that the word "rat" was once again featured prominently, being used three times in the seventeen-word message.

"Do you have any idea what the word signifies?" I asked.

"It is only a guess, Watson, but I would imagine that it is my code name."

"Really? Do you suppose I have a code name as well?"

"Probably. Let us only hope it is more attractive than mine!"

Early in the evening, Holmes received another message—a telegram from Wooldridge in Chicago that proved to be, in Holmes's words, "full of useful information." For reasons of security, the telegram was sent in a code of Holmes's own devising with which Wooldridge was intimately familiar. Translated, the message read as follows:

MR. SHERLOCK HOLMES, HOTEL ALBERT, NY: HERE IS INFORMATION YOU REQUESTED. LETTER WITH MORE DETAILS TO FOLLOW. JAKE SLANEY IN EVERY WAY A MATCH FOR ABE. GAMBLING, ROBBERY, EXTORTION AND MURDER REMAIN HIS GANG'S LINE OF WORK. AS TOLD YOU EARLIER, NO EVIDENCE ABE STILL ALIVE AND IN CHICAGO. WOULD KNOW IF HE WERE. DEARBORN ADDRESS IS EVERLEIGH CLUB, EXPENSIVE BROTHEL FREQUENTED BY RICH AND POWERFUL. CLUB "PROTECTED" AND NO COPPER CAN TOUCH IT. KNOW OF NO JOHN SMITH WHO WORKS THERE BUT NAME OBVIOUS ALIAS. KNOW NOTHING OF WOMAN YOU ASKED ABOUT BUT WILL MAKE INQUIRIES. BEST TO YOU AND DR. WATSON. WOOLDRIDGE.

After reading the message, Holmes said, "Detective Wooldridge has, as usual, outdone himself, although there are one or two points in his message which I will need to clarify with him. I was particularly struck—as I am sure you were, Watson—by the reference to Jake Slaney as being 'in every way a match' for his brother. I wonder if Wooldridge was referring to their physical features, their characters, or perhaps both. I would also like to know the names and ages of other members of Abe Slaney's family, along with physical descriptions."

"Perhaps Wooldridge will provide that information in his letter," I said.

"Let us just hope we are still here to receive it."

Holmes normally possessed boundless self-confidence and the idea of failure seldom occurred to him. I was therefore quite shocked by his seemingly fatalistic remark.

"What on earth do you mean, Holmes? Surely you do not think we shall soon be dead."

Holmes shook his head and patted my shoulder, then said, "My dear Watson, you have misinterpreted me. By 'here,' I mean in New York. You see, I believe we will be traveling again soon, perhaps as early as tomorrow. Believe me, I have no intention of dying."

One final message—the most startling and significant of all—was delivered to our hotel at half past eight that night. The message was purportedly from Slaney himself, and it was especially surprising in that Holmes had been most alert to the possibility of being followed. Nonetheless, the sender knew not only where we were staying but even Holmes's room number, for the envelope containing the message was addressed only to the "Gentleman in Room 322."

The message employed the familiar dancing men code, which Holmes translated as follows: THIS IS YOUR LAST CHANCE, BRING $10,000 U.S. TOMORROW NIGHT, WASHINGTON STATUE, UNION SQUARE, 10 P.M. YOU WILL BE CONTACTED THERE. COME WITH WATSON. NO PO-LICE, NO DOUBLE CROSSES OR SHE DIES. SLANEY.

Holmes studied the message for some minutes, crumpled it up and then threw it on the floor. He said, "I am sick of these games, Watson! I will not be played the fool."

"So you believe this message is designed to mislead us?"

"Of course it is! Elsie Cubitt's kidnapping has nothing to do with money. It is about revenge. There will be no ransom exchange tomorrow or any other night. You may count on that. No, it is all too clear that we are being invited into a trap, Watson."

"How can you be so certain of that?"

"Because it is the only sensible reading of the evidence before us. The fact that I have been instructed to bring you along tomorrow night only confirms that an ambush of some kind is being planned."

"Then we must not go," I said as forcefully as I could.

Holmes made no immediate reply. Instead, he folded his arms and stood for well over a minute in silent thought. Finally, he said, "Perhaps you are right, Watson. Perhaps we shouldn't go. You, however, must."

"What do you mean?"

"I mean that we must buy some time, Watson, by meeting our adversary halfway. If we ignore his summons, then it is possible—though not, I believe, likely—that he might carry out his threat to murder Mrs. Cubitt. On the other hand, if you go alone, it just may throw our antagonist off stride and will leave me free to maneuver. Besides, I have no doubt that once you reach Union Square, you will be directed to another location, and quite possibly several more after that, until you are finally led to the place where the trap has been set."

"I will be completely at the kidnapper's mercy," I pointed out.

"On the contrary, I shall make certain that you are watched every step of the way. Moreover, I intend to alter the rules of the game our adversary wishes to play."

"How do you propose to do that?"

"By acquiring more information, Watson. Mme. DuBois is the key. It is imperative that Hargreave and his men find her as soon as possible. In the meantime, I will talk with the inspector to make arrangements for the rendezvous at Union Square."

There followed a lengthy telephone conversation between Holmes and Hargreave, but as I was extremely fatigued, I fell asleep and did not awaken for many hours.

The next morning, a warm and humid Sunday, began with a telephone call from Hargreave, who reported that he had finally found Mme. DuBois. One of his men had located her at the Hotel Manhattan on Forty-second Street and Madison Avenue. By a certain irony, this hotel was within a stone's throw of Grand Central Station, and Holmes openly wondered why it had taken so long to track down a woman "as distinctive in appearance as Mme. DuBois." Even so, he was greatly pleased to learn that the police had found her and that she was now in her hotel room under guard. Hargreave said he would meet us there.

On our way to the hotel, Holmes went over the plans he had made with Hargreave regarding the supposed ransom exchange at Union Square. I was to receive ten thousand dollars in cash, courtesy of the New York Police Department, to take to the rendezvous, "for purposes of authenticity," as Holmes put it. Hargreave would also provide a full complement of his best men to watch my every move and thereby make sure I came to no harm.

"And where will you be?" I asked Holmes.

"Nearby," he said but offered no further explanation.

The Hotel Manhattan, which we reached after a ride of nearly half an hour, turned out to be a new building, well over twelve stories in height and with a luxurious lobby of the usual American type. Once inside, we were directed to a suite on the tenth floor, where we found Hargreave, two detectives and Mme. DuBois, resplendent in a swirling flowered dress and seated upon a richly upholstered divan. She had dyed her hair and removed the facial markings we had seen in England but otherwise looked much the same. As we entered, she registered a look of surprise, her thick eyebrows arching up and her small black eyes inspecting us as though we were some great curiosity.[3]

"Ah, the gentlemen from England!" she said. "How strange to see you here. Am I to assume you have followed me all the way to America?"

We took seats across from her. Holmes said, "You are the seer, Mme. DuBois, so I must presume you can answer that question for yourself."

"In such an idea you are mistaken, sir. I do not choose the questions I answer. They choose me, for I am merely a humble servant of the world beyond."

"I am of this world, madame, and I care nothing for any other," said Holmes sternly. "Now, as time is precious, you will tell us at once where to find Elsie Cubitt. It is the only hope you have of leniency in this affair."

Mme. DuBois settled back on the divan and said, "I have not the need of leniency, sir, for I have done nothing that would require it. This charming gendarme"—she nodded toward Inspector Hargreave—"has asked me already the very same question. I have no knowledge of where Mrs. Cubitt has gone to, though I am naturally distraught to learn that she is still missing. The poor dear, I always feared that her troubles might one day overwhelm her. But why is it you think I would know where to find her?"

"Because you were involved in kidnapping her in the first place," said Holmes.

"Oh, but that is untrue, and I am shocked to think that you could believe such a terrible thing. May I ask, what is your proof?"

A very good question, I thought, for aside from meager scraps of circumstantial evidence—most notably the locket bearing Hilton Cubitt's picture we had discovered in Mme. DuBois's Liverpool hotel room—there was nothing except Holmes's suspicions to connect her to the kidnapping. Holmes knew this better than anyone, but he forged ahead, perhaps hoping he could frighten Mme. DuBois into an admission of guilt. I frankly doubted he would succeed, for she struck me as a woman who had been around the world more than once and knew its many treacheries.

Holmes now brought up the locket, although he did not mention where we had found it, stating only that it "was known to have been" in Mme. DuBois's possession.

"Ah yes, there was a locket which she gave to me once in the hope I might be able to divine from it any emanations from her dear late husband. Alas, I was not able to do so, for the aura, it was not right, and so the locket did not speak to me. Mrs. Cubitt for some reason never reclaimed it and I lost it somewhere during my recent travels. Where did you find it, Mr. — why, I believe I do not even know your name, sir."

"Holmes, as you well know. Where the locket was found is immaterial. I must warn you again, madame, that it will go hard with you if you do not cooperate."

"But I am cooperating," she protested. "Still, I have not yet heard to my question a satisfactory answer. What is your evidence that I am somehow involved in Mrs. Cubitt's disappearance?"

Holmes ignored her question and said, "It is only a matter of time, madame, before we learn your true identity and then you will not be so comfortable or confident in your deceit. I should imagine you are connected with the Slaney gang in Chicago."

Mme. DuBois turned to Hargreave and said, "You must help me, inspector, for I have not the faintest idea what this gentleman is talking about. Now, as I have business this afternoon, I must ask you to leave."

"What sort of business?" Holmes demanded.

"I will be meeting with a client who wishes to avail herself of my services."

Said Hargreave, "Is that right, toots? Who's this client of yours?"

"You have perhaps heard of her—Mrs. William Astor. I am to meet her at noon at her mansion on Sixty-fifth Street. Caroline, as she insists I call her, is a great believer in the spirit world, and we have become the best of friends. It is to help her in her quest for knowledge that I have come to New York. However, she will be most unhappy if I am late for our appointment."

"She'll get over it," Hargreave growled.

"Perhaps," said Mme. DuBois. "However, she would be even more upset if I were to inform her that I had been detained, for some strange reason, by the police. I do not doubt she would express her dissatisfaction in no uncertain terms to her favorite member of the police board, Mr. Hess. I also believe she would be offended to learn that there is among the police of New York a supposedly civilized inspector who addresses a dear friend of hers as 'toots.' That is all I have to say. You may leave now."[4]

I wondered how Holmes and Hargreave would react to this imperious dismissal. The answer came quickly, for Hargreave—with a slight bow—stood up and announced, without consulting Holmes, that we would indeed be leaving immediately.

Once we had got back out into the hallway, Hargreave apologized for his precipitous decision but said he had little choice. "I'm a brave enough fellow," he said to Holmes, "but the last copper in this town who got in the way of the almighty Astors ended up walking a beat near Five Points and took a knife in the back for his trouble. Money don't talk in this town, it shouts at the top of its lungs, and when it does, a poor man such as myself had better listen."[5]

Holmes said, "I understand, inspector. But how do you know Mme. DuBois is telling the truth about her supposed friendship with Mrs. Astor?"

"I don't. I do know that Mrs. Astor is crazy for spiritualists, mediums, palm readers and all their ilk, so I can't take any chances. I'm already dangling on a long, thin branch in this business, Mr. Holmes, but it's certain my career would be ruined if the likes of Mrs. Astor brought me up before the commissioner. Still, I'll have one of my men follow Mme. DuBois to see where she goes."

"No, I think you had best leave that job to Watson and me," Holmes replied, "as I do not wish to put you, or your career, in jeopardy. You have already gone well beyond the call of duty in assisting us."

"Think nothing of it. One more thing: if the lady does go out, I'd be happy to have one of my men take a little tour through her suite."

"Why that would be burglary, inspector."

"Only if my man gets caught, and that won't happen. Besides, he won't steal anything."

"Then by all means, have your man take a look."

"No problem," said Hargreave. "I'm going back to headquarters. Ring me up if you find out anything. By the way, I'm sure you know this already, but Mme. DuBois is no more French than I am. I've seen her kind before. She's running a con of some kind, and her story don't make an ounce of sense. For one thing, why would she sail to Boston instead of New York if she was coming to see Mrs. Astor?"

"An excellent question, inspector, and there are many more that might be asked about the lady," said Holmes. "Well, we had best let you go about your business. I will inform you as soon as possible what we find out about Mme. DuBois."

We went outside and took up a discreet station in a doorway across from the hotel, waiting to see if Mme.

DuBois would indeed leave for her supposed appointment. We did not wait long, for at half past eleven she swept through the front door of the hotel and spoke briefly to the doorman, who summoned a cab.

Holmes had already secured a cab for us and moments later we were proceeding up the grand sweep of Fifth Avenue. Near Fiftieth Street we began to encounter rows of mansions of such size and splendor as would have embarrassed even Croesus. Our driver, a droll and lively fellow of uncertain age and few teeth, pointed out the owners of these houses — most of whom seemed to be Vanderbilts by birth or marriage.[6]

At Sixty-fifth Street, across from the great green swath of Central Park, Mme. DuBois's hansom came to a stop. We were about a block behind and Holmes instructed our driver to pull forward so we could have a better view. We watched as Mme. DuBois stepped down from the cab in front of a gigantic mansion which resembled a French chateau.[7]

"Who owns the house the lady has gone into?" Holmes asked the driver.

"Why, that would be Mrs. William Astor herself. Number One of the Four Hundred, she is. Cream of the cream, swellest of the swells and the richest woman in New York, or so the newspapers claim. That house of hers is said to be the most luxurious in town, though believe it or not I have yet to be invited in for tea. An oversight on Mrs. Astor's part, don't you think?"[8]

Holmes grinned at this bit of badinage and said, "Well, perhaps one day she will rectify her error. Ah, what have we here?"

We now saw that as a liveried servant prepared to escort Mme. DuBois into the mansion, she suddenly turned around, apparently at the behest of her cabman, who said something and pointed to the ground. The servant then went back toward the cab, retrieved an item that had fallen and handed it to Mme. DuBois. I could not make out what it was, but Holmes—whose eyesight was uncanny—said the object appeared to be a pamphlet of some kind. We continued to watch until Mme. DuBois was admitted into the house and her hansom driver began to pull away from the curb.

"Quick, overtake that cab," Holmes instructed our driver.

We raced forward, nearly striking a carriage at the intersection of Sixty-fifth before pulling up in front of Mme. DuBois's cab. This maneuver was greeted with a long volley of oaths from its driver, but he became far more respectful when Holmes and I approached him.

Holmes came around directly beneath the driver and said, "I have five dollars for you, sir, if you will answer a few simple questions."

The driver was a small, middle-aged man with ruddy cheeks, sharp little ferret eyes and a high forehead crowned by the top hat usual to his trade. I thought he might question Holmes's request, or at least ask for some identification, but the prospect of quick money to a man of his station apparently was sufficient to stifle any outbreak of curiosity.

"You produce the money, sir, and I'll gladly answer any questions you wish."

Holmes took out a five-dollar gold piece and displayed it in the palm of his hand. He said, "You may begin by telling me exactly what it was that your last fare dropped after leaving your cab."

"It was a pamphlet, sir. I saw it in the lady's hand when I picked her up at the hotel. When she got out, why, she must have dropped it, so I pointed it out right away. Would have gone down and got it myself for her—could be a tip in that, you know—but the servant beat me to it."

"Did you happen to notice what the pamphlet was about?"

The driver nodded and said, "Why, it was a guide to St. Paul's Chapel, down on Broadway. Very popular item it is, sir. Lots of folks want to see where old George Washington had his pew. Taken many a fare there in my day."

"I see. Where could I obtain one of these pamphlets?"

"Well now, as far as I know, you can only get them at the chapel. They're in a little rack by the door. The lady must have gone down there for a visit."

"So it would appear. One more question: Did the lady mention anything to you about visiting the chapel?"

"Not a word, sir. All she said to me was that she wished to go to Mrs. Astor's house at Sixty-fifth Street."

Holmes handed the driver his gold and said, "You have been most helpful, sir, and I will trouble you no further. Good day."

We now returned to our cab to await Mme. DuBois's next move. Just past two o'clock, as I was beginning to feel very hungry, we saw her leave Mrs. Astor's house and step into a cab hailed by a servant. Again we followed but with disappointing results, as she returned directly to the Hotel Manhattan.

Holmes found a public telephone and called Hargreave to report on our activities and Mme. DuBois's return to her hotel. After he hung up, Holmes told me Hargreave would have Mme. DuBois watched until further notice.

"Then perhaps we will have time for lunch," I said.

"You are a slave to your stomach, Watson, and I can see by your growly look that you will not be denied. Very well, I shall drop you off at our hotel so you can satisfy your appetite."

"Where will you be going, Holmes?"

"On a little tour. I shouldn't be more than a few hours."

I asked what sort of "tour" Holmes had in mind, but he would say no more, and I knew it would be fruitless to press for further details. Upon reaching my room at the Hotel Albert, I ordered cold ham sandwiches and ale from the kitchen, then awaited Holmes's return, which did not occur until after eight o'clock.

Holmes at first offered no information as to where he had been on his tour, but having had several hours to ponder the matter, I thought I knew.

"I imagine you rather enjoyed visiting St. Paul's Chapel," I observed.

Holmes arched an eyebrow in characteristic fashion and said, "Pray tell, Watson, what makes you think I visited the chapel?"

"Because you are a man who likes to be prepared for any eventuality, because you are man who will leave no possible clue unconsidered, because it would be the logical thing to do and more than anything else, Holmes, because I have known you now for the better part of two decades."

Holmes cocked his head and stared at me, his bright eyes burning like lamps. Finally, he smiled and said, "My dear Watson, you do indeed know me too well. Yes, I made the long trip down to St. Paul's. I looked around the old church and, of course, purchased the descriptive pamphlet mentioned by Mme. DuBois's driver."

He handed me the pamphlet, which he described as "nothing out of the ordinary."

"So you think it is of little significance?"

"On the contrary, I think it most significant, for why would Mme. DuBois suddenly become interested in an old church? The pamphlet, as you can see, includes a plan of the chapel as well as a map of the surrounding streets. You will also note the chapel's proximity to the Astor House hotel. Curious, is it not, how the Astor name seems to be cropping up in this investigation?"

"I suppose so, although I cannot believe the family would have anything to do with Mrs. Cubitt's abduction."

"Nor could I, Watson, since in my experience the Astors spend every waking hour arguing among themselves."[9]

"Now, Holmes, I am still waiting to hear why a pamphlet about St. Paul's Chapel should be of such great interest to you," I said. "Is the chapel linked in some way to Mrs. Cubitt's abduction? Did you find a clue there?"

"Time will tell, time will tell," Holmes replied. "Still, I must ask you, as a precaution, to familiarize yourself with the contents of this pamphlet at once."

"Very well, but —"

"Please, no more questions, Watson, for the clock is ticking and we have much to do. I should tell you that after leaving St. Paul's, I contacted Inspector Hargreave once again. He informed me that his detectives found nothing suspicious in Mme. DuBois's hotel room, but that hardly came as a surprise."

Holmes paused and looked at me in his usual frank and perceptive way, much as an officer might inspect a soldier on the eve of combat. I could only trust he would not find me wanting in any way. Then he said, "Well, my dear Watson, the time is at hand to play out the game. You must be my eyes and ears tonight. Are you up for such a task? I will not lie to you. There could be great danger."

"That has never stopped me, as you well know, Holmes. As always, I am ready to perform whatever tasks you require of me. It is my honor and privilege to do so. Still, I must ask you again, where will you be?"

Holmes patted me on the shoulder and said, "I intend, my dear Watson, to be one step ahead of the Conspirator and his accomplices. This dark business has already gone on for far too long, and I fully expect that before this night is over, Elsie Cubitt shall be free at last."

Chapter Fourteen

"We Shall Have Him Too"

The basement where Elsie Cubitt lay—in an old house in Brooklyn—was dark, damp and cool, and she found it strangely pleasant to be out of the light and in a quiet place. Although she remained heavily sedated, she was coming to realize that the drugs, which at first had left her either unconscious or in a stuporous daze, had begun to lose some of their potency as her body adjusted to them.

Even so, she was far from fully alert and she still felt like a stranger in her own body. Her skin itched, her eyes did not want to stay open and her limbs seemed as heavy as millstones. Worst of all, her head felt as though it were encased in a heavy helmet, and the slightest movement produced the sensation that her skull was an anvil upon which a very large blacksmith was pounding with all of his strength.

Her mental faculties, however, were showing signs of significant improvement. Although her normally acute intellect was still dulled by barbiturates, she was beginning to think more clearly. Her memory, which for days had been a sieve in which she managed to catch only scattered grains of recollection, was also improving. She could now recall more details of her kidnapping—the inside of a wagon, a cloth soaked in chloroform, the man with the black beard. She still couldn't identify him but his name was so close to popping up into her consciousness that she could almost see it. She was certain it would come to her soon.

In the meantime, she had been doing her best to feign sleepiness whenever her kidnappers came in to check on her, administer more drugs or take her to the bathroom. She had, of course, thought of trying to escape, but she realized that it would be futile given her physical condition. Even if she somehow got her hands on one of the pistols that her captors carried—and she was very familiar with weapons of all kinds—she doubted she would have the strength to pull the trigger. So she had adopted a strategy of waiting and listening, hoping to learn as much as she could about her abductors and then finding a way to make an escape.

She had already learned a great deal by listening to the younger of her two abductors, a despicable man who went by the name of Coffin. She found him to be as creepy as his name. He had thinning blond hair, a small mustache, pointy teeth and chilly hunter's eyes, and he was fond of leaning over her as she feigned sleep and touching her breasts. On other occasions, he would whisper perverted thoughts into her ear, even though she never gave any indication of hearing them. Coffin seemed to enjoy talking to a woman who could not talk back, and from his idle and salacious conversation she had gleaned several significant pieces of intelligence.

Among other things, she learned that she was in New York—a city she had passed through several times before and which she knew to be the main port for ocean liners going to and coming from England. She had even lived for some months in Manhattan before sailing off to England to make her new home. Although she could not be sure exactly where she was, she had heard Coffin refer once to Orange Street. The street was unfamiliar to her, and she wondered if she was in a borough—Brooklyn perhaps, or the Bronx—other than Manhattan.[1]

It was also clear from Coffin's remarks that the other man—the one with the beard—was behind her kidnapping and that he hated her fiercely.

"You'll regret the day you were born when he gets through with you," Coffin had whispered into her ear one night. "Too bad you're so beautiful, Elsie, for I would like to have you before he does."

Elsie Cubitt had no doubt what he meant by "having" her and she had already made up her mind that she would die, if necessary, before allowing that to happen.

The last thing she learned, also gleaned from eavesdropping at the edge of consciousness, was at once the most hopeful and most terrible of all. It had to do with why she had been abducted. Although Coffin and the bearded man detested her, there was someone else they despised even more. The night before, both men had come down to the cellar to "tuck her in," as they mockingly called it, and she had listened as they discussed their plans.

"Well, we have the bait," the bearded man had said, touching Elsie's forehead. "And now that Holmes has arrived, we shall have him, too, just like a skunk in a trap. I cannot tell you how long I have waited for this day."

The men had then gone on to discuss their plans in more detail, and the more Elsie heard—especially regarding how cleverly Holmes and Watson had been "set up," in the bearded man's parlance—the more worried she had become. Now, as she lay alone in the moist darkness of the cellar, Elsie Cubitt knew that time was running out and that she must find a way to warn Holmes and Watson of the danger that lay ahead. The question was how, and so far she had not hit upon an answer. Even so, the revelation that Sherlock Holmes was in New York had given her spirits a mighty boost and she was determined to make certain, by whatever means possible, that she would not be the cause of his undoing.

She had barely drifted off to sleep again when she heard the heavy wooden cellar door open and saw, through barely open eyes, her two captors coming down the steps with a lantern.

"Time to get up, dear Elsie," said the bearded man as he approached her makeshift bed. "You're going on a little trip with us."

Since there was no point in feigning sleep now, she said, "Where?"

"To Chicago," said the bearded man with a malignant chuckle, and at that instant the final curtain fell away inside her brain and she knew at last the identity of her chief tormentor.

Chapter Fifteen

"Where Is Holmes?"

FROM THE NARRATIVE OF DR. JOHN WATSON:

It was quarter to ten when I prepared to leave the Hotel Albert for the short ride—a mere three blocks—to Union Square. Inspector Hargreave had by then stopped at the hotel to deliver the ransom money, after which he and Holmes thoroughly apprised me of their plan and my duties as part of it. Among many other things, my instructions included specific steps I was to take if confronted by the kidnappers and asked to turn over the ten thousand dollars, which I carried in my medical bag. Although Holmes readily admitted that he could not anticipate every possible contingency, he reiterated his belief that there would be no "actual exchange" during the course of the night.

"I expect, Watson, that you will see a good deal of New York before the sun rises," he said, "but be assured that either I or Inspector Hargreave's men will always be close at hand. Now, are you ready?"

"I am."

"What of your revolver?"

This was a question Holmes always asked me before dangerous missions and although he knew the answer perfectly well, he must have found some value in the ritual of it.

"It is in my coat pocket and fully loaded."

"Then Godspeed, Watson, and before this night is done you shall, I think, have quite a tale to tell."

After shaking hands with Holmes and Hargreave, I went downstairs and out to the front of the hotel, where the doorman hailed a cab. The driver, I had been told, would be one of Hargreave's men and identified himself as such when I entered the hansom. He told me to "sit back and relax"—advice I found impossible to follow given the circumstances.

We proceeded up University Place to Union Square, a pleasant and well-wooded oval of greenery which, according to *King's Handbook*, was a favorite spot for mass demonstrations by the city's laboring class. I soon saw, near the center of the park, the equestrian statue of George Washington. The general and his horse were mounted atop a tall stone pedestal illuminated by a ring of bright electric lights. My driver let me off on the Broadway side of the square and I followed a winding walkway to the statue, which was protected by a high iron fence.[1]

The atmosphere was very close, and white wisps of fog hovered over the square like mysterious angels. A good many strollers, mostly couples, were enjoying the night air, and I even passed a uniformed patrolman just before I reached the statue. Once I had positioned myself by the fence, I consulted my watch and saw that it was five minutes to ten. Lighting a cigar, I waited as patiently as I could, all the while keeping a sharp lookout for any suspicious activity. However, I could see nothing which appeared to be out of the ordinary. Inspector Hargreave's men, I knew, must be somewhere nearby, but they did their work of observation so skillfully that I had no idea who among all the people I saw might actually be police detectives.

As ten o'clock came and went I began to wonder whether the supposed ransom exchange might be nothing more than a hoax. Then, at ten after the hour, a shabbily dressed man appeared out of the shadows, walked directly up to me and handed me an envelope.

"Read this," he said, "and do exactly what it says."

The man left as quickly as he had arrived, walking west toward Broadway. I tore open the envelope and found, just as Holmes had predicted, a message containing further directions. It said: GO NORTH TO 17TH ST. LOOK FOR HANSOM DRIVER WITH RED FEATHER IN HAT. DO AS HE TELLS YOU. REMEMBER, NO POLICE. SLANEY.

I had been told by Holmes to obey whatever instructions I received, and so I set off at once for the north end of the square, trusting that Hargreave's men would follow. At Seventeenth Street I spotted my cab at once, for the driver—a rough-looking fellow with a thick black beard—sported the requisite red feather.

"Would you be the man looking for Mrs. Cubitt?" he asked as I approached.

"I would."

"Get in, then, and be quick about it."

"Where are we going?"

"None of your business."

I had hardly settled into my seat before the driver whipped his horse forward. He immediately turned north on Broadway, and so began the second leg of my journey. We proceeded with surprising ease through Times Square but it was slower going up to Columbus Circle, where the great black void of Central Park loomed into view. The driver left Broadway at the circle and went north on Eighth Avenue along the western edge of the park. Traffic here was surprisingly light, and the short blocks clipped by in rapid succession. Within a matter of minutes, the driver made a sharp left turn onto a side street (the number of which I did not catch) and then immediately turned right into the arched carriageway of a tall, craggy building which overlooked the park.

The carriageway led into a large courtyard surrounded by sheer walls of brick and stone which seemed to tower hundreds of feet overhead. My driver came to an abrupt halt and shouted at me, in a very rude way, to get out. As I did so, I saw two men closing the large iron gates guarding the carriageway, and for a moment I wondered whether I had now fallen into the trap Holmes so greatly feared. But I soon discovered that if there was a trap, it lay elsewhere, for another vehicle—a small coach pulled by two handsome black steeds—now pulled up. My new driver hustled me into the coach without ceremony and off we went, this time leaving by a narrow, alleylike passageway at the other end of the building.[2]

As we raced away through the night, I realized that my situation had suddenly become extremely perilous. Hargreave's men, I knew, could not have seen the quick change of coaches in the courtyard, nor could they have possibly anticipated that I would leave by a different way than I had come in. As a result, I thought it highly unlikely any of Hargreave's men could now be following me. Whatever happened now, I would be on my own, with only my wits and my pistol to protect me.

After leaving the courtyard, the coach proceeded only a short distance before the driver turned back onto a wide avenue that I recognized as Broadway. I glanced through the back window to see if anyone was following us, but I saw no evidence of the police. The switch in the courtyard, it appeared, had indeed accomplished its purpose.

As we proceeded farther north on Broadway—which cut through the great loaf of Manhattan like the diagonal slice of a knife—the city itself began to thin out. By the time we passed 100th Street, I was surprised to see black patches of open land beyond the glow of gas lamps. I had somehow thought that all of Manhattan would be dense with building, as was London. Here, however, traces of the rocky old island of Dutchmen and Indians lingered in the form of rugged outcrops which formed small, picturesque crags in the vacant fields between streets. Looking west, I also caught glimpses of the Hudson Valley and lights atop the distant cliffs of New Jersey.

At 114th Street we turned west to Riverside Drive, which ran atop steep bluffs overlooking the Hudson. There was a scattering of mansions along this thoroughfare, although it was by no means completely built up and the houses grew farther apart as we continued northward. Despite the area's remoteness and the lateness of the hour, I noticed several people strolling along pathways in the park, while the drive itself supported a fair amount of carriage and bicycle traffic. I also saw several motorcars of the type Holmes had often talked about buying.[3]

As we passed 120th Street I caught my first glimpse of an enormous, brilliantly illuminated stone structure which seemed to rise like a mirage out of the darkness. Surmounted by a high colonnaded drum and a conical roof, the structure commanded a magnificent site on the bluffs. At first, I could not fathom what it might be, given its remote location. Then, something sparked in my memory and I realized that I must be looking at General Ulysses Grant's spectacular new tomb.

I had read about the tomb in my *King's Handbook*, which described it as the largest mausoleum on the continent, built at a cost of six hundred thousand dollars. The guidebook, as I recalled, stated that although General Grant had died in 1885, the tomb itself was not finished until 1897, when it was dedicated following a parade and naval flotilla, which supposedly drew a crowd of one million people. President William McKinley, whom Holmes and I had been of some service to only recently in Minneapolis, led the parade and spoke at the dedication. The tomb had immediately become one of New York's great attractions, more popular with visitors, it was said, than even the Statue of Liberty.[4]

As it turned out, I would soon have a chance to see the famous tomb firsthand, for my coach now stopped before a broad walkway leading to the mausoleum. I got out and went up to the driver, who remained in his seat.

"You're to go inside," he said, pointing toward the tomb, which occupied an oval site formed by a split in Riverside Drive.

"But why on earth—" I began.

"I don't know anything," the driver said as he gave the reins a shake. "Just do as I've told you." And with that final word, he and his coach clattered off into the night.

I watched as he vanished down the hill on Riverside, hoping I might see a carriage or two—perhaps with some of Hargreave's men—coming my way. Yet I knew in my heart that it was a forlorn hope. I was indeed alone, and I would simply have to deal with whatever—or whoever— awaited me inside the tomb. Checking my watch, I saw that it was now just eleven o'clock, even though it seemed like many hours since I had left the comfortable confines of the Hotel Albert.

I now turned my full attention to the tomb, which in the suggestive light cast by lampposts along the drive rose up like a great relic of imperial Rome, unaccountably transported to the New World. It seemed far too grand for Grant, often described as a reticent man uninterested in pomp and ceremony. During the afternoon, I imagined, the tomb had been crowded with its usual complement of visitors, but now it looked curiously forlorn despite its obvious strivings for grandeur. Although a carriage still passed by now and then on Riverside, the grounds around the tomb were deserted—a situation that only added to the gloomy feel of the place.

Of course, I could not help but wonder whether Elsie Cubitt was somewhere inside the great white monument, and if so, how the "game," as Holmes liked to call it, would play out. And what of Holmes himself? Was he in fact somewhere close at hand, having anticipated my arrival at the tomb? I could only pray that such was the case.

Keeping my hand in my coat pocket, with one finger on the trigger of my revolver, I now walked slowly up toward the tomb's main entrance, located behind a columned portico at the top of a wide set of steps. I knew that Slaney or his confederates might be waiting in the dark recesses of the portico, which was poorly illuminated by a single light, but duty demanded that I go forward, regardless of the risk.

As I neared the steps, I noticed a message carved on the parapet above the entry portico. Illuminated by a small row of lights, it read: LET US HAVE PEACE. I fervently wished this could be so, although in consideration of the possible dangers at hand, I cocked my revolver. I paused for a moment, taking care to look all around, before proceeding up the stairs and into the portico, where a pair of bronze doors afforded entrance to the tomb.

One of the doors, I noted at once, was slightly ajar. Clearly, someone had gone inside ahead of me. This circumstance struck me as a perfect invitation to an ambush, and I hesitated, wondering if it would be wise to enter the tomb. I did not hesitate for long, however, since I knew what Holmes, the bravest man I have ever known, would have done if he were with me. I therefore pulled open the door and cautiously stepped inside.

Immediately I felt a rush of cool, damp air and saw a faint glow in the rotunda straight ahead. The guidebook had shown plans of the tomb and I knew that Grant's marble sarcophagus, and another intended for his wife, lay side by side below me in a well at the base of the rotunda. I crept forward toward a balustraded walkway encircling the crypt, listening for the slightest sound in the purple shadows all around me. I heard nothing, for the hush of death prevailed, and the park outside now seemed as distant as Baker Street in London.[5]

I went up to the balustrade, still straining to hear any sound, and leaned over to look down upon the twin sarcophagi, which were so close together that they nearly touched. The sight which greeted me was one I will remember to my last day, for sprawled across the smooth black marble lids of the sarcophagi was the body of a man, clad in what looked to be a military uniform. The man lay face down as though he had been dropped from the high dome overhead. Two kerosene lanterns next to the motionless figure illuminated this grim and puzzling scene, for which none of Holmes's instructions had prepared me.

My first instinct was to go back outside and use the police whistle I had been given by Hargreave in hopes of summoning help. Then I recalled a piece of advice I once received from Holmes. "The good detective," he said, "is much like a good general in that he must exhaust every possibility of going forward before even considering retreat." It occurred to me that Grant himself would have heartily agreed with this advice, and so I decided to advance against the enemy, wherever he might be.

Guided by what little light the lanterns provided in such a cavernous space, I went around the balustrade to a staircase which led down to the floor of the rotunda, where the sarcophagi—set in a well behind a low, encircling wall—presented the timeless pose of death. I set down the bag with the money and climbed over the wall to see if I could be of any help to the sprawled figure.

Once I reached the sarcophagi, which were beautifully sculpted of lustrous dark marble, I examined the man who lay upon them, his head and one arm dangling over the edge. He wore a dark blue uniform, possibly that of a soldier, and I presumed he must be one of the tomb's honor guards. A clump of blood on the back of his head suggested that he had been struck with a club or some other blunt instrument. I placed my hand on the guard's carotid artery and detected a faint pulse. He was alive, though barely.[6]

I was just about to lift the guard's head in hopes I could

bring him back to consciousness when I suddenly heard footsteps behind me. Swinging around, I encountered a thin, pale young man dressed from head to toe in white — an angel of sorts, but not from heaven. He had come over the circling wall so quietly that I had not heard him until he was only a few feet away. The young man held a pistol of the new automatic type in his right hand and there was something in his watery blue eyes which bespoke a particularly cold and vicious disposition.

"Where is Holmes?" he demanded, leveling the pistol at my chest.

"He is nearby," I replied, which for all I knew was true. "Now, sir, who are you and where is Mrs. Cubitt?"

"My name will mean nothing to you," the man said. "As for Mrs. Cubitt, why, she is — let me see, what would be a good word — why, she is 'nearby,' Dr. Watson. But it seems you have not upheld your end of the bargain. Holmes was supposed to come here. Instead, he sent his lackey. We figured that might happen."

"I am no one's lackey," I said, rather hotly, even if I was staring down the barrel of a gun. "Now, I must ask you again, where is Mrs. Cubitt? If there is business you wish to conduct, let us get on with it."

I started to slip my hand into my coat pocket, hoping I might get a drop on the insolent fellow, but he would have none of it.

"Don't," he said, aiming the pistol directly at my head. "I will kill you right here if I have to. Indeed, I would take great pleasure in doing so. Alas, that is not the plan."

He came forward and, pressing his pistol against my temple, withdrew the revolver from my pocket. Then he stepped back and casually examined my weapon. "You are a Colt man, I see, Dr. Watson, but not very up-to-date in your choice of pistols. You really should consider the new automatic."[7]

"I did not come here to discuss pistols," I said. "Now, about Mrs. Cubitt—"

"Yes, by all means, let us get back to the lovely Elsie," the man said, cutting me short. He then reached into the vest pocket of his immaculate white jacket and withdrew an envelope, which he tossed on the floor at my feet.

He said, "You and Mr. Holmes will follow these instructions precisely. Otherwise, I will have to slit Mrs. Cubitt's beautiful throat. Well, don't just stand there, Dr. Watson. You may read the instructions after you've left the tomb."

I picked up the envelope, and I do not mind admitting that I was quite mystified by this latest turn of events. Why on earth had I been dragged all the way up to Grant's Tomb, even after it must have been clear to Slaney and his gang that I had lost my police escort? I could think of no good reason, but I also knew that I had no choice but to follow these latest instructions—no matter how fruitless they might prove to be.

"What about the guard?" I asked before I turned to leave. "He will need medical assistance."

"He'll be fine," the pale gunman replied. "I'll take good care of him. Now, goodbye doctor, and this time make sure you follow orders. If we see any more signs of the police, Mrs. Cubitt will die. That is a promise. Oh, and don't forget your ransom money."

My bag was right where I had left it, and I could only puzzle why the gunman had not taken the ten thousand dollars when it would have been so easy to do so. However, as it was beginning to seem as though nothing would make sense this night, I retrieved the bag and left the tomb. Back out on the front steps, I opened the envelope and read the following message: YOU CANNOT FOOL ME. YOU CANNOT STOP ME. 110TH & 9TH, UNDER EL, MIDNIGHT. WAIT THERE FOR NEW INSTRUCTIONS. USE BICYCLE. THIS IS YOUR LAST CHANCE AND HERS. YOU HAVE BEEN WARNED. SLANEY.

I looked at my watch and saw that it was already almost half past eleven, leaving but half an hour to reach the new destination. For a moment I considered searching for a telephone or trying to flag down a passing policeman in order to alert Hargreave's men to my whereabouts. Yet Slaney and his confederates had thus far proven so masterful in outwitting the police that I had no doubt my actions would be discovered and that Elsie Cubitt might indeed be murdered by the cold-eyed killer I had met in the tomb. Yet if I made no attempt to bring the police back into the chase, what chance would there ever be of catching Slaney or saving his captive? How I wished now that Holmes was by my side, and I wondered more than ever why he had elected to stay in the shadows.

I finally decided that I could not risk having Mrs. Cubitt's blood on my hands. Therefore, I saw no choice but to follow my latest instructions and pray that my mission might yet meet with success. Folding up the message, I peered out toward Riverside Drive and saw a bicycle lying on the grass not fifty feet away. I ran over to the bicycle—conveniently equipped with a front basket to hold my bag—climbed upon the seat and began to pedal south along Riverside as quickly as I could.

I had done very little cycling in recent years and my balance was somewhat unsteady. Once, I nearly lost control when the wheels hit a patch of heavy sand, but as necessity always spurs quick learning, I soon began to feel more comfortable. The cyclists I had seen earlier were gone now, but there were still carriages out on the drive, their bright running lamps cutting through the darkness. I had no idea what awaited me at the intersection of 110th Street and Ninth Avenue, but I was thankful that this part of New York—unlike all of London—was a place where finding one's way depended only on the ability to count and read signs.

When I reached 110th and Riverside, I again consulted my watch and saw that it was now twenty to twelve, leaving me plenty of time to pedal the several blocks to Ninth Avenue. As I turned east on 110th and began ascending a slight rise leading away from the river bluffs, I glanced back several times but saw no signs that anyone was following me in a carriage or other type of vehicle.

My uphill ride soon gave way to a long descent past largely open land, although to the north I could make out the lights of several large buildings and what looked to be the ruins of an old cathedral. I coasted downhill to Ninth Avenue, arriving there well before the deadline.[8]

The intersection I now entered was most peculiar, for it lay beneath an enormous iron railroad trestle which came north on Ninth, swung abruptly east on 110th and then quickly veered north again before disappearing into the darkness. I had never seen in any city a structure quite like this trestle, and only later did I learn that it was the famous "Suicide Curve," where the tracks of the Ninth Avenue elevated line took two sharp turns before continuing north on Eighth.[9]

As I stopped at one corner of the intersection, fog began rolling in from the east like great curls of cigarette smoke and quickly infiltrated the forest of slender iron pillars supporting the trestle. These pillars and the latticed cross members connecting them were so delicate that they hardly seemed strong enough to support the tracks a good sixty feet overhead. Lamps shone out at regular intervals along the trestle, marking its sinuous path through the night and creating a most remarkable effect.

This striking scene was utterly devoid of people, however, for reasons that made themselves immediately clear. There was no station nearby—at least none that I could see—nor had any buildings been constructed along 110th Street beneath the trestle, presumably because of the noise and smoke of passing trains. Moreover, much of the area around the curve (again, something I learned only later) was undeveloped parkland, so it was in every respect a desolate corner of Manhattan. This is why it must have appealed to Slaney. To make matters worse, the fog appeared to be thickening, and I felt triply blind, for I was in a place I did not know, to receive a message by unknown means, in a fog which threatened to obscure everything around me.

I looked for anyone who might come out to meet me, but the streets all around were deserted. Midnight soon went past without incident. At ten after, a tall man in a powder blue suit emerged out of the fog on 110th Street. I inspected him closely but he walked past without a word. By twenty after the hour, I was beginning to wonder whether I had deliberately been led astray by the man in the tomb.

As I debated what to do next, I heard a low, distant rumble, which gradually grew louder, and I realized that a train must be approaching high above, from the north by the sound of it. I moved out from under the trestle in time to see the engine's headlamp burst out of the fog before the turn at Eighth Avenue, which was accomplished amid a horrible screeching of brakes. Then I felt a tap on my shoulder and was so startled that I jumped nearly to the top of the trestle, or so it seemed.

I spun around, almost expecting to see the dark visage of Abe Slaney himself. Instead, I was confronted by a boy of no more than twelve, wearing the patched clothes and billed cap of a street urchin and looking at me as though I must be perfectly insane.

"Geez, you're jumpy mister," he said.

"Good God, lad, you scared me half to death, sneaking up on me like that. Where did you come from?"

The boy, who obviously had been recruited for his impudence, said, "Where I come from don't matter, mister. I'm to ask if you're looking for Mrs. Cubitt."

"I am, but—"

"Then take this and do exactly what it says."

Like just about everyone else I had met during my night's adventures, he handed me an envelope. Inside was yet another communication from Slaney. The message, which I had to read with the aid of a match, said, SO FAR, SO GOOD. TAKE 9TH AVE. EL SOUTH TO END OF LINE AT SOUTH FERRY. BE THERE NO LATER THAN 1 A.M. NO POLICE OR YOU KNOW THE RESULTS. SLANEY.

"Who gave you this message?" I asked the boy.

"A gentleman," he responded. "That's all you need to know."

"I see you do not wish to be helpful."

"Not unless there's money in it."

"All right, I will give you five dollars if you will tell me where you got this message."

Said the boy contemptuously, "Well, aren't you the big spender, mister. You don't know these people, do you? I'd be at the bottom of the river over yonder in five minutes if they thought I'd told you anything."

"Very well, I will double my offer."

The boy shook his head and said, "Forget it, mister. You ain't got the money I need. I can see that. By the way, if you're looking to go somewhere, the closest el station is at 104th. Should be a train south in ten or fifteen minutes. See you around, sucker."[10]

I had half a mind to grab the boy by the neck and choke the truth out of him, but I thought better of it. He was clearly worldly wise beyond his years and quite fearless, and I doubted he would believe for a minute that I would harm him. As the boy melted away into the fog, I heard horses approaching and loud voices. Were Slaney's confederates arriving to make sure the message had been delivered? I could not afford to wait and find out, so I mounted my bicycle and set off down Ninth Avenue.

Chapter Sixteen

"Love Is a Strange Thing"

At the Astor House hotel, in a luxurious old suite where — she had been informed by the desk clerk — "kings and queens once stayed," Mme. Simone DuBois stood at a large window and gazed down at the Chapel of St. Paul across the street. It was eleven o'clock at night, and miles away on the other end of Manhattan, Dr. John Watson was just entering Grant's Tomb in hopes of securing Elsie Cubitt's freedom. He was in the wrong place, however, as Mme. DuBois knew only too well.

She had checked into the Astor House only an hour earlier, after leaving her rooms uptown at the Hotel Manhattan. In making her departure, she had easily shed the police detective — a small Irishman with a monkey face and the bloodshot eyes of a hard drinker — who was supposed to be watching her.

Although she continued to use the name, she was pleased that she no longer had to play the role of the fortune-telling Mme. DuBois — a role that over a period of months had sent her from Chicago to New York, then to England, and now back to New York, where the penultimate scene of the drama would be played out in a matter of hours. It had been the most arduous role of her career, but also the most satisfying, for it would soon bring her the ineffable pleasure that comes only of vengeance perfectly achieved.

Ever since Abe Slaney had been taken from her by Elsie Cubitt and Sherlock Holmes, she had dreamed of a way to see that the two of them would one day suffer as she had and then pay for their crimes with their miserable lives. She had considered traveling to England and killing them herself, but there would have been only limited satisfaction in that. No, she wished them both humiliated first—their names spoken with contempt, their actions subject to derision in every corner of the globe, their achievements turned to bitter ashes by the fire of scandal and death that would ultimately consume them.

Her hatred was powered, as is so often the case, by love. Abe Slaney was her godson and had always occupied a special place in her heart. He was only seven—a darling, serious, strong-willed little boy—when she had left Chicago for good, to begin the stage career that ultimately led her to establish a new home in faraway San Francisco. Still, she wrote to him almost weekly, and he never failed to reply, invariably addressing her as "Dear Auntie," even after he had become a full-grown man. He confided in her—she was the loving mother he had never really had—and she advised him, in her surprisingly steely way, to always take what was rightfully his.

She could still vividly remember their last visit together, only months before he went off to England to pursue Elsie Cubitt. They met in St. Louis, where she was performing, and had dinner at the Planter's Hotel. He told her all about his plan to "reclaim"—that was the exact word he used—Elsie Cubitt. Mme. DuBois had strongly advised against it, of course. Elsie, she knew, was far too unruly and headstrong for a man of Abe's dominating temperament. Indeed, Mme. DuBois had never cared for the Cubitt girl, who seemed to think she was too good for the world she had been born into. But

Abe was obsessed with her and there had been no talking him out of his plan.[1]

Later, when the terrible news came—first of Abe's conviction and imprisonment, and then of his apparent death—Mme. DuBois knew where the blame lay. Elsie Cubitt, she fervently believed, was a temptress who had led Abe astray, and Sherlock Holmes had been her willing helpmate.

And so, when the great plan of revenge had been presented to her and the "boys"—as she liked to call the other members of Abe's old gang—they had all signed on at once. She had found the scheme breathtaking in its malignant scope and beautiful in the arching symmetry of its design. The boys had agreed—the plan was perfection. Even now, she could hardly believe their good fortune in stumbling upon so brilliant and creative an ally. Still, the drama in which she had played such a large part was not quite over. She knew only too well that Sherlock Holmes would do all in his power to thwart her and her confederates, just as he had thwarted Abe by breaking the code of the dancing men.

This time, however, Holmes would not be so lucky, for Mme. DuBois firmly believed he was now up against a mind in every respect superior to his own. She had known and consorted with many criminals in her day, but never had she encountered anyone as clever as her ally in Chicago. So far, the plan had worked brilliantly, except for the failure to delay Holmes and Watson in Liverpool. But that had been no more than a minor setback. Since then, everything had gone smoothly, and Mme. DuBois was convinced that only something approaching divine intervention could now save Holmes from the fate that awaited him.

Much to her displeasure, the divine suddenly showed signs of intervening. As she took in the scene outside her window—where the tide of activity on lower Broadway was at low ebb, as it usually was on Sunday nights—she noted with consternation that light fog had begun to filter in from the East River. As yet, it only slightly obscured the view from her suite and certainly would pose no problem for her confederates, one of whom would be joining her at the hotel around midnight. If the fog began to thicken, however, there could be real trouble.

Feeling anxious now, she looked at her diamond-studded watch—a gift many years ago from Abe—and prayed that the fog would dissipate or, at least, grow no denser. So much work had been required to reach this moment that she refused to countenance the idea that the heavens might suddenly turn against her. No, the fog would simply have to wait.

She peered out the window again and took a deep breath. If the fog would cooperate, and if everything else went as planned, the great Sherlock Holmes would soon be in for the surprise of his life, and the beginning of a long nightmare. What Mme. DuBois did not know was that Holmes was also planning a surprise for her.

Far to the west in St. Paul, Shadwell Rafferty was enjoying a different sort of Sunday. He had gotten up just before noon and consumed a hearty late breakfast of pancakes, bacon and eggs while he read his usual complement of newspapers. Then he had gone to the St. Paul Cathedral to light a votive candle for his long-dead wife—something he did every day. After attending a matinee performance of *Dr. Jekyll and Mr. Hyde* at the Metropolitan Theater, he had called James J. Hill—to whom he had already reported on his conversation with Holmes—to wish the Empire Builder good luck on his annual fishing expedition to Quebec. Finally, late in the afternoon, Rafferty had taken the streetcar to Minneapolis to enjoy a quiet dinner with his friend Majesty Burke, whom he was rumored to be courting—a rumor he took great pains to deny, although no one believed him.[2]

When he finally returned to his apartment at the Ryan Hotel just after ten o'clock, he was surprised to find a telegram waiting for him. He was even more surprised by its contents. The message said: WILL BE FORCED TO LEAVE NEW YORK SOON AND MUST HAVE YOUR HELP WHEN I DO. CANNOT EXPLAIN NOW BUT HAVE NOT TOLD YOU FULL TRUTH ABOUT WHY I CAME TO AMERICA. LOVE IS A STRANGE THING. YOUR DEAR FRIEND, SHERLOCK HOLMES.

Rafferty had received more than a few odd telegrams in his day, but this was surely the oddest, especially the last line. Whatever did Holmes mean by "love is a strange thing"? Try as he might, Rafferty could make no sense of the message, which seemed entirely out of character for Holmes, who was about the last man in Rafferty's estimation to become entangled in the tribulations of love.

Wondering whether the message was a hoax, Rafferty went up to his apartment and placed another call to the Hotel Albert in New York. But this time there was no answer.

Chapter Seventeen

∫ ∿

"It Was a Tiger"

FROM THE NARRATIVE OF DR. JOHN WATSON:

My ride on Ninth Avenue was all uphill, and the elevated line overhead seemed to bear down on me more oppressively with each passing block as its height above the street diminished. The avenue here was only lightly traveled—no doubt because the elevated tracks made it such an unpleasant thoroughfare—but despite the hill I was able to reach 104th Street in less than ten minutes. After spotting an illuminated sign for the station, which was difficult to see in the fog, I left my bicycle in the street and, bag in hand, climbed up two long flights of wooden steps to catch my train.[1]

The station was small, dingy and unkempt, and it appeared unoccupied save for an attendant in the fare booth. I purchased a nickel token, passed through the turnstile and went out to the platform, which was also made of wood and gave evidence of years of hard use. At so late an hour on Sunday I hardly expected to encounter many other riders but was surprised to see a half-a-dozen people waiting for the southbound train. The group included an elderly bearded man in a shabby gray suit, a man and woman of middle age whom I took to be a married couple, two young men wearing bowlers who appeared to be street toughs and, at the far end of the platform, a slender man of perhaps thirty years of age fastidiously attired in a seersucker suit, white shoes and a panama hat.

Naturally, I made it my business to look closely at each of these people, using certain tricks I had learned from Holmes about spotting what he calls "the incongruous detail." The man in the seersucker suit soon attracted my attention. He carried a folded newspaper, which he clutched to his chest as though it contained something precious and irreplaceable. I had never seen anyone hold a newspaper in quite this way, and I at once became suspicious. Was another message from Slaney hidden within the newspaper, thereby accounting for the man's apparent fear of dropping it? Or was I, as sometimes even Holmes was inclined to do, making too much of an insignificant detail? I stared at the man, hoping he would meet my gaze and give a signal, but he seemed oblivious to my presence, as did the other passengers.

After several minutes of waiting, which I found to be nerve-wracking given the uncertainty of my situation, I heard the familiar low rumble of an approaching train. Next came the awful shriek of brakes, and I realized the train must be rounding Suicide Curve. As the last squeals stabbed through the heavy air, the platform began to vibrate, as though resonating to the blows of a giant hammer. Moments later, amid much clattering and shaking, the train's surprisingly small engine appeared through the fog, its headlamp radiating an eerie nimbus and heavy black smoke pouring from its funnel. The engine pulled only three cars, the last of which rolled to a stop directly in front of me.[2]

It was now ten minutes to midnight, which meant I should have ample time to reach South Ferry by the one o'clock deadline. Since I did not know whether I was to receive another message before boarding, I let the others who were waiting go first. I paid particular attention to the man in the seersucker suit, but he took no notice of me as he stepped into the last car. Others on the platform followed and I finally joined them only when two whistle blasts indicated the train was about to leave.

The train car, plainly furnished with wooden seats, was not crowded. I counted only ten other passengers, including those who had come aboard with me at 104th. I took a seat in the rear, in order to see everyone in the car, but none of my fellow riders appeared to pay me any heed. Again, I studied the passengers for some distinctive feature which might give them away but my efforts were to no avail.

Holmes by this time would have memorized every passenger's face and probably deduced as well their occupation, matrimonial state and, for all I knew, country of origin. Being a mere mortal, I was incapable of such feats and decided to sit back and wait for Slaney to come to me. However, I suspected that I would receive no further instructions from him until I reached the end of the line at South Ferry, which was many stops away.

As the train picked up speed, I glanced out the window but saw nothing except the blur of lighted windows from tenement buildings, which were so close to the track that I might well have reached out and touched them. In a matter of minutes the train began to slow for the next station, which according to a map posted in the car was Ninety-third Street. The couple I had seen waiting at 104th and who were sitting several seats ahead, got up to leave. The woman smiled as she and the man walked past me toward the rear door.

Once the train had stopped, a few new passengers boarded at the front of the car. Then, as the whistle sounded and the train began to inch forward, a small white envelope suddenly fluttered down on the seat beside me. I craned around just in time to see the couple going out the rear door. Through my window I caught one more glimpse of them as they hurried away on the platform and disappeared down the steps to the street.

Wondering what new instructions I would receive, I opened the envelope and read the following: GET OFF AT WARREN ST. TALK TO NO ONE. YOU ARE BEING WATCHED. SLANEY.

I quickly consulted the map again. Warren Street, I discovered, was far down in Lower Manhattan but several stops north of South Ferry, where I was originally to have left the train. It was now obvious to me that the whole purpose of my complicated travels was to make absolutely certain that no policemen—or Holmes himself, for that matter—could possibly be following me. Slaney's precautions in this regard had proved to be entirely successful from what I could tell. Indeed, I had seen no sign of the police since leaving the courtyard where I had switched vehicles, and it seemed unlikely that even Holmes could have picked up my trail thereafter.

I felt much anxiety as I rode south through the fog, believing as I did that Holmes and Hargreave's plan had gone seriously awry and that our adversary now controlled the game. At the same time, I wondered who in the car, if anyone, might be "watching" me. Again, I scanned the occupants of the seats in front of me—there were perhaps twenty passengers now in all—but I spotted no one who looked particularly suspicious.

It was half past midnight when the train arrived at Warren Street. I waited until the last instant to exit in the event I was to receive another communication aboard the train. No one approached, however, and I was the only passenger to alight at the station. I stood on the platform until the train had gone and then went inside the station, which was even smaller and more drab than the one at 104th. It was also deserted except for a uniformed attendant manning the fare booth. He was an elderly man, with a dusting of white hair at the edges of his blue cap, and the sad, drawn face of someone who had spent too many nights alone. I looked at him expectantly and he spoke up at once.

"Would you be the fellow from England?" he asked.

"Yes."

"Then I've got something for you here."

He pulled open a drawer beneath the counter, fished about for a moment, then handed me a white envelope of the type with which I was by now all too familiar. The envelope was sealed just as the others had been.

"May I ask where you got this?" I said.

The attendant, who seemed eager for conversation, replied, "Don't see no harm in that. Fellow came up here about fifteen minutes ago and handed me that envelope. Told me an English gent—that would be you, I guess— was to arrive on the next train and that I was to give it to him, no questions asked. Well, now you've got it. You're a detective, aren't you?"

"Why do you say that?"

"Seems obvious. I've been stuck up here ten years now and nobody ever asked me to deliver an envelope like that before. Nobody ever paid me five dollars, either. So I figure there must be some skullduggery going on, if you catch my drift. What kind of case are you on?"

"I'm afraid I cannot say. Could you describe the fellow who gave you this envelope?"

Said the attendant, "Well, truth is, he was mostly about as average looking as a fellow can get. Face-in-the-crowd type, that's what I'd call him. Wore a derby hat, plain white shirt rolled up at the sleeves, dark pants, had brown hair and eyes. Maybe forty-five, give or take a few years. Like I said, nothing stood out about him, except maybe for one thing."

"What was that?"

"The fellow had a little tattoo on his right arm just below the elbow."

"What kind of tattoo?"

"Well now, it was a very distinctive tattoo, as I recall, though my memory, sir, just isn't what it used to be. Of course—"

I had by now been in New York long enough to realize that information was just another commodity to its citizens, to be bought and sold like anything else on the open market. I reached into my pocket and extracted several silver dollars, which I jingled in my palm.

"Perhaps this will help restore your memory," I said.

"I believe it would, sir."

"Good. Now, be so kind as to describe the tattoo to me without further delay."

"All right. It was a tiger, sir, and a fierce looking one at that."

"Were there any words on the tattoo?"

"No, it was just the tiger."

"Have you seen tattoos like it before?"

"Maybe, but now my memory is starting to go again, if you must know the truth. It is difficult being old, sir, very difficult."

I am not proud to report that I now became exceedingly angry. Perhaps it was the stress of the night's events, or simply the oppressive heat and humidity, but I momentarily lost control of myself. I reached across the counter, grabbed the old man by his shirt collar, shook him violently and promised all manner of dire consequences if he did not answer my question immediately.

This display of outrage had its desired effect, for the startled attendant, terror etched on his wizened face, responded at once.

"It was a Tammany tiger, sir, and that is God's truth," he said. "He must have been one of Croker's men, for they are the only ones who have such tattoos."

"Who is Croker?" I demanded.

"Why Boss Croker. He's the head of Tammany Hall, which is them that runs this city."[3]

I let the attendant go, feeling sheepish that I had resorted to such crude force, although the information I had obtained was certainly interesting.

"Very well," I said. "Now tell me this, had you ever seen the man in question before?"

"No, sir, I can't say that I have, but then an awful lot of people come through here every day, as I'm sure you understand."

"Of course. Did the man say anything about what the envelope might contain?"

"No, and for five dollars, I didn't ask. But he made it clear that if I didn't deliver the envelope or if I opened it up, I'd regret it. I believed him. He had a pistol, he did, under his coat"—here the attendant paused before adding—"just like you. I can always tell."

"You are very observant, sir. Perhaps you can now tell me whether you've noticed any policemen around here in the last hour or so."

"No, I never see coppers unless there's a fight or something like that. They don't like walking up all those steps. Too much work and no money in it, if you know what I mean."

I could think of no other useful questions, so I thanked the attendant, who had been quite cowed by my outburst of anger, and added another five dollars to his night's earnings. Then I went outside to read Slaney's latest message under a lamppost. It said: FOLLOW WARREN EAST TO BROADWAY. GO SOUTH ON BROADWAY TO VESEY. YOU WILL SEE CHAPEL OF ST. PAUL. ENTER BY GATE ON BROADWAY. WAIT IN PORTICO. YOU WILL RECEIVE NEXT INSTRUCTIONS THERE. REMEMBER, NO POLICE OR SHE DIES. MAKE SURE YOU HAVE THE MONEY. SLANEY.

I read the message a second time, noting that it was the first in a while to mention money, and I wondered if this meant I was at last getting closer to the actual ransom exchange—if there was indeed to be one, which Holmes of course doubted. Nonetheless, Holmes and Hargreave had given me very specific instructions about what to do should someone demand the money from me in exchange for Mrs. Cubitt.

But with the police no longer behind me, I knew how dangerous any exchange would be and how readily I might be attacked. Indeed, Holmes had warned that the kidnappers might well use the exchange as a pretext for an ambush or simply as a way to obtain money for their criminal enterprises. I thus made sure to maintain an iron grip on my bag as I walked down to Warren Street, although I greatly wished that I still had my revolver.

Dense clumps of fog rolled along Warren as I walked east, adding to my sense of unease. This was largely a commercial district, and massive brick and stone warehouses crouched like staunch bulldogs to either side of the narrow street, which on a work day would have been jammed with carts, drays and wagons. Such was not the case now. Indeed, I appeared to have the street to myself, for there were no taverns or other establishments to draw visitors at this late hour, nor were any houses or apartments visible. Not until I reached Broadway, after a walk of less than three blocks, did I begin to see signs of life— mostly in the form of wagons and other night delivery vehicles—although even this great thoroughfare was hardly lively.

Turning south on Broadway, I suddenly plunged into a bank of fog as impenetrable as any I had ever encountered in London. Had it not been for the straight line of sidewalk at my feet, I would have been lost, for all nearby landmarks had vanished in an instant. I knew city hall and its surrounding park were almost directly across Broadway, but both were invisible through the murk. Nor could I make out the bulbous mass of the post office at the south end of the park. New York, the mightiest city of a mighty continent, had been swallowed up!

I proceeded south on Broadway, navigating more by sound and feel than sight. Now and then the rumbling and creaking of wagons echoed out of the fog, and once I thought I heard laughter up ahead of me. I saw no one, however, and the laughter soon died away. Indeed, I passed not a single person until I crossed Barclay Street and reached the brightly lighted entrance to the Astor House, where Holmes and I had gone only hours after arriving in New York.

A pair of well-dressed gentlemen were smoking and chatting outside the hotel's entrance as I went by. I nodded in their direction and they returned my gesture, one of them remarking to me, "You'd better be careful, my friend, or you'll walk right into the harbor. Ain't this the damnedest fog you've ever seen?"

I agreed that it was and moved on, aware that I had completed a great circle since coming to New York with Holmes. Was it mere coincidence, I wondered, that our adversary's trail led back to the very place where he had once planned to stay with his captive and where Holmes and I had first looked for him? Holmes would have been suspicious in this regard, for he was a great believer in what he called "the secret pattern of events"—hidden connections among seemingly disparate occurrences which were visible only to the most astute detective. There seemed to be just such a pattern in this case, with the Astor House at its center, and I sensed that the enemy was close at hand, lurking somewhere in the darkness and fog.

Once past the hotel, I crossed Vesey Street. The Chapel of St. Paul now stood directly before me, set back from the sidewalk behind an iron fence and gate. I could barely make out the columns of the chapel's front portico, while the tall tower to the rear was utterly invisible. I paused, fearful once again of an ambush, but well aware that I was no longer master of my fate. I went up to the gate, which was open, and walked into the portico.

Chapter Eighteen

§ ₹

"I Hope You Are Safe"

Fifty feet above Watson, in a room adjoining Mme. DuBois's suite, John Coffin prepared for what promised to be a most enjoyable night of hunting. With his fair, almost boyish features, Coffin might easily have passed for a schoolteacher or perhaps an energetic young minister, but his real line of work had nothing to do with education or God. Coffin's profession was murder for hire, and he was very good at it. He also excelled at intimidation, kneecapping, the administration of savage beatings and all the other dark arts required of a well-rounded Chicago enforcer.

On this night, however, shooting was to be his only business and he had brought along his weapon of choice for murder at a distance. It was a single-shot Creedmoor sporting rifle, specially made by Remington, with a long-range Vernier sight, a thirty-four-inch barrel, a fancy-grained walnut stock and a silver butt plate engraved with its owner's initials. In capable hands, it was among the most accurate and deadly rifles in the world, and Coffin had yet to miss a shot with it when it counted.[1]

Barely a year earlier, he had used the rifle to kill Harry Varnell, who ran the policy rackets in Chicago. Varnell had been dropped at a range of five hundred yards, as he and his mistress enjoyed an afternoon of sailing—and other more vigorous pursuits—on Lake Michigan. His death had been ordered after it became apparent he was underreporting proceeds, an offense his silent but by no means unobservant partners could not forgive. The old gambler had feared he was a marked man and had surrounded himself with well-armed bodyguards. All his precautions, however, had proved to be useless against the Creedmoor and the marksman who wielded it.[2]

It had been a difficult shot, not because of the range but because of the boat's irregular motion. Even so, Coffin had put the slug right through the rings of fat encircling Varnell's thick neck, the bullet severing the old man's carotid artery. Blood had pumped out of the wound like water from a high-pressure hose, showering Varnell's mistress in a crimson spray. The "Policy King," as the Chicago newspapers had dubbed him, was dead before he hit the deck.

Compared to that shot, Coffin's assignment this night would be sinfully easy—if the fog ever dissipated. All he needed was a view down to the street at the right time and his lethal work could be done in a matter of minutes. Soon thereafter, the world would learn of a great tragedy.

As Coffin laid his plans, so did Sherlock Holmes, who— had it not been for the fog—would have been within easy rifle shot of the Chicago assassin. Holmes was stationed just around the corner from St. Paul's front portico, in the narrow section of graveyard along Vesey Street. Originally, he had intended to wait inside the chapel, but the fog had forced him outside, where he expected to hear Slaney coming, even if he could not see him.

Like Slaney and his confederates, Holmes had not anticipated the fog, and the careful plans he had made with Hargreave to establish proper sightlines for his men were in shambles. Indeed, he had already debated whether to call off the ambush. In the end, however, he had decided that his adversaries would be no better off in the fog than he was, and that an equally good opportunity to end the whole business might never present itself.

Still, uncertainty gnawed at him in a way that it never had before. Once Holmes had laid his plans, he was normally the epitome of confidence, for he believed—rightly—that few if any criminals could match his daunting powers of deduction. He drove events where he wanted them to go, and even the most hardened and clever criminals invariably found themselves crushed by the stampede he had unleashed. But this case was different, so different that Holmes could liken it to none other in his experience. Not even some of the early and brilliant crimes orchestrated by the malign genius Dr. James Moriarty could compare with Elsie Cubitt's kidnapping.

What distinguished the case from all others, Holmes thought, was the level of premeditation that had been woven into its very fabric. At every step, beginning on the plains of Norfolk and continuing through London and Liverpool to New York, the case gave evidence of planning so thorough, so intricate, so maliciously brilliant that Holmes could only view it with a certain professional admiration. Whoever was behind the crime was not merely a tactician but a master strategist. This mastery revealed itself in his adversary's ability to pollute the entire environment of the case with doubt, which clung to every piece of evidence like black soot.

The clues that had led Holmes to St. Paul's Chapel formed a case in point. There was, to begin with, the name itself, which his adversary had played on throughout the case. Elsie Cubitt (or at least her impersonator) had been seen at St. Paul's Cathedral in London after her kidnapping. She had then been taken to America aboard a ship named the *St. Paul*, by a man calling himself Rafferty. The real Rafferty, of course, lived in the city of St. Paul, Minnesota. Finally, there had been the pamphlet about the chapel of St. Paul that Mme. DuBois had dropped outside Mrs. Astor's mansion.

The dropped pamphlet, Holmes believed, was one of the few genuine clues in the case, and it had been enough to convince him that St. Paul's would be the scene of the final ambush. It was a daring leap of a deduction, of course, but Holmes was convinced that the whole line of the case, with its many references to the name "St. Paul," pointed to the chapel as the place where the Conspirator would make his final move. The fact that Mme. DuBois was now ensconced at the Astor House, just across the street, only served to strengthen Holmes's theory.

Holmes was also certain that the lady did not know she had been followed to the Astor House. In order to mislead her, Holmes had asked Hargreave to have two men watch her. She had easily lost the first man, who in any event had been instructed not to pursue her too vigorously. The other man—Hargreave's most skilled shadow—had then taken over and followed her to the Astor House, where her suite was now under surveillance.

Within the past few minutes, Holmes had also learned—from Hargreave, who was stationed nearby and in contact with his men—of a visitor to Mme. DuBois's suite. This visitor, Holmes realized at once, matched the description of the young "Dr. Watson" who had accompanied Elsie Cubitt across the Atlantic and later brought her to the apartment in Greenwich Village. Only the Conspirator himself, and of course, Elsie Cubitt, were still unaccounted for, but Holmes had no doubt they were nearby. The ransom exchange, he knew, was a ruse, since the Conspirator would not give up, for a mere ten thousand dollars, the woman he had gone to such lengths to abduct.

Now, however, the damnable fog had thrown many of Holmes's calculations out the window. The ring of policemen surrounding the chapel would be blind in the fog and would have to rely on sound — Holmes carried a police whistle — when the time came to close in. Even worse, he had just learned from Hargreave that his detectives had lost track of Watson and had no idea where he might be. This was very bad news indeed, and if anything should happen to Watson, Holmes would never forgive himself.

Holmes had debated whether to send Watson on such a risky mission but saw no other choice. The Conspirator, Holmes had reasoned, would be instantly suspicious if someone unknown to him showed up to make the supposed ransom exchange. On the other hand, the appearance of Watson would, in theory, trigger no such concern, since the Conspirator might well assume that Holmes was simply exercising appropriate caution by staying in the background.

Even so, Holmes was well aware that if he was wrong — if the Conspirator and his confederates did not plan to converge at St. Paul's Chapel — Watson would be in mortal peril. This was doubly true now that Hargreave's men no longer shadowed Watson.

"Wherever you are, Watson, I hope you are safe," Holmes said quietly to himself as he peered into the suffocating fog, which seemed to drench everything it touched in uncertainty. Holmes, in fact, felt as uncomfortable as he had in a very long time. But there could be no turning back now, and as he waited in the graveyard, alert to every sound in the dense unknowable darkness beyond, he could only hope that he had not made the worst mistake of his life.

His thoughts were suddenly interrupted by the sound of footsteps, coming toward him along Broadway. Holmes listened intently as the steps, undoubtedly those of a man, continued to a point just past him before suddenly stopping. Then, just after he heard the creak of the old iron gate as it swung open, Holmes sprung into action.

Chapter Nineteen

ᔓ ᔓ

"I Will Be Fine, My Dear Watson"

FROM THE NARRATIVE OF DR. JOHN WATSON:

As I stepped up into the portico of St. Paul's, expecting at any instant to confront the kidnappers, I was immediately accosted from behind by someone who had materialized out of the fog with Indianlike stealth. A bony hand was cupped over my mouth while another grabbed my right arm. Then, as I was pushed back toward the front of the chapel, I heard whispered words which sent my heart soaring. It was Holmes!

"Ah, Watson, you have made it," he whispered. "You do not know how pleased I am to see you."

"My God, Holmes, but you gave me a fright!" I whispered back, for my heart had nearly leaped out of my chest.

"My apologies, but I did not wish to have you cry out and give away my position, or yours," said Holmes. "Now, tell me what happened to you tonight. But do so quickly, for the Conspirator may be here at any moment."

I gave Holmes a brief account of my many adventures, including the curious episode at Grant's Tomb. I concluded by relating how my final set of instructions from Slaney had directed me to the portico.

"Ah, then I was right all along," Holmes said. "It will be here—and nowhere else—that the Conspirator makes his move. Now, listen carefully, Watson, for here is what you must do. Go around to the north side of the chapel and find a place to hide in the graveyard. I shall stay here to await our adversary. When you hear my police whistle, come running here as fast as you can. Inspector Hargreave already has a ring of men elsewhere around the chapel and they will converge once they hear the whistle."

"But wouldn't it be better to stay here with you?" I protested.

"No. You have carried more than your fair share of the burden tonight. It is I who must come face to face with the Conspirator."

"Then you will need my bag, which has the money," I said.

Holmes, however, refused to take the bag, saying it would be safer with me.

"Very well," I said, "but are you sure it is wise for you to take on such desperate men alone, even if it is only for a matter of seconds?"

"I will be fine, my dear Watson. Have no worries about me. Now, go to your post and listen for the whistle."

"Still, Holmes, in this fog, anything could happen and—"

"I know, Watson, I know. It is a dicey business all the way around. But if we are blind, so too is the Conspirator. He has tried to lay a trap here, but if we have any luck at all, he is the one who shall fall into it. Now, off you go, Watson, and be as careful as you have ever been in your life. Our enemies will not hesitate to kill if they think they are cornered."

Despite premonitions of disaster, I acceded as always to Holmes's wishes and went without delay into the graveyard. There, I quickly discovered—by nearly bumping into it—a large tree which provided some measure of cover. Once I had taken up this position, I set down my bag and waited for what seemed like many minutes, although I could not be certain of the time, since it was too dark to read my watch and I dared not strike a match.

Waiting, as any soldier will confess, is the worst part of war, as I recalled all too vividly from my experiences at Maiwand. In advance of battle a man's imagination grows uncommonly active, and when the time comes to step forward it is almost a relief to face real bullets at last. The great metropolis of New York, I sensed, was now waiting with me, for with each passing minute I became more aware of an eerie stillness, as though the entire city had drawn in a long, deep breath and was waiting to exhale.[1]

Just when it seemed I could bear to wait no longer, something curious happened. The fog, pushed by the invisible hand of a wind which had stirred on the East River, began to swirl and lift, causing a large break to appear, like a clearing hewn from a dense forest. Suddenly, I could see at least one hundred feet in all directions, and as I peered through the graveyard toward Broadway I noticed a faint light flickering in the chapel's side windows. Had someone inside just turned on the lights or had they been on all along but hidden by fog? Before I could consider this question I was startled by the shrill, urgent call of a police whistle from in front of the chapel. Holmes had signaled!

Chapter Twenty

"Shoot the Bastards If You Can"

John Coffin left his room at the Astor House just after midnight, carrying his disassembled rifle in what looked like a violin case. He went to the back stairs and walked up to the attic, where many of the hotel's maids and bellboys lived in cramped rooms under the eaves. After making sure no one had seen him, Coffin jimmied open a heavy wooden door that gave access to a narrow flight of steps ascending to the roof.

Once outside, Coffin stopped a moment to get his bearings. He had gone up to the roof several days earlier to identify the best place to carry out his mission, but the fog was so thick now that he had to negotiate by memory and feel. Fortunately, the spot he had chosen to do his murderous work was no more than ten feet from the stairway entrance, behind one of the numerous tall chimneys that resembled a line of battlements around the roof's perimeter. Under normal conditions, Coffin's position commanded an excellent view straight across Vesey Street to St. Paul's, and he would be able to pick off anybody who moved along the street or in the chapel's surrounding graveyard.

After assembling and loading his rifle—a task he could easily accomplish blindfolded—Coffin settled in to wait for the fog to lift. His orders were simple. Once Coffin heard the call of a police whistle, he was to open fire immediately, spraying bullets around but being careful not to hit any uniformed policemen. Nor was Coffin to take a shot at Sherlock Holmes under any circumstances. There were, however, at least two targets he was free to take dead aim at should an opportunity present itself.

"Shoot the bastards if you can," his employer had said, and Coffin would be only too happy to comply. Still, he wasn't especially pleased with his orders. It seemed extremely odd to him that he had been hired *not* to shoot Holmes or any coppers in uniform. His employer had offered no explanation for these orders, and Coffin knew enough not to ask for one. Still, it was all very strange, especially considering that this was to be the best-paid job of his career.

Of course, now that the fog had blotted out everything, Coffin wasn't really sure how he would carry out his orders or, for that matter, how long he should remain on the roof. He couldn't even see Vesey Street, or St. Paul's, and if a police whistle sounded out of the gloom he'd have nothing to shoot at. He considered going down to the street, where he might be able to use his Colt automatic pistol to good effect. After mulling over his options, he decided to stay where he was, hoping the fog would clear before anything happened below.

His wish was soon to come true, for around one o'clock he felt the first stirrings of an easterly breeze. Almost at once, holes began to develop in the fog. Encouraged, Coffin readied himself for action, standing up by the chimney and bracing his left shoulder to ensure the steadiest possible shot. Within minutes, as the wind continued to pick up, he was able to see down to the street, helped by a bright moon that had suddenly popped out of the heavens like a light being switched on in a dark room.

He noticed at once that a figure was crouching in the graveyard along Vesey Street. Coffin got the figure in his sights and saw that it was Dr. John Watson, the faithful servant of Sherlock Holmes to the very end. Bringing him down would be child's play, Coffin thought, as he waited to take his shot.

Then he heard the high-pitched warble of a police whistle slicing through the damp night air. It was an invitation to mayhem and Coffin did not intend to miss the party. Watson had responded instantly to the whistle by running toward the front of the chapel. Even so, Coffin kept Watson in his sights and prepared, with an easy squeeze of the trigger, to put a slug through the back of his head.

He would have been successful had it not been for the pair of police detectives who, thanks to the foresight of Sherlock Holmes, were stationed near Mme. DuBois's room. They had been told to watch for any visitors, who might be accomplices of the kidnapper, and to be alert for other suspicious activity. The detectives had seen Coffin go into Mme. Dubois's room and had decided to place him under surveillance. When he later emerged from his own room with the violin case, and went up to the roof, the two policemen—by then extremely suspicious—had followed.

Now, as the fog suddenly cleared and they saw Coffin aiming his rifle, the detectives drew their revolvers and burst through the roof door, shouting at him to drop the weapon. This sudden hubbub was enough to disturb Coffin's concentration and his shot went just wide of Watson. Cursing, he reloaded his rifle with a speed borne of years of practice and spun around to face the policemen who had so inconveniently interrupted his work.

Although there was only one policeman he was supposed to shoot, nobody had told him that coppers would be gunning for him on the roof. It was now a matter of self-defense. In one fluid motion, Coffin fired the Creedmoor from his hip. The bullet tore through the right shoulder of one of the detectives, and he dropped to his knees, his heavy revolver clattering on the slate roof. Coffin now discarded his single-shot rifle and reached for his Colt automatic, intending to shoot his way off the roof.

The second detective, however, did not intend to suffer his partner's fate, and he opened fire, even though Coffin was only a silhouette in the moonlight. Like most of his brethren, the cop wasn't an especially good marksman, and his first few rounds went wide and high. Coffin by this time had his seven-shot automatic in hand and was ready to shoot the second cop down. But as he started to squeeze the trigger, a bullet—the very last fired by the policeman before his revolver was empty—struck Coffin square in the forehead.

The force of the impact knocked Coffin back from the chimney and over the roof. The notorious Chicago assassin plummeted soundlessly through the night. He was already dead by the time his body slammed into the sidewalk on Vesey Street, bounced once and finally rolled to a rest, face down, in the gutter.

Chapter Twenty-one

"Let the World Know What I Have Done"

FROM THE NARRATIVE OF DR. JOHN WATSON:

At the sound of Holmes's police whistle, I started to sprint toward the portico. I had gone only a few feet when a loud report rang out and I heard a hiss just behind my head, followed by the unmistakable thwack of a bullet slamming into the side wall of the chapel. Fearing that a second bullet might come my way at any moment, I ducked behind the nearest large tombstone. Then, from somewhere well above me, I heard the crackle of pistol fire—perhaps half-a-dozen shots in all—echoing through the darkness. I looked across Vesey Street and saw to my astonishment a man, who had apparently plummeted from the upper floors of the Astor House, crash to the sidewalk with sickening force.

To add to the chaos, two large men armed with pistols came running up from Broadway toward the body. Were these Hargreave's men, or the kidnapper's? I did not wait to find out, for Holmes was now my only concern. I ran through the graveyard and around the corner of the chapel, hoping to spot Holmes in the portico. He was not there. Instead, I saw two more armed men coming at full speed through the sidewalk gate. Both immediately shouted at me to raise my hands, even though I was not armed. Their manner and tone of voice identified them as police. I did as I was told, knowing I would surely be shot otherwise. As the two officers approached, I informed them in no uncertain terms who I was but they appeared dubious and kept their guns trained on me.

I now saw other men—presumably all police—arriving as well. Among them was Hargreave himself, looking at once harried and deeply perturbed. When he saw me, he ordered his men to let me go at once.

"By God, it's good to see you, doctor," he said, his big face flush with excitement. "Was that you who walked in through the fog awhile ago?"

"It was."

"Well, you gave me a scare, you did. Almost sent my boys in to check. But Mr. Holmes was very insistent that we were not to converge until he blew the whistle. Now, do you know what in blazes is going on here?"

"I do not," I readily admitted. "Tell me, where is Holmes? He was standing in the portico just minutes ago. Has anybody seen him?"

Hargreave repeated this question to his men, but all shook their heads. They had not seen Holmes, or anyone else, in the portico after the fog lifted.

"Is it possible, inspector, that he came around the other side of the chapel and got past your men?" I asked.

"No, we were all on the alert and I don't think that's likely. I see only one possibility. Mr. Holmes must have gone inside. There's a light shining in the chapel and it's got no business being on at this hour. I tell you, something funny's going on."

I was all for entering the chapel immediately, shooting open the door if necessary. Hargreave, however, advocated caution.

"Before we do anything, we must secure the area. There's already been gunplay tonight—did you hear it?— and heaven only knows what happened to my men at the Astor House."

This remark was mystifying, as neither Holmes nor

Hargreave had mentioned anything to me earlier about sending police to the hotel. However, I cared little about what might have occurred there. Holmes's well-being was all that mattered.

"I heard the shooting, inspector, and saw the body fall," I said. "Indeed, a bullet just missed me. But our first goal must be to find Holmes."

I now called out Holmes's name as loudly as I could. There was no answer and I repeated to Hargreave that we must break into the chapel without further delay, for I felt a growing sense of alarm. If Holmes had gone inside the chapel, why hadn't he used his whistle again or responded to my call?

"You're right, doctor," Hargreave finally said. "Ah, what's this?"

I followed Hargreave's gaze to a large window which took up much of the wall between the two doorways in the portico. The window had numerous small panes of opaque, colored glass. Hargreave had noticed that one pane along the bottom row was missing. He walked over to it and glanced inside.

"The chapel looks empty from what I can tell," he said, "but there's not much light in there and somebody could be hiding out."

"We will have to take that risk," I told him.

Hargreave nodded in agreement and turned to his men—a small crowd of them had by now gathered around us—to issue orders. One group of officers was to go around to the east end of the church and enter through the door there. Hargreave, I and two of his men would go in one of the portico doors, while the remaining officers would watch outside in case anyone tried to escape through the windows.

"Very well, gentlemen, you have your assignments, and I warn you to be alert," Hargreave said. "If Abe

Slaney is in there, and if he has Mr. Holmes, he will not go down without a fight."

Hargreave and I went up to the nearest set of entry doors, which were made of stout oak. The doors were locked. The two officers with us then tried the doors on the other side of the portico, but they were secured as well.

"Well, I guess it's to be breaking and entering," Hargreave said. "All right, boys, put your shoulder to it."

The two burly police officers did just that and after several attacks the lock gave way and the doors burst open.

"All right, we're going in," Hargreave announced. "Stay together, boys, and be ready for anything."

We entered a small vestibule, from which I could see portions of the chapel beneath a low gallery. Another gallery ran along the opposite wall. Pews, divided by a central aisle, filled the main floor. The light was so dim, however, that the rear of the chapel vanished into the shadows. I called out Holmes's name several more times. There was still no answer, nor did any other sound break the stillness of the old church.

We now went up into the chapel itself. I had assumed the sanctuary would be at the far end of the chapel but soon learned otherwise, for a high pulpit loomed immediately to my left. A single light shone down from an ornate coronet above it. This was, as far as I could tell, the only illumination in the chapel. To the rear of the pulpit, behind the communion rail, was a small sanctuary containing an altar and a sunburst ornament in front of the main window.[1]

Peering off into the gloom beyond the feeble arc of the pulpit light, I called out for Holmes yet again, to no effect. I then turned to Hargreave, who stared blankly into the darkness, as though not quite believing what he saw, or perhaps I should say, what he did not see.

"Where do you suppose Holmes could have gone?" I asked.

"I don't know, Dr. Watson, but this is a rum business if you ask me. Well, let's have a thorough look around, beginning with the galleries. If somebody's hiding up behind those railings, we'd be sitting ducks."

The two policemen with us had each brought lanterns and they now went up to examine the galleries, which proved to be empty. Next, we went down the center aisle, Hargreave's men shining their lanterns along every row of pews, including the one where—a wall plaque informed us—George Washington had sat. Once again, we saw nothing. When we reached the back of the chapel, Hargreave opened the massive doors there to admit more policemen, who had been unable to force their way in.

They joined in our search, although it quickly became clear that no one could be secreted anywhere in the chapel proper. Two officers then climbed up into the bell tower, while others examined the cellar, all to no avail. Holmes had vanished as though by some malignant act of magic. Hargreave—who was not easy to impress, or to fool—could only shake his head in amazement.

"It's the damnedest thing I've ever seen," he said. "How does a man just disappear like that? It's like the earth swallowed him up and he's down there with old General Montgomery under the porch."

"Who are you talking about?"

"Oh, I guess you wouldn't know about that, doctor. General Richard Montgomery—Revolutionary War hero, killed storming Quebec in 1775, I think—well, he's buried right under the porch where Mr. Holmes was standing last time you saw him. But I was just being facetious, doctor. There's nothing down there but a gloomy old crypt. My men have already checked it out."[2]

"Then we must assume that Holmes and Slaney slipped by us in the fog," I said.

"Perhaps, but I ain't ready to lay any money on that idea," Hargreave replied. "You and I were out there, as were my very best men, and somebody would've heard or seen something, fog or no fog. I'd stake my life on that."

I now found myself once again recalling Holmes's famous aphorism that once the impossible has been ruled out, whatever remains, no matter how improbable, must be the truth. The trouble was, in this case no possibilities— even improbable ones—seemed to present themselves.

Amid these disturbing thoughts, I heard a voice shout down from the pulpit: "I've found something in here, inspector. You'd better come have a look."

I followed Hargreave to the altar rail as a policeman came down from the pulpit to meet us. He was holding a large silver cufflink in one hand and a small envelope in the other.

My heart skipped a beat, for I recognized the cufflink immediately. It was embossed with the letters RTM (for Ridling Thorpe Manor) and had been a gift to Holmes from Elsie Cubitt.

"They were on the floor in the pulpit," the policeman said, handing the items to Hargreave. "Looks like they were left for us to find."

"Why do you say that?" I asked.

"Because of what's written on the envelope," said Hargreave. "Have a look for yourself, doctor."

The envelope was addressed to the "Police of New York City."

Hargreave said, "Go ahead and open it, doctor, though I have a bad feeling we'll not like what we find."

In this Hargreave proved correct, for inside was a message written in the same blocky letters as all the others I had received. It said: I HAVE HOLMES AND MRS. CUBITT. YOU WILL NOT FIND THEM. LET THE WORLD KNOW WHAT I HAVE DONE. SLANEY.

I felt a deep chill penetrate to the very core of my being, for I feared that the finest man I had ever known might be lost to me forever. Hargreave, however, was by no means ready to give up the fight, nor was I.

"By God, sir, I will prove Slaney wrong if it is the last thing I ever do," said Hargreave. "Mr. Holmes is somewhere in this city and I will find him."

A policeman I had not seen before now approached Hargreave with news of what he called "the big fight at the hotel."

I listened with great interest as the officer narrated his story, describing how an unidentified assassin had wounded a policeman and then been shot dead on the roof of the Astor House. I also learned that Mme. DuBois had been staying at the hotel and was now in police custody.

After the policeman had completed his report, Hargreave said, "Well, I guess I'd best have a look at the fellow who went diving off the roof. Why don't you come along, doctor? Maybe it's somebody you know."

Although I was not anxious to leave the chapel, believing that the answer to Holmes's seemingly unaccountable disappearance must lie somewhere within its old walls, I went out with Hargreave. We found several policemen gathered around the body, which lay in a gutter on Vesey Street and was covered by a blanket. Dark pools of blood had oozed out from under the blanket and flies were already gathering to begin their dreadful work.

Hargreave, who had probably seen as many dead men in his time as any coroner, signaled for one of the officers to lift up the blanket. Even though the man's skull was broken into bloody pieces and a bullet hole formed a small red medallion in the center of his forehead, I had no trouble recognizing him.

"My God, I know this man," I said. "He accosted me at Grant's Tomb."

I now told Hargreave how I had been driven to Grant's Tomb, only to find the injured guard and the gunman who now lay dead at our feet. I further explained how the man had held me at gunpoint, taken my revolver (but not the ransom money) and then set me on the course which ultimately led to St. Paul's.

"What a peculiar story," Hargreave remarked. "It doesn't on the face of it make any sense."

"I agree, but that is what happened. Is the man familiar to you at all, inspector?"

"No, and there's not a single piece of identification on him. But he was carrying a Creedmoor rifle and one of the new Colt automatic pistols. It's not every day you see guns like those out on the street. My guess is that this fellow was a professional shooter, maybe hired by Slaney out of Chicago."

"But who was he shooting at?"

"You for one, doctor, or so it would appear," Hargreave said. "In any case, I'll arrange to get some men up to the tomb to see what they can find out."

Feeling overwhelmed by the night's strange and violent events, I now walked back across Vesey toward the chapel, where I wanted to sit and think for awhile. I noticed that my bag was sitting by the tree where I had left it and I went over to pick it up. The ransom money had proved useless, just as Holmes had feared, and I thought I might as well return it to Hargreave.

I opened the bag, only to receive the final shock of what had been one of the most puzzling nights of my life. The ten thousand dollars in police money had vanished, much like Holmes, with no obvious explanation. I called Hargreave over to explain this unfortunate circumstance, which was as surprising to him as to me. As we began to discuss how—and where—the theft might have occurred, one of Hargreave's detectives approached and pointed to a man who had just arrived at the scene.

Tall and portly, the man had the largest cigar I had ever seen dangling from his mouth. He wore a distinctive white hat above an elegant suit of the same color and appeared to be well-known to the police officers who gathered around him on the sidewalk next to the Astor House. I later learned that the man was none other than New York Chief of Police William Devery, and that white in his case did not equate with purity or goodness.[3]

What Hargreave did next was quite unexpected. He whispered instructions to his detectives and then told me I was to leave at once.

"But there is—"

"No arguments, doctor!" said Hargreave sharply. "Go now or I can't be responsible for your safety. Michael here will lead the way. I will explain later."

Without another word, Hargreave turned away while a detective—who was obviously one of Hargreave's most trusted lieutenants—took me in tow. He led me around to the opposite side of the church, out through a gate along Fulton Street and then south on Broadway. We eventually found a cab—no easy task at half past two on a Monday morning, even in Manhattan—and went at once to Hargreave's house. My escort, whose last name was Bissen, would not explain why I had been spirited away from St. Paul's, telling me only that Hargreave "would have all the answers."

I lay down on a couch in Hargreave's front parlor and fell asleep at once, such was my exhaustion of both mind and body. My rest did not last for long, however, for at five in the morning I was aroused by Bissen. He told me Hargreave had telephoned and that I was to be taken to another residence several blocks away owned by a certain Miss Katherine Parry. This woman, Bissen informed me, was "a longtime acquaintance of Inspector Hargreave who happens to be out of town at present."

Bissen went on to say that the move was for my own safety. Naturally, I asked what he meant, but he again deferred all explanations to Hargreave. Once I had settled in, Bissen departed and I was left alone except for the company of Miss Parry's two large and ill-tempered dogs, which Hargreave had been caring for in her absence.

Since I was by this time thoroughly awake, I brewed a cup of tea and set to work on my journal while events were still fresh in my mind. Around nine o'clock Bissen came back to report that Hargreave would be delayed because he was "on the hot seat down at headquarters." As was his usual practice, he would not explain what he meant by this startling statement, although he promised that Hargreave himself would answer all of my questions upon his arrival.

With little else to do, I occupied myself by preparing messages to be telegraphed to Detective Wooldridge in Chicago and Shadwell Rafferty in St. Paul. I informed both men of Holmes's disappearance and asked for their aid. Specifically, I asked Wooldridge to supply more information about the Slaney gang, including the location of their lair in Chicago, in the event Holmes was to be taken there. I also gave Wooldridge a description of the gunman killed at the Astor House, since it seemed possible he was from Chicago.

As for Rafferty, I could only ask him in a general way for his assistance, which I knew would be offered in an instant. However, I told him there would be no point in him coming to New York until I had a better idea as to Holmes's whereabouts.

Bissen came by before noon and took my messages to the nearest Western Union office. Then I sat and waited, wondering when—or if—I might see Sherlock Holmes again. Not since seeing him disappear into the gloomy chasm of Reichenbach Falls had I felt so bereft or so fearful for the fate of my dearest friend on Earth. Still, I determined to remain hopeful at all costs, and I prayed that at any moment Holmes would walk through the door, throw down his hat, loosen his collar, light his favorite pipe and then — pacing in his accustomed manner — launch into a marvelous tale of his night's adventures. It was to be the dream which sustained me in the terrible days ahead.

Chapter Twenty-two

"I Like Those Odds"

Elsie Cubitt had always known that her kidnapper, if he had the chance, would in the end take her to Chicago. She held the image in her mind of the great city by the lake, its rude towers and roaring els, its majesty and filth, its impossible gathering of nations, its stockyards and abattoirs where the work of destroying living things had been brought to industrialized perfection. City of hope and death—that was Chicago—and as her train rolled out of the Pennsylvania Railroad station in Jersey City, she found herself wandering through the haunted realms of her own history, back to the place that had given her life.

Chicago was where both she and the whole Slaney clan had been born and raised, and she had known Abe since childhood. Eban Patrick, Elsie's father, was in his own way the model of a loving parent (Elsie was only three when her mother died) and he had always provided the best of everything for his only child. Unfortunately, his line of work—robbery, extortion, prostitution and even murder—did not endear him to his strong-willed daughter.

She had never understood how a man could be so kind to her and yet so barbaric in his dealings with others. Although she loved him, she had finally refused to become part of his cruel and brutal world. She had not even gone back to Chicago for his funeral earlier in the year. Elsie had always expected her father would die violently, and while she privately mourned his passing she could not bring herself to return to the city where he and his henchmen — the Slaneys particularly — had caused so much human misery.

Once, she had even thought she loved Abe, who was handsome in a dangerous way. He could be funny and charming, danced beautifully, was highly intelligent and clearly loved her. But like Elsie's father, he seemed to have an incomplete heart — a fact that had been brought home to her one night at a cafe when he took offense at a how another man looked at her and all but beat him to death before her unbelieving eyes. It was then that she had decided to take some money she had saved and begin a new life in England, where her mother's family had come from. Not long after arriving in London, she had met Hilton Cubitt — who like Abe was dashing, clever and a wonderful dancer — but who in addition possessed a sweet and gentle disposition.

She could never quite forgive herself for Hilton's death. Even though Abe Slaney had pulled the trigger, she had been the magnet who drew him to England in the first place. And if she had not been so proud and foolish — if she had only told Hilton that Slaney was in England — everything might have turned out differently. For weeks after her husband's death, and her own attempted suicide, she had been disconsolate.

Then she had met Sherlock Holmes and the world suddenly seemed to brighten. She treasured his letters, which were so wise and understanding, and she found him to be a delightful companion. Indeed, she thought she loved him, but she also wondered whether — for all of his

kindness—he could truly love her as well, for his sentiments lay deeply buried under a hard crust of reason.

She wondered where Holmes was now and hoped that
he had not suffered some awful fate at the hands of her
kidnappers. Already she had lost one man to Abe Slaney's
insane hatred, and now she could only pray that she
would not lose another.

The first sound Sherlock Holmes heard, when he
struggled toward consciousness some hours later, was
vague and distant, like wind clattering through bare trees
in a faraway forest. He was lying on his back, and his
head throbbed with pain. Holmes also had a peculiar sensation that he was being rocked, or perhaps shaken, in a
giant cradle. It was not an altogether unpleasant feeling,
especially in his condition. His mind, normally so sharp
that many an unsuspecting criminal had been cut to rib-
bons upon it, felt heavy and dull—a consequence of the
hefty dose of barbiturates he had been given after his encounter with the kidnappers at St. Paul's.

Floating between sleep and wakefulness, Holmes experienced small, intense bursts of memory that popped in
his head like exploding flashbulbs. He remembered seeing the man in the pulpit, his mouth twisted into a malevolent grin. Holmes also recalled the glow of kerosene
lanterns in a long dark corridor, and something—what
was it?—dropping from his pants pocket. Then there was
a face, a woman's face, peering down at him. The woman
had said something—he couldn't remember what—but
he would never forget her harsh laughter. And then?
There was nothing, or at least nothing more Holmes
could tease out of his recalcitrant memory.

Holmes tried to keep his eyes open, to will himself into
a state of full consciousness, but the rocking of the cradle
was too persistent, the steady noise (what was it?) too

comforting and, like Elsie Cubitt—who unknown to Holmes lay less than a hundred feet away—he dropped back into a deep yet hardly restful slumber.

That same morning, a telegram arrived in Chicago, addressed to the owner of a nondescript tavern on Dearborn Street. The message, for which the tavern keeper duly signed, was in fact intended for someone else. Within a matter of minutes, it was delivered to its real recipient, a certain Mrs. Mary Mortimer, at the Potomac Apartments on the city's south side.[1]

Mrs. Mortimer, who was entertaining a gentleman in her front parlor when the message arrived, occupied a spacious suite atop the building. From her apartment, Mrs. Mortimer had a fine view of Lake Michigan, shimmering like dark metal in the high summer sun as it rolled out from the eastern margins of the city. She could also see, directly to her north, the source of her riches—Chicago's infamous Levee district, said to be the largest concentration of vice on the continent, if not the world. Now, as she tore open the message she had been waiting for, she would know if her great labors of the past year were close to fruition.

The brief message was exactly as Mrs. Mortimer hoped it would be. It said: HAVE BOTH PACKAGES. WILL DELIVER TUESDAY AS PER INSTRUCTIONS. J. S.

"Well, you look pleased," said the tall, portly man who sat across from her and who, as always, looked even more pleased with himself. Bathhouse John Coughlin, as he was called, was a handsome man in his forties, with a strong squarish face, a bushy black mustache and a full head of equally black hair from which all traces of gray had been carefully dyed away. If his features were rather four-square, his attire was not, for he was dressed with his usual discordant flamboyance in a shrieking green frock coat, a plush satin vest studded with diamonds, a white shirt with ruffled sleeves and striped maroon-and-gold trousers.

Mrs. Mortimer, whose own attire—a long blue dress of elegant cut that accentuated her voluptuous figure—was always impeccable, stared at the Fat Peacock, as she liked to call Coughlin, and said, "Yes, it appears everything is going as planned, despite the complications in New York. In any event, our guests are now on their way and should arrive in the morning. I trust, John, that you will be prepared for them."

Coughlin, one of Chicago's most famously corrupt aldermen, replied that he was indeed ready. "They will have quite the surprise, Mary, quite the surprise. You can count on it."

Mrs. Mortimer smiled and said, "I knew you would not fail me, John."

In truth, she had known no such thing. Bathhouse John—so named because he had once worked as a rubber in a Turkish bath—was in fact a buffoon in her eyes. However, he was a useful buffoon, with that mixture of low animal cunning and clear-eyed ruthlessness that all good street criminals possessed. What he didn't have, Mrs. Mortimer knew all too well, was a strategic intellect—his cohort and fellow crook, Mike (Hinky Dink) Kenna, supplied that element of the partnership—and together the two of them ran the entire Levee district. Or at least, they thought they did.[2]

But the real power in the Levee—if power could be measured in terms of dollars extracted from its carnival of vice—was Mrs. Mortimer, who in a remarkably short period of time had insinuated herself into almost every aspect of the precinct's flourishing trade. Yet despite her rapid rise to a position of wealth and influence, little was known about her.

In this respect, she was a darkly fascinating mystery in an otherwise wide-open city where hoodlums regularly killed one another in the lurid light of day. She had arrived sometime in the summer of 1899, from the East Coast it was said, and rented an apartment at the Potomac. At first, it was assumed that Mrs. Mortimer was merely a high-priced courtesan, for she immediately attracted a steady stream of corrupt politicians, gamblers, brothel owners and other gangsters to her quarters.

Kenna and Coughlin, as two of Chicago's duly elected aldermen (at the going rate of fifty cents a vote), were naturally among Mrs. Mortimer's first notable visitors. Both were soon reported to be infatuated by the strikingly beautiful new arrival. She also entertained Jake Slaney, one of Coughlin's closest associates. In time, Jake Slaney became the most regular of all visitors to Mrs. Mortimer's apartment.

Over a period of months it became apparent to sharpeyed observers of the local crime scene that Mrs. Mortimer was more than she appeared to be. For one thing, she seemed to have money—a great deal of it—and with the blessing of Kenna and Coughlin, she began to invest in the Levee, securing a majority interest in several of the district's higher-class brothels. By the turn of the new century, she took an even larger step, purchasing a building near Twenty-second and Dearborn streets and quickly transforming it into a palace of sin without precedent in Chicago. Her own name, however, was never directly linked to the club, for she had recruited two well-bred young brothel keepers, Ada and Minna Everleigh, to run the operation.

The Everleigh sisters, daughters of a wealthy Kentucky lawyer, had opened their first brothel in Omaha in 1898 before moving on to Chicago, where the "sporting" population of randy males was much larger. Chicago also had the advantage of being the nation's great railroad transfer point, which meant traveling men could easily find their way to the Levee, conveniently located within blocks of several of the city's rail stations. Mrs. Mortimer hired the Everleighs as her "front women" because they were elegant, chaste (neither one was ever known to have a lover, unlike most madams) and excellent, if not necessarily honest, bookkeepers.[3]

When the Everleigh Club opened in February of 1900, it instantly became the brothel of choice for the richest men in Chicago, as well as from elsewhere around the country, and it netted over twenty-five thousand dollars a month, a phenomenal figure by the standards of the time. Much of the profit flowed directly into Mrs. Mortimer's purse. As her own tastes were not exceptionally lavish, she set some of the money aside for a rainy day but poured most of it into the vendetta that had come to consume her life.

Among her first steps, after she had cemented her power, was to arrange the murder of Eban Patrick, Elsie's father. This had been easy, since Mrs. Mortimer excelled at the fine art of playing one greedy criminal off against another. Her hope had been that Eban's death would cause Elsie to return to Chicago. But that had not happened, and so Mrs. Mortimer, working with the Slaney family, had devised a far more elaborate scheme to bring Elsie—and Holmes—to Chicago.

Coughlin had signed on to Mrs. Mortimer's plan simply because there appeared to be the possibility of amusement in it, and also because of the opportunity it afforded for a sexual conquest he had long dreamed of. To Mrs. Mortimer, on the other hand, it was war, and she intended to win it at any cost and to dispose of Sherlock Holmes once and for all. By contrast, she cared nothing for Elsie Cubitt and would let the Slaneys take their own revenge upon the woman they hated.

Mrs. Mortimer now stood and walked over to one of the big parlor windows overlooking the lake. Then she turned around and said to Coughlin, "Just be careful, John. Mr. Holmes is full of tricks. You must never underestimate him."

Coughlin, who knew it was time to leave, got up and put on his silk top hat. "Ah, don't worry, Mrs. Mortimer. He is but one man and every scoundrel in the Levee, not to mention the police themselves, will be arrayed against him. I like those odds."

"Yes," said Mrs. Mortimer, "I like them as well."

Book Three

The Pennsylvania Limited

Chapter Twenty-three

§ ᶘ

"They Will Not Escape New York"

FROM THE NARRATIVE OF DR. JOHN WATSON:

I spent Monday morning in a state of nervous expectation, pacing back and forth, smoking cigars, and hoping with each step that I would hear some word of Holmes. But as the clock ticked past noon, silence prevailed. It was as if Holmes had literally tumbled off the face of the planet and into the trackless ether of space. I now found myself eager to do something—anything!—to find him, even though there was not a scintilla of evidence which might explain his seemingly miraculous disappearance. Compounding my restlessness was the fact that I was marooned at Miss Parry's house in Brooklyn, where I felt as removed from the great events of the world as Selkirk on his lonely island. Despite my protests, Hargreave and his trusted detective, Bissen, insisted that I remain in hiding.[1]

By three o'clock, I had become so anxious that I finally left the house—something Bissen had expressly warned against—and walked several blocks until I found a store where newspapers were sold. I bought copies of the *Sun* and *Times* and was about to leave when a delivery boy came in with the latest edition of the *World*.

Nothing could have prepared me for the series of shocks I now received. Atop the *World*'s front page was a headline which said: SHERLOCK HOLMES DISAPPEARS. This was followed by a series of smaller headlines stating that Holmes was suspected of masterminding Elsie Cubitt's kidnapping while the police wished to question me about a murder! I felt a sense of stunned disbelief as I read the story:

In a sensational turn of events, the famous English consulting detective Sherlock Holmes has himself become a criminal suspect here in New York, the *World* has learned exclusively. Holmes and his longtime companion, Dr. John Watson, are being sought by police for questioning in a series of crimes that span two continents. Chief of Police William Devery stated this morning that while "it is naturally strange to think of Sherlock Holmes as a criminal, the evidence in this matter is quite overwhelming and we must therefore do our job and bring him in. If he is not guilty of any wrongdoing, he will certainly have every chance to demonstrate his innocence."

Holmes and Dr. Watson are wanted for questioning in connection with a kidnapping and murder in England, as well as two bizarre and deadly incidents this morning. The first of these occurred at Grant's Tomb, where a guard, Walter Smith,

was found beaten and shot to death shortly before 2 A.M. The guard's lifeless body, blood still oozing from a fatal gunshot wound to the heart, was discovered lying atop Gen. Grant's sarcophagus—an obscene and heartless act of desecration that the nation will not easily forgive.

A revolver found at the scene is believed to be the murder weapon, and police sources have told the *World* that initials engraved on the weapon identify it as belonging to Dr. Watson. At least two eyewitnesses also report seeing Dr. Watson leave the tomb, alone, at about 11:30 P.M. and rush off on a bicycle, as though fleeing the scene of a crime. It has also been learned that $10,000 in police money entrusted to Watson's care, supposedly for the ransom of Mrs. Cubitt, is missing.

"We don't know of any motive for the killing of the guard at the tomb and we don't know what happened to the money," said Chief Devery, "but we would certainly like to talk to Dr. Watson about both matters. He has much explaining to do." Asked whether the doctor was a suspect, the chief replied, "How could he not be?"

An equally strange incident occurred only an hour or so later at the Astor House on Lower Broadway. An assassin possibly hired by Holmes was shot to death by the police after wounding an officer in a gunfight on the hotel roof. Both Holmes and Watson were at the scene but mysteriously disappeared after the shooting. Though many details remain unclear, this much is known about the incident at the Astor House and the circumstances leading up to it:

Holmes, renowned for his brilliant solutions to some of the era's most baffling crimes, allegedly became entangled some months ago in a torrid love affair with a former client's wife, Mrs. Elsie Cubitt, of Norfolk, England. She, however, apparently wished to break off the relationship and told Holmes of her intentions. Not long after making this announcement, Mrs. Cubitt, said to be a woman of great beauty, mysteriously disappeared from her large rural estate. This occurred about 10 days ago and

evidence found at the scene suggests she might have been kidnapped by Holmes, with Dr. Watson's assistance.

Scotland Yard tracked the two men to the city of Liverpool, where a woman whose connection to the case is uncertain was found murdered on the very same floor of the hotel where Holmes and Dr. Watson were staying. Rather than answer questions regarding this strange incident or the whereabouts of Mrs. Cubitt, the two men hastily boarded the White Star Line's *Oceania* and set sail for New York. The police now believe that Holmes also made arrangements to take Mrs. Cubitt to New York, but aboard a different ship.

The *World* has been told that Scotland Yard alerted police here to snare the duo when the *Oceania* berthed Friday morning at the Gansevoort pier. However, the police inexplicably failed to bring in the pair for questioning, or to search other incoming ships for Mrs. Cubitt, according to knowledgeable sources, who state that Inspector William Hargreave is the officer who must answer for these failures.

In the meantime, Chief Devery, acting on information from Scotland Yard, began an investigation of his own into the activities of Holmes and Dr. Watson. A trap was finally set early this morning at St. Paul's Church, across from the Astor House, but heavy fog allowed the two men to elude the police net. However, a sniper posted atop the hotel, possibly to help cover Holmes's escape, was shot to death in a fierce gun battle with police. Detective James Hurley, 32, of Brooklyn, was seriously wounded in the engagement but it is believed he will recover from his wounds. The sniper's identity is unknown, but the *World* has been told by sources in the police department that the man had in his pants pocket a message from Holmes.

Chief Devery said today that Holmes may already have fled the city with Mrs. Cubitt, who apparently remains his captive. The chief based his suspicion on a report that a man answering Holmes's description was seen rushing toward a Boston-bound train at Grand Central Station about 7 A.M. this morning. Police in Boston have already been notified to be on the lookout, and if Holmes did indeed flee to that city it is almost certain he will be captured there.

Meanwhile, the whereabouts of Dr. Watson and Mrs. Cubitt remain a complete mystery, though Chief Devery said he has over 100 men scouring the city for them. "They will not escape New York," said the chief. "We will find them one way or another."

The story sickened me, for it was apparent that the poor guard had been shot down in cold blood after I left the tomb. I had been lured to the tomb, it appeared, solely for the purpose of implicating me in a murder which, because of its hallowed setting, was certain to outrage the public. The guard had simply been a pawn in it all—his life worth nothing to the madman responsible for the crime. Feeling at once angry and betrayed, I returned to Miss Parry's house and read the story a second time, trying to fathom how such a vicious farrago of lies and half-truths could be published in a respectable newspaper. I then went through the *Times* and *Sun* but found nothing about Holmes or any supposed criminal investigation.

However, I was familiar enough with newspapers to know that come tomorrow every daily in the city would be trumpeting the "news" of Sherlock Holmes's new status as a fugitive, not to mention mine. I now understood why Hargreave had wanted me to stay at Miss Parry's, for he must have seen the storm coming after talking with Police Chief Devery outside the Astor House. My only hope now was that Hargreave himself would not be the next victim of the great deceit which had been perpetrated in the city of New York. If that were to happen, then I would truly be alone and my chances of finding Holmes would be no better than finding a kernel of truth in the pages of the New York *World*.

Chapter Twenty-four

$\int$ λ

"He'll Be All Mine"

At nine o'clock on the morning of Monday, July 16, as Dr. Watson paced the floor at Miss Parry's house in Brooklyn, the luxurious passenger train known as the *Pennsylvania Limited* eased out of the huge Exchange Street station in Jersey City and headed west for its twenty-four-hour journey to Chicago. The train's "consist," as railroad men called it, usually included a baggage car, a combined buffet-smoking car, a dining car, four sleeping cars and an observation-lounge car. On this run, however, the *Limited*, powered by one of the Pennsylvania Railroad's new Atlantic-type locomotives, had an addition in the form of a luxurious private car.[1]

The car was owned by Mrs. Caroline Astor, who used it once or twice a year to cross the continent in imperial splendor for no other reason than that she could afford to do so. Equipped with all the immodest amenities that great wealth could provide—French tapestries, cut-glass chandeliers, fine mahogany furniture, intricately woven Persian rugs and even a pair of servants specially trained in England to cope with the casual lunacies of the rich— the car had been dubbed "Versailles on wheels" by a wag for one of the dailies in New York.

The sumptuous excess of the car had often been cited

by the fractious penny press as yet another example of how uncaring men (and women) of wealth played while the poor eked by in squalor. These criticisms so upset Mrs. Astor's blossoming social conscience that, in a gesture of untrammeled munificence, she had announced one day in 1899 that she would make her giant railroad toy available free of charge to "any charitable or civic organization which might have legitimate need of it."

On this morning it had been made available to the Women's Relief Society of Chicago, an organization that, according to its handsomely printed brochure, was devoted to the care and well-being of young females who had become pregnant but who inconveniently lacked husbands. Mme. Simone DuBois, who in addition to her self-proclaimed psychic powers was a dedicated social activist (or so she had informed Mrs. Astor), had requested use of the car to bring a contingent of "fallen and destitute" women to Chicago, where the society would come to their aid and make a new, better life for them. Naturally, Mrs. Astor had assented at once to so noble a use of her largesse, telling Mme. DuBois that she could have the car for a week if she needed it.

What Mrs. Astor did not know was that the Women's Relief Society was in fact a front for Chicago brothel owners who regularly brought pregnant young women into the city, paid for their abortions and then forced them into lives of prostitution. Four women, all pregnant and the oldest barely twenty, were now aboard Mrs. Astor's car, as was Mme. DuBois, who had been detained for less than an hour by the police in New York before being sent on her way.

Another woman was also aboard. She was represented as the "sickly wife" of a prominent British businessman traveling to Chicago. The businessman—who was tall, angular and handsome in a tweedy sort of way—constantly attended to his wife, the two of them sharing a small private sleeping compartment at the rear of the car. The four young women being taken to Chicago had no way of knowing, of course, that the supposedly ill woman was in fact Elsie Cubitt. As for her devoted husband, the women noted that he spoke with a distinctive British accent, was rather brusque in his manner and altogether looked a great deal like the famed English detective, Sherlock Holmes.

It was around four o'clock in the afternoon before Sherlock Holmes finally began to awaken for good and regain his usual state of alert consciousness. He had always been notably resistant to soporific drugs — it was as though his very nature opposed the idea of sleep — and Watson had once remarked that in this regard Holmes "must be regarded as a freak of nature." Now, as his head started to clear, he became much more aware of the sound that had pulled him out of his slumber. A metallic clickety-clack, it grew loud and insistent. Holmes also felt a familiar rhythmic swaying. He soon realized that he was aboard a train, and one that was moving at high speed judging by the sound of it.

Holmes opened his eyes but saw nothing. For a terrifying instant, he wondered if he had suddenly gone blind. Thinking he might still be in a dream, he tried to lift himself up, only to strike the top of his head against something hard enough to cause a sharp stab of pain. Holmes attempted to raise one arm to rub the sore spot but found he could not move his limbs, or any other part of his body, without immediately encountering a barrier. His sense of smell was for some reason the last to return, but when it did he immediately detected the odor of new wood. Once he knew what the walls confining him were made of, he understood his circumstances. He was lying in what was either a coffin or something much like one.

Holmes possessed extraordinary reserves of courage and discipline, and over the next several minutes he drew them down as far as they would go to avoid being overwhelmed by panic. He had faced many dangers in his life, survived any number of tight scrapes, but he could think of no worse fate than being shut up alive in a coffin.

As a child, Holmes had read Edgar Allan Poe's "Premature Burial" and he now recalled, with an involuntary shudder, its grim descriptions of "the rigid embrace of the narrow house" and "the blackness of the absolute night." Holmes was also well-acquainted with the immense amount of popular literature devoted to the subject, including Dr. Franz Hartmann's recent tome, with its numerous lurid stories of living victims trying to claw their way out of sealed coffins.[2]

Holmes felt his heart accelerate as the primal fear of being buried alive coursed like poison through his blood. Before panic could overwhelm him, however, a small calm voice somewhere in his head made an observation at once intriguing and obvious. The voice said, "A man cannot be buried alive in a moving train." This simple statement brought Holmes's initial fears to heel and let reason shine its clear light through the darkness. Taking a deep breath—in itself, he soon realized, another good sign—Holmes quickly came to three conclusions.

The first was that the final act of revenge would be undertaken (Holmes could not help but smile at his own choice of words) elsewhere—presumably in Chicago. Otherwise, Holmes thought, why would he have been loaded aboard a train when his body could easily have been disposed of in New York City?

A second conclusion—that there must be an air hole somewhere in the coffin—flowed logically from the first. Without provision for air, Holmes would suffocate long before reaching Chicago, which he knew from experience was about a day's travel by rail from Manhattan. The Conspirator, Holmes was certain, wished to wreak his ultimate vengeance face to face, no doubt with Elsie Cubitt present as well, and he would take no pleasure in it unless Holmes were alive to suffer whatever dark fate awaited him.

Holmes's third conclusion was less a matter of logic than faith. He didn't know yet how he would do it, but he believed he could find a way out of his "narrow house." Closing his eyes, as naturally as if he were resting on his day couch at Baker Street, he began to think long and hard—despite the damnable inconvenience of having no tobacco—upon the problem of the coffin.

At first, however, Holmes's attempts at thinking his way out of the box, as it were, showed little promise, since pure logic will not—without the aid of a saw or crowbar—pry apart a well-made and tightly secured coffin. It was only after some minutes of unproductive thought that Holmes suddenly realized he had made a critical mistake by violating the first rule for solving any problem, which is determining exactly what the problem is—and isn't. So it was with the quandary of the coffin. Opening it, Holmes saw, wasn't really the problem at all. The coffin would be opened—perhaps in a matter of minutes, perhaps not for many hours—but it would be opened. The critical question was what Holmes would do once this happened.

To find the best answer, he started with what he liked to call the "hard facts" of the case. What could he deduce, based on the senses available to him—touch, smell, hearing and taste—about the coffin itself, its location on the train and the circumstances under which it was likely to be opened? He began by calculating that the box, which was of the simple rectangular variety as opposed to the tapered form of the so-called shoulder coffin, was about seventy-eight inches long (giving Holmes only a few inches of clearance at either end), twenty-four inches wide and eighteen inches deep. These were approximate measurements, of course, but Holmes thought they were reasonably close to the coffin's actual dimensions.

By digging his thumbnail into one of the side panels, Holmes next determined that the coffin was made of pine as opposed to a harder wood such as oak or walnut. From this he went on to speculate that the coffin's lid might be nailed on, since pine took nails easily while hardwoods usually required screws. To test his theory, he tried pushing up against the lid but made no headway, leading him to deduce that the lid was probably secured by clamps or straps as well.

Holmes then sought out the coffin's source of air. Using his feet to feel, Holmes found a slit extending across the coffin's end panel, directly beneath the lid. By means of twisting one of his long and exceptionally limber arms behind his head, Holmes immediately established that the other end panel had a similar feature, thereby providing sufficient cross ventilation to keep him alive. Holmes even managed to poke a finger through the slit, from which he learned that the coffin was made of wood about an inch thick.

But perhaps the most interesting conclusion Holmes arrived at had to do with light, or rather the lack of it. Because he was in pitch blackness, Holmes reasoned that the coffin could not be in a coach, parlor or even sleeping car, all of which came with numerous windows. Were he in any of these passenger cars, he would have seen some light through the slits in the coffin, even at night, since the train would pass many lighted stations. Holmes therefore concluded that the coffin must be in one of the baggage cars that were a feature of most long-distance trains. These cars, he knew, were usually equipped with large sliding doors on both sides and standard vestibule doors at either end. However, they typically did not have windows.

Satisfied with this conclusion, Holmes moved on to consider the most critical questions of all, which concerned when, how and by whom the coffin would be opened. He began with the essential assumption that he was indeed on his way to Chicago, a trip that would consume a full day. How long would even the largest non-lethal dose of barbiturates or other sleep-inducing drugs last? He went through the layers of accumulated information in his memory, which was still vague as to recent events but much clearer on matters going further back.

He soon recalled a case—the bizarre affair of Lord Huntington's blue toes—in which the administration of phenobarbital had played a key role. Watson had remarked at one point during the case that a normal man might stay under for anywhere from eight to twelve hours with a maximum dose of the drug. Assuming he had received just such a dose, Holmes calculated that with his known resistance to sleep-inducing drugs, he might have been under for only half that time.[3]

Unfortunately, Holmes had no way of knowing the time of day, for his watch had been removed, along with everything else in his pockets, including his pistol and his matches. Nor was he able to hazard a guess as to when he had been placed aboard the train, since his memory of recent events remained cloudy at best. Still, he reasoned that at least once on his journey to Chicago, someone would have to enter the baggage car, open the lid of the coffin and administer a second injection of drugs to make sure he stayed quiet for the remainder of the trip. This would provide his best—perhaps his only—chance to make an escape.

Holmes was certain that whoever was charged with administering the drugs was not yet in the baggage car. After awakening, he had hit his head on the coffin lid with a loud thump, and the sound would have alerted anyone standing guard to his revived condition. He had heard nothing, however, and was therefore convinced that no one else was in the car.

Holmes next pondered the question of who would give him the drugs and exactly how it would be done. Here, he could only resort to informed speculation, based on how his adversary had conducted himself to date. The Conspirator had proven himself to be a brilliant planner, attentive to every detail of his criminal enterprise, and Holmes could only assume that he would exercise equal care when it came time to open the coffin.

After thinking through the possibilities, Holmes concluded that at least two men—perhaps even three, but certainly no more—would do the job. Since they would be American thugs, from a city famed for the violence of its gangsters, they would undoubtedly carry guns. They might also have other weapons, such as brass knuckles and saps. Holmes further expected that one of the men would be entrusted with the task of injecting the drug, while the other—his gun drawn—would stay back to watch for any sign of trouble. If there was a third man, he would also function as an armed guard. The Conspirator himself, Holmes believed, would not be one of the men, since he would likely be staying with Mrs. Cubitt, if he was aboard the train at all.

Holmes concluded there would be no more than two or three men for the simple reason that a larger number would draw suspicion, while a single man would be insufficient for the job from the Conspirator's cautious point of view. Presumably, Holmes's coffin had been presented to the baggage car handlers as the remains of a beloved relative being transported to Chicago for his funeral. The men assigned to administer more drugs would doubtlessly offer some pretext, such as communing with their dear relative, to gain access to the baggage car. They might even bribe the conductor to ensure they would not be disturbed.

When the men entered the car, Holmes would certainly hear them. The men would also have to turn on one of the car's lights before making their way to the coffin, which Holmes believed was sitting directly on the floor, given how noisy and rough his ride was. All of this meant he would have several seconds, perhaps longer, to prepare himself.

He was counting on surprise as his most powerful ally. The men, not knowing Holmes's resistance to drugs, would expect to find him asleep, or at the least, in a dazed and sluggish state. One of the men, or perhaps both, would use a hammer claw or crowbar (another weapon Holmes had to be aware of) to pry open the coffin's lid. Holmes further reasoned that the man giving the injection would not have a gun in his hand, for the simple reason that it would make his job—tricky enough on a swaying train—even more difficult.

The man with the needle, in other words, would be vulnerable to attack, and if he could be quickly disabled, Holmes might then have a fair chance against the other man. This would be especially true if the men, as Holmes suspected, had been instructed not to kill him—a pleasure the Conspirator would have reserved for himself. But how would Holmes make his initial attack and what weapon could he use for maximum effect? He thought through the problem in his usual methodical way and discovered that he did indeed have a potentially powerful weapon, one that could inflict great pain if used in exactly the right way.

For the first time since awakening, Sherlock Holmes permitted himself a slight smile and then began making his preparations. When the men came to inject him with drugs, he would definitely be ready for them.

The Conspirator, however, did not expect more trouble, for he believed the most difficult part of his work was already done. He had both Holmes and Mrs. Cubitt in his possession, and he intended to deliver them on schedule to Chicago. There, in a matter of days, the intricate plan he and his ally had put into effect months earlier would have its final flowering. Elsie Cubitt and Sherlock Holmes would be destroyed, in every sense of that word, and the great act of vengeance would at last be complete.

Still, as he sat smoking a cigar in his compartment aboard one of the *Limited*'s deluxe Pullman cars, the Conspirator knew just how close he had come to failure in New York. At first, everything had gone very nicely indeed. The quick switch of carriages had thrown off the pursuing police and the little sideshow of Grant's Tomb had worked wonderfully. True, the Conspirator had hoped that Holmes would be the one at the tomb, but he had anticipated that Watson might be sent out instead. It didn't really matter, since implicating either man in the crime would, in effect, implicate the other, at least in the eyes of the public. And what could be more ruinous to a man's reputation than being suspected of killing a guard at the tomb of America's most revered soldier? Holmes's name, and Watson's, would be soiled forever.

But after the success at Grant's Tomb, events had not gone nearly as smoothly for the Conspirator and his confederates. Holmes had proved his usual clever self, somehow sniffing out the ambush at St. Paul's ahead of time and nearly bollixing the whole plan in the process. There had been other problems as well. The fog had confused everything and then the coppers had killed Coffin on the roof of the Astor House before he could rub out his two main targets—Watson and Hargreave.

With all these complications, the entire operation could easily have come to naught had not Holmes decided to station himself in the chapel's portico, where the Conspirator and his helpers were able to spot him despite the thick fog. Luck had been on their side, although the Conspirator knew that his powerful ally in Chicago put no stock in good fortune. In the end, however, what mattered was that Holmes had been captured, and the Conspirator had already received a congratulatory telegram from his ally, who promised him a memorable night in Chicago upon his return.

Stubbing out his cigar, the Conspirator consulted his pocket watch and saw that it was nearly six o'clock in the evening—time for an important piece of business. The *Limited* had just pulled into Altoona, Pennsylvania, where it would take on a second locomotive to help pull the train up the long grade through Horseshoe Curve and across the main ridge of the Alleghenies. After that, it would be an easy downhill run to Pittsburgh and then a fast twelve-hour dash across the Ohio and Indiana flatlands to Chicago.

It was a good time, the Conspirator thought, for Belgian Jack and Little Pete—two associates who had come all the way with him from England—to pay a visit to the baggage car where Holmes lay in his coffin. The two men were in an adjacent Pullman car, since the Conspirator wished to maintain as much separation as possible from his subordinates, should questions arise later.

Slipping on his suit coat, the Conspirator left his compartment and walked to the next car. There, he carefully looked around—the passageway was empty—before knocking twice on the door of his confederates' compartment. He was admitted at once and saw that the two men had been playing pinochle, which was their favorite pastime next to robbery, mugging and murder.

Belgian Jack—a heavyset man with massive arms and shoulders, dull black eyes, rotting teeth yellowed by tobacco and a nose so mangled from years of street brawling that it looked like a gob of putty—would be losing, of course, since anything that involved even modest mental exertion was not his strong suit. Little Pete, on the other hand, was small, wiry, clever with figures, extremely handy with pistols and knives and the possessor of a temper as fiery as his abundant red hair.

"All right boys, it'll be time pretty soon to update Mr. Holmes's prescription," the Conspirator said as he took a seat across from the men. Little Pete nodded, stood up and pulled down a bag from a rack overhead. Inside was a small case containing hypodermic needles and a solution of barbiturates. With the death of John Coffin, Little Pete had been prevailed upon to serve as the gang's new "injection specialist," as he called himself, using drugs obtained from an unscrupulous doctor in New York.

The doctor—whose practice included such specialties as abortion and the treatment, no questions asked, of gunshot wounds—had given assurances that the prescribed dose would be "sufficient to knock out a horse for eight hours and a man for much longer than that." After showing Little Pete how to administer the drug, the doctor had also promised that the dose, if administered no more than every six hours, would not be lethal.

Little Pete had given Holmes his first injection at six in the morning, just before he was loaded into the coffin, and the drug had worked beautifully, sending Holmes into a deep, quiet sleep. Indeed, Holmes had not even stirred when he received a second shot around noon.

As Pete slipped the case into his coat pocket, Belgian Jack double-checked the Smith and Wesson revolver he always carried. It was fully loaded. He had also brought along a small sap, as had Little Pete, in the event Holmes became obstreperous. But they had checked him just a couple of hours earlier and he had given no sign of being awake, so they expected no problems.

Even so, the Conspirator reminded them to "follow procedures. You know the drill. Use your saps if you have to, but no guns. I want him alive when we reach Chicago. Then he'll be all mine."

"No problem," said Belgian Jack, so named, as far as anyone knew, because in size and temperament he resembled a big Belgian draft horse. "If he tries anything, I'll take care of him."

"Just be careful," the Conspirator cautioned as he pulled up the window shade and looked outside. Light drizzle was dripping down from a low deck of clouds, adding an extra touch of dreariness to the Pennsylvania Railroad's vast complex of shops and yards in Altoona. In the distance the long, steep escarpment of the Allegheny Mountains rose to meet the lowering clouds.

The Conspirator pulled the shade down and said, "I want the two of you to wait until we get moving again, just in case somebody decides to inspect the baggage car now that we're stopped. Once we're underway, we'll be up on Horseshoe Curve in a matter of minutes. You'll feel the train slow down. That'll be the time to give Mr. Holmes his injection. Understood?"

"Sure," said Little Pete. "You can count on us."

"I know," said the Conspirator, and left to return to his own compartment. As he did so, he felt a sudden lurch, and the *Pennsylvania Limited,* now with two locomotives to pull it, began to chug west, toward the mountains.

Chapter Twenty-five

§ ₹

"Do You Remember Alfred Beach?"

FROM THE NARRATIVE OF DR. JOHN WATSON:

Inspector William Hargreave, his eyes bloodshot and dejection marking his face like a scar, finally arrived at my "safe house," as he called it, late in the afternoon. We took chairs in the front parlor by a large oriel window offering splendid views of Manhattan, after which Hargreave poured out his story of "the big trouble," as he called it.

"Well, Dr. Watson, we are in for it now, and I must warn you that I can't protect you much longer from what is happening here."

"You have seen the newspapers then," I said, showing him my copy of the *World*. "I hope you can explain to me what this is all about."

"You shouldn't have left the house, doctor," Hargreave said as he glanced at the newspaper's blaring headline. "That was a very risky thing to do and I must ask you not to do it again. We're all in great danger from the powers that be — Tammany Hall, the mayor, the chief of police and all the other crooks in fine clothes and shiny shoes who run this city. You see, the fix is in, doctor, and Mr. Holmes, you and I are the ones to be fixed. It's that simple."

I now thought back to what the attendant at the Warren Street station had told me about the messenger with a

Tammany tiger tattooed on his arm. If Tammany Hall itself was somehow allied with our adversary, then the case
took on a new and deeply troubling aspect. Although I
knew Holmes's role in tracking down the Tammany Hall
fugitive in London might have angered the bosses back in
New York, I still could not comprehend how this could
have led to an alliance with Mrs. Cubitt's kidnappers.[1]

"I fear I do not understand," I said. "Why would—"

Hargreave cut in, "Don't try to understand, doctor.
There's no understanding it when the fix is in. It's just
something that happens, like a storm blowing up at sea or
a meteor hurling down from the heavens. That's the way
it is with the fix in this city. Somebody has it in for somebody else, and pretty soon deals are made, money changes
hands, mysterious forces move like shadows through the
night and the next thing you know, the fix is in, and
there's nobody that can stop it. The only hope you have,
doctor, is to get out of this city before the police—myself
and a few of my loyal men excepted—track you down.
Same goes for Mr. Holmes, assuming he's still . . . well,
what I mean to say is, assuming he's—"

"Alive? Is that what you were going to say, inspector?"

Hargreave, turning to look out the window, said, "Yes,
I'm afraid it is."

"Well, I refuse to believe Holmes is dead, and I will
hear no such talk. Now, please tell me what happened this
morning after you sent me away from St. Paul's."

"I will," said Hargreave, "but first you must understand
something. I have not been completely honest with you."

"Whatever do you mean?"

"I have been a dupe, Dr. Watson," said Hargreave
with a pained expression. "You see, I was ordered by
Chief Devery himself to meet you and Mr. Holmes at the
pier when you arrived from England. The chief knew I
was someone Mr. Holmes would trust, and I was in-

structed to keep a watch on the two of you and file daily reports. Naturally, I wanted to know why I was being asked to do such a thing. I was told that it was for your own benefit."

"How so?"

Hargreave smiled wanly and said, "According to that snake Devery, there had been an 'incident' in England, and because of it your lives were in jeopardy. Mrs. Cubitt and several other conspirators, I was informed, were attempting to lure you and Holmes into a trap. My job, supposedly, was to stop this from happening. However, I was specifically warned not to reveal the true nature of my assignment to the two of you, since the chief believed Mr. Holmes might object to the idea of being 'protected' by the police. Devery told me everything I was doing would be for 'the good of Mr. Holmes' and I was foolish enough to believe him. I am ashamed to say he played me for the sucker."

This was most unsettling news, yet I could tell by Hargreave's expression that he felt worse about it than anyone else. I thanked him for his honesty and asked when he had begun to suspect he was being misled by his own superiors.

"My first inkling that something might be amiss came when Mr. Holmes mentioned the cable he had sent to me from Liverpool but which I never received. I'm guessing now that one of Devery's men at headquarters intercepted it. But the truth is, doctor, I really didn't know I'd been conned until after all hell broke loose this morning at St. Paul's. I started seeing that a lot of things didn't add up. Then the chief himself confirmed that I'd been snookered like a regular babe in the woods."

Hargreave now told me about the conversation he'd had with Devery moments after I was hustled away from the chapel. The chief—whom Hargreave described as "one of the biggest thieves and liars in New York, which is saying a lot in view of the competition"—began by announcing that Holmes and I were to be arrested immediately on suspicion of engineering Mrs. Cubitt's kidnapping! Hargreave pointed out the absurdity of this order in view of the night's events, but Devery paid no heed. Instead, the chief claimed that he had been "personally informed" by Scotland Yard that it wanted to question us in connection with the kidnapping and with "the suspicious death of a woman in Liverpool."

Hargreave said he was then instructed to sign a report which would be prepared by one of Devery's lieutenants and which would implicate Holmes and me in the kidnapping and other crimes.

"My God," I said. "What happened next?"

"I told Devery I'd do no such thing, that's what happened. He would've had me arrested right on the spot but I called in a marker. There's a certain powerful figure in Tammany Hall, for whom I once did a very great favor, and I used his name to buy some time. But I'm still cooked, and there's no getting around it."

"I'm not sure I understand."

"My days with the New York police are numbered," Hargreave responded. "Devery will find a way to get rid of me—maybe permanently—unless I do him the favor of resigning first. The truth is, I've had enough of it anyway. Policing is no profession for an honest man, not in this city. I admit to doing my share of dirty work over the years, but I will be damned to hell—damned to hell, sir—before I turn you or Mr. Holmes over to the likes of Bill Devery."

Hargreave's noble declaration sent chills of gratitude down my spine and I leaned over to shake his hand warmly. I knew that, were it not for Hargreave's bravery and quick thinking, I could at this very moment be under police interrogation, languishing in some filthy jail cell or, for that matter, a newly admitted member to the fraternity of bloated corpses which convened daily in the foul waters of the East River.

"Neither Holmes nor I will ever forget what you have done for us, inspector," I said.

"Think nothing of it. I've no doubt you'd do the same for me. Now then, doctor, let us turn to the business at hand and consider how we might find Mr. Holmes before Devery and his lackeys do. We've also got to figure out what to do about you."

"What do you mean?"

"Why, you're hot property, doctor, the mad killer at Grant's Tomb. I'm sure a full account of your perfidy will be in all the papers tomorrow. Devery will see to that."

"I am not worried about myself," I replied. "Finding Holmes comes first. In that regard, I have an idea. We must talk with Mme. DuBois. I am sure she knows everything."

Hargreave shook his head and said, "That won't be possible, I'm afraid. You see, Mme. DuBois has already given her story to Devery, or so I'm told, and it's her testimony that she's been working all along for Mr. Holmes—and you, of course."

"Why that is so plainly ridiculous I cannot imagine—"

"Save your breath, doctor," said Hargreave. "You and I know what a whopping big lie it is, but it don't matter. When the fix is in, and in as deep as it is now, the truth gets buried six feet under and it won't be rising from the dead anytime soon. Whatever story Mme. DuBois is peddling, or whatever story's been made up for her, it will be the Tammany truth, which bears no resemblance to the real thing."

"This is simply incredible," I protested. "What about the gunman who murdered the guard at Grant's Tomb and then tried to kill me?"

"He's as yet unidentified, at least officially. As I said

before, I suspect he's a Chicago hoodlum brought in by the Slaney gang, if they're the ones behind all of this."

"I've already sent a message to Detective Wooldridge in Chicago asking, among other things, if he knows the man based on a description I provided."

"Good. You've saved me some work, doctor. There's something else you need to be aware of. It has to do with that message supposedly found in one of the gunman's pockets, which you and I both know were empty, despite what the *World* says. My sources on Mulberry Street say Devery is showing around a cable from England that he claims the gunman had on his person. The message, sent some time ago, allegedly instructs the assassin—who used the alias John Coffin, by the way—what he was to do at the Astor House. I haven't seen this message, but I'm told it's signed by 'S. Holmes.'"

"Good Lord, there is no end to it," I said.

"It would seem not. Here's something else for you to chew on, though it won't aid your digestion in the least. I'm sure that the supposed sighting of Mr. Holmes at Grand Central Station yesterday is as phony as they come. You can be sure that wherever Sherlock Holmes is, he ain't in Boston. That was just a dodge to send people going in the wrong direction. For all I know, Devery may have Mr. Holmes tied up in the basement of police headquarters as we speak."

"It appears our adversaries have thought of everything," I said, suddenly feeling very glum.

"Maybe not everything," said Hargreave, "for I have a trick or two up my sleeve yet. Still, there's no denying we are contending with a very clever lot of people, doctor. They also must have money to burn, since the one thing that's impossible to buy cheap in this town is Tammany Hall. A lot of money must have changed hands already, enough to make that ten thousand taken from your bag a pittance, or maybe just a down payment. However, I suppose it didn't surprise you to read that you're suspected of stealing the money yourself as part of Mr. Holmes's great kidnapping plot."

"Of course. Thievery, kidnapping, murder—why Holmes and I are a regular pair of gangsters, and if the Crown Jewels suddenly went missing, I imagine we should be accused of that crime as well. By the way, inspector, I believe I know where and how the money was stolen from my bag."

"I'm thinking it must have been at St. Paul's, when you left your bag in the graveyard."

"That is possible," I admitted, "but with so many people around, taking the money there would have been risky. No, I think it happened at Grant's Tomb. I distinctly remember putting down the bag before I ran to assist the guard and was confronted by the man we now know to have been this Coffin fellow. An accomplice could easily have removed the money while I was distracted."

"That would mean there was another conspirator at the tomb, maybe even Abe Slaney himself. I just wish I knew where he was now."

"As do I. If we can find Slaney, or whoever is using his name, we will find Holmes."

Hargreave and I now turned to a discussion of how Holmes might have been abducted from St. Paul's. I said a brick-by-brick and stone-by-stone inspection of the chapel would be in order, since we had not had time to do so earlier in the morning. However, Hargreave told me that policemen loyal to Devery now guarded the chapel and that it would be impossible for us to make any sort of search without risking immediate capture.

"Well, we must do something," I said. "What do you suggest, inspector?"

"I suggest we sit right here and keep our heads low for

a bit. I've been calling in every chip I have and after twenty-five years of being in the police game, I built up a nice pile. There's got to be people besides Devery and the big bosses at Tammany who know what really happened at St. Paul's. I'm hoping one of them will send a little birdie my way. It's the best chance we've got."

As it turned out, Hargreave proved to be remarkably clairvoyant, for at about seven o'clock, just after we had finished supper and retired to the parlor to smoke our cigars, Detective Bissen arrived with intriguing news. He told us that he had just had a mysterious encounter with a man outside the central police station. The man, whom Bissen did not know, had stopped him and asked for directions to Washington Square. After Bissen had fulfilled this request, the man shook his hand, passing on a crumpled piece of paper in the process.

Said Bissen, "Then this fellow looks me right in the eye and says, 'See that this gets to your friend, Inspector Hargreave. He will find it to be a most valuable piece of information.' Finally, he says, 'Don't try to follow me,' and then he tips his hat and walks off like he ain't got a care in the world. I suppose you'll want to know what this fellow looked like—"

Hargreave said, "Don't bother, Michael. You may be sure he was merely hired for the job. Now, more importantly, did you keep a sharp eye out for any shadows on your way over here, since this message could be nothing but a Trojan horse?"

"I was very careful, inspector. I'm sure no one followed me."

"Well, if anyone did, it's too late now. All right, let's see what this fellow gave you."

Bissen handed over the piece of paper, which—after Hargreave had smoothed it out—revealed a message in small, crablike handwriting. I looked over Hargreave's shoulder as he read the following: "Do you remember Alfred Beach and his secret construction project? I'm told it leads to some interesting places. Start in the basement of Devlin's old store at Broadway and Warren. A friend."

"I presume you know what this means," I said.

A broad smile spread across Hargreave's face. He said, "You're damned right I do. It means we're back in business, doctor."

Only when Hargreave told me the story of Beach's "secret construction project" did I understand his sudden excitement, and I could hardly wait to begin our exploration in the bowels of Manhattan.

Chapter Twenty-six

ʃ ₹

"Your Presence Is Requested"

"Having a nice sleep, are you, Elsie?" asked the man portraying Sherlock Holmes.

Elsie Cubitt struggled to look up but could offer only a low groan in response. This pleased the fake Holmes—whose real name, she had come to learn, was Charlie—and he bent over and fluffed up her pillows.

"Well," he continued, "enjoy yourself while you can. You'll regret waking up soon enough." He straightened up, looked at her one last time and stepped out of their compartment to have a smoke.

Once he was gone, Elsie managed to open her eyes and take in her surroundings. She lay in a narrow berth along one side of the compartment, her head facing the window, its shade drawn. Across from her was another berth, which Charlie used as a seat, and a small fold-out table where he kept a pitcher of water, a package of the biscuits he liked to eat and several newspapers.

Elsie Cubitt tried to commit all of this to memory, despite the fact that her head still felt incredibly heavy, as though her skull had been replaced by a thick block of granite that at any moment threatened to crush her neck and shoulders. Still, she was not quite as sleepy, or as dull of mind, as she must have appeared to Charlie. Since the moment of her kidnapping—a kind of nightmarish blur now—she had fought the drugs given to her and she had slowly built up some degree of tolerance. Her strategy, however, was to look and sound as drowsy as possible so that her captors would have no reason to increase her dose of what she assumed to be powerful barbiturates.

So far, her strategy had allowed her to gather, like an explorer in some vast cavern equipped with only one dim lantern, small bits of information amid the general darkness. Among other things, she had learned Charlie's first name and that he was from Chicago, where he had once been an actor. She had gleaned this from overheard conversations between Charlie and a confederate named Little Pete, who had taken over the task of administering her drugs.

Elsie had also seen Mme. DuBois in her compartment. She had jettisoned her French accent and usually referred to Elsie as "the little bitch." What Elsie didn't know was why Mme. DuBois seemed to hate her so much. The one person Elsie hadn't seen was Slaney. She assumed he must be aboard the train, although she thought it possible he had taken some other route to Chicago.

That she was riding on the *Pennsylvania Limited* was perhaps the most important fact she had deduced. Some hours earlier, when Charlie was relieving himself at great length in the adjoining toilet, she had managed to pull herself up toward the window, lift the shade and take a brief look outside. The train was slowing for a tight turn and up ahead she saw—on one of its distinctive green, cream and red Pullman cars—the name proudly emblazoned.

Elsie had also caught a glimpse, further ahead, of a gigantic arched bridge, which appeared to be under construction across an exceptionally wide river. She had traveled between New York and Chicago any number of times and she recognized the river as the Susquehanna, presumably somewhere near Harrisburg, Pennsylvania, on the Pennsylvania Railroad's main line to Chicago.[1]

She was well past that point now, and she had an idea exactly where she was. Some minutes earlier the train had come to a stop—it could have been a station anywhere—and then gone forward for only a brief time before halting again. During this second stop, she had felt the clanging jolt of another car—or perhaps an engine—being coupled to the train. Now the train was moving again, but slowly and with much labor, judging by the deep-throated roar of the locomotives. She couldn't be certain, but she guessed the train had taken on an extra locomotive and was climbing up toward Horseshoe Curve, a famous attraction in the Pennsylvania mountains.

Thinking back to earlier—and far happier—train trips, Elsie Cubitt realized that she was now nearly halfway to Chicago. In the time left to her, she had to find some way to either escape from the train on her own, or alert rescuers. And if she failed—well, she preferred not to think what Slaney had in mind once he brought her home.

Hundreds of miles to the northwest, another train—operated by the Chicago, Burlington and Quincy railroads—was making its way south to Chicago through the wide gash of the Mississippi River Valley. The train had left Minneapolis at four o'clock on the afternoon of Monday, July 16, stopped ten miles away in St. Paul and then begun its long run down the river. Among the train's passengers on this warm, drowsy afternoon were Shadwell Rafferty and his partner, George Washington Thomas.

Rafferty and Thomas had decided to go to Chicago after a day of bizarre and disturbing developments. The cryptic telegram from Holmes on Sunday night had caused Rafferty considerable alarm, and he had spent much of Monday morning trying to reach him by telephone in New York. But all of his efforts had proved futile, with the police in New York proving to be particularly uncooperative.

Then, early in the afternoon, Rafferty had finally heard from Watson via a telegram. The message not only informed Rafferty of Holmes's mysterious disappearance but also went on to speculate that the conspirators might attempt to take both Holmes and Elsie Cubitt to Chicago. Yet it was not this telegram that had caused Rafferty to pack his bags and head off to Chicago with Thomas on the briefest of notice. Indeed, Watson had not asked them to go to Chicago, saying that he "had no firm evidence" as to where Holmes might be.

What had prompted Rafferty's departure was another message, which arrived—perhaps by coincidence, perhaps not—less than an hour after Watson's telegram. The message had been delivered directly to Rafferty at his saloon by a lad of ten or so. Under questioning, the boy said a man he did not know—and whom he could describe only vaguely—had stopped him on the street and offered him "a whole silver dollar" to carry a message to "Mr. Shadwell Rafferty, the famous detective and friend of Sherlock Holmes."

Rafferty had never made it a point, except among close friends, to talk about his earlier adventures with Holmes and Watson, and so the man's statement—which the lad insisted he had quoted exactly—was highly curious. The message itself was even more so. Printed in the elegant manner of a formal invitation, it read, "Your presence is requested at the Everleigh Club, Chicago, at five o'clock in the evening, on Friday, July 20, 1900, when Mr. Sherlock Holmes, of London, England, will be united in holy matrimony with Miss Elsie Patrick, of Chicago."

All in all, Rafferty thought, it was just about the most astonishing message he had ever received in his life.

Chapter Twenty-seven

§ ₹

"I Think I Know What We've Found"

FROM THE NARRATIVE OF DR. JOHN WATSON:

It was just after ten o'clock on Monday night when Hargreave and I set out on our mission to the Manhattan underworld. Hargreave had insisted that we wait until after dark to minimize our chances of being followed, and the wait had been excruciating, given my eagerness to solve the mystery of Holmes's disappearance. Just before we left, Detective Bissen had gone out ahead of us to observe the area around Miss Parry's house on Joralemon Street. Once he had given us the all clear, we felt confident that we would not be followed.[1]

Both Hargreave and I—again with aid from Bissen, who proved himself to be a skillful scrounger of odd objects—had dressed ourselves in light raincoats, shabby suits, battered wide-brimmed hats and well-worn shoes. We had also splashed our faces with gin found in Miss Parry's surprisingly well-stocked liquor cabinet. In addition, we carried, as conspicuously as possible in our coat pockets, flasks filled with the same substance. The idea was that we would deflect any undue suspicion by passing ourselves off as a pair of wandering tosspots—a not uncommon sight on the streets of New York—should we be stopped and questioned by a patrolman. Hargreave had also acquired a large false mustache and spectacles so that any patrolmen we encountered would be unlikely to recognize him.

The night was humid and overcast, and I immediately worked up a sweat as we walked north on Henry Street toward the Brooklyn Bridge. We passed several large churches, many apartment buildings and commercial structures, and at every intersection I saw rows of elegant townhouses along the side streets. Looking down one of these streets, I noted a sharp flash of lightning off to the west.[2]

Hargreave, who had also seen the lightning, said, "Looks like we may be walking into the eye of a storm, doctor."

"I fear we are already there," I replied.

At half past one we reached the approach to the Brooklyn Bridge, which curved upward in preparation for its noble leap across the East River. A station for the small trains which ran across the bridge occupied the middle of the approach. Although Hargreave informed me that these trains ran all night, he said it would be safer for us to walk, since the police generally did not venture too far out on the bridge unless called to an emergency.[3]

To my surprise, the walkway ran in an elevated position down the very center of the bridge. We continued up the approach, crossing over several streets and many small buildings until we at last reached the bridge's gigantic east tower and passed under its great Gothic arch. I felt an exhilarating touch of sea breeze as we stepped out across the longest span in the world, and I found myself wishing Holmes were with me to enjoy the incomparable views of Manhattan which the bridge afforded.

As we made our crossing, Hargreave went over—in much greater detail than he had earlier—the curious saga of Alfred E. Beach. He told me Beach was "an eccentric Yankee" best known as the publisher, until his death some years earlier, of *Scientific American* magazine (which Holmes often read with great interest). Beach was also something of an inventor, and like many other New Yorkers he had long been appalled by the city's horrendous traffic problems. Convinced that horses could no longer be relied upon to move the city's growing masses, Beach finally decided to take matters into his own hands by building what later came to be known as his "pneumatic railway."[4]

"Mind you, this all happened back in 1870," Hargreave said. "I was a lad of eighteen then, just finding my way in the world, though I'd already latched onto a job with Tammany Hall. It was your typical Tammany job, which is to say I did nothing and was paid handsomely not to do it, so I had plenty of free time to scuff about the city. Anyway, I had a friend named Donny O'Rourke who always seemed to know what was going on, and one afternoon he says to me, 'Will, how'd you like to see something absolutely amazing?'"

"I do not suppose you said 'no,'" I observed.

Hargreave laughed and replied, "I surely didn't, for what lad with a little vinegar in his veins would refuse such a fine offer? So, I said to Donny, 'Lead the way,' and after he'd sworn me to secrecy, he took me down into the basement of Devlin's clothing store on Broadway, through a heavy door and, lo and behold, there was the damnedest thing I'd ever seen! It was a tunnel, doctor, perfectly round, lined with bricks and big iron hoops, and curving off into the darkness like the path to hell itself. This was just a month or so before the secret subway, as people called it, opened for business. Beach's men were working like demons, laying track and installing the big fan—the Western Tornado, they called it—that ran the whole contraption."[5]

"As I understand, the subway only ran for a block."

"That's right. It went from Warren to Murray streets, about three hundred feet in all, I would guess. Beach built it strictly as a demonstration, just to show that the thing could be done."

"Yet he was able to do the work in secret, from what you told me earlier. How on earth did he manage that in the heart of Manhattan?"

"Ah, that was his stroke of genius, doctor! You see, he'd already gone up to Albany to get permission from the legislature to build a pair of small pneumatic tubes under Broadway to speed mail to and from the new post office, which was being planned at the time. But instead of building small tubes, he built his subway tunnel. He pulled off his little trick because he knew that if the boys at Tammany Hall ever got wind of his subway, he'd be chest-deep in bribery and boodle in a minute."

"I take it his scheme worked."

"It did. When he completed the thing, he called in the press and public and said, 'Look what I've done, ladies and gentlemen. How'd you like to take a ride in my fine little subway?' Well, it was quite an attraction for a while. He charged a nickel a ride, and people would pile into a car and get blown through the tunnel by the Tornado. Then they'd reverse the flow of air, and back the car would come. Oh, it was something to see all right."

"What happened to the subway?"

"I guess you could say Tammany happened to it," Hargreave said. "The big shots at city hall were furious that they hadn't got their mitts in the business, and Beach couldn't raise more money to lengthen the subway. Of course, other things happened, too. Boss Tweed went down in flames a year or so later and then came the big financial panic. I guess there were problems with the pneumatic system, too. In any event, the subway closed in only a few years. I remember it became a shooting gallery for a while and then, I think, some kind of storage vault. I don't know what's down there now. Fact is, doctor, I haven't been inside the tunnel for twenty years or more."[6]

"But do you really think it might offer some sort of passage into the basement of St. Paul's?"

Hargreave shrugged and said, "Well, as far as I know, the tunnel itself never went past Murray Street, which is three blocks north of St. Paul's. But it's worth checking out."

We now reached the Manhattan side of the bridge and descended down another long approach. As we neared the bridge terminal across from city hall, Hargreave pointed out the domed skyscraper of the *World* newspaper, which had caused us so much trouble.

"Joseph Pulitzer's got his office way up in that dome," Hargreave said. "Sits there like God Almighty, from what I've heard."[7]

"Well, if you ask me, his business is far more profane than godly," I said with some feeling.

Once through the bridge terminal, we made our way down to Park Row. The streets were busy, although less so than during the day, but in our guise as amiable drunkards we attracted no attention from passersby and only a brief look from a patrolman standing in front of the *World* Building. We crossed Park Row and cut through city hall park toward Broadway. When we had reached that fabled thoroughfare, Hargreave pointed out a five-story building across from us.

"There it is—Devlin's old store. The outfit in there sells typewriters now. Let's cross over. See any coppers around?"[8]

I looked up and down Broadway but saw only the usual bustle of trolley cars, carriages and coaches, delivery wagons, pushcarts and pedestrians of all rank and stature.

"All clear, I would say."

As we stepped onto Broadway, Hargreave said, "All right then, let's go around to the back of the store. If I remember right, there's a service door there that should pose no problem to a pair of fine gentlemen such as ourselves."

We reached the alley behind the building without incident and slipped into its dark recesses. Hargreave lit a long match to guide us and we soon found the door he had remembered. It was secured with a hasp and one of the largest padlocks I had ever seen.

Hargreave bent down to look more closely at the padlock. He said, "This is interesting. Both the lock and its clasp look brand new. Makes a man wonder if somebody else might have broken in here recently. We're going to have to do the same, by the looks of it. I can jiggle a lock with the best of them, but I'd need a pick the size of an axe handle to work this one."

"Perhaps we could enter by the door out front," I said. "I would imagine its lock is much smaller."

Hargreave blew out his match, leaving us in almost complete darkness, then said, "Too risky, even at this hour. No, it'll have to be brute force. Be so kind, doctor, as to go back out to the end of the alley and see if anybody's coming. If they are, let them pass and then make sure the coast is clear. Once it is, light up a cigar where I can see you, wait a few seconds and then come join me. Oh, and while you're waiting, it wouldn't hurt to sing something at the top of your lungs. Got all of that?"

As I was used to dealing with Holmes, whose requests were often outlandish and inexplicable, I found no difficulty in complying with Hargreave's rather peculiar instructions. I walked back out to Warren Street, looked around and saw several pedestrians coming toward me from Broadway. I waited for them to pass, made one more inspection of my surroundings, then lit a cigar to signal to

Hargreave that all was well. After performing these duties, I launched immediately into a wretched version of an old drinking song which had been a favorite of my fellow soldiers in the dreary wastes of Afghanistan.

As I sang, I heard a sharp splintering noise from the alley. After waiting as instructed, I walked down to rejoin Hargreave, who lit another match to show me his handiwork. Using a stout metal bar—part of his "standard burglary kit," he informed me—he had pried off the door latch, thereby rendering the padlock useless.

"After you, Dr. Watson," he said when he had pushed open the door. He then followed me inside.

We had taken small lanterns along in our raincoats, and Hargreave lit his while I kept mine in reserve. His light revealed a large, high-ceilinged workroom, presumably directly behind the shop, with tables upon which typewriters sat in various stages of assembly.

Hargreave shined his light on a door to our right and said, "As I recall, that's the way down to the basement."

The door was locked, but Hargreave withdrew a ring of skeleton keys from his coat pocket and had it open in a matter of seconds. We walked down creaky wooden steps to the cellar, which was disagreeably moldy and, we discovered, home to a small army of rats, some of which were the largest I had ever seen.

"My God, they're huge," I said.

Hargreave grinned and said, "Buildings aren't the only things we grow big in New York, doctor. Detective Bissen claims he once shot a rat so big it had to stoop over just to get through doorways. I imagine he was exaggerating. Ah, here's a light."

The inspector pulled a chain overhead and a single electric bulb came on, illuminating a large room with a dirt floor, heavy wooden columns and joists and rough stone walls damp from seeping water. Boxes filled with rusting metal parts, piles of wood and old pieces of furniture were strewn all around the room, which was decorated with an intricate network of spider webs.

"Does any of this look familiar to you, inspector?" I asked.

"I'm afraid not, doctor. As I told you, it's been a long time since I was down in the subway tunnel. The entrance was probably sealed off years ago."

We now moved deeper into the room and turned on a second light which illuminated an area around the boiler and a large coal bin along the north wall, paralleling Warren Street. Past this bin an old wooden cabinet, perhaps eight feet high, was pushed up against the wall, and the dirt floor in front of it immediately caught my attention. The dirt had been disturbed, leaving behind a semicircular depression which suggested that someone had pivoted the cabinet away from the wall and then swung it back into place. I also noted footprints, although there were so many that only Holmes himself might have been able to make sense of their pattern and significance.

"This could be the place all right," Hargreave said. "I know the subway station was along Warren and that when you got into the car it made a turn before taking you under Broadway. Well, let's see if we can move this cabinet."

Putting our backs into the job, we managed to pull the cabinet away from the wall, revealing a jagged opening with a jumble of bricks scattered on the floor of a chamber inside.

Hargreave said excitedly, "This is it, I'm sure. I remember now. There was a door here—see the old frame around it?—that led into the subway's station, if you could call it that. The doorway must have been bricked up years ago."

"Someone obviously has reopened it."

"So it would seem. Well, let's have a look."

With Hargreave in the lead shining his lantern, we stepped into the narrow chamber, which was elegantly plastered. An old chandelier still hung from the ceiling.

"My God, would you look at that, doctor," Hargreave said. "It's all coming back to me now. This was the waiting room, and old man Beach had it as nicely furnished as grandma's front parlor. He wanted to show folks just how elegant riding a subway could be. There were paintings hung on the walls, mirrors, settees, all the comforts of home. He even had a fish tank in here if I remember right. Well, let's move along."[9]

We went to the far end of the chamber, where radiating rows of bricks formed a circular portal leading into a tubelike tunnel perhaps eight feet in diameter.

"That's the subway," Hargreave told me. "There were rails, of course, and the car fit into the tunnel as snug as could be. When they turned on the Tornado, there was a big whoosh and off you went."

We went into the tunnel, which Hargreave informed me was about twelve feet below street level, and followed it around a curve until it straightened out to run directly beneath Broadway. The rails were long gone, and the floor was coated with a disgusting layer of guano, rat droppings and other animal excretions, which combined to produce a foul stench. Even so, I was buoyed by hope and determined to proceed, for I noticed footprints in the slime which looked as though they had been made only recently.

Hargreave told me that as far as he knew there was no waiting room at the Murray Street end of the tunnel. Instead, once the car reached that point, the Tornado was reversed and the car was sucked back to Warren Street. As we neared the end of the subway, however, we saw that someone had broken through the brick wall which originally sealed off the tunnel. Hargreave held out his

lantern and we made our way through the narrow opening. The sight which greeted us was entirely unexpected.

"Well, I'll be damned, doctor," said Hargreave. "Would
you look at this?"

We were in a continuation of the subway, constructed
exactly like the tunnel we had just left.

Hargreave said, "Old Alfred Beach had a final trick up
his sleeve, it seems. The first tunnel was just a teaser. He
must have planned to go all the way down to the Battery.
I wonder how far he got."

As it turned out, Beach had gotten quite far. Since
there were no landmarks to guide us, we counted off
paces as we walked down the tunnel. This would give us
at least a rough idea as to how far we had traveled beyond
Murray Street. Hargreave estimated that blocks in this
part of Manhattan averaged about three hundred feet
long, which meant that the basement of St. Paul's would
be perhaps nine hundred feet, or three hundred paces,
away. The tunnel's atmosphere was extremely close, and
both Hargreave and I were sweating profusely by the
time I had marked off two hundred and fifty paces.

Hargreave's lantern provided illumination only ten
yards or so ahead of us—the circling walls of dark red
brick seemed to soak up light—and as we moved along
we had no way of telling just how far the tunnel might extend. Then, as I stepped off my three hundred and fifth
pace, Hargreave's light caught an exposed brick wall
straight ahead. It looked as though we had reached a
dead end. I felt a surge of disappointment, fearing that
our journey through the bowels of Manhattan would lead
to naught. However, as we pressed forward, I saw an alcove off to the west side of the wall.

Hope restored, I rushed forward and discovered that
the alcove opened into a narrow passage, built—none too
carefully—with heavy wooden shoring. The floor was lit-

tered with cigarette and cigar stubs, food tins, newspapers and pint bottles of whisky and other ardent spirits. Hargreave came up behind me and bent down to pick up one of the newspapers.

"This little side tunnel was built not long ago, doctor," he said. "Look at the date on this edition of the *Sun* — June 12, 1900."

I said, "This is simply unbelievable, inspector. Think of the trouble the conspirators must have gone through to dig this tunnel, just so they could use it to spirit away Holmes."

Hargreave, who had gotten down on his knees to look more closely at the objects on the floor, said, "I'm betting there's more to it than that. Why would someone as meticulous as the kidnapper leave all this stuff around?"

"Perhaps he wanted it to be found."

"Exactly! Ah, and here's the evidence, planted as neat as can be."

Getting back up to his feet, Hargreave showed me a torn notebook page he had found next to a whisky bottle. The page contained handwriting which looked remarkably like Holmes's, although it was different in a way I could not easily describe. I knew it had not been written by Holmes. The message, which was incomplete because much of the page had been ripped away, said, "Work to be completed by July 1 and in absolute secrecy. . . . Payment in sum of $500.00 to be rendered upon satisfactory . . ." The signature below, in a familiar flourish, was that of Sherlock Holmes.

"I must tell you, inspector, that Holmes did not write this message," I said.

"Of course he didn't. But don't you see the beauty of it? The official line will be that Mr. Holmes had this tunnel dug to stage a spectacular escape and to disguise his real purpose, which was to vanish with Mrs. Cubitt."

"I am appalled to think anyone could give any credence to such nonsense."

"Well, as I said before, when the fix is in, the Tammany bosses could say night is day, up is down and black is white, and Chief Devery would find no cause to argue about it."

"Is there anyone in this city who will listen to the truth?" I asked.

Hargreave emitted a sigh and said, "At the moment, you're talking to him, for all the good it will do you. But there's no sense standing here and bemoaning our fate. Since we've come this far, we might as well try to figure out how this passage leads into St. Paul's."

We now proceeded into a chimneylike room, which appeared to mark the end of the passage. Here, a ghoulish surprise awaited us, for scattered around the floor were pieces of a human skeleton, including a skull, several ribs, a tibia and pelvic bones. I was relieved to see that the skeleton was very old and decayed, and I wondered whether the diggers had disturbed an ancient cemetery. Hargreave, meanwhile, called my attention to a ladder propped up against one wall of the chamber.

Directing his lantern toward the top of the room, he said, "Well now, would you take a gander at that."

What his light had illuminated was a large slab of white marble forming a kind of trapdoor overhead.

"By God, doctor, I think I know what we've found here," Hargreave continued. "Give me a hand, will you? I want to go up and have a look."

I braced the ladder and watched as Hargreave climbed. I could not see past him, but I soon heard the metallic snap of a latch or some similar device. This was followed by a loud scraping sound, intermixed with Hargreave's equally loud grunts, and I realized that he must be trying to move the stone slab.

"What have you found?"

As he climbed down the ladder, Hargreave said, "I've found how the deed was done, that's what. Take a look for yourself. They tunneled right into old Gen. Montgomery's tomb. Those are his remains all over the floor."

I went up the ladder and found that the slab we had seen was in fact the lid of Gen. Montgomery's marble sarcophagus, located beneath St. Paul's porch. The tunneling crew had knocked a hole through the floor of the tomb and into the sarcophagus, unceremoniously dumped the general's remains and then pried open the lid to gain entry into the basement of the chapel.

I asked Hargreave whether his men had thought to check the sarcophagus earlier.

"They did," he replied. "The lid couldn't be budged. Now I see why. It was latched from the inside with anchors driven into the stone. Whoever did this job thought of just about everything. They also had to have help from important people at city hall."

"Why do you say that?"

"Because of that second tunnel we found. Somebody from Tammany had to know that Beach tried to extend his subway. In fact, it must have been Tammany Hall that finally put a stop to the whole scheme."

I could only shake my head in disbelief, as I had so many other times during the past twenty-four hours. It seemed that our adversaries not only had unlimited resources but also the complete support of the largest and most corrupt municipal organization in America.

"Cheer up, doctor," Hargreave said. "We'll fight this thing no matter how long it takes. Let's take a careful look around and then call it a night. We know now how Mr. Holmes was taken from the church, but we still can't be sure where he was taken."

"I still believe the final destination will be Chicago," I said. "I know Holmes himself assumed that to be the case."

As I spoke, I spread apart Gen. Montgomery's remains to see if the tunnelers might have left any other clues.

When I idly picked up the general's skull, feeling rather like Hamlet amid the gravediggers, a box of matches tumbled out. Curious, I brought up the box to Hargreave's light and made two discoveries. The first was gold-embossed lettering on the box cover stating that the matches had come from the "Everleigh Club, Chicago," which was described in smaller writing as providing "entertainment for gentlemen of means."

Far more important was what I found inside. Instead of matches, the box contained Holmes's other silver cufflink. Its twin had already been found in the pulpit upstairs. How, I wondered, did the second one come to be inside a matchbox?

Hargreave and I puzzled over this question for some minutes before it finally occurred to me what must have happened.

"I am not sure you know, inspector, but Holmes is an expert pickpocket, a skill he uses now and then as an aid to investigation. Indeed, among the light-fingered brigades of London his dexterity is regarded with something like awe. Therefore, I am guessing that he lifted the matchbox from one of his captors and managed to put one of his cufflinks inside as a clue for us or the police to follow. I am more certain than ever now that he is being taken to Chicago."

Hargreave was about to reply when we heard, echoing through the darkness far behind us, the faint sound of voices. We stood still, straining to hear, until it became apparent the voices were coming closer.

Taking out a scrap of paper and scribbling on it, Hargreave whispered, "I have a hunch who our visitors might be. You must get away at once, doctor. Go up the ladder and into the chapel. Leave by the back door on Church Street and whatever you do don't go back to Miss Parry's house, or mine. Find a public telephone and contact

Bissen"—Hargreave pressed the piece of paper into my hand—"at this number. He will provide whatever help you need. You may also send telegrams to him at the address I've given you. Of course, I assume you will want to go to Chicago in the morning to look for Holmes. If you do, you must travel in disguise, for Devery's men will be at all the train stations looking for you. Is that understood?"

"Yes, but—"

"Then be on your way," Hargreave said. "You have not a second to waste."

"But what will you do?"

"I'll close up the trapdoor after you and stay here to stall for time. I suspect it's Devery's agents who are coming after us. Now, go!"

I shook Hargreave's hand and promised I would keep him posted as to subsequent events. Then I scrambled up the ladder and into the chapel's basement. I paused to look down at Hargreave, his noble face showing great resolution but no sense of fear as he slid back the lid of the sarcophagus. Just before it shut completely, I heard voices, much louder now, approaching from below. Lighting a match for illumination, I made my way out of the crypt and up into the chapel, where almost twenty-four hours earlier I had seen Sherlock Holmes for the last time. As I steeled myself for what I knew would be a long day ahead, I wondered when, and under what circumstances, I would see him again.

Chapter Twenty-eight

"He Won't Be Trying Anything"

A mile or so after pulling out of Altoona, the *Pennsylvania Limited*, bolstered by a second engine, took a sharp turn to the northwest and began climbing toward one of the most celebrated stretches of railway in America — Horseshoe Curve. Built in the early 1850s by Irish laborers equipped with little more than hand tools and black powder, the curve was one of the nation's first great feats of mountain railroading, and a brilliant piece of engineering. The curve, by which trains climbed along one side of a narrow valley and then doubled back over a fill to continue up the other side, allowed the railroad to ascend almost all the way to the crest of the Alleghenies at a rate of under one hundred feet per mile.[1]

Crew members aboard the *Limited* always gave notice of the approaching landmark, since passengers enjoyed the sensation of seeing the train snake back upon itself after it reached the center of the curve at Kittanning Point. But as the *Limited* began its arduous climb out of Altoona, one passenger — Sherlock Holmes — had no opportunity to take in the scenic view. Shut in his coffin, he was busy trying to calculate where the train might be, and his conclusion turned out to be remarkably accurate.

The clue that sent his mind racing had struck him,

quite literally, in Altoona. There, when the helper engine was coupled to the train, he had felt a jolt and heard the clang of metal meeting metal. These physical sensations served to jar his memory, and he soon found himself in possession of an intriguing idea as to his whereabouts. Although the idea seemed to strike Holmes like the proverbial bolt of lightning, it was in fact the product of a long chain of deductions.

Holmes had begun with the assumption that he was being taken from New York City to Chicago, Slaney's native city. Then came the realization that this was a journey Holmes had undertaken four times before, on his way to investigations in Minnesota, and that in each case he (and Watson) had taken the fastest available express train, known initially as the *Pennsylvania Special* and later as the *Pennsylvania Limited*. Next, he recalled that this luxurious train always left Jersey City, across from Manhattan, at nine o'clock in the morning. Finally, he remembered that in early evening the train stopped in the gritty industrial town of Altoona, Pennsylvania, to pick up more passengers and an additional engine to pull it over the mountains via Horseshoe Curve. He therefore concluded that the distinctive jolt he had felt might well be an engine being coupled on at Altoona.[2]

It would be easy to verify this conclusion. Holmes knew from his earlier trips that if the train was climbing through the curve, its speed would slow markedly and its wheels would squeal as it negotiated the tight turn. He would also feel the inward pull of the train around the curve. Final proof, if needed, would come some minutes later, for Holmes also knew that only a few miles past the curve a long tunnel awaited. Even though Holmes couldn't see anything, he would certainly hear a change in the sound of the train once it slipped inside the tunnel.[3]

Holmes's deductions were soon borne out, for within minutes of getting underway again, the train began to labor, its locomotives throbbing as they struggled up the long grade. He listened intently, waiting to hear the protest of the wheels as the train began to turn. Instead, he heard the unmistakable sound of a door being pulled open. This was followed by a whoosh of air, after which the clatter of wheels briefly grew much louder. Then a light came on, its faint glow visible through the breathing slit above Holmes's feet. To Holmes, who had been in darkness ever since awakening, it was as welcome as the rising sun, although it took a moment for his eyes to adjust to even this small intrusion of light. Moments later, Holmes heard the door close, dampening the sound of the train wheels below. He also heard a voice.

"Well, let's see how Sleeping Beauty is doing," said a familiar tenor. Holmes recognized the voice as belonging to the small red-headed man who'd given him his last injection.

"He's no beauty if you ask me," came the reply in a hoarse basso that Holmes had also heard before. It was the voice of the oversized thug who had knocked Holmes senseless with a sap and then dragged him into the basement of St. Paul's Chapel before Watson and the police could come to the rescue.

The thug now continued: "I'll tell you what, Pete. There ain't a palooka in Chicago couldn't clean Mr. Sherlock Holmes's clock in a minute, and that's a fact."

"Well, Jack, in case you haven't noticed, it's people with brains that run the world, not palookas like you and your pals," Little Pete replied.

Belgian Jack weighed in with another carefully considered opinion: "Is that so, Pete? Then you tell me what good Mr. Sherlock Holmes's big brain is doing him at this very moment. I'd like to know, I would."

"Ah, forget it," said Little Pete. "Come on, let's have a look at him. Now remember what the boss said."

"Don't worry, he won't cause no trouble. I'll see to that."

Holmes was ready for them. He had carefully prepared for the encounter to come, and he knew he would have only one chance. Yet he felt remarkably confident, for Holmes was one of those rare men who could seamlessly transform thought into action. His confidence lay in the fact that he had already seen exactly what would happen in his head, much as Mozart was said to have composed an entire piece of music before committing it to paper. To Holmes, waiting patiently in his coffin, everything seemed preordained.

He now heard the two men approaching. When their footsteps stopped, something blotted out the light coming through the coffin's air slit. One of the men, Holmes realized, must be standing directly in front of it. Holmes immediately closed his eyes and did his best imitation of a deep, narcotic sleep, taking long slow breaths and allowing his head to fall over toward one shoulder. He had barely gone into this act when he felt a blast of bright light on his face. One of the men obviously had shined a lamp through the slit. After a few seconds, the light went away.

"Looks like he's still enjoying his nap," said Little Pete, who had gotten down on one knee to look in on Holmes. "All right, let's get this done, so we can go eat. I hear they serve mighty fine roast beef in the dining car."

There was more movement now, and Holmes heard clasps being opened above him, followed by the screech of nails as one of the men used a crowbar to pry open the lid. Light flooded into the casket, as did something equally valuable to Holmes—fresh air, or at least the freshest he had enjoyed in many hours. Holmes, however, gave no hint of being awake, although he slowly opened one eye just a crack to look at the men who stood between him and freedom.

He saw that the small redhead, whose name he now knew was Pete, stood next to the coffin but had turned away, perhaps to prepare the injection. The other man—Jack—was stationed a few feet farther back. He smacked a sap repeatedly into the palm of his hand, as though anxious to inflict some punishment. Holmes assumed that both men were armed with other weapons as well—probably a knife in Pete's case, while Jack no doubt preferred the comfort of a pistol.

"All right, Jack, stay alert," said Little Pete, who took out a hypodermic syringe from the case he had brought along. "I'm just about ready here."

"I'm watching," said Belgian Jack. "Like I said, he won't be trying anything."

Little Pete double-checked the syringe, making sure he had the correct dose of phenobarbital, and then turned back toward Holmes, who by all appearances remained in a profound sleep. The train was moving very slowly, still fighting its way up the grade toward the curve, and the ride was about as smooth as it could be. This will be a piece of cake, Little Pete thought as he steadied himself beside the open coffin.

Little Pete didn't know, however, that Holmes was awake, nor did he notice that Holmes had removed the belt from his trousers. A gift from Elsie Cubitt, the belt—which had come with Holmes's now vanished cufflinks—was made of fine Moroccan leather and had a heavy silver buckle embossed with an image of Ridling Thorpe Manor. Now, as Holmes lay with his arms resting on his stomach, one hand cupped over the other, he clutched the belt—hidden under his arms—in his right hand, holding it well back from the buckle.

As Little Pete leaned over to administer the injection, Holmes—in a move so quick it would have impressed a sleight-of-hand artist—slid away his left hand and with his right snapped the belt upward like a whip. The heavy buckle caught Little Pete square in the right eye, from which blood began to squirt with surprising force. Unleashing a fierce yelp of pain, Little Pete dropped the syringe and staggered back into Belgian Jack, who was too stunned to react immediately to this surprise attack. At the same time, Holmes gave a hard shove with his left shoulder, knocked the coffin onto its side and rolled out. As he did so, nails from the open lid tore into him, but he ignored the pain and struggled to his feet, which felt distant and rubbery after the long confinement.

Once on his feet, Holmes glanced around to orient himself. As he had suspected, he was in a long, windowless baggage car, with electric lamps at either end providing the only light. There were sliding freight doors on both sides of the car and vestibule doors at the ends. Double rows of stanchions, to which pieces of baggage were secured with ropes, ran the length of the car. However, some especially large items — Holmes's coffin fortunately among them — simply rested on the wooden floor.

Toward the far end of the car, past Pete and Jack, the luggage was piled particularly high — trunks, crates, suitcases and other items forming a small mountain range that peaked along the center line of the car. There could be no escape in that direction, nor did the closest freight door, which undoubtedly was locked against theft, offer favorable prospects. Holmes concluded that he would have to go out the way Pete and Jack had come in, via the vestibule door behind him that presumably connected to another car.

Holmes arrived at his decision in a matter of seconds, all the while watching his adversaries. Little Pete, blood still coming from his eye, had gone down to one knee and would not be causing any mischief for a while. Belgian Jack, however, was ready for a fight. With a great animal bellow, he raised his sap and prepared to attack Holmes. He didn't get far. Displaying strength borne of desperation, Holmes lifted up one end of the coffin and used it like a battering ram, driving Belgian Jack back until he lost his footing and tumbled over a crate.

Then Holmes turned around and made a run for it, praying he wouldn't trip over his own unsteady legs. He reached the door well ahead of Belgian Jack and went into the vestibule of the next car, where he hoped to find help. What he found instead was an extraordinary surprise.

When Charlie went out for his smoke, Elsie Cubitt decided the time had come to attempt her own escape. She couldn't say exactly how she had come to this decision, since a kind of narcotic fog still lingered in her head and she couldn't think with her accustomed clarity. Still, she had a plan, and Horseshoe Curve, she knew, would be as good a place as any to carry it out.

Despite the heaviness that still lingered in all of her limbs, she rolled out of her bed and onto the floor of the compartment. She sat there for a few moments, then crawled over to the door, which she assumed—correctly—that Charlie had locked. This proved to be no barrier, however, because lock picking was one of many illicit skills the precocious Elsie Cubitt had learned as a child from her father. She already had a hairpin in her hand and, still on her knees, used it to open the flimsy, easily worked lock.

Now came the critical—and unpredictable—part of her plan. She had no idea what sort of a car she might be in, but her intention was to leave the compartment, find the nearest vestibule, get to it as quickly as she could and then jump from the train. She was wearing only a nightgown and a light robe—attire that would obviously call attention to her and might even inhibit her escape. But she had no other clothes and, truth was, no other choices either. Once off the train, she would at least have a fighting chance of being rescued before her kidnappers came looking for her.

Using the compartment door's small knob as a handhold, she slowly pulled herself up to her feet, an act that required enormous exertion. She felt wobbly and nauseous but was determined to go on, for she intended to walk out of the compartment no matter how much her body objected. Taking a deep breath, she cracked open the door and saw that her compartment was in a plush private car of some kind. She thought she heard voices off to her right but couldn't see anyone. To her left, however, was a vestibule door no more than thirty feet away.

Freedom was now within reach, and Elsie decided she could not delay. She stepped outside the compartment. Without even looking to her right, she turned toward the vestibule door and suddenly found herself staring through the door's large window into the startled eyes of Sherlock Holmes.

Holmes could scarcely believe that he had finally found Elsie Cubitt, and a deep, satisfying joy leaped into his long-suppressed heart. Elsie, however, was not the only person he saw at that moment. A black-bearded man loomed up behind her and when he spotted Holmes his features contorted into a look of grim astonishment. It was the Conspirator himself, the man Holmes had last seen in the pulpit at St. Paul's Chapel.

Stepping forward, the man knocked Elsie to the floor with a tremendous blow to the side of her face. Enraged, Holmes was about to rush to her aid when he saw a pistol leveled directly at him. The Conspirator fired just as Holmes ducked. The bullet tore through the thin wooden door, just missing both Holmes and the glass.

Holmes retreated back to one side of the vestibule, realizing he had no chance of rescuing Elsie with armed men coming at him from two directions. The train had by now slowed to a crawl, wheels screaming, as it rounded the sharpest portion of Horseshoe Curve. With no other choice, Holmes decided on a desperate expedient. There were exit doors on either side of the vestibule, and he went to the one on his right, pulled it open, and looked out just as a pair of massive locomotives roared past on the adjacent track. They were hauling a long freight downhill toward Altoona, smoke rising like mist from the cars' red-hot brakes.[4]

Silently cursing his bad luck, Holmes turned to try the exit on the other side, only to see Belgian Jack burst through the door from the baggage car. The big man shouted out something but Holmes couldn't hear his words over the din of the passing trains. Holmes had already sworn that he would never allow himself to be kidnapped again, yet he knew that his chances in a hand-to-hand fight with a brute the size of Jack weren't good, especially with the Conspirator coming up to help.

Holmes still had his belt in his hand, and he prepared to use it against Belgian Jack, hoping to buy enough time so that the freight would pass by and he could jump from the train without being instantly mangled. But his fight was not to be with Belgian Jack. The Conspirator now came through from the other car, pushed his hired hand out of the way and turned toward Holmes with a baleful glare. Then he raised his pistol, and there was no doubt he intended to use it again, despite the elaborate measures he had already taken to bring Holmes to Chicago. Anger burned in the man's dark, hard eyes and he would kill Holmes before allowing him to escape.

Once again, Holmes found his belt to be an effective weapon. He snapped it with all his strength into the Conspirator's face, striking him on the bridge of the nose. The vicious blow threw off the man's aim and a shot whistled past Holmes's ear before shattering the exit door's window. Holmes lunged forward and got one hand on the barrel of the gun, a large-caliber revolver, and lifted it upward as the Conspirator squeezed off another round, which went harmlessly into the ceiling. Then the gun clattered to the floor. By now, Belgian Jack was trying to join the fray, but the tiny vestibule gave him little room to maneuver as Holmes and his mortal enemy clawed at each other.

The Conspirator was smaller than either Holmes or Belgian Jack, but he was lean and sinewy and surprisingly strong. He now got a hand under Holmes's chin and pushed him back into the exit door with such force that it flew open. Holmes saved himself by grabbing a handhold, but not before a shard of shattered glass caught him in the back of the head and opened up a scalp wound that began to bleed profusely. The Conspirator now charged at Holmes, head low like a bull taking aim at a matador's cape, and this time he intended to shove the man he hated all the way out the door and to certain death beneath one train or the other.

But Holmes, who had exceptionally long arms and a wiry strength of his own, got a good grip on the handhold and, pushing off with his foot, swung out and away just as the Conspirator arrived to deliver the final blow. With nothing to break his momentum, the man suddenly found himself teetering over the edge of the open door, desperately reaching for something to hang onto, his face frozen in terror. Holmes showed no mercy. He reached over and, with a quick tug on the Conspirator's coat, sent him tumbling off the train. The fall pitched the man forward under the passing freight, and he was instantly decapitated by the first set of wheels that struck his neck.

Holmes had no time to react to this gruesome spectacle, for he still had to contend with Belgian Jack, who like his dead employer would be out for blood and who now would almost certainly use his gun. Out of the corner of his eye, Holmes saw an empty flatcar up ahead amid the freight train's long procession of boxcars. Without pausing to consider what Belgian Jack might be up to, Holmes took one of the biggest risks of his life.

As the flatcar approached, Holmes again pushed off with his legs and hands. Only this time, his aim was to leap across three feet of potentially lethal space, from one moving train to another going in the opposite direction. It was all a matter of timing, and Holmes's turned out to be superb. He landed in the middle of the flatcar, just back from the edge. His worries weren't over, however. Although both trains were traveling slowly, their opposing motion was strong enough to send Holmes tumbling out of control as he landed. Carried by the freight train's momentum, he rolled over twice before coming to a rest at the far end of the car. One more roll, and he would have fallen between cars, with assuredly fatal results.[5]

Then he felt a bullet zip past his head and embed itself with a thwack in the flatcar's wooden flooring. Holmes looked up to see Belgian Jack, firing wildly with his pistol just before he disappeared from view. Soon thereafter, the entire *Pennsylvania Limited* vanished around the bend.

Holmes rolled onto his back and looked up at the sky, where clouds were gathering over the mountains, portending a night of storms. He would welcome them, welcome whatever darkness would bring, for he was lucky to be alive, although he would never have acknowledged such a possibility. A man *earned* luck, Holmes believed. If pressed, however, he might have admitted that on this particular evening, high in the Alleghenies, he had perhaps received a sizable bonus.

As Holmes rode down to Altoona, he took careful stock of his situation. He had a bloody head wound, cuts from the coffin nails, torn and tattered clothes, no belt (he had finally dropped his "weapon" before leaping onto the flatcar), no money, no shelter from the rain that appeared ready to pour down at any minute, and he was, for the moment, all alone against a band of ruthless enemies, even if their ranks had recently been thinned by one. He also thought back to the moment when he had hurled the man he knew to be Jake Slaney, Abe's brother, to his death, and felt a belated chill at the coldness of his act. But there had really been no choice — someone had to die, and Holmes had only done what was necessary to preserve his own life.

Even before the events at St. Paul's Chapel, Holmes had been all but certain that the Conspirator was not Abe Slaney. Then, when he saw the bearded man in the pulpit, he knew instantly that his nemesis must be Jake, who looked a great deal like his older brother, although he was a bit shorter and thinner than Abe. Even so, it had been no problem for Jake to masquerade as his brother, given their overall resemblance.

Jake Slaney had also proved to be a far more subtle, patient and devious man than Abe, and therefore a far more formidable foe. Yet Holmes knew his trials — and Elsie Cubitt's — were far from over. Mme. DuBois was still on the loose, as were Jack and Pete. Most important, Elsie Cubitt remained a captive and might even have been seriously injured by Jake's brutal blow. As Holmes let his mind wander through a fortnight of extraordinary events, he was more convinced than ever that Jake Slaney had not acted alone in devising the great scheme of revenge. There was a co-conspirator, Holmes believed, who was the real mastermind and who — using Elsie Cubitt as bait — now lay waiting for him at the end of the line, in Chicago.

Chapter Twenty-nine

♫ ♫

"You Are British to the Core"

FROM THE NARRATIVE OF DR. JOHN WATSON:

After leaving St. Paul's, I walked quickly away, as Hargreave had instructed me to do, until I found a public telephone at a raucous tavern in the Bowery. There, I placed a call to Detective Michael Bissen. It was obvious when he answered that I had gotten him out of bed, but he made no protest. After I had explained my circumstances, Bissen—who seemed to be not in the least surprised by anything I had told him—provided directions to his apartment in the Chelsea neighborhood of Manhattan.[1]

It was approaching midnight by the time I reached his apartment, located amid a row of modest brownstones on West Twenty-third Street. Bissen's wife—an attractive, smiling woman who also seemed utterly unperturbed by my late arrival—greeted me at the door and had a full meal waiting! As I downed a plateful of excellent sausage and potatoes, Bissen with his usual efficiency explained how he would arrange for me to leave New York.

"Inspector Hargreave has figured everything all out," Bissen said. "He assumed Devery's men are posted at all the railroad stations and ferry terminals, so you'll have to travel in disguise. You've missed the last night train to Chicago so you'll have to go out in the morning on the *Pennsylvania Special*. Now, let me show you something."

I followed Bissen into a small sewing room where, he proudly informed me, he maintained his "costumes." As part of his work, Bissen—like Holmes, Wooldridge and other detectives—often found it necessary to adopt a disguise, and so he kept numerous "theatrical goods" from which he could create whatever new appearance suited his mission. These "goods" included an astonishing array of items, from clothes (sewn entirely by Mrs. Bissen) to artistic makeup to false noses and chins. Bissen also stocked a ready supply of beards, mustaches and hairpieces.

"You have missed your calling, Detective Bissen," I remarked. "Surely you belong on the stage."

"The same has been said of Mr. Holmes, I imagine," Bissen replied. "All right then, let's think a bit, doctor, and see what we can do for you."

Bissen called in his wife, whose name was Jenny, and she joined in the consultation over my appearance. Several ideas were tried and rejected, and the two of them clucked over me as if I was being outfitted for the lead role in a Shakespearean drama.

"You are British to the core, doctor," Bissen complained, at one point, although I took his remark as a compliment. "You must be made to look more American."

It took nearly an hour for Bissen to decide that I would look best as, in his words, "a high-class sort of drummer on his way to do business in Chicago." My disguise therefore was to include a large bag (which announced that I was the exclusive purveyor of "Dr. Smith's New Model Corsets—a Lady's Best Friend"), heavy paste-on eyebrows (which gave me, I thought, a rather sinister look), a broadened nose, spectacles and an "American-looking suit" to replace what Bissen described as my "British duds."

Bissen then said, "Come morning, Jenny will dye and pomade your hair to a nice deep black so you'll look just as slick and slippery as a good salesman should. And, of course, you'll have to shave off that mustache."

"My God, I've had it since my days in Afghanistan," I protested.[2]

"Well, it must go," Bissen repeated. "Now why don't you get some rest, doctor, for you'll have a long trip tomorrow."

I was exhausted and took his advice. Sleep, however, did not come easily, for all my thoughts were still concentrated upon the fate of my dearest friend in the world.

Nonetheless, I felt at least somewhat refreshed when Bissen awakened me some hours later to begin my transformation into an American traveling salesman. Once Bissen and his wife had finished their task, they handed me a mirror and I gazed upon a new man! Holmes, of course, would have seen through my disguise in an instant, but anyone who did not know me well would certainly be fooled. I complimented the Bissens on their work, after which talk inevitably turned to the pressing business at hand.

"Will you be able to make any further investigation into Holmes's whereabouts without being thwarted by Devery's men?" I asked Bissen. "If Holmes has been kidnapped and taken to Chicago with Mrs. Cubitt, as I fear, then it surely should not be difficult for you and Inspector Hargreave's other detectives to pick up the trail here."

"You're right," Bissen said. "Under normal circumstances, we'd canvas the train stations and it probably wouldn't take too long to figure how they'd been taken out of the city. But with Devery doing his best to cover things up, and with Inspector Hargreave out of commission as it were, there's not much we can do anymore—at least, officially."

"I understand," I said. "You have already done more than anyone could ask of you. Now, what about Inspector Hargreave? Is he going to be in great trouble because he helped Holmes and me?"

"There's no telling what will happen," Bissen said, "for in this city everything is politics. Willy [Hargreave's nickname, I learned] will certainly be in deep Dutch at headquarters but he also has angels in high places at Tammany. So I think he'll be all right in the end."

"Given all the inspector has done for us," I said, "I can only hope that will be the case."

At seven o'clock on Tuesday morning, after eating a large breakfast prepared by the estimable Mrs. Bissen, I said my farewells. I thanked the couple profusely for their help and promised to inform Detective Bissen of my whereabouts once I reached Chicago. He in turn vowed to let me know as soon as possible about Hargreave's circumstances.

As a precaution, I left the Bissens' apartment by the back door and walked a few blocks before hailing a cab to the Pennsylvania Railroad ferry station, conveniently located less than a mile away at the foot of Twenty-third Street, just upriver from where Holmes and I had landed in New York five days earlier aboard the *Oceania*. I reflected upon all that had happened since then and was struck by the tremendous velocity of events in such a short period. Indeed, it seemed I had hardly enjoyed a moment's rest since setting foot in Manhattan.[3]

I encountered nothing suspicious at the ferry and made a quick trip across the Hudson to the railroad's huge station in Jersey City. There, I secured a private berth on the *Pennsylvania Limited*, which departed promptly at nine o'clock. My trip was without incident, although as we pulled out of Altoona, Pennsylvania, that evening, I learned from a porter that a man had been killed the evening before at Horseshoe Curve when he apparently fell, or jumped, from the *Pennsylvania Special* and was horribly mangled under the wheels of a passing freight train.

Curious, I asked the porter what the man looked like. The victim's description perfectly matched that of Abe Slaney. I was, I will admit, quite stunned by this news, although I assumed the resemblance could be nothing but a coincidence. In hopes of gaining more information, I bought a copy of the Altoona newspaper but found only a brief story about the death, which did not identify the victim. Unfortunately, I also found a much longer wire story, filled with the usual half-truths and innuendoes, linking Holmes and me to Mrs. Cubitt's kidnapping.

As the *Special* rounded Horseshoe Curve and made its final climb to the top of the Alleghenies, I put aside the newspaper and lay down to rest in my berth. A hundred questions, or so it seemed, jostled for attention in my thoughts, but I knew that my best hope for finding answers would not come until morning, when I reached Chicago.

Chapter Thirty

"Something Like That"

Mme. Simone DuBois's pendulous form disguised an inner armature of iron, as she was to demonstrate only minutes after Holmes's daring escape. When all the excitement broke out, she had been in the dining car, enjoying supper with the four unsuspecting young women being taken to Chicago. The women then went on to the lounge, and Mme. DuBois was alone when she arrived back at the private car only to encounter the chaotic aftermath of Holmes's seemingly impossible escape. As she stepped through the vestibule door, Mme. DuBois saw Charlie and Belgian Jack at the far end of the car, dragging Elsie Cubitt toward her compartment. She saw Little Pete hunched over in a nearby chair, holding a towel to his face and sobbing, "My eye, he ruined my eye!" She didn't see Jake Slaney.

"What on earth has happened?" she asked.

Belgian Jack then came forward and blurted out the bad news—Holmes was gone, Jake dead—almost like a child confessing to some petty theft. It took all of Mme. DuBois's fortitude to stay calm and coherent. But that had always been the Slaney way—never give in, never show pain, always get even—and she had lived by this hard philosophy all of her life.

So she stepped in at once and took command of the sit-

uation. First, she helped return Elsie, who was unconscious and bleeding from the mouth, to her bed. After determining that Elsie's bleeding stemmed from nothing
worse than a broken tooth, Mme. DuBois gave her another injection, since Little Pete was in no condition to
perform this vital task. Finally, she made certain that all
signs of Holmes's escape were cleaned up so that none of
the train crew would become suspicious.

Only after she had thus restored order did Mme.
DuBois turn her attention to the men—Belgian Jack,
Charlie and Little Pete—who had ruined everything, and
her icy control quickly gave way to fierce anger.

"You morons!" she screamed, so angry that her words
came out in a spray of spittle. "You can begin, Jack, by
explaining to me how you and Little Pete managed to allow an unarmed, half-dead man locked in a coffin get
away from you."

Belgian Jack did his best to do just that, but if he expected sympathy after recounting Holmes's surprise attack with the belt, he got none.

"A belt!" she repeated, shaking her head in a fury of
disbelief. "I knew Jake should never have brought the
two of you along. Stupid, stupid, stupid!"

She then turned her wrath toward Charlie, who was
dressed in his full Sherlockian regalia but had lost any
semblance of his old self-confident posture. "And you let
a woman who can barely stay awake wander away. How
did you manage that?"

Charlie admitted going out for a smoke but said he
did not anticipate any problem because Elsie Cubitt
seemed fast asleep. He also noted that he felt perfectly
secure because Jake had come into the car to enjoy
a cigar as well. The two of them were talking, he said,
when Jake spotted Elsie leaving her compartment. After
that, Charlie reported, "I don't know what happened
except that Jake ran to stop her and then he started

shooting and pretty soon there was a big uproar all around."

"And what were you doing while all this was going on?" Mme. DuBois demanded.

"Ducking," Charlie answered.

Belgian Jack now spoke up. "What should we do about Little Pete? His eye's hurt pretty bad."

"Let him suffer," Mme. DuBois said. "It's just too bad all three of you weren't thrown from the train instead of Jake. There would have been some justice in that."

"Well, I'm sorry," Belgian Jack said. "I—"

"Oh, for God's sake shut up and spare me the excuses," she said. "I want the three of you to stay right here until I tell you otherwise. Now get out of my sight. I need time to think."

Once Belgian Jack and Charlie were gone, Mme. DuBois went back into her compartment, sat down on her bed and began to cry softly. It was hard to accept that Jake, like Abe, was now dead. Though she wasn't as close to Jake as she had been to Abe, she still loved him like a son. Mme. DuBois didn't cry for long, however, because there was too much to do. Although Jake was dead and Holmes had escaped, Mme. DuBois knew that she and her ally in Chicago still held the most critical card—Elsie Cubitt—in the game that had begun so many months before.

Holmes, Mme. DuBois was certain, would not under any circumstances abandon the secret love of his life. No, he would come flying to her as quickly as he could, and therein lay the genius of the plan so cleverly prepared by Mme. DuBois's ally. The trap could still be sprung in Chicago, where the powers that be had already been bought and paid for and where Mme. DuBois and her ally would at last be on familiar ground.

Mme. DuBois wasn't sure what Holmes would try next, but thought it possible he might look for a way to delay the *Pennsylvania Limited*—perhaps at its next stop, about three hours away in Pittsburgh—so he could mount a rescue effort. At first glance, this scenario didn't strike her as all that likely, since Holmes officially remained a fugitive from justice and thus could count on no help from authorities. Then again, he had managed to escape from a locked coffin, eluding two armed men and killing another, so the idea could not be dismissed out of hand.

As she thought through the problem, Mme. DuBois decided she had no choice but to switch trains at Pittsburgh, if at all possible, and bring Elsie Cubitt with her. And as it so happened, there was, she saw, an easy way to accomplish the switch. Satisfied that the situation might yet be made right, she left her compartment and once again told her three incompetent subordinates to stay put. Then she went looking for the conductor to see what other trains might be available from Pittsburgh to Chicago.

That night, as Mme. DuBois plotted her response to Holmes's escape, a small crime wave struck Altoona, Pennsylvania. Not long after dark, near the sooty brick mass of the Pennsylvania Railroad Station, a man hurrying to catch a train arrived at his destination only to learn that his wallet had been filched from his pocket. Minutes later, a few blocks away on busy Seventh Avenue, two more men—both local citizens of some repute—suffered similar fates. All three thefts were immediately reported to the police.[1]

The investigating officers quickly discovered that each of the victims had been bumped while on the sidewalk by a tall, dirty man in tattered clothes who appeared to be more than several sheets to the wind. The man, who held a newspaper under one arm, apologized in each case for his carelessness, tipped his hat and shambled away into the night. Because the suspected pickpocket had managed to keep his face in the shadows, none of the victims was able to give police a good description of his features.

Had the police been on hand to observe, they would

soon have seen three more crimes committed that night in Altoona. At a large downtown clothing shop someone picked a lock to gain entrance and walked off with an entire outfit of clothes—shirt and pants, belt, suspenders, two ties, a linen jacket suitable for summer and a black hat. As it so happened, one of the shop's specialties was clerical apparel, and the thief also took a complete priest's outfit. Next door, a druggist's shop was entered, the burglar escaping with hair dye, various items of makeup, a comb, a pipe and tobacco, several packs of cigarettes, matches, a small notebook, a good pen and a bottle of ink. The final burglary occurred at a leather goods store, where a suitcase and a billfold were stolen.

At three o'clock the next morning, well before the burglaries were discovered, a tall priest with ruddy features, and carrying a single small bag that matched the color of his black outfit, walked into the Pennsylvania Railroad station in Altoona. Pronouncing himself new to the area, the priest chatted amiably with the young ticket agent, displaying a fine Irish lilt. The priest asked many questions about train connections and the best way to send telegrams before he finally got down to specifics.

"Now, tell me if you would, my son, what would be the fastest way for a poor traveling man of God such as myself to reach Chicago at this hour of the night?"

"You don't have many good choices, father," the agent replied. "The next train through is the *Western Express*, which should be here shortly. Trouble is, the *Western* is a crawler compared to the *Limited*. It'll take you eighteen hours to get to Chicago, but it's still the fastest way to get there right now. So what will it be, father?"[2]

The tall priest smiled and said, "Why, I will take the *Express*, my son, for I am wanted in Chicago."

"Ah, so it is God's work that calls you," the clerk remarked.

"Something like that," said Sherlock Holmes.

Book Four

Chicago

Chapter Thirty-one

§ ₹

"Big Wheels Continue to Turn"

FROM THE NARRATIVE OF DR. JOHN WATSON:

At quarter past nine on Wednesday morning I arrived in Chicago in the midst of a roaring thunderstorm, which reflected my troubled state of mind. The long train journey had given me ample time to think. Although I remained hopeful that I would find Holmes and Elsie Cubitt, I knew that great difficulties lay before me. The sheer immensity of Chicago made it, like London or New York, a city where any search would be challenging, especially to an outsider such as myself. Moreover, I still possessed no incontrovertible evidence that Holmes was in Chicago, since the match box found in the tunnel beneath St. Paul's Chapel could have been planted, like so many other clues, by our enemies.

Instead, I was relying—as Holmes had—on the fact that the direction of the case, from the very beginning, had followed a westerly course, toward the city where both Abe Slaney and Elsie Cubitt were raised. Holmes clearly believed that Chicago would be the terminus of our great adventure, just as it was for so many of the railroad lines radiating across the American continent, and I could only proceed on the assumption that he was right. Still, I found myself feeling very much alone and bearing a great burden of expectations which in all our previous cases Holmes himself had shouldered.

After my bags had been retrieved, I took a taxi through the pounding rain to the Sherman House, an old but comfortable establishment on Randolph Street in the heart of Chicago's Loop. My first order of business was to place a telephone call to Detective Wooldridge, whom I intended to rely upon for help in finding Holmes. The detective was not in his office, however, and I left a message asking him to contact me immediately. Next, I wrote out a telegram to be sent to Bissen at his home, confirming my arrival in Chicago and asking for any news.[1]

Still weary from my travels, I took a nap, woke up refreshed shortly after noon and ate lunch in the hotel's restaurant. Before returning to my room, I took aside one of the bellboys, who looked to be a clever lad, and made inquiries regarding the Everleigh Club, of which I knew almost nothing.

The boy was not at all reluctant to discuss this establishment, which he informed me had been open for less than two years yet was already considered "*the* place for sporting gentlemen so long as they ain't shy about spending money." I was told the club was so opulent that princes and potentates were among its regular visitors and that, as the boy put it, "the ladies there are the finest money can buy and not your usual cheap harlots."

When I inquired how I might be admitted to this elegant brothel, the boy said "all a man has to do is show up at the front door with a wad of cash in his hand and he'll have no trouble." I then asked for his definition of "a wad of cash" and the boy said he had heard that "any gentleman expecting to spend under one hundred dollars for the evening would not be welcome." The lad added that the club was owned by "a pair of respectable sisters from Kentucky" who made sure everything was "on the up and up."

I thanked the boy and returned to my room, hoping

that Wooldridge might call at any moment. By three o'clock, however, I had heard nothing from the detective and was considering whether to go look for him at the police station when I received a most surprising message from Bissen in Manhattan. Indeed, the message contained several surprises, beginning with the fact that it consisted not only of his telegram but two others as well.

These additional messages—from Wooldridge and Shadwell Rafferty—were in response to the telegrams I had sent them before leaving New York. Bissen did not say how he had obtained their responses but I could only surmise that he had learned of them from an informant in the local Western Union office. I began by reading Bissen's telegram, which he had sent at noon:

> DR. WATSON: GLAD TO HEAR YOU ARE SAFE. AM
> FORWARDING MESSAGES FROM RAFFERTY AND
> WOOLDRIDGE, WHICH I THINK YOU WILL FIND
> INTERESTING. INSP. HARGREAVE FINE, THOUGH
> DEVERY'S MEN WERE NOT HAPPY TO SEE HIM IN
> TUNNEL. *SUN* AND *WORLD* HAVE RUN STORIES ABOUT
> DEVERY'S SUPPOSED "DISCOVERY" OF SECRET
> TUNNEL AND ARE AGAIN POINTING FINGER AT YOU
> AND HOLMES. AM TOLD BY FRIEND AT *WORLD* THAT
> THERE WILL BE EVEN MORE "ASTONISHING" NEWS IN
> TOMORROW'S EDITION. HE WOULD NOT ELABORATE.
> THIS TELLS ME BIG WHEELS CONTINUE TO TURN.
> YOU MUST BE VERY CAREFUL NOT TO BE GROUND
> UNDER THEM. WILL HELP FROM HERE IN ANY WAY
> POSSIBLE. INSP. HARGREAVE SENDS HIS BEST BUT HE
> IS NOW BEING WATCHED CONSTANTLY AND THERE IS
> LITTLE MORE HE CAN DO. GOOD LUCK! BISSEN.

The telegram from Wooldridge, sent at half past six on Monday night, was as follows:

DR. WATSON: DEVASTATED TO LEARN OF HOLMES'S
DISAPPEARANCE. WILL DO ALL POSSIBLE TO HELP.
IF HE IS BEING TAKEN HERE, SITUATION WILL BE
DIFFICULT. JAKE SLANEY HAS POWERFUL FRIENDS
AT CITY HALL AND ALL BUT UNTOUCHABLE BY
POLICE. HIS GANG BASED AT EVERLEIGH CLUB,
BEST-PROTECTED BROTHEL IN LEVEE. AS TOLD
HOLMES, HAVE SEEN NO SIGN OF ABE SLANEY SINCE
PRESUMED DEATH IN ENGLAND. GUNMAN KILLED
IN NEW YORK SOUNDS LIKE BILLY WAINWRIGHT,
ASSASSIN WHO WORKS FOR GANGSTERS HERE. WILL
CHECK ON HIS WHEREABOUTS. ALSO WILL KEEP EYE
OUT FOR HOLMES AND MRS. CUBITT. BUT WITH SO
MANY RAIL STATIONS IT WILL BE BIG JOB. CALL OR
WIRE IF YOU NEED MORE INFORMATION. SHALL
PRAY HOLMES IS FOUND SOON. LET ME KNOW IF YOU
PLAN TO COME HERE. REGARDS, WOOLDRIDGE.[2]

Rafferty's message was the last I read and certainly
contained the most extraordinary piece of information.
Sent on Monday afternoon, it said:

MY DEAR DR. WATSON: SHOCKED TO HEAR OF
HOLMES'S ABDUCTION BUT MORE SHOCKED
WITHIN LAST HOUR TO RECEIVE INVITATION TO
HIS WEDDING TO ELSIE CUBITT! DO YOU KNOW
ABOUT THIS? NUPTIALS SAID TO BE IN CHICAGO
FRIDAY. PERHAPS SOME KIND OF JOKE BUT I THINK
NOT, GIVEN MESSÁGE I RECEIVED SUNDAY NIGHT,
SUPPOSEDLY FROM HOLMES. DESCRIBED LOVE AS
"STRANGE THING" AND SAID HE WOULD LEAVE
NEW YORK SOON. DID NOT SAY WHY. ALL VERY,
VERY PECULIAR. WASH AND I ARE LEAVING FOR
CHICAGO ON FIRST AVAILABLE TRAIN AND SHOULD
ARRIVE BY MIDNIGHT. IF HOLMES HAS BEEN

BROUGHT THERE, WE WILL DO ALL IN OUR POWER
TO FIND HIM. PASS ON ANY NEW DETAILS AS YOU
GET THEM AND PLEASE EXPLAIN EXACTLY WHAT IS
GOING ON! WE WILL BE AT HOTEL ST. BENEDICT
NORTH OF LOOP. GOOD LUCK AND GODSPEED,
RAFFERTY.[3]

The news of a supposed wedding between Holmes and
Elsie Cubitt was the most bizarre development yet in a
case that had already produced more than its share of
outlandish events. Naturally, I gave no credence to the
idea that the wedding could be genuine. Yet the message
was also cause for hope because it provided additional
evidence—though admittedly of a very suspicious sort—
that Holmes and Mrs. Cubitt were indeed in Chicago. At
the same time, I wondered why Rafferty had received an
invitation when no one else apparently had. It then occurred to me that more sham invitations might already be
in the mail as part of the continuing campaign to harass
and embarrass Holmes.

I did not puzzle long over the curious matter of the invitation, however, since the telegram's most important
news concerned the arrival of Rafferty and Thomas in
Chicago. I walked downstairs at once to place a telephone
call to Rafferty at the Hotel St. Benedict. A clerk there
told me there was no answer in his suite.

Disappointed, I turned to walk back to my room when
I saw, coming into the lobby of the Sherman House, the
beaming red face of Shadwell Rafferty, with George
Washington Thomas beside him. I cannot describe how
much it meant to me to see them again. After my long
journey, and with so many dire questions hanging over me
like heavy swords, I was wonderfully relieved to be once
again among friends. Because of my disguise, however,
Rafferty did not spot me immediately, and only when I

came up to him and expressed my warmest sentiments did he realize who I was.

He greeted me with a bear hug which nearly squeezed the air out of my lungs, while Thomas offered a more restrained handshake. Not wishing to make a prolonged public scene, we retired at once to my room to talk. After we had taken seats and lit cigars, Rafferty looked at me with undisguised curiosity, then spoke up in his usual spirited manner.

"I'm hopin', doctor, that you are travelin' in disguise, since I can't say you're especially charmin' as a snake-oil salesman, which is what you look like in that get-up," he said with a broad grin. "I must also remark that you look downright naked without your mustache."

"As did you, Mr. Rafferty, the last time we met, when you were without your beard. I see, however, that you have let it grow back."

"I have, but I've tried to tame it a bit, as you can see. The last time you saw me with it—why, that must have been during the rune stone affair—it was hangin' halfway down to my knees."

This amiable badinage continued for some minutes—I think all of us felt need of relief from the tense circumstances which had brought us to Chicago—but we soon turned to far more significant matters. After Rafferty briefly explained why he and Thomas had decided to come to Chicago, I asked how they had located me at Sherman House.

"'Twas no mystery," Rafferty said. "After he'd intercepted my telegram and forwarded it to you, Detective Bissen in New York wired me at the St. Benedict and told me where you'd be stayin'. Wash and I came over as soon as we got his telegram. This Bissen fellow sounds like quite a pip. He works for your friend Hargreave, I take it."

"He does, Mr. Rafferty, and he is definitely a 'pip,' as you put it. In any event, you do not know how happy I am to see the two of you. I could not think of better men to have with me at this critical hour."

"The feelin' is mutual, doctor, for these are indeed strange times. By the way, have you seen the latest newspapers?"

"No, I was just going to get one when I ran into you."

"Well, you won't like what you'll find in the *Tribune*," Rafferty said. "I'll grab one for you."

After Rafferty returned from the newsstand, he handed me a copy of the Chicago *Tribune*, which on the front page carried a story which began as follows:

One of the most curious and shocking stories of recent years is now being played out in New York City, where the famed English detective Sherlock Holmes and his longtime companion Dr. John Watson are being pursued by police on suspicion of murder, kidnapping and theft.

According to authorities in New York, Holmes and Dr. Watson arranged the kidnapping in England of a woman with whom Holmes is said to be passionately in love. The woman, Mrs. Hilton Cubitt, was transported to New York aboard a liner and then spirited away from the docks before police could intervene.

Holmes and Watson are said to be suspects in the kidnapping, as well as the murder of a

guard at Gen. Grant's Tomb in New York, where a $10,000 ransom was apparently to be paid for Mrs. Cubitt's safe return. Instead, police allege Holmes and Watson disappeared with the money and with Mrs. Cubitt.

It has also been learned that authorities in England are seeking the two men for questioning in connection with the murder of a woman in Liverpool.

"Mr. Holmes appears to have become unhinged," said New York Chief of Police William Devery. "We are not certain where he is keeping Mrs. Cubitt at the moment, or exactly what he intends to do, but we will leave no stone unturned in our effort to track him down."

There is some thought that

Holmes, with Dr. Watson's assistance, may be taking the woman to Chicago, since that is where she reportedly was born. However, other sources believe that Holmes and his captive may already have fled to Canada. Holmes is said to have become infatuated with Mrs. Cubitt after investigating the death of her husband some years ago in England.

Holmes first made a name for himself . . .

I could read no more. "It never ceases to amaze what lies can be told in the newspapers. To think that even a respected paper like the *Tribune* could report such blatant falsehoods is simply incredible."[4]

"That it is," said Rafferty. "Still, the fact that you're officially a fugitive means that we must be doubly careful. Now, why don't you tell us everything you know about this case and we'll do the same."

Although the tale of Elsie Cubitt's kidnapping and Holmes's disappearance was so tangled as to defy description, I composed myself and launched upon as complete an account of the affair as I could muster. It was nearly three quarters of an hour before I finished.

Rafferty, who had listened with the utmost attention, said, "Why, 'tis a tale worthy of Homer, doctor, and all it needs now is a happy homecomin'. As for this Slaney fellow, I don't like him appropriatin' my name but it tells me that I'm a target in this affair, just like Mr. Holmes. That explains why I got the wedding invitation. Slaney wants me to be here, and I imagine the same is true of you, doctor. We are bein' invited to take part in our own demise. 'Tis a creepy business all the way around."

"That is why we must find Holmes and Mrs. Cubitt as quickly as possible, since it is apparent Slaney will stop at nothing to satisfy his thirst for revenge," I said.

Thomas said, "Well, one thing's sure, which is that we'll need all the help we can get. Chicago's a mighty tough town." He then asked me if I had talked to Detective Wooldridge. I said I had been trying but to no avail.

"'Tis the same story with us," Rafferty complained. "We've been calling him since we got here, but the coppers don't seem to want to tell us where he is. He's off on what they call 'special assignment'—that's all they'll say."

"My God, do you think something has happened to him?"

"There's no way of telling, but from what you've told me about this business, I'd say anything is possible. Maybe it's time we brought in some heavy guns to see if we can soften up the enemy's position."

"What did you have in mind?"

"Well, I'm thinkin' Mr. Hill up in St. Paul would have something to say about what goes on in this city. He's got plenty of business interests here, and he's also got experience dealin' with city hall. If the word were to go out that he would like to find Mr. Holmes, and that he'd pay handsomely for the right information, why I imagine all manner of creatures with an itch to talk would come scurryin' out of the woodwork. He could also put some pressure on the police to cooperate. You know what he can do when he gets his dander up."

Indeed I did, for it was a sight to behold when the railroad baron turned that fierce eye of his (he had only one) upon some object of his wrath. I was about to second Rafferty's motion when Thomas issued a caveat.

"You're forgettin' something, Shad. Mr. Hill's up at his fishing camp in Quebec and won't be back in St. Paul for a week. You know how hard he is to reach up there."

"Ah, you're right, Wash. Still, I'll call Mr. Pyle in St. Paul and see if he can track down the famous salmon fisherman. In the meantime, I guess we're on our own."

"Well, if nothing else, you and Mr. Thomas have a head start on me here," I said. "Have you learned anything of value since your arrival?"

"Maybe," Rafferty said. "Yesterday, we went nosin' around the Levee district where the Everleigh Club is located. As you know, that's the place where Mr. Holmes is supposedly goin' to be married in two days."

"What a preposterous notion that is. Surely, you don't believe Holmes is actually going to appear at some brothel on Friday night with Mrs. Cubitt?"

"No, I don't, but I was still curious why the club had been selected to host the supposed matrimonials. So Wash and I did some checking. Trouble is, Dr. Watson, the Levee is a very secretive place and findin' anybody to talk about the club wasn't easy, especially since I wasn't carryin' enough cash to satisfy the steep price of truth in that part of town. Then Wash had a better idea, which was to go over to Bed Bug Row—that's the black part of the Levee—and see if the folks over there might be helpful. They were, and Wash got the information for a price that didn't break the bank."[5]

"What did you find out, Mr. Thomas?" I asked.

"Well, I just moseyed around a bit, chatting with folks here and there, and I finally ran into a fellow who operates one of the establishments that caters to white men looking for what I guess you could call an exotic experience. This fellow told me that he'd heard about the big wedding at the Everleigh and that it was supposedly being planned by the 'mystery lady'—that's what he calls her—who runs the place."

"But isn't the club owned by two sisters?" I asked, recalling my conversation with the bellboy. "I believe their names are Minna and—"

"Ada Everleigh," said Rafferty, completing my thought. "Well now, that's the odd thing, doctor. From what Wash found out, the famous twin madams are just figureheads. The real boss of the place is said to be a certain Mrs. Mary Mortimer, known to be—and you'll be interested to hear this—an intimate of Jake Slaney, who as you know is Abe's younger brother."

"And just who is this Mary Mortimer?"

It was Thomas who provided the answer: "The fellow I talked to said nobody seemed to know much about where she came from or how she got to be 'so high and mighty so quick,' as he put it. But it's well-known that she and Jake Slaney, among others, have a hand in running the Everleigh Club."

"All of which may explain why the mock wedding is planned there," Rafferty noted, "since the Slaney family obviously has an interest in the establishment. There's something else we found out about this mysterious woman, which is that she's also an intimate friend of the two crooked aldermen who control the entire vice district."

"For your infomation, doctor, that would be Bathhouse John Coughlin and Hinky Dink Kenna," Thomas said. "Known far and wide, they are, as Chicago's champions of corruption."

Rafferty chimed in, "They're also two of the more vicious criminals you'll find on this side of the Atlantic, or the other, as far as that goes. 'Tis common knowledge they will not stop at murder to maintain their grip on the business of vice. 'Tis also no secret that they and their cronies have the mayor, the police department and every other branch of government in this city bought and paid for, and that puts them for all practical purposes beyond the reach of the local law. Which is why I'm telling you we are in very deep water if those two scoundrels are tied in with the kidnapping of Mr. Holmes and Mrs. Cubitt."

It now seemed that I had escaped the sickening corruption of New York City only to encounter an even worse situation in Chicago. "Well then, what are we to do, Mr. Rafferty?" I asked. "Are you saying that not even a policeman like Wooldridge can be relied upon?"

"No. He may be honest as the day is long but as you found out in New York, one or two honorable coppers can only do so much when everybody else is crooked. All I'm saying is that whatever we do here, we can't expect much help from the police. We'll have to find Mr. Holmes and Mrs. Cubitt ourselves, and I have an idea how we might do it."

"I was hoping you would say that, Mr. Rafferty."

"Well, Wash and I were talkin' about that this mornin', askin' ourselves just how a fellow might go about shanghaiin' someone all the way from New York to Chicago without arousin' suspicion. Remember, it's a trip of twenty-four hours by train at best, and your captive isn't likely to be in a cooperative mood, so you've got to take precautions. The captive would have to be kept out of public sight and probably drugged, or bound and gagged. That means you'd need a private Pullman compartment or even a private rail car. But even if you made all those arrangements, you'd still have one big problem."

"I see what you're driving at, Mr. Rafferty. The question is how to get your captive on and off the train."

"Exactly. 'Twas the same problem facing Slaney when he had to take Mrs. Cubitt from the ship in New York."

"Of course! He would need an ambulance. Now, if we check the ambulance services here—"

"Hold your horses, doctor, for there's another possibility, which Wash suggested. Tell him what you're thinkin', Wash."

"Well, what occurred to me is that there'd be an even safer way to slip somebody off a train if he was all drugged up. You see, I worked one summer, way back when, unloading baggage cars for the New York Central. As it turned out, some of the heaviest items we had to handle were coffins. Corpses were always being shipped to New York for burial, and we'd take out the coffins and put them in a special spot for the mortuaries, who'd send hearses to pick them up. Like I said, it was very common."

The image this conveyed—of Holmes and Mrs. Cubitt imprisoned in a coffin—was utterly repugnant. Yet I knew Thomas's idea was not beyond the realm of possibility.

"Then you are saying we should also talk to mortuaries, which may have picked up caskets at one of the rail stations?"

"That would be one way of doin' it," Rafferty replied, "but there must be dozens, or maybe even hundreds, of funeral parlors in Chicago, and it could take us days to track down the right one. Besides, we don't even know that a coffin was used to transport either Mr. Holmes or Mrs. Cubitt. No, I think we must try another approach, just as Mr. Holmes would do if he were in our situation."

"Ah, and what have you concluded?" I asked.

With a grin, Rafferty said, "That we must cut the odds, doctor, by makin' some deductions based on what we know, or believe we know."

The series of deductions which Rafferty now laid out before us was, I can state with confidence, worthy of Holmes himself. Rafferty's reasoning went thusly:

The kidnappers would have left New York as quickly as possible, probably by the first available express train with Pullman cars. The two fastest trains Rafferty knew of were the New York Central's *Twentieth Century* and the *Pennsylvania Limited*, which I had taken. These, he said, should be the first trains we check. However, the kidnappers—to throw off any pursuers—might have transferred somewhere to another train bound for Chicago. We would thus have to be alert to that possibility as well.

Once in Chicago—and Rafferty assumed the kidnappers must already be in the city—they would have used either an ambulance or a hearse to transport Holmes and Mrs. Cubitt to some hideaway. Given the match box I had found in New York, and the fact that the Everleigh Club was also to be the scene of the supposed wedding,

Rafferty concluded that Holmes and Mrs. Cubitt were probably being kept somewhere in the Levee district.

"I'm willing to admit that I could be wrong about all of this," Rafferty said, "but I don't have any better ideas at the moment. How about you, doctor?"

"No."

"How about you, Wash?"

"You'll get no argument from me, Shad."

"Very well then," Rafferty said, "it is settled, and I see no reason to delay. I suggest we go at once to Union Station and look for coffins."

Chapter Thirty-two

♪ ♫

"How Nice of You to Join Us"

"It sounds like you had quite a time of it," said Mary Mortimer as she offered a cup of tea to Mme. Simone DuBois.

"That would be an understatement, I think," replied Mme. DuBois, who had arrived in Chicago only a few hours earlier after her harrowing trip from New York.

The women were in Mrs. Mortimer's apartment, sitting in the big parlor that offered a panoramic view of Lake Michigan. It was early in the evening of Tuesday, July 17, and Mme. DuBois had already provided a full account of the trip, including her decision to leave the *Pennsylvania Limited* at Pittsburgh and take a later train — the *Chicago and St. Louis Express* — to her final destination. Elsie Cubitt had been secreted in Holmes's coffin aboard the *Express*, and had been so heavily sedated that she was still sleeping, as far as Mme. DuBois knew.

Mrs. Mortimer had learned much earlier of the unfortunate events in Pennsylvania, first in a telegram from Mme. DuBois and later from Belgian Jack, who had been summoned for an interview after he, Little Pete and Charlie — along with the four young prostitutes-to-be — arrived in Chicago that morning aboard the *Limited*. Like Mme. DuBois, Mrs. Mortimer had been appalled by the men's inexcusable mistakes, and she had already decided that all three would have to be dealt with severely.

All was far from lost, however, for Elsie Cubitt still remained in her hands and was now safely under lock and key. "How is our Helen of Troy?" Mrs. Mortimer asked her guest. "I trust you were not too unkind to her."

"She's fine. I imagine she's still sleeping at the stockade. I told the gentlemen there to let her sleep as long as she likes. Tomorrow evening, I think, they will take their pleasure," said Mme. DuBois, who delighted to think of what would soon happen to the "beautiful princess," as she sardonically referred to Elsie. "Do you still believe, Mary, that Holmes will try to rescue her?"

"Of course he will, and we shall be ready for him," said Mrs. Mortimer. "His friend Rafferty, I have been informed, is already in town, and I imagine the ever-loyal Dr. Watson will be along shortly from New York. Too bad he wasn't taken care of there as planned. However, we'll have the whole lot of them soon enough."

Mme. DuBois, who was breathing slowly and looked as though she might tumble over into sleep at any moment, nodded her head. "That shall be the long-awaited judgment day, Mary, and I cannot wait to see it. It's just too bad that Belgian Jack, Little Pete and Charlie failed me. They can be of no use to us anymore, as far as I'm concerned. No use whatsoever."

"Have no worries about those three bumblers," Mrs. Mortimer said. "I have already made suitable arrangements to deal with them."

Mme. DuBois was pleased to hear this, for she remained bitterly angry about what had happened aboard the *Pennsylvania Limited*. "If they had simply done their job, dear Jake would still be alive and we would have Holmes in our grasp at this instant," she said. "You must be heartbroken, my dear."

"Yes," said Mrs. Mortimer, trying to sound suitably bereaved, "I shall miss Jake until my dying day. But we must go forward with our plan, or he will have died for nothing."

Mrs. Mortimer had always been expert at voicing the proper feminine sentiments, although the truth was that she felt no different about Jake than she did about any of the other men in her life. Jake had definitely been useful—and had possessed the added advantage of being a vigorous and practiced lover—but there would always be another man, perhaps better and even richer, somewhere down the road. Sherlock Holmes remained the only real passion of her life, for he was the one man she had been unable to bend to her fierce will. His escape from the train upset her far more than the fact that, in doing so, he had killed Jake.

"When do you think Holmes will be here?" Mme. DuBois now asked.

"Tomorrow at the latest, I should think. He will come running after his beloved Elsie, and when he does he will run right into our trap. I look forward to his ruination. Now then, dear, will you have more tea?"

Much later that night, well after Mary Mortimer had gone to the Everleigh Club, a curious thing occurred outside the entry of the Potomac Apartments, where she lived. The building, on Michigan Avenue a mile or so south of the sin-drenched precincts of the Levee, was one of Chicago's most elegant addresses, and was staffed round-the-clock by a concierge. Normally, the work offered little excitement, but on this night a fracas broke out on the building's front steps. It appeared to involve half-a-dozen drunken men, who made an awful racket as they brawled and screamed at one another. The concierge, a forceful young man who had been on the job for less than a month, went out to deal with the problem.

"All of you, get out of here," he shouted as he came out onto the steps, "or I shall call the police."

Most of the fighters ignored this warning but one man broke free from the mob and confronted the concierge, who was beginning to have second thoughts about his boldness. "Why, this is none of your damn business, sonny boy," the man said, grabbing the startled concierge by the lapels of his coat and shoving him up against a wall.

"Get your hands off me," the concierge said, trying to free himself from the drunk's powerful grip.

"Say please," said the man, "and be nice about it."

While the concierge was thus occupied, he failed to notice that one of the brawlers—a lanky man dressed in overalls and wearing a short-billed cap—disengaged himself from the melee and slipped inside the lobby.

Not long thereafter, the fight broke up as quickly as it had started, and the brawlers melted away into the night. Feeling rather proud of himself, the concierge dusted off his coat and went back to his desk in the lobby. As he took his seat, he didn't bother to glance at the indicator above the building's elevator. Had he done so, he would have been surprised to note that someone was riding up to the top floor.

Some hours before the concierge's great adventure, Joseph Pyle hung up the telephone in his large apartment at the Aberdeen Hotel in St. Paul and paused to consider the remarkable story he had just heard. Pyle, editor of the St. Paul *Daily Globe*, had certainly been privy to his share of fantastic tales over the years and had even printed quite a few of them. But none held a candle, he thought, to the story that had been laid out for him over the past twenty minutes. He had also received explicit instructions from his caller, and he intended to carry them out to the letter despite the difficulties they presented.

Pyle's most pressing task was to reach James J. Hill, the railroad tycoon whose power and influence were now desperately needed. Like most newspaper editors, Pyle was a quick and impatient man, characteristics that more than a decade earlier had recommended him to Hill, who possessed similar traits. It was Pyle, acting on Hill's orders, who had traveled to London in 1894 to persuade Sherlock Holmes to investigate the strange affair of the Red Demon. Since then, Pyle had become involved, to one degree or another, in all of Holmes's investigations in Minnesota, earning his respect as a man who could be relied upon in a pinch. Pyle was also well-acquainted with Shadwell Rafferty and was aware — although not in great detail — of Rafferty's mission in Chicago.[1]

Normally, Pyle would have had no trouble reaching Hill, whose mansion was but a few blocks from the Aberdeen. At the moment, however, Hill was over a thousand miles away at his fishing lodge along the River St. John in eastern Quebec. The railroad tycoon had made arrangements to bring telephone and telegraph lines into the remote lodge, but the service in Pyle's experience had been spotty at best. Pyle could only hope that the lines would be open tonight.[2]

He got back on the telephone and gave the operator the number of Hill's lodge. Then he waited as the call was routed through a maze of switchboards and interchanges. Finally, he heard the unmistakable voice of Jacque LeClair, who ran the lodge for Hill.

"Jacque, this is Joseph Pyle. Is Mr. Hill at the lodge?"

"Of course, Joseph. Where else would he be at such an hour? He is sleeping."

"You must wake him, Jacque."

There was a pause on the other end of the line. LeClair had worked for Hill long enough to know that he needed an extremely good reason to disturb the great man's sleep. In the best of moods, Hill could be difficult but when he was tired and out of sorts—well, it could be very unpleasant.

"I think you must tell me what this is about, Joseph. Is it an emergency or is it something—"

"It's more than an emergency," Pyle said impatiently. "It is a matter of life and death, Jacque. Now, wake Mr. Hill at once!"

Just before she became fully conscious, Elsie Cubitt found herself in a twilight world of memories and dreams centering around her long train trip from New York. She recalled, in brief flashes, being in the Pullman car with a man who looked like Sherlock Holmes. Then, she seemed to remember, she had actually seen Holmes, or was this only a dream? No, it was real. It had to be real. She had walked toward him, reached for his hand, so close to safety and freedom, and then . . . then she had plummeted over a high cliff, down, down, down into a great void. Then . . .

Elsie Cubitt awoke with a start, suddenly aware that something had changed. There was no swaying, no noise and clatter, just quiet. She was no longer on the train. Where was she now? She struggled to open her eyes, but this simple task seemed all but impossible, for she felt paralyzed by the weight of her own body. Her head and neck, arms and legs, even her fingers and toes seemed like great clumps of lead. Her mind felt equally slow and heavy, as though her very thoughts had acquired the heft of real things. She could do nothing but lay in silence and hope her own body would release her.

In time, it did. As minutes and then hours passed— Elsie could not say how many—the burden on her body began to lighten, while her intellect, long dulled by drugs, started to regain its customary sharpness. Her return to consciousness, however, brought with it a terrible pain in her jaw, where she had been struck by Jake Slaney moments before his death. She didn't remember the blow, but as she gingerly felt around her jaw she was pleased to find that it didn't appear to be broken.

When she finally managed to open her eyes, what she saw brought her no comfort. She was lying on a mattress in a large room, alone, and wearing nothing save for a gauzy shift of the kind favored by the occupants of brothels. The gloomy and decrepit room was dimly lit by two flickering gas jets, and as Elsie looked around she grew extremely apprehensive. With its peeling wallpaper, water-soaked plaster ceiling and gaudy but threadbare crimson carpet, the room had the hard-worn look of a place from which hope itself had been evicted long ago. However, something else had been kept inside, for Elsie Cubitt noticed that the room's three windows—arranged in a row along one wall—were all heavily barred. But the most remarkable, and disturbing, feature of the room was that it appeared to contain no furnishings other than mattresses.

A half-dozen or so mattresses, whose purpose Elsie Cubitt could not fail to understand, lay haphazardly scattered around the floor, but there were no chairs or tables or lamps or anything else in the way of ordinary furniture. There was, however, plenty of litter in the form of cans and bottles, empty tins of tobacco, cigarette and cigar stubs and what looked to be torn pieces of women's underclothing. The room also had a stench to it that reminded Elsie of the vile saloons where her father often did business.

Elsie now concluded that she must be somewhere in Chicago, very probably in the Levee district. She had grown up near the unspeakably sordid world of the Levee, and—against her father's express instructions—had gone one day to see the infamous vice precinct for herself. Accompanying her were two guides from the

Chicago Civic Federation, an anti-corruption group. Among other things, her guides had pointed out several of the district's stockades—prisonlike buildings where young women were "broken in" for a life of prostitution.[3]

This brutal work, the guides had told her, was accomplished by beatings and repeated rapes until the women became "used to their lot in life." She had also been informed that all the stockades were controlled by Bathhouse John Coughlin, who bragged of personally "supervising" the work on occasion. It was after her tour of the Levee that Elsie Cubitt had finally renounced her father and left Chicago, going first to New York and then to London. Now, she feared, she might well be in one of the Levee's stockades, set to become the latest victim of Coughlin and his hired rapists.

Although she still felt slightly dizzy and her head ached right down to her neck, she began to look for some means of escape. She managed to get to her feet and wobbled over to one of the barred windows. Using all her strength, she pulled at the thick bars but could not budge them. The other two windows, she soon discovered, were equally well-protected. There were doors at either end of the room and she decided to try them both, even though she held out little hope that either would be open. She went to the nearest door and attempted to turn the knob without success. The door was securely locked. She then started toward the other door, only to see it suddenly swing open. Four men entered the room and closed the door behind them.

Elsie recognized two of the men at once. The tallest and stoutest of the foursome, wearing a bizarre outfit that included lime green pants and a candy-striped coat, was Coughlin. Behind him was a tall, sinister-looking man with a wide face cut by several scars, a nose twisted out of shape by a long career of brawling and heavily lidded black eyes. This was Billy Perdue, also known as Bang-

Bang, who for a time had been a member of her father's criminal gang. She didn't recognize the other two men, both large and feral looking, but assumed they were some of Coughlin's so-called "professional rapists."

"Ah, my dear Elsie, how nice of you to join us," Coughlin said, making a slight bow and then adding with an undisguised leer, "and may I say you look very fetching in your little outfit."

Elsie said nothing and began slowly backing away, despite the fact that she had nowhere to go. The men only laughed as they watched her edge toward the far wall.

Coughlin said, "Where are you going, Elsie? There's no reason to be afraid. Why, you might even enjoy yourself. Mr. Perdue, I am sure, will be very gentle. Besides, he has long looked forward to getting better acquainted with a woman of your charm and beauty. Isn't that right, Bang-Bang."

Perdue smiled and said, "That is a fact, Bathhouse, that is a fact. Why, ever since I first saw the little lady years ago, I thought she would one day be a fine peach of a woman ripe for plucking."

"Well then, we certainly won't stand in your way," said Coughlin. "We'll just sit back and watch for a while. I'm sure Mrs. Cubitt—or should I say, the Widow Cubitt—will have no objection."

Elsie Cubitt had always been a fighter—more than once Eban had remarked how his daughter was the most fearless member of the family—but she did not see how she could hope to ward off four vicious men intent on violating her. Perdue now slowly approached, a crooked grin on his ravaged face, and she kept backing away until her back was literally against the wall. Glancing down, she saw a broken whisky bottle on the floor and picked it up.

"You stay away," she said, waving the end of the bottle at Perdue, who appeared far more amused than frightened by her show of resistance.

"Oh, she's a fighter, boys," he said, turning round to address the other men, who now broke out in raucous laughter. "Why, I've always liked a fighter. It adds to the fun."

He now turned around to face Elsie. His face darkened and he said grimly, "Now, be a good girl and drop that bottle, or I will have to hurt you with it. Didn't your old man ever tell you about me, Elsie? I like to hurt people, especially people like you."

A memory now emerged from some far corner of Elsie's mind, only it didn't involve her father, who had never talked at home about Perdue or any of many other brutal associates. But the two guides who had shown Elsie around the Levee had in fact mentioned Perdue, who was infamous as the district's most vicious rapist. Elsie had thought his nickname referred to his sexual activities but in fact it derived from something else.

Her guides had told her that Perdue acquired the moniker because of a sadistic trick he liked to play with his victims. He always carried a pistol, and as he prepared to assault his latest prey he would deliberately let the woman or, more often than not, girl see the weapon tucked in his pants pocket. If the victim was especially brave, she would grab the gun as Perdue started to attack and threaten to shoot him. He would leap back, feigning fear, and even go so far as to tell the woman he would have to let her go. Then, he would suddenly lurch toward her, even as she tried to pull the trigger, take the pistol away and, releasing a trigger safety on the specially modified revolver, fire off a round into the ceiling. He would conclude by pistol whipping the woman, berating her for her stupidity and then having his way with her.

Now, as Perdue bore down on her, Elsie Cubitt saw that, behind his vest, which he had made a display of unbuttoning, was a small ivory-handled pistol lodged under his belt. He *wanted* her to see it, she realized, wanted her to play his sadistic little game. She decided she would do just that. She caught his eye before staring down at his belt to signal that she had indeed seen the pistol. Then, when Perdue lunged for her, she grabbed the pistol from his belt and pushed him away.

The next few moments went according to Perdue's perverted script. "Oh please, please, don't shoot," he said, stepping back and raising his hands.

Then he turned around once again to address Coughlin and the other two men, who did their best to look equally frightened. "She has us now, boys. I do not know what we can do, except beg for mercy."

"Ah, so it would seem," Coughlin agreed. "It is our only hope."

But as Perdue spun back around to face Elsie, his manner suddenly changed. He began to walk slowly toward her and said, "Or maybe you will just have to shoot me, if you have the courage. Go ahead, Elsie, show me how brave you really are."

Perdue, who as always before one of his "breaking-in" sessions had imbibed large quantities of alcohol along with a jolt of cocaine, felt invulnerable as he approached Elsie Cubitt. She appeared to be fumbling with the revolver, and Perdue assumed that like all his other victims, she knew nothing about guns. In this belief, he was entirely wrong.

Elsie Cubitt was in fact extremely familiar with guns of all kinds. Her father had associated with many violent men, and reprisals against a gangster's family were not unheard of among the Levee's criminal classes. As a precaution, Eban had carefully trained his wife—and his headstrong daughter—in the use of firearms. She still had, back in England, a .32 caliber revolver Eban had given her when she turned eighteen. Later, with Hilton, she had taken up hunting at Ridling Thorpe and had quickly become a crack shot with both rifle and shotgun.

Now, as she held the small revolver in her hand, she

carefully felt around the trigger guard and then near the hammer for some kind of safety device. It did not take long for her thumb to come across a small lever behind the cylinder and just below the hammer. No revolver of her acquaintance had such a lever and she guessed it must be the safety. She tried pushing it with her thumb. Nothing happened. Next, she tried to push up the lever. Again nothing. Then, just as Perdue came almost close enough to grab her, she pushed down on the lever and heard a little click inside the pistol.

Raising the pistol and pointing at Perdue, she said, "Stand back or so help me God I will shoot."

But Perdue, who seemed to be in a kind of libidinous trance, ignored her command and, with a wild whoop, lunged toward her.

Elsie Cubitt did not hesitate. She squeezed off two rounds just as Perdue got one hand on her throat. The slugs struck him just below the breastbone. One tore through his ribcage and lungs, and probably would have killed him in a matter of minutes. The second bullet, however, did its lethal work more quickly, severing Perdue's aorta and sending out a plume of blood that drenched Elsie in its pulsing spray. Perdue staggered back, and Elsie would remember until her last day the look—part astonishment, part stark fear—that spread across his cruel face before he dropped to his knees and then, without a word, toppled over at her feet, as dead as a man could be.

The effect of this scene on Coughlin and his companions was electric. The three of them turned and made for the nearest door but were stopped when Elsie, who was not in a forgiving mood, fired off another round, which nearly parted Coughlin's luxuriant head of dark hair before it slammed into the wall.

"Stop," she shouted, "or Bathhouse dies."

She now had Coughlin's undivided attention, and he immediately complied with her order, raising his hands. His companions did the same.

"Whatever you want, Mrs. Cubitt, we shall do," he said, this time a genuine quiver of fear in his voice. "Just be careful with that pistol."

Being careful was, in fact, the last thing on Elsie Cubitt's mind. Although she was all alone in arguably the worst hellhole on the continent, half-naked, covered with a dead man's blood, hungry, cold and tired, she was also—for the first time in a fortnight—free, and what she really wanted to do was put a few chunks of lead through Coughlin's miserable hide. Yet she also knew that revenge of this sort, however pleasant to contemplate, would not get her out of her predicament. For that, she would need Coughlin's cooperation, whether he wished to give it or not.

"Don't any of you move," she said, coming up closer behind the three men but staying back far enough so that they couldn't try to grab away her gun. She was thinking, as fast as she ever had in her life, about what to do next, and she suddenly recalled something Holmes had told her, just a few months earlier, before her nightmare journey back to Chicago.

They had met one Sunday afternoon—just the two of them—at a little beach hotel at Great Yarmouth and talked at great length about many things. Holmes had been his usual dazzling self, with many wonderful stories, including an account of his recent adventures with the missing rune stone in Minnesota. She had then asked Holmes whether he ever worried about "thinking too much" and perhaps not leaving room for intuition and imagination in solving a case. To her surprise, he had said that despite his devotion to logic, he always left "clear space" in his mind for "the possibility of inspiration. Indeed, I have often found that the best ideas are rather like disobedient dogs—the harder you try to summon them, the less likely they are to come."[4]

Elsie Cubitt now realized that she must do the same— open her mind to inspiration and trust to her best instincts. It would be her only hope of finding a way out of the Levee alive.

"You two," she said to Coughlin's companions, "get down on the floor, face down. Spread your arms. Do it at once or you will be as dead as Mr. Perdue."

Once the men had obeyed, a sudden thought—her first inspiration—darted into her mind. Watching the other two men out of the corner of her eyes, she told Coughlin to go over to Perdue's corpse and look in his pocket for extra ammunition. "But first," she said, "give me that coat of yours, your shirt and your pants."

Elsie had looked around for her own clothes but saw no sign of them. They must have been taken away—part of the "breaking-in" strategy designed to so thoroughly abase its victims that they lost all self-respect. Since her clothes might be anywhere, she saw little choice but to borrow Coughlin's. It would also be a way of seeing whether, as she thought likely, he was carrying a pistol.

The big man balked at the idea of disrobing but Elsie would have none of it. She cocked the hammer of the revolver and said, "If I have to shoot you at this very instant, Bathhouse, I will do so and gladly. Now do as you are told, as I am not in a patient mood. And if you have a pistol do not try to reach for it."

Coughlin slowly removed his striped coat, his cream-colored shirt with pearl cufflinks and studs, and his green trousers. No weapon revealed itself but Elsie was astonished to discover that beneath his colorful outfit Coughlin wore, in addition to the usual underwear, an elaborate corset designed to rein in his pendulous belly.

Elsie could only laugh at the absurd spectacle Coughlin

presented in his tightly laced undergarment. She said, "I had heard you were quite the ladies' man, Bathhouse, but I did not suspect that you also dressed as they do."

"Go ahead, Elsie, laugh while you can," replied Coughlin, who despite his embarrassment seemed to be regaining his nerve. "But I assure you that your amusement at my expense will be short-lived. Don't you know what will happen if you try to leave here? Why, a thousand of the roughest men in Chicago, not to mention every copper this side of Harrison Street, will come looking for you as soon as the alarm is sounded. I fear you will not leave the Levee alive this night unless you give yourself up at once, Elsie. I promise I will see to it that you are not molested. That was not my idea in any case."[5]

"Really? Whose was it then, Bathhouse, if not yours?" Elsie asked, even though she had known since her moment of recognition in New York that Jake Slaney was the man who had kidnapped her. But she still suspected that Abe himself had planned the crime.

"Was it Abe's idea?" she now asked Coughlin, hoping he might give something away.

Coughlin looked genuinely astonished and said, "I don't know what you're talking about, Elsie. Abe is dead, as you must be aware. The truth is, Elsie, I don't know why you were brought here. I was simply asked to accompany Mr. Perdue tonight. I had no idea what he had in mind, believe me. I just went along because I was afraid to cross him. You were right to shoot him, Elsie, absolutely right, and I'm glad you did it. He was a terrible man. Now, before you do something foolish, you must let me help you. I can get you out of here. All you need to do is put down that gun."

"So that you and your men can have your way with me? I think not," Elsie said. "I would go to hell first. You are a liar to the core, Bathhouse, and always have been.

But I promise you this: if I die tonight, you will die with me. Now, go find that ammunition and don't try any tricks. I assure you I am an excellent shot and that you are a very large target."

Elsie slipped on Coughlin's shirt and coat as he went over to search Perdue's body. The coat, she noticed, had a heavy item in one pocket that turned out to be a .32 caliber Colt revolver almost identical to the one she had left behind in England. She left the revolver where it was, pleased that she had now added a second weapon to her arsenal.[6]

Coughlin's coat was so big that it came down to her knees, and Elsie decided there was no point in trying on his pants as well, since she would drown in them. With the shirt and coat, she was at least decently covered, even if in a most ridiculous fashion.

"I can't seem to find any bullets," said Coughlin, who had bent down over Perdue's body and was rummaging through his pockets.

"Fine," Elsie said. "I will just shoot you now and find them myself. Do you doubt my words, Bathhouse?"

"Now take it easy, Elsie, take it easy. I'm looking. Ah, here we are."

She kept her gun trained on Coughlin as he came back toward her, holding a half-dozen or so bullets in his hand. Then, when he got within about six feet, she said, "That's far enough. Just set the bullets on the floor and then go stand over by your friends. Oh, and you'll keep your hands in the air if you know what's good for you."

As she scooped up the bullets, Coughlin made one more attempt to talk her out of trying to escape.

"You really should listen to me, Elsie," he said. "If you try to leave now, there'll be a price on your head in five minutes, and word travels fast through the Levee. Every street will have a hundred eyes looking for you, and every building, every yard, every nook and cranny will be swarming with men eager to claim you as their prize. It will be but the work of an hour at most to hunt you down, and then, even I will not be able to protect you from a terrible fate."

Elsie, however, was not interested in further talk about surrendering. "Put on your pants, Bathhouse," she said. "You're leaving with me right now."

"Where are we going? As I told you, there's no hope of escape. I'm sure that a thousand dollars"—he placed particular emphasis on the amount—"will go to the man who can bring you in, dead or alive. What chance will you have, Elsie?"

"Better than yours if you cross me," she said. She pointed to the door at the far end of the room, opposite where Coughlin and his men had entered. "Where does that lead?"

"Outside, to the backyard," Coughlin said.

"I trust you are not trying to deceive me, Bathhouse."

"I'm not lying," he insisted.

"Good, then we will be on our way," Elsie said, marching Coughlin over toward his two henchmen, who still lay with arms outstretched on the floor. She said, "If either of you try to follow us, I will kill Bathhouse. If I ever see either of you again, I will kill Bathhouse. If anybody tries to approach us, I will kill Bathhouse. The only way Bathhouse will survive this night is if I do as well. Tell that to those who would come searching for us."

Then, with a wave of her pistol, she directed Coughlin to the door, which he opened with a key, and they went down a set of rickety wooden steps and into the humid Chicago night.

Chapter Thirty-three

§ ξ

"It Was Strictly a Delivery Job"

FROM THE NARRATIVE OF DR. JOHN WATSON:

Before we left my room at the Sherman House, Rafferty placed a call to Joseph Pyle in St. Paul. Unfortunately, the editor could not be reached at either his apartment or office, leaving us no choice but to try him later in hopes he could bring the might of James J. Hill to bear upon our situation.

It was just before six o'clock by the time we walked out onto Randolph Street, which was aglow in the early evening sunlight streaming in from the vast prairies to the west. The great stone pile of Chicago City Hall, its closely paired columns casting intricate shadows, loomed directly across from us, while to the east skyscrapers formed impressive escarpments of masonry along either side of the street. Even though a streetcar line ran down Randolph, we elected to walk, since Rafferty assured me that our destination — Union Station — was less than a mile away, just on the other side of the Chicago River.[1]

The evening was hot and unsettled, with dark skies to the northwest holding out the possibility of a storm. Despite my anxiety over the fate of Holmes and Elsie Cubitt, I enjoyed the opportunity to stretch my legs after my long travels. Both of my companions knew Chicago well — Thomas even had "a lady friend" in the city, according to Rafferty—and so I was content to let them lead the way.

We went down Washington Street and into the city's wholesale district, which proved surprisingly quiet. At Wells Street we passed under the elevated line, which forms a giant loop in the center of the city. As I looked up at the forbidding iron structure and heard the roar of passing trains, I could not help but recall my adventures on the Ninth Avenue elevated line in New York on the previous Sunday night, which also marked the last time I had seen Holmes.

Two blocks past Wells we reached the approaches to the south branch of the Chicago River. To my surprise, we did not cross over the river but instead went *under* it, through a tunnel reached by a long descending ramp in the middle of the street. Once we emerged from the tunnel, it was but a walk of two blocks to Union Station.[2]

The station, a surprisingly dingy structure which sported an awkward array of towers and pavilions, was perhaps the busiest of Chicago's numerous railroad depots. It was used by all of the Pennsylvania Railroad's trains, as well as those of several other lines arriving from or departing to the East. If Holmes and Mrs. Cubitt had been taken to Chicago by train, then the odds were that they had arrived at this station.[3]

Our plan was to split up so as to use our time as efficiently as possible. We hoped to find someone—a conductor, porter, teamster, hackman, freight handler or other worker—who might have seen a coffin being taken from a train in the last day or two. Rafferty planned to talk to teamsters and hackmen outside the depot, while Thomas was to interview porters, conductors and other railroad personnel. My assignment was to locate a freight agent or anyone else who might have records of recently shipped coffins.

However, before we had a chance to split up, Rafferty noticed a hearse parked outside the station amid the usual line of hansoms. The name stenciled on its side identified the hearse as belonging to "Livingston Mortuary, Chicago." A suitably somber-looking man, dressed in a black coat and matching stovepipe hat, sat in the driver's seat.

We walked over to the hearse, where Rafferty with his usual bonhomie introduced himself.

"Evenin', sir, and what a fine one it is," he began. "You must be waitin' for a customer. I imagine you're often called upon to pick up corpses here."

The undertaker, who had a long pale face with sunken cheeks and dark sorrowful eyes, replied rather stiffly that he did indeed make occasional visits to the station on business.

"Have you been here in the past day or two by chance?" Rafferty asked.

"Why do you ask, sir?"

"Well, I'm mighty embarrassed to admit it, but I was supposed to be here on Monday, or maybe it was Tuesday, to take receipt of my dear Aunt Emma, from New York, who is to be buried up at Graceland tomorrow. The sad fact is, I got involved in a most intriguin' poker game—you know how such things go—and, before I knew it, I'd forgotten all about my sweet old aunt, may she rest in peace. Now, I can't seem to find her corpse—the railroad for some reason has no record of the body leavin' New York—and I'll be damned if I can remember which funeral parlor here was supposed to pick her up. It wouldn't have been you, would it?"[4]

The undertaker stared suspiciously at Rafferty and said, "I have never known the railroads to lose a corpse, sir, and in any event it is the policy of the Livingston Mortuary to exercise the utmost discretion when dealing with families in their time of grief. As you are a complete stranger to me, and as your story is so highly improbable as to be unbelievable, I can tell you nothing about any corpse which may have been transferred by our mortuary."

Rafferty nodded and said, "I see. Well, sir, just let me say that it's a regular marvel to find here in Chicago a man as honest and discrete as yourself. I'm impressed, sir, powerfully impressed. In fact, I'm so impressed that I would like to reward you with a personal donation"—here he took out a ten-dollar gold piece and rolled it around in the palm of his hand—"since I imagine you're always looking for a bit of extra money with which to aid widows, orphans and others in need of charity. Naturally, I'd still be interested in hearin' anything you might know about my dear departed aunt."

The undertaker's icy manner abruptly changed and he said, "I must say it is most kind of you, sir, to contribute to those in need. It is obvious that you are a gentleman of the best sort, and so perhaps I can be of some assistance to you after all."

"I thought so. Now then, about my aunt, can you tell me anything, Mr.—ah, I don't think I caught your name."

"Van Ness, sir. Timothy Van Ness. It is a pleasure to be at your service."

"All right, Mr. Van Ness, let us see if you can earn the donation I have in mind. Am I right in thinkin' you've picked up a coffin here in recent days?"

"You are, sir. I picked up one yesterday and transported it, though I do not know the name of the deceased."

"I see. Which train did the corpse arrive on?"

"The *Chicago and St. Louis Express*, at about four in the afternoon."

My heart sank at this news, since I believed that Holmes and Elsie Cubitt would have been smuggled aboard the *Pennsylvania Limited*, the fastest train between New York and Chicago. Certainly, I reasoned, they could not have been on any train traveling from St. Louis to Chicago. However, I soon learned that I had committed a cardinal sin—one that Holmes himself always warned against—by leaping to a conclusion ahead of the facts.

"I have not heard of that train," Rafferty said. "Where does it come from?"

"The afternoon train comes in from the East—I believe it originates in New York City—and then goes on to St. Louis," Van Ness replied.

"Very well. Now, who hired you to pick up the coffin here?"

"The person who ordered the pickup identified himself over the telephone as a Mr. Holmes—he gave no first name—and sent along payment in cash. That is all I can tell you. He said only that the deceased was a relative. Judging by the weight of the body, I'd say it was a woman or a very small man."

By this time, I was so used to Holmes's name being misappropriated that I hardly paid heed to this latest reference. Instead, I felt a burst of excitement to learn that we appeared to be closing in on Elsie Cubitt and perhaps Holmes as well.

"Incidentally, did you notice anything unusual about the corpse?" Rafferty now asked Van Ness.

"Unusual, sir? What do you mean?"

"Well, to be blunt, I've always had a great fear of being buried alive. There was nothing to indicate to you, I suppose, that a living person might be inside the casket?"

"Good gracious, sir, had there been even the slightest hint that such was the case, I assure you the casket would have been opened at once."

"But I take it that absent such evidence, you saw no reason to inspect the corpse."

"No reason whatsoever, sir."

Now came the question which I had been waiting for, knowing that Rafferty would get around to it in due time.

"By the way, Mr. Van Ness, am I safe in assumin' you're still in possession of the corpse?"

"Oh, no sir. It was strictly a delivery job. I took the casket, as per Mr. Holmes's request, to the Everleigh Club."

Even Rafferty seemed surprised by this news. "Since when are caskets delivered to whorehouses?"

"I must admit, sir, that it was an odd sort of request," Van Ness said. "However, it is not my place to dispute with a paying customer. I agree that the Everleigh hardly seems a fit place for a wake, but as I said, I just took the casket where I was told to."

"What time did you drop the casket off?"

"It would have been about six o'clock last night."

"Who took receipt of it?"

"Two large gentlemen who met me at the back door. They were not overly friendly and I did not linger, since there is nothing but trouble to be found in the Levee."

Rafferty asked several more questions, but it became apparent that Van Ness could tell us little more, so Rafferty paid him and we went on our way. I remarked that it had been "great good fortune" to find the undertaker. Rafferty, however, was not so sure, nor was Thomas.

Said Rafferty, "Do you not find it odd, doctor, that we were able to waltz right up to the station and find the very answer we were lookin' for without so much as breakin' a sweat?"

"Holmes has often stated that luck comes to those who are best prepared to receive it," I noted. "You may call it luck, Mr. Rafferty, but I prefer to believe that we deserved the luck that came our way just now."

Rafferty scratched his head and stopped to light one of his execrable cigars. Then he turned to Thomas and said, "What about you, Wash? What do you make of our good fortune today?"

"I'm with you on this one," Thomas said. "Something doesn't smell right."

Rafferty nodded in agreement as he looked out over the crowded scene in front of the station, where hackmen were constantly arriving or leaving with passengers and baggage.

"Maybe there's a way to find out if we were lucky or if we just got taken," he said. "Follow me."

We walked back toward the front of the station, where a heavyset doorman armed with a police whistle and wearing a dark blue uniform was busy directing passengers to cabs lined up at the curb. Rafferty strode up to the man and without preamble pressed a five-dollar gold piece into his hand.

"If you can give me a minute of your valuable time, sir, to answer one or two simple questions, there will be another five dollars in it for you."

The doorman, who had a broad creased face and wary gray eyes, let the whistle fall from his mouth and said, "Ask away, friend, but don't try to stiff me or you'll pay for it."

Rafferty pointed to the hearse, which I now saw was pulling away, and asked, "How long was that undertaker parked here today?"

"He's been here since I came on duty at eight this morning. He was here yesterday, too."

"Do you know him by name?"

"Can't say that I do. This was the first time I've seen him here. Now, by my count, that's two questions."

Rafferty handed over another gold piece and asked, "Did you have occasion to chat with the fellow at all while he was waiting?"

"I did, as I was curious what he was doing. I asked him if he was waiting for Methuselah to die. He thought that was pretty funny."

"Ah, you are indeed quite the wit, sir. Did the undertaker say who he was really waiting for?"

"He did."

The doorman suddenly went silent, like a clock that had wound down. With a sigh, Rafferty dug deeper into his pocket and produced another gold piece. "All right," he said to the doorman, "let's hear it."

"Certainly. The undertaker told me he was waiting to pick up the casket of a very important gentleman from New York who was to have his wake at the Sons of Hibernia Hall."

"I see. Where is this hall and what is it?"

"It's down at Twenty-first and South Dearborn, right across from the car barns. You can't miss it. As to what it is, I've heard it's a clubhouse of sorts for all the gangsters who infest the Levee."

Rafferty rubbed his chin and asked, "How far would the hall be from the Everleigh Club?"

"It's on the same block," the doorman said. "Now, if you have any more questions—"

"I think not," Rafferty said, "or I will soon be bankrupt."

"Well then, have a pleasant day, sir."

When we had stepped back away from the curb, Thomas said, "Damn, Shad, I knew it. It was a set-up all the way."

"So it was, just like the invitation to Mr. Holmes's supposed wedding. We're being led like sheep to the slaughter, Wash, and that's a fact."

"Are you saying that Van Ness was simply waiting for us to show up and ask about a coffin so he could direct us to the Everleigh Club?" I asked.

"Precisely. The person who plotted the abduction of Mr. Holmes and Mrs. Cubitt wants to make sure that we're part of the big show, too."

"Then there will be a trap waiting for us at the Everleigh Club."

"You can count on that, doctor. But if we play our cards right, maybe we won't be the ones caught in it, especially if Mr. Van Ness was telling the truth about delivering the casket to the Sons of Hibernia Hall."

"He could be lying about that as well," I pointed out.

"True enough," said Rafferty. "But why would he, since he presumably wasn't paid to tell the doorman a lie, as was the case with us? In any case, I think we'd best go back to your hotel, doctor, and make some plans before we venture out tonight. It'll also give us a chance to shed the spies who've been followin' us."

"Spies?" I repeated. "Do you mean—"

"There's at least two of them," Rafferty said. "Been trailin' Wash and me ever since we got to Chicago. I imagine someone's been following you, too, doctor. Didn't you notice?"

I confessed that I had not.

Chapter Thirty-four

"Perhaps I Am Being Too Hard on You"

When Elsie Cubitt and Bathhouse John Coughlin reached the bottom of Hibernia Hall's back stairs, she ordered him to stop. "Let's just see if your friends have decided to follow us," she said.

They had, and as the door at the top of the steps swung open, Elsie Cubitt pressed her pistol into one of the folds of skin at the back of Coughlin's neck and said, "If I were you Bathhouse, I would tell them to leave at once."

"Now, don't do anything foolish, Elsie," Coughlin said. "I'll take care of the problem." He shouted out, "Don't come this way, boys, or the lady will shoot. She means business. Go back and do what you need to do. I will be all right."

Once she heard the door above slam shut, Elsie Cubitt took a deep breath and turned her attention to what lay ahead. They were in a small rear vestibule, and she pushed open the door to look outside. It was not an encouraging view. The door opened onto a small backyard that ended in a junk-strewn alley hemmed in by low brick buildings. There were no lampposts in the alley, and what little light there was came through the windows of adjoining buildings and from a single electric bulb over the hall's back door.

Elsie Cubitt said, "Now, Bathhouse, you will tell me three things. I wish to know the day and the time and also exactly where we are. If I find you have lied to me, I will kill you."

Coughlin, who more than once had disarmed a patron of his famously tough tavern with a few well-chosen words, tried the same approach with his captor. "Listen, Elsie, you've got to be reasonable about this. As I told you before, there's no escaping unless you let me help you. If you kill me, why—"

"Spare me," Elsie Cubitt said, pushing the barrel of her pistol deeper into Coughlin's fleshy neck. "You have missed the point, Bathhouse. Do you think I wish to live so that you and your cutthroats can enjoy the opportunity to violate me? Now, I will not ask you again. Answer my questions or so help me I will end your miserable life right here. Do not try my patience further."

Coughlin was a good judge of men, but much less so in the case of women, whom he believed to be delicate, easily cowed but unpredictable creatures. Yet even he could sense that Elsie Cubitt meant every word of what she had said.

"All right, Elsie, take it easy," he said. "It's Wednesday, July 18, and it's about half past ten. We're at the back of Hibernia Hall, on Dearborn just south of Twenty-first."

It was just as Elsie Cubitt had suspected, and feared. She was in the very heart of the Levee, surrounded by saloons, brothels, gambling halls and opium dens. The two men she had left behind in the hall would quickly spread news of her escape—and of the ransom offered by Bathhouse—to every criminal, vagrant and drunkard in the area. The district's streets would quickly swarm with men desperate to obtain the ransom, and even with her valuable hostage, the odds of escaping were infinitesimal. Nor did she think the police would be of any help, since she knew from her father's criminal career that the cops in Chicago had long since been paid off by men like Coughlin.

Her only chance, she realized, was to buy some time by finding a place to hide, in the hope that Sherlock Holmes, if he was still alive, might come to her aid. But where to hide? And how would she reach such a place without being seen? As she pondered these questions, her mind racing, she noticed a second door to one side of the vestibule. The door was ajar and all beyond was dark.

"Where does that door lead to?" she demanded.

"The cellar," Coughlin said.

"What's down there?"

"It is just an old storage room, full of rats and spiders."

Elsie Cubitt had an inspiration. Backing away from Coughlin and warning him not to move, she reached beneath the long coat she was wearing and ripped off a piece of the flimsy shift beneath.

"All right, John, let's go," she said, pushing him out the door and into the alley, where they turned south, in the direction of the Everleigh Club at the far end of the block. Somewhere in the distance Elsie could hear the mad tinkling of a piano and drunken voices singing a wildly off-key rendition of a sentimental song whose chorus repeated the words "Dear Midnight of Love."[1]

"Ah, they're singing my song, Elsie," Coughlin said. "You see, I'm not such a bad fellow after all. If you would only trust me—"

"I'd put my faith in Satan first," said Elsie. "That's far enough, Bathhouse."

They were halfway down the alley, behind a two-story brick building typical of those on the block. A rat's haven of trash and debris—boards with nails sticking out, bricks, broken furniture and old pieces of pottery, all garnished with discarded food and other household offal—

lay heaped up into a ragged pile beside the building's back door, illuminated by a single overhead light.

"Why are we stopping here, Elsie?" Coughlin asked.

Elsie Cubitt ignored the question as she draped the torn piece of her shift on a long nail protruding from one of the boards. The effect was to make it look as though the cloth had torn off and become snagged as she walked past.

"All right, we can go back now," Elsie Cubitt said.

"Back? What do you mean?"

"You'll see, Bathhouse. It's my intent to hide in the last place anybody will look for us."

They retraced their steps to Hibernia Hall where, to Coughlin's surprise, he was directed to go back into the building.

"We'll go down into the basement," Elsie said. "Light a match so that I can see the way."

"Very well," Coughlin said, striking a match, which showed a flight of steep, narrow steps leading down into the gloom. "But it's really unpleasant down there, my dear. Why, I have seen rats the size of—"

"The biggest rat of all is right before me," Elsie said. "Now, down you go and be quiet about it."

Coughlin had taken only a few steps when he turned around and whispered, "Perhaps you should shut the door, Elsie, so that no one will be able to hear us from above."

Elsie almost complied before she realized that Coughlin was up to a crude attempt at trickery. The door to the cellar was badly warped and had probably been ajar for years. Any searchers seeing it closed would immediately suspect that someone had gone down the basement.

"We will leave it just as it was," she said, "and if you try to call for help, Bathhouse, you know what the result will be."

When they reached the bottom of the steps, Coughlin struck another match and Elsie saw that the cellar was as he had described it—damp, dirty and littered with odds and ends. There were rusted tools, lamps and other fixtures, several old tables and chairs, and—most incongruously— a beautifully carved wooden horse, its head severed from its body, that must have come from an old merry-go-round. She wondered how it had ended up in the basement. Coughlin soon provided the answer.

"Ah, will you look at that," he said, sounding genuinely nostalgic. "Lady Godiva's horse. That's what we used to call it, Elsie, as it could only be ridden by ladies not burdened by clothes. Yes indeed, there were some fine parties in the old days up in the hall. Fine parties! Too bad you weren't here to enjoy them."

The latest leering comment was almost enough to make Elsie want to shoot Coughlin on the spot, as a general service to womankind, but she knew she must not succumb to her desire for revenge while there was still a chance, however small, to make an escape.

She instructed Coughlin to light one more match. In its flickering light, she saw, near the doorway they had just come through, the outlines of a large wooden bin—probably used for coal—extending out from the basement wall. She also saw, on one of the tables, a candle resting in a cracked saucer.

"Over there," she said, motioning to Coughlin with her pistol. "Light that candle, leave it on the table and then move, very slowly, over behind the coal bin and sit down."

"Your wish is my command," Coughlin said, following her instructions without protest.

Elsie then picked up the candle and came around to one side of Coughlin, who sat with his back to the wall and his hands resting on his knees. Making sure to stay far enough away so that he couldn't grab the pistol, she sat down and let the candle rest between them, her pistol all the while trained on Coughlin.

"Well, then, what's it to be, Elsie?" he asked. "Do you really think the two of us can hide out here for long? This will be the first place my men look."

"Possibly. But it could also be the last."

Coughlin hated to admit it, but he knew she was right. Leaving a piece of her clothes in the alley had been a clever stroke, and it would send his men off in the wrong direction, at least for a while. Still, he believed it only a matter of time before they were found. The question then was what she would do. Coughlin knew that if Elsie Cubitt was pushed into a corner, with no hope of escape, she might indeed shoot him out of spite. As there was nothing dearer to him than his own skin, he wanted desperately to avoid such a fate. Talk had always been his best ally, and he still believed she might be vulnerable to his blandishments since she was, after all, a woman. Besides, Coughlin was of the opinion that no woman could resist his many charms for long.

"It is a fine fix we are in here, Elsie," he whispered, "and I've been wondering just what your father Eban would have done in a situation like this. Of course, his first goal would be your well-being, and believe it or not, my dear, that is also mine. Your abduction, as I've told you, was not my idea—indeed, I had nothing to do with it—and I've only been playing along with the kidnappers because, frankly, I was afraid not to."

Elsie Cubitt responded with a withering look. Who, she wondered, could possibly fall for such ridiculous lies? She said, "Is that so, Bathhouse? Then why is it that I did not notice any protest on your part as Mr. Perdue prepared to do his brutal work? Indeed, you seemed quite willing to join in with him."

Coughlin gave his big head a slow shake and tried to fix a look of absolute sincerity on his handsome face. "I was merely waiting for the best opportunity to try and stop him. But as you saw, he is a frightful man when aroused. Why— and this is the God's truth, Elsie—I didn't even know you were the woman to be broken in. I simply went up to the hall with Mr. Perdue at his request, as he said he had something he wished to show me. When I saw that you were his intended victim, I played along at first but I swear to you I was all the while trying to figure out how I might stop him from satisfying his vicious lust. That's not important now, however. What is important for you to know is that I'm in a position at this moment to help you, if you will only let me."

Elsie Cubitt's first instinct was simply to laugh at Coughlin's absurd, almost childish mendacity, but she quickly thought better of it. Coughlin was clearly one of those men who had listened so long to his own bombast that he had lost all ability to distinguish it from the truth. She was also struck by a certain dim obliviousness in his manner—Hinky Dink Kenna, Elsie's father had always said, was the real brains behind the Levee's spectacularly profitable vice trade.

Now, Elsie realized, Coughlin might prove useful if he could be led into revealing who was behind her kidnapping. Coughlin's look of honest bewilderment in response to her mention of Abe's name earlier had convinced Elsie that the murderer of her husband truly was dead. That seemed to leave Jake as the culprit, and Elsie now looked for final confirmation that he was indeed the man who had caused her such misery and terror.

She said, "Perhaps I am being too hard on you, Bathhouse. My abduction required the most careful planning, not to mention enormous patience and resourcefulness. At first, I thought Abe might be behind it, despite the fact he was thought to be dead. But now I realize how wrong

I was. After all, Abe—as you well know—was not a patient or calculating man."

"Ah, you have spoken the truth there, Elsie. Abe was quicksilver. He always hated waiting for anything, which is why he went chasing after you in England as soon as he had the chance."

"And it cost him his life. I confess that I have always felt bad about that, Bathhouse. I really did love Abe. I imagine his death sent Jake into a rage, and you and I both know how Jake would feel toward anyone he held responsible for the death of his big brother. He would want revenge and he would go to the ends of the earth to get it, no matter how long it might take. Jake was always a schemer, unlike poor Abe. Isn't that so, Bathhouse?"

"Yes, I guess you could say Jake was like that," Coughlin agreed, but there was something about the way he spoke of Jake in the past tense that caught Elsie's attention.

She now took a wild stab in the dark. "Too bad Jake's dead as well," she said. Elsie spoke these words with such matter-of-fact assurance that Coughlin was caught completely off guard, "How did you—I mean, what makes you think that?"

"Your face," she replied, adding, "I have seen better liars than you in grade school, Bathhouse."

Elsie had not been surprised to discover that Jake Slaney was her kidnapper. In the old days Jake had pursued her even more ardently than his older brother. Once—in a drunken rage—he had even tried to take her by force. He was also far more sly and manipulative than Abe, one of many reasons why Elsie had rejected him from the very start. Yet despite his cleverness, Jake had never struck Elsie as a brilliant criminal mastermind. That kind of intelligence, she believed, simply didn't run in the Slaney family.

"So what happened to Jake?" Elsie asked, trying another tack. "Did he run afoul of Mr. Holmes?"

Coughlin now had his own moment of inspiration. "Yes," he said. "Fact is, the both of them are dead, Elsie, killed in a fight on the train. There is no one to save you now, is there?"

Elsie felt her stomach tighten into a knot but did not give Coughlin the satisfaction of thinking she might actually believe him. "As I have said all along, Bathhouse, you are a poor excuse for a liar."

"Ah, the truth hurts, doesn't it Elsie. Your lover is gone and—"

Elsie broke in, "I will hear no more of this, for if I believed that Mr. Holmes was dead, I would have no reason to go on living under the present circumstances. Neither," she added ominously, leveling her pistol at Coughlin's forehead, "would you."

After a period of silence, Elsie continued, "Now, then, why don't you try telling the truth, Bathhouse, while you still have the chance? Since you have promised to help me, I would like to know who besides Jake and yourself arranged for my kidnapping."

"I understand," Coughlin replied, "but I think we should get to a place of safety before we do anything else. There must be hundreds of men already combing the Levee in hopes of finding you. Now, if you'd just put that pistol down and—"

"No, you must answer my question first, Bathhouse. Otherwise, how can I be sure that you are really my friend?"

"Oh ye of little faith," Coughlin intoned. "The pistol, Elsie, you must at least put it down or there is nothing I can do for you."

It was now obvious Coughlin had no intention of telling her more, and Elsie realized that he must have finally figured out that she could not afford to give their position away by firing her gun. At the same time, she was convinced that he did indeed believe she would shoot him if left with no other choice.

"We are at a stalemate, aren't we Bathhouse," she said.

"So it would seem," Coughlin agreed. "Well, what do you intend to do now, Elsie? You can't wait here forever."

"True, but I can wait here for a while, and that is what I intend to do."

"Wait for what?"

"Deliverance," Elsie Cubitt said calmly, "or death."

Chapter Thirty-five

§ ℞

"Trouble Is, We're Not the Indians"

FROM THE NARRATIVE OF DR. JOHN WATSON:

Rafferty, Thomas and I returned to the Sherman House at half past seven — our shadows not far behind, according to Rafferty — and went up to my room. We smoked and talked, reviewing once again the extraordinary series of events which had brought us to America's great inland city in search of Sherlock Holmes and Elsie Cubitt. Then, as darkness began to nestle into the windy canyons of the Loop, we made final preparations for our visit to the Levee.

We would start at the Sons of Hibernia Hall, where we believed the coffin used to transport Elsie Cubitt — or perhaps Sherlock Holmes — had been taken. From there, we intended to go wherever the evidence led us, quite possibly to the Everleigh Club. Because Rafferty was convinced that a trap of some kind lay waiting, he insisted that we "go fully prepared into battle." In his case, that meant arming himself with a daunting array of weaponry.

His "personal arsenal," as he called it, included a large .44 caliber revolver tucked into his belt, a spring-loaded derringer hidden beneath his left coat sleeve, a curious long-barreled pistol with a detachable stock which he referred to as his "pocket rifle" and a knife strapped above one of his ankles. Thomas was also well-armed, equipping himself with a small club, a pistol and a short-barreled shotgun which could be secreted under his long raincoat. My Colt revolver, of course, had been taken in New York, but Rafferty provided me with an almost identical model from his private armory.[1]

While we waited for the last traces of daylight to give way, I asked Rafferty how difficult it would be to rescue Holmes and Mrs. Cubitt from the Everleigh Club, if they were indeed being held there. "From your description," I noted, "the place sounds as well-protected as a bank vault. It cannot be so with all the brothels in this city."

"No, the Everleigh is unique, from what I know, simply because of how much money it rakes in. There's a regular at my saloon who subscribes to the Chicago *Tribune*, and he often leaves it behind for me to read. I saw a story not long ago estimatin' that the Everleigh, on a good Saturday night, might do five thousand dollars or more worth of business."

"I think we might have grossed that much in a month—once or twice," Thomas said, referring to the saloon he and Rafferty owned in St. Paul.

"Ah, you're dreamin', Wash," Rafferty said with a grin. "Be that as it may, five thousand dollars for one night's business is an awful lot of money. When it comes to the eternal business of carnal recreation, 'twould seem the Everleigh is a regular golden goose. That's why it's so well-guarded. The fact that the club is strictly for swells— the story I read called it the 'millionaires' whorehouse'— means it'll be protected by the police in exchange for the usual payoffs. The place will also have its own crew of hired toughs to make sure only the right people get in. I'm afraid we'll have a devil of a time gettin' Mr. Holmes and Mrs. Cubitt out of there, if that's where they are."

"So what shall we do?"

"Improvise," said Rafferty, who went over to the window and peered out across Randolph Street toward city hall. "Well, it looks dark as can be out there, so we should be on our way."

Rafferty, who could be as ingenious as Holmes in his own way, had already hit upon a method of "shaking" the two men he believed would follow us from the hotel. We put his plan into effect in the lobby, where Rafferty assumed the "spies," as he called them, would be waiting for us. The lobby of the Sherman House was one of those large, boisterous and somewhat garish rooms favored by American hotels of a certain class. The hotel was said to be a favorite of salesmen and other business travelers, and the lobby was abuzz with knots of men engaged in animated—and presumably lucrative—conversations. I glanced over the lobby as we came down the steps but saw no one who looked notably out of place or who seemed to take any unusual interest in our arrival.

Even so, in accord with Rafferty's instructions, the three of us made a point of stopping in the lobby, talking as though engrossed in some profoundly important matter and then conspicuously separating. Rafferty and Thomas slipped out a rear entrance while I waited awhile before going out the front door. Once outside, I turned east on Randolph and north on Clark Street until I reached an alley at the rear of the hotel. A single light burned some distance down the alley over the hotel's back entrance. The feeble light was just sufficient for me to make out a large, shadowy figure walking toward me. Then, somewhere in the gloom behind the figure, I heard a loud thump, followed by a strangled cry.

The figure, who had paid no heed to the noise behind him, continued walking toward me until I could make out the unmistakable features of his face. "Ah, doctor, it appears there has been an accident in the alley," said Rafferty. "A certain gentleman who came out the back door of the hotel has somehow bumped his head into a billy club. I fear the poor fellow will be out of commission for some time."

Thomas now came running up the alley to join us, carrying the small club which had been the cause of the "accident." He made a point of tapping the weapon into the palm of his hand as though to show us exactly how he had dispatched the "spy." Rafferty patted him on the shoulder and said in his booming voice, "Well, gentlemen, we will be bothered no more tonight. Now, let us be about our business."

As we walked up toward the elevated station on Lake Street, Rafferty said to me, almost in a whisper, "That's one down, doctor, and one to go. But if we've done a good job of actin,' the other spy, who undoubtedly followed you out of the hotel, will think we've let our guard down. That'll make it easier to get rid of him when the time comes."

"What does this second 'spy' look like?" I asked.

"Why, I have no idea," Rafferty said with a shrug. "Fact is, I've never seen him."

"Then how do you know he exists?"

"Because he has to," Rafferty replied with blithe assurance. "'Tis impossible for one man to follow anyone, as Mr. Holmes well knows. There are just too many ways to lose your quarry. No, whoever has gone to all the trouble of plannin' this gigantic caper would not be stupid enough to make do with a single spy watchin' all three of us. There must be at least two, and perhaps even more than that. Shakin' them will be our next task."

At Lake Street, we walked up a covered stairway to the elevated station, which resembled a small house incongruously perched above the street amid the ranks of towering office blocks all around it. While we waited for a train, Rafferty explained that two sets of tracks formed the downtown loop. Trains on the inner loop went in a clockwise direction, while those on the outer loop ran the other way.

"'Tis time for us now to do the loop-de-loop," Rafferty said as a train approached.

There were perhaps two dozen people on the plat-form—including at least half that number who had come up to the station only after our arrival—and the "spy" whose existence Rafferty had postulated was presumably among them. I saw no one who looked particularly suspi-cious, although I realized that the very purpose of any "spy" would be to appear as ordinary as possible. Lights now approached down the tracks, and the wooden plat-form vibrated as a train pulled in with the usual sonic fan-fare. We boarded and were soon off on what was to be one of the shortest and most curious series of train rides in my life.

The "loop-de-loop," which Rafferty had spoken of proved to be just that, for minutes after boarding the first train and rounding a tight curve amid much squealing and screeching, we alit at another downtown station, on Wabash Avenue. We then walked under the tracks and back up to the station on the other side. As we waited for the next train, I scanned the crowd, trying to spot anyone who looked familiar but had no success. Rafferty later told me, however, that he recognized one man who had boarded with us at Lake Street.

All told, we repeated this crossing maneuver three times, the last of which allowed us to slip into a northbound train just seconds before it left the station. As we were clearly the last persons to board the train, Rafferty felt certain that we had lost whoever might be following us.

"All right, doctor," he said as the train lurched for-ward, "we have but one more switch to make and then we can head toward the Levee."

As it so happened, we proceeded to the very station on Lake Street where we had started our circling tour. We again crossed to the other platform and boarded a train bound for the south side. A few blocks after we had finally left the downtown loop, the train took a sharp turn, and I was surprised to see that we were proceeding down what looked to be an alley, as opposed to a street.

"Now you see why they call this the Alley El," Rafferty said. "'Twas too expensive, I'm told, to secure street rights so the builders went down alleys instead. It won't be long now until we reach our stop."[2]

Although there was a station at Twenty-second Street, within a block or so of the Sons of Hibernia Hall, we got off at Eighteenth, to give us "a little wiggle room," as Rafferty put it. We were now near the northern boundary of the Levee, said to offer the most concentrated collection of vice establishments on the continent. It was also known to be a very dangerous place, its streets teeming with footpads, pickpockets, hooligans, dope fiends, cadets (as the district's procurers were known) and all other manner of human refuse.

Even so, I did not feel completely uncomfortable in this sordid environment, for I had seen it in some detail four years earlier, after Holmes had been called to Chicago to investigate a sensitive matter for Potter Palmer, the hotel and real estate tycoon. Holmes, who was fascinated by the criminal mind in all of its manifestations, had insisted on visiting the Levee. Detective Wooldridge had served as our guide on that memorable tour, and I found myself wishing that he could be with us now.[3]

We took a circuitous route toward the Sons of Hibernia Hall, since Rafferty continued to fear an ambush. The streets were busy, and the sounds of merriment—piano music, laughter, loud voices—wafted out from open windows into the warm, and increasingly windy, night. The establishments which made up the Levee were housed in a maze of old brick buildings, some with surprisingly elegant facades, others looking close to ruin. Many of the clubs sported gaudy signs, but a few gave no indication of their purpose.

"'Tis a known fact," Rafferty said, "that the larger the sign, the cheaper the entertainment. I imagine a club like the Everleigh would require no sign at all."

After walking several blocks, we saw large streetcar barns off to our right, an indication that we were at last approaching Dearborn Street. Holding down the corner at Twenty-first was an unremarkable brick building, two stories high, with large windows on the upper floor. A faded sign announced it to be the Sons of Hibernia Hall, and lights shone through every window.

"Looks like a busy night at the hall," Rafferty said. "I'd like to know who's in there and what they're doing."

"I can find out," Thomas said.

"Perhaps we should all go in," I cautioned. "There may be safety in numbers."

"No, 'twould not be wise," Rafferty said, then turned to Thomas and said, "Are you plannin' what I think you are, Wash?"

"It's worked before," Thomas said cryptically.

"All right, but be careful and don't stay any longer than you have to."

"Just what do you intend to do?" I asked Thomas.

"Play the invisible man," he said, and began at once to disarrange his clothes, after which he pulled out a small flask of whisky and splashed a few drops on his face. He also took off his light raincoat and, to my surprise, handed his shotgun, pistol and billy club to Rafferty.

"If they were to find a weapon on Wash, the situation inside could get nasty in a hurry," Rafferty explained. "He'll be safer without them."

"I'll whistle if I need any help," Thomas said and then walked up to the front entrance of the hall, on Dearborn.

We waited a few moments and crossed to the other side of the street. "What does Mr. Thomas mean by being invisible?" I asked Rafferty.

"He means, doctor, that a black man can move almost invisibly in the white world. Whoever answers his knock won't see a potential threat as he might if it was you or I poundin' at the door. He'll see only a poor black man—and one who appears to be drunk, at that—and he'll figure such a fellow can be of no danger or consequence."

We watched from across the street as Thomas pounded on the door with his fists until it was opened by a very large man, dressed in dark trousers and a white shirt. Thomas shouted something incomprehensible and then barged inside past the startled man.

"Should we go in after him?" I asked.

"Not unless we have to," Rafferty said.

The door remained open and I soon heard more yelling inside the hall. Not long thereafter, the man who had answered the door and an equally large companion reappeared, holding Thomas between them.

"Go on, get out of here, you drunken coon," one of the men said as they literally tossed Thomas into the gutter, "and stay out if you know what's good for you."

After the door had slammed shut, Thomas got to his feet and came over to join us.

"Are you all right?" Rafferty asked, for Thomas appeared to have a cut lip.

"I'm fine," he said. "But those are a couple of rough customers in there, I'll tell you that."

"We noticed," Rafferty said with a smile. "What did you see inside?"

"Well, I wasn't in there for long, but I can tell you that I saw no one except for the two bruisers who escorted me out the door. There's certainly no big event going on in the hall, because I didn't hear any noise coming from up-stairs."

Rafferty nodded and said, "What were the two gents doin' when you made your appearance?"

"I don't know what the fellow who answered the door was up to, but the other one was on the telephone. I didn't hear what he was talking about."

"Then I guess we'll have to go in and find out," Rafferty said. "Do you agree, Wash?"

"I do."

"Dr. Watson?"

"I am ready to do whatever is necessary."

"Very well," said Rafferty. "Then I see no choice but to make a frontal assault."

"But what if there are more men inside than just the two Mr. Thomas saw?" I asked.

"Then they'll be much surprised by our boldness," said Rafferty. "Now, here's what we must do . . ."

Some minutes later, after we had made one last check of our weaponry, we walked across the street to the hall. Thomas stationed himself on one side of the door and I on the other. Rafferty, planted squarely between us, then de-livered a series of sharp knocks.

We waited for what seemed like many seconds before the door swung open, revealing the same big man we had seen before. "I told you—" he began, no doubt expecting to encounter Thomas again. Instead, he found himself staring down the barrel of Rafferty's big revolver.

"In you go," Rafferty said, pressing the barrel against the man's forehead and forcing him back into a large foyer.

Thomas and I followed, looking for the second man. But there appeared to be no one else in the foyer, which opened onto a wide staircase presumably leading up to the meeting hall. Draped doorways were located on either side of the foyer. I also noticed a telephone table in one corner, with a straight-backed chair beside it.

"Now, who would you be, sir, and where's your friend?" Rafferty asked the big man, who was nearly Rafferty's size but whose dull brown eyes and lowering brow suggested that he possessed little of Rafferty's intelligence.

"Take it easy with that thing," the man said, his eyes cast upward toward the gun barrel. "The name's Danny Banion. If it's money you're looking for, we don't have any here."

"'Tis not money I'm after, Danny," said Rafferty. "'Tis information, and you're the man who's going to give it to me."

Thomas, shotgun at the ready, now went to check the curtained doorway to our right. I interpreted this as a signal to do the same on the left.

Rafferty, meanwhile, searched Banion for weapons, confiscated a pistol and then cocked the hammer of his own revolver to impress upon Banion the urgency of his inquiries. "Now then, Danny boy, you can begin by tellin' me all about Elsie Cubitt—"

What happened next was yet another remarkable example of Rafferty's talent—I can call it nothing else— for survival. As I approached the draped doorway to his left, I heard a slight rustling sound and was about to shout out a warning when I heard the deafening report of a gunshot. This was followed by a loud cry, after which a man staggered through the curtain, a shotgun dropping from his hands and clattering onto the hard tile floor. The man stumbled, pulled the curtain free of its rod and then, as though wrapping himself in his death shroud, spun around before falling to the floor with a heavy thud. He lay on his back, still breathing, but his eyes were already taking on the fixed glaze of the dead. It was only after I had watched this startling scene that I noticed the smoking derringer in Rafferty's left hand.

While Thomas provided cover in the event other gunmen were nearby, I bent down to look at the man, but it was clear I could do nothing for him. The bullet had gone into the center of his chest, undoubtedly piercing the heart. Whether Rafferty had somehow heard the man or detected a slight movement behind the curtain I was never to learn, for he would later tell me only that he had "felt the man's presence" and had decided it would be "better to shoot than be shot." That his aim was so unerring, despite having to fire through a curtain that concealed his target, only confirmed what Holmes had once told me, which was that Rafferty in the heat of battle was "by far" the most dangerous man he knew.

Rafferty took no interest in the dying man. Instead, he turned to Thomas and said, "Wash, maybe you'd better check the building to see if any more assassins are lurkin' about. I'll deal with our friend Danny."

"Sure thing," said Thomas, who was every bit as fearless as his partner.

As I stood guard by the front door, Rafferty backed Banion up against a wall beside the staircase and said, "By God, Danny, I have killed one man tonight and you will be the next unless you speak the truth and speak it now. Where is the Cubitt woman and where is Sherlock Holmes?"

"I don't know," Banion insisted, the dullness of his eyes replaced by the unmistakable sheen of high terror. "She's not here, I swear it."

Rafferty put one hand around Banion's throat and all but lifted him—and he was, I guessed, easily two hundred pounds—off the floor. "I will not ask you again. Where are they? Tell me now or die. The choice is yours."

"She escaped," Banion blurted out once Rafferty had released his grip. "It is God's truth. It happened not long ago."

Banion looked so sincerely frightened that I could not help but believe him. I suspected Rafferty was of a similar mind, although he gave no indication that this was so.

"What do you mean she escaped?" Rafferty demanded.

Banion now recounted a most remarkable story about how Elsie Cubitt, who as we suspected had been brought to the hall in a coffin, had not only escaped her captors but had killed one of them and kidnapped another! Equally stunning was the news that her captive was none other than John Coughlin, the corrupt alderman said to be one of the bosses of the Levee. Banion, under Rafferty's relentless questioning, also explained just why Mrs. Cubitt had been taken up to the hall . . .

After hearing Banion's sordid story, I felt a surge of anger to think that in our supposedly civilized world there were men as vile as he, Coughlin and their companions. At the same time, I was gratified to know that Elsie Cubitt had escaped their clutches. But as Rafferty questioned Banion at greater length, we soon learned disturbing news, which was that a bounty had been placed on Elsie Cubitt's head and that scores of the most vicious and desperate criminals in the Levee were already hunting for her.

As to Sherlock Holmes's whereabouts, Banion was of no help whatsoever, saying only that he had heard Holmes was supposed to be at the Everleigh Club for an "event" on Friday.

"And just who was plannin' this event?" Rafferty asked.

"Why Bathhouse I suppose," Banion said. "He runs the place, along with Hinky Dink."

Thomas now returned to tell us that he had found only

one other person in the building. "But he won't be bothering us on account of he's got two big holes in his chest. He got shot at very close range by the looks of it."

"Ah, that would be the man killed by Mrs. Cubitt, I suppose," said Rafferty, looking at Banion, who quickly nodded in agreement.

"Now then, Wash, what else did you find?"

"Not much. There's a bunch of small rooms on this floor—probably used as club rooms at one time. They're mostly empty from what I could tell. A hallway between them leads to the back door. There's also another stairway there that goes to the big hall upstairs. I've never seen anything like it. Gives me the creeps, if you want to know the truth."

"What do you mean?" I asked.

Thomas now described the hall and its peculiar furnishings in considerable detail.

"So, 'twould appear we have found one of the Levee's infamous stockades," Rafferty said, directing a murderous stare at the increasingly nervous Banion. "Too bad Mrs. Cubitt didn't put a couple slugs in you as well, Danny boy, though I may yet do it on her behalf."

Rafferty was about to continue his interrogation when there was a loud rap at the door. The door had a peephole and Rafferty bent over to use it.

"Who's out there?" Thomas asked after Rafferty had straightened up.

"At least eight men from what I can see, and they don't look like they're Quakers. All right, Danny, your turn. Go on, take a look."

Banion, prodded by a pistol at the back of his head, peered through the peephole just as a voice from outside shouted, "Come on, open up! We know you've got her, you scumbags."

Rafferty said, "Friends of yours, Danny?"

"I . . . I don't know," Banion replied, but Rafferty had caught the hesitation in his voice.

"You're lyin', Danny, and I am *not* the man you wish to lie to. Now, who are these men?"

The beads of sweat which had long since formed on Banion's forehead were now coalescing into rivulets, and he had taken on the desperate look of a man with no good choices left. "They're cadets," he said, "and I guess they want the reward. They were here before, you know, just to see the woman. But now that she's got away, they're suspicious. I suppose they think me and Joe"—the man shot by Rafferty, I presumed—"pulled a put-up job to get the reward. They've already been drinking and smoking dope half the night and they'll be crazy. For a thousand dollars, they'll kill us in a second, and that's God's truth. We've got to get out of here."

"Open up, goddamnit!" another voice shouted out, followed by a terrific bang as something heavy hit the door.

Rafferty looked through the peephole again and said, "'Twould appear they've found part of an old power pole and intend to batter down the door."

"Let them come," said Thomas, chambering a shell in his shotgun. "I would not mind sending a few pimps to hell."

"Nor would I," Rafferty said, "but I would just as soon not go with them."

There was another loud crash as the frenzied gang outside took a second run at the door. This time they succeeded in punching a gaping hole through one of the upper panels, sending a shower of splinters into the foyer where we stood. Events had obviously taken a dangerous and unexpected turn, and for the first time I began to wonder if we would leave Chicago alive.

Rafferty, however, appeared to have no such doubts, perhaps because he had on so many other occasions cheated death.

"All right, Wash, let's give the cadets somethin' to think about," Rafferty said. "You know what to do. Dr. Watson, I want you to go to the doorway over there"—he pointed to the curtained opening opposite the one in which the dead man lay—"and take cover, as I expect the bullets may start flyin' very soon. Oh, and get out some matches, for we'll have to turn off the lights."

"But what are you and Mr. Thomas—"

"Just go, doctor," Rafferty said. "Wash and I will join you shortly."

"What about me?" Banion complained, panic contorting his features. "I ain't staying here."

"Go with the doctor," Rafferty replied, "but if you get in our way I will take great pleasure in shootin' you down. Understand?"

"Sure, sure," Banion said. "I'm not lookin' for any more trouble tonight."

With Banion rushing ahead of me, I went to the doorway and just had time to see Thomas fire three shotgun blasts through the hole in the door before the lights went out. This was followed by the flash and noise of another weapon—Rafferty's pistol, I presumed—and I immediately heard a series of horrible screams outside the door, followed a few moments later by the cacophony of many weapons being discharged. Only this time, I realized, the shots were coming in rather than going out.

As bullets pounded like leaden raindrops into the wall of the foyer, I was startled to feel a giant hand grab my right arm. It was Rafferty, of course, crawling on his hands and knees through the doorway. His form of locomotion in any other circumstance would have been richly comic, but now it was simply a matter of survival. "C'mon, doctor, strike a match and let's move to the rear while we can."

I did as I was told and saw, in the light of my match, that Thomas, also on his hands and knees, was scurrying behind Rafferty. Once through the doorway, we all got to our feet and Thomas said, "Follow me. I know the way to the back."

I noticed now that Banion was gone but supposed he had already fled to the rear amid all the confusion. As we passed through a small room and then into a hallway, I also noticed that the gunfire from outside had slackened.

"Maybe they're reloading," I said.

"Or they're goin' around to the back to cut us off," Rafferty replied. "'Tis what I would do."

The back door—located in a small, windowless vestibule—was just as Thomas had described it. To one side of the door a staircase came down from the hall upstairs, while on the other side another stairway led into the cellar.

"I thought we'd find Banion here," I said to Rafferty, who had already gone over to look at the door, which was secured by a lock and a heavy bolt.

"Well, he didn't go out. Maybe he's cowerin' in the basement, not that it matters. The question is whether we should be goin' out the door ourselves. Trouble is, we can't see a thing from here. There's got to be some rear windows on this floor."

"They're all bricked up, Shad," Thomas said. "I looked already. The people who run this place like their privacy."

"And we know why," Rafferty said grimly, just as there was a tremendous bang and the entire door seemed to shudder. Then we heard voices shouting: "Hand her over! Hand her over!"

"Well, that settles it," Thomas said. "They're out there but they'll be in here before long."

I now saw a look on Rafferty's face which I had never seen before. It was not dejection, nor was it anything like fear. It was resignation, and at that instant I feared we were all about to die.

"You're right, Wash," Rafferty said. "'Tis beginnin' to

look like Custer's last stand, and we're not the Indians. Well then, we'll go down fightin', just as old George Armstrong did."

At this moment, when the last flickering light of hope seemed to have been extinguished, I suddenly experienced an astonishing vision—the first of two great surprises that were to come our way in a matter of minutes.

Chapter Thirty-six

§ ₹

"My God, I Don't Believe It"

Governor John Tanner of Illinois wasn't used to being scolded, but then again, he had never been exposed before to James J. Hill in high dudgeon. The governor, a stout Republican who had been elected in a landslide following what to his mind was the disastrous tenure of the Democrat John Altgeld, had just arrived at his home in Springfield late Wednesday afternoon when the telephone rang. Tanner had been intrigued to hear that the caller was Hill, whose farflung railroad empire included hundreds of miles of track in Illinois.[1]

But it quickly became apparent when Tanner picked up the telephone that the famous tycoon was not interested in talking about his railroad business. Instead, without so much as a minute's worth of small talk, he all but ordered Tanner to call out the National Guard to suppress what he called "an extreme episode of lawlessness" in Chicago. To Tanner, lawlessness and Chicago were already synonymous, and he therefore asked Hill to spell out his concerns in more detail. The story that followed was so utterly fantastic that Tanner was taken aback.

When Hill had finished, Tanner said, "So, let me see if I have this straight, Mr. Hill. You believe a woman from England has been kidnapped, that Sherlock Holmes is trying to rescue her, that a vast conspiracy is afoot to thwart him and that the police of Chicago, and apparently New York as well, are part of this invidious scheme."

"Exactly," Hill replied, ignoring Tanner's skeptical tone, "and given the breakdown in law enforcement that obviously has occurred in Chicago, it is your duty, governor, to restore order by any means at your disposal, including the National Guard. I suggest that a regiment be summoned at once from the nearest armory."

"That is not a thing to be done lightly, Mr. Hill, especially—"

"I will have no excuses," Hill thundered. "You must do your duty, sir, or face the consequences."

Tanner thought for a moment and said, "Are you aware, Mr. Hill, of what is being said about the situation in the newspapers here? Why, just today, the *Tribune*—"

"The newspapers lie," Hill said with great exasperation. "I have known Sherlock Holmes for six years now and there is no man on earth in whom I would put more trust."

"Of course. Still—"

"You must not delay," Hill broke in. "Dispatch a unit of Guardsmen at once to the Levee district. Have them lay siege if necessary to the Everleigh Club, where I believe Mrs. Cubitt will be taken."

Tanner was known in Illinois political circles as an amiable man, a longtime party regular who had worked his way up the ladder and could be counted upon not to do anything extreme. But he had already been burned once by calling up the National Guard, in a coal miners' strike in 1898, and he did not wish to encounter similar trouble again.

"I will look into the matter," Tanner finally said, "but I can promise you no more than that."

What followed, Tanner told a friend later, was the most impressive display of invective he had ever heard. Even so, the governor stood his ground, since even though James J. Hill was a rich and powerful man, he controlled few votes in Illinois.

When the shooting started upstairs, Elsie Cubitt had been fighting off sleep, knowing that Coughlin would pounce the instant she nodded off. Days of exposure to powerful sleeping drugs were taking their effect, as was the furious burst of energy she had summoned up to achieve her escape. She felt completely drained, and no matter how hard she tried to stay awake, it seemed as if an invisible hand was pressing down on her eyelids, trying to force them shut.

The gunplay therefore had come, oddly, as something of a tonic. It seemed to energize her again, although she had no idea who was waging what sounded like a full-scale battle upstairs. Coughlin, who like most blowhards grew soft in the presence of danger, seemed to be unnerved by the gunfire, dropping his head between his knees and curling up as though he feared a slug might at any moment come crashing through the floorboards.

The shooting stopped momentarily, and Elsie listened as footsteps raced overhead, the building's old floor joists creaking under their weight. Whoever was upstairs—several people, by the sound of it—was coming toward the back and perhaps, she feared, into the basement.

"Be absolutely quiet and do not move so much as an inch," she whispered to Coughlin before blowing out the candle that flickered between them.

The basement now became pitch black, and Elsie worried that Coughlin might try to use the situation to his advantage. But given that he was such a large and clumsy man, she did not think he could make a rush at her without her hearing him. If that happened, she would start shooting at once, no matter what the consequences. And at a range of no more than five feet, she could hardly miss her target.

It was not Coughlin, however, who made the first move in the darkness. Instead, Elsie heard the heavy footsteps of a man coming pell-mell down the basement stairs. The man stumbled over something in the darkness, cursed, then walked toward the coal bin. Elsie's heart was now pounding in her chest like a booming drum, and her hand was shaking as she tried to steady her pistol.

Suddenly, a match flared up, revealing the unpleasant features of Danny Banion, who was looking for a place to hide after slipping away from the men upstairs. Banion, who had already seen two men shot dead under extraordinary circumstances, received yet another shock as his eyes adjusted to the match's flaring light.

"Jesus," he said, spotting Coughlin first and then Elsie, "what the —"

"Sit down," Elsie commanded, bringing up the barrel of her revolver so that it pointed directly at Banion's chest, "and be quiet, just like your friend Bathhouse. You have seen me shoot one man tonight and I will shoot another if I have to."

Banion, who had lost his taste for armed combat, complied at once, raising his hands to indicate that he would cause no trouble. Elsie didn't know Banion's name but she recognized him as one of her would-be rapists. She also knew that her situation was now complicated by the fact that she had two dangerous men to watch instead of one. Even though she still had no clue what was happening upstairs, she decided that she needed light to protect herself.

"Light that candle next to Bathhouse," she instructed Banion, "and keep your hands where I can see them."

Banion obeyed without objection and took a seat on the floor beside Coughlin. Elsie was about to ask him about the gunfire when she heard men's voices coming from the top of the steps. To her amazement, one of the voices sounded remarkably familiar.

The more she listened, the more certain she became that she knew the voice, and yet the more unbelievable it seemed.

"Who are those men talking?" she asked Banion.

"I don't know who they are," Banion answered, truthfully. "I swear."

Elsie had taken risks all her life and she took one now. "Stay where you are," she told her two captives, then stood up and crept around the coal bin toward the doorway at the bottom of the stairs. Coughlin and Banion were out of sight, and there would be nothing to stop them from sneaking off into some dark corner of the basement and shouting for help.

Still, there was that voice, so soothing and familiar! She stopped by the doorway, listening for the sound of her salvation. But she didn't hear it. Instead, there were two other, unfamiliar voices—one with an Irish lilt, the other deep and sonorous. Now Elsie wondered if her mind had been playing tricks on her. Was it possible she hadn't heard that voice so well-known to her after all?

Then she heard it again and this time she was positive. She poked her head around the door and looked up toward the rear vestibule, just as Dr. John Watson—his appearance curiously altered but his voice unmistakable—turned to glance down the stairway.

"My God, I don't believe it," he said as she ran up into the light and embraced him.

Chapter Thirty-seven

"For God's Sake, Do Not Shoot"

FROM THE NARRATIVE OF DR. JOHN WATSON:

I shall never forget the look on Elsie Cubitt's face—a mixture of surprise, delight and relief—as she came up from the darkness at the bottom of the stairs, as though returning from a long tour of the underworld. Her garb, which consisted of little more than a huge man's coat that came down to her knees, and the deep weariness evident in her normally sparkling eyes, left little doubt she had been through a terrible ordeal, as did the revolver in her hand. Yet her own circumstances seemed not to concern her, for we had hardly embraced before she asked, "Where is Mr. Holmes? Please tell me he is all right."

I greatly wished that I could provide her with solace but I felt compelled to state the truth: "He is missing, Mrs. Cubitt. But now that we have found you, perhaps he shall turn up as well."

There were innumerable questions I longed to ask her, but the desperation of our situation prevented me from doing so. Indeed, I had only managed to introduce her to Rafferty and Thomas, whom she greeted warmly, when a makeshift battering ram smashed through one of the door panels.

"Quick, up to the hall," Rafferty said as Thomas fired a blast from his shotgun through the jagged opening. "We're sittin' ducks here."

When we got upstairs, Rafferty sent Thomas to the other end of the hall to guard the front stairs. Then he got out his pocket rifle, expertly assembled the stock and chambered a round.

"What is happening?" Elsie asked.

"I'm afraid there's no time to explain," Rafferty said, positioning himself so he had an easy shot down the stairs. "We're fightin' for our lives."

"Then I will fight with you," Elsie Cubitt said, pulling a second pistol out of the pocket of her oversized coat.

Even Rafferty was impressed by this bravura display. "I've no doubt you will," he said. "Then go join Mr. Thomas, if you would, and don't hesitate to shoot anybody who tries to come up the front stairs."

Just after she left, there was another crash below, and as I looked over Rafferty's shoulder I saw the back door give way and a man tumble into the vestibule. The man, who was armed with a pistol, tried to scramble to his feet. He never made it. Rafferty leveled his pocket rifle and shot the man through the head, no doubt killing him instantly. An ear-splitting salvo of gunfire followed, all directed harmlessly into the vestibule, but Rafferty's shot had served its purpose, for none of the other cadets were anxious to risk their comrade's fate.

Rafferty shouted to Thomas, "Anybody comin' up the front, Wash?"

"Not yet," came the reply.

Although Rafferty had never gone beyond the rank of sergeant in the American Civil War, he had been at many great battles, including Gettysburg, and possessed the commanding presence of a general—a trait he shared with Holmes. He now instructed me to see if I could find a stairway or trapdoor to the roof. "'Tis our best hope, doctor," he said calmly. "Otherwise, we'd best start prayin' for the cavalry. While you're at it, take a look out the windows and see if you can tell how many men are out there."[1]

Three large windows, all barred and shaded, looked out from the rear of the hall. I went to the nearest one, cracked open the shade and peered through the bars. What I saw did not augur well for our hopes of escape. There appeared to be twenty or more men milling around in the small yard and alley behind the building. One knot of men had formed a huddle of sorts, and I could only assume they were planning their final assault upon us. The wind we had noticed earlier seemed to have picked up, causing paper and other debris to swirl around the alley like dirty snow.

"I'd say there are close to two dozen men out there," I told Rafferty.

"And no doubt more out front," he said. "All right, see if you can get us to the roof, doctor, for they'll be comin' at us again soon enough."

I was about to comply when I heard what sounded like the crack of a rifle from somewhere outside. I glanced back down at the yard just as one of the men in the huddle clutched his stomach and fell to the ground. Before his companions could react, there was another crack, and another man went down.

Other shots followed in rapid succession, more men went down, and panic ensued. Some of the cadets scurried for cover, others scattered and ran, firing wildly with their pistols as they disappeared down the alley.

"What's going on?" Rafferty shouted.

"Somebody is out there with a rifle," I said. "He seems to be picking off men left and right, but I cannot tell where the shots are coming from. The cadets are scattering to the winds."

"Well, I guess the cavalry has arrived," Rafferty said. "I wonder—"

I cut in, "Wait, I see something. A man is running toward the back door. I do not know—"

"He'll not get through if I have anything to say about it," Rafferty said.

As I watched the man race across the yard in great long strides, his head bent low and turned ever so slightly to the left, I experienced a thrilling moment of recognition. There was only one man in the world—at least only one man I knew—who ran in precisely the same way, with precisely the same tilt of his head.

"For God's sake, do not shoot," I yelled. "It is Holmes!"

The reunion which followed was as joyful as any in my life. Holmes was as surprised to see us as we were to see him, and it seemed little short of a miracle that we had all found one another in the midst of such chaos. Yet even my great elation paled in comparison to Elsie Cubitt's. She seemed to fairly fly across the hall and all but leapt into Holmes's arms when she saw him at last.

"You are alive!" she said, touching a hand to his cheek as though to prove his presence was not a dream. She then hugged him and said, "All this time, I feared—"

"As did I," said Holmes, who looked flustered as he gently disengaged himself from Mrs. Cubitt.

There were so many questions I wished to ask Holmes that I scarcely knew where to begin. Holmes must have seen the questioning look in my eyes, for he said, "I know, my dear Watson, you are anxious to learn all that has happened and how I came to be here. I in turn am anxious to learn why you have dyed your hair and removed your mustache! I am even more curious as to how you, Mr. Rafferty and Mr. Thomas found your way to this place. We shall all have much to talk about when this business is done. Our priority now, however, must be to make our escape."

Rafferty said, "We're thinkin' you brought along some help, Mr. Holmes, or did you mow down all those cadets out there?"

"No, you have our friend Mr. Wooldridge to thank for that bit of work. He is quite a hunter and an expert marksman. But his rifle alone will not suffice if we are to get out of here alive. There are a great many men outside who wish to claim the bounty for Elsie's capture."

"Good God, that reminds me of something," Mrs. Cubitt now said. "Bathhouse Coughlin, the man who posted that reward, is down in the basement, as is one of the men who tried to assault me earlier. I left them when I heard your voice, Dr. Watson."

"I'll go down and get them," Rafferty volunteered. "The other fellow must be Danny Banion, with whom I've already had some friendly words this evenin'. They can't have gotten away or I'd have seen them by the back door."

"Do not bother," said Holmes. "They are irrelevant. We must leave here as quickly as possible."

"But what about all those men outside?" I asked. "Perhaps we could use that Coughlin fellow as a hostage."

Elsie Cubitt seconded the idea but Holmes said, "I'm not at all sure that the mob out there cares whether Mr. Coughlin lives or dies. Besides, I think there is a way the men can be persuaded to leave."

"And what might that be?" Rafferty inquired.

Holmes smiled and said, "As I recall, Chicago was once the scene of a great fire. Perhaps it is time for another one."[2]

Chapter Thirty-eight

"We All Must Leave at Once"

From the daintily curtained window in her penthouse suite atop the Everleigh Club, Mary Mortimer looked down upon the chaos that had erupted on Dearborn Street and wondered whether it was time for her to leave. She had come so close to triumphing once and for all over Sherlock Holmes that she did not want to abandon her grand plan quite yet. Even so, she realized that events were careening out of control and that the likelihood of finally gaining the vengeance she craved was growing more remote by the minute.

Her plan, she thought, had been perfect in every detail—only the execution was wanting. How Pete and Belgian Jack had allowed Holmes to escape from the train was beyond her ken, and the two of them—along with Charlie, Holmes's look-alike—would soon pay for their mistakes. Still, all might have been salvaged had not Elsie Cubitt somehow managed to get away as well. Now the whole Levee had turned into a madhouse, and both Holmes and Mrs. Cubitt remained at large. Even if they were found, the wild disorder in the streets, which the police would inevitably be forced to quell, almost certainly precluded her from carrying out the final—and most important—part of her plan.

She closed the curtains and walked out to a narrow hallway that ran the length of the penthouse. At its far end was the pink boudoir, as it was called, the room where the club's wealthiest patrons enjoyed, for two hundred dollars a night, whatever it took to satisfy their lust. The room lived up to its name, for everything in it was some shade of pink. There was a pink carpet from one of the best mills in France, a Venetian chandelier with rose-tinted glass, heavy floral wallpaper featuring pink and red petals and a huge four-poster bed with a pink quilt made, at considerable expense, by a lady's sewing circle in Muscatine, Iowa. Even the customary brass spittoon had been replaced by a special pink porcelain model.

It was in this hothouse of love that Sherlock Holmes and Elsie Cubitt, just before their supposed wedding, were to have been found dead—victims of a murder-suicide guaranteed to shock the world. Mrs. Mortimer had already written the story line for this culminating event, which would be promoted to the newspapers as Holmes's final act of madness. Spurned to the end by the woman he had kidnapped, Holmes—or so the press would be told—had finally shot her in a rage and then turned the gun on himself. Dr. John Watson, of course, was supposed to have been killed earlier in New York City while abetting Holmes's escape, but his death could easily have been arranged in Chicago as well. The meddling Shadwell Rafferty was also to have been taken care of, which was why he had been invited to the "wedding."

Mrs. Mortimer knew full well the world might or might not choose to believe this version of events, but it hardly mattered. What was certain was that Holmes would not only be dead but that his reputation would be forever soiled. Now, however, it appeared that this dream was not to be, and as Mrs. Mortimer considered her circumstances, she decided that it was indeed time to move on.

As always, she had made careful plans in the event she needed to make a sudden departure. She had already deposited more than twenty-five thousand dollars in cash—much of it skimmed from the Everleigh Club's proceeds—in a special bank account known only to her, and she had made arrangements to have a carriage waiting for her at a nondescript, but secure, livery stable within walking distance of the club. A single bag—she always traveled lightly—was already packed and stored at the livery stable.

Mrs. Mortimer consulted her watch and saw that it was already well past midnight. She went back to her suite, intending to write a letter, but noticed that the commotion outside seemed to be growing louder. Peering out the window again, she was met by an extraordinary sight. Borne by high winds, burning embers were swirling down Dearborn like huge fireflies, while just to the north an ominous glow lit up the normally dark street. Then she heard the clanging of bells. Fire!

She went down to the second floor, where a series of ornate parlors provided various forms of entertainment, and saw that panic had already begun to spread throughout the club. Gentlemen, not all of them completely dressed, were fleeing down the hallways, as were a number of young women who wore hardly anything at all. Mrs. Mortimer saw Minna Everleigh, dressed as usual in a long flowing dress with a choker collar, directing customers to the staircase.

"What is happening, Minna?" she asked.

"There is a big fire at the Hibernia Hall," came the reply, "and it's coming right this way. Van Bever's and French Em's are sure to go with it, and the whole block is in grave danger. We all must leave at once."[1]

"Very well," said Mrs. Mortimer, who was certain that the fire was no accident.

As revelers continued to pour out of rooms on the second floor, she calmly went back up to her suite, changed clothes and put on a dark wig and a pair of glasses. Then she went downstairs and left by the servant's entry in the alley.

The fire, she saw when she got outside, was raging out of control, and a stiff wind was sending it south, toward the Everleigh Club. A large, excited group of men had formed a bucket brigade around Monohan's, which was the next brothel down the line and just two buildings away from the Everleigh. A few of the braver men had climbed up to Monohan's roof and were trying to stamp out embers before they could set the entire building ablaze.

Mrs. Mortimer heard the steady clang of bells amid the howling wind, signaling that the fire department would soon be on the scene. Perhaps the firemen would be able to save the Everleigh; perhaps not. In either case, it hardly mattered to her. She had made her decision to leave and she would have no trouble starting over somewhere else. After all, she had done it several times before.

Dodging embers and larger chunks of burning debris, she turned south, away from the fire. At Twenty-second Street, she went east, toward the Chicago River and the carriage that would take her out of the city, to a place where even Sherlock Holmes would never find her.

Several blocks to the north, another vehicle—a black maria belonging to the Chicago Police Department—also awaited its occupants. The wagon had been "borrowed" for the night by Detective Clifton Wooldridge, whose superiors would not be happy when they learned of his unauthorized requisition. But Wooldridge, a cocky bantam of a man, didn't really care what his bosses thought, nor did he have to, for the simple reason that he was by far the most famous policeman in Chicago and was adored by both the public and the press.

Like other prominent detectives of his era, Wooldridge had achieved fame in part through the convenient device of bestowing it upon himself. Not content with newspaper accounts of his daring deeds, he took to penning his own books, in one of which he modestly described himself as the "world's greatest detective, the incorruptible Sherlock Holmes of America." Although it is doubtful Holmes would have entirely agreed with this assessment, he was an admirer of Wooldridge's work and knew him to be a truly honest officer in a city not famous for the probity of its police.[2]

The two detectives had first met in Chicago in 1896 prior to the case of the ice palace murders. Since then, they had maintained a regular correspondence. Wooldridge was also used to responding to telegraphed inquiries from Holmes, such as the three he had received within the past two weeks. Then had come the disturbing message from Dr. Watson regarding Holmes's disappearance. As a result, Wooldridge had been quite unprepared for the telephone call from Holmes late Tuesday night. The story Holmes related was almost unbelievable, but Wooldridge did not hesitate for a moment in offering his help.

Now, however, as he walked up State Street toward the paddy wagon, which was being watched by an officer personally loyal to him, Wooldridge greatly feared that both Holmes and Elsie Cubitt were dead. He had known from the start that the night would be full of risks, for both himself and Holmes, but as he thought back on events he realized how the unexpected had caused their plans to go badly awry.

In accord with Holmes's plan, Wooldridge had begun by establishing a sniper's nest behind the brick parapet of a building across the alley from the Sons of Hibernia Hall. The idea was to provide cover for Holmes if he needed it. As it turned out, he did, for a large crowd of cadets inexplicably materialized just as Holmes was preparing to enter the hall. With his high-powered Remington, Wooldridge wounded several of the cadets and sent the rest scattering like birds flushed from cover. Holmes, who believed Mrs. Cubitt was being held prisoner inside the hall, then went to the rescue.

After that, however, more problems had developed. One group of cadets—the bravest or perhaps drunkest of the lot—found cover behind a small shed off the alley and sniped at Wooldridge with increasing accuracy. Worse, the cadets were in a position to have a clear shot at Holmes and Mrs. Cubitt when they came out the back door, as was the plan.

Then, as he continued to exchange gunfire with the cadets, Wooldridge was startled to see a bright geyser of flame spout from the roof of the hall. Fanned by stiff winds, the geyser quickly became a raging fire. Wooldridge had no idea how the blaze had started, although it occurred to him that Holmes himself might have set it in order to effect his escape. If so, Wooldridge was ready to do his best to keep the remaining cadets at bay.

"Come on, Mr. Holmes, get out of there," Wooldridge said to himself as the fire, feeding on the old hall's wooden beams and joists, continued to intensify. The fire at first proved to be Wooldridge's ally, for a red-hot ember soon ignited the wooden shed where the last of the cadets were stationed. Seeing that they either had to abandon their cover or risk incineration, the men—firing to no effect with their pistols—ran out toward the alley.

Moments later, Wooldridge saw another man fleeing through the yard after emerging from somewhere behind the shed. Then, to the detective's utter astonishment, he saw a familiar figure—dressed only in trousers and an undershirt—come out from the same place and make a run for it. What caused Wooldridge to stare in disbelief was that the man was none other than Bathhouse John Coughlin.

Moments later, the wind shifted slightly and a wall of heavy, acrid smoke suddenly engulfed Wooldridge. Fighting for breath and blinded by the smoke, he crawled along the roof toward the front of the building on State Street. He was nearly overcome but finally got clear of the thickest smoke. He lay coughing and wheezing for some minutes, feeling as though he had just had a taste of hell, before he was ready to move again. Once he reached the front of the building on State, he shinnied down a drainpipe and made his way back toward the hall.

Wooldridge went around the corner to Twenty-first Street, which he was surprised to find all but deserted, and headed back toward the alley. He had left his rifle on the roof—it would have instantly aroused the mob's suspicion—but still kept two pistols tucked under his coat for self-defense. When he reached the alley he saw why Twenty-first was so empty. The mob had moved south, following the fire, which had already spread to a brothel adjoining Hibernia Hall.

It was clear to Wooldridge, and everyone else, that the fire might well consume the entire block, or an even greater part of the Levee district. That would be a disaster for the Levee's criminal population, which understood that once gone, the Levee and its immensely profitable vice trade could never be replaced. Fire bells now began clanging in the distance and Wooldridge observed half-dressed women and men—prostitutes and their clientele—fleeing from the burning brothels. Farther down the alley, a bucket brigade had been formed in what looked to be a futile attempt to halt the fire's seemingly inexorable advance down Dearborn toward the Everleigh Club.[3]

Amid the chaos of fire and flight, Wooldridge saw no signs of Holmes, and he became deeply worried. Was Holmes in fact trapped in Hibernia Hall? Or was he planning to get out another way? Had he already done so? Or was he simply waiting to leave at the last moment? One thing was certain, which was that the hall—engulfed in a roaring storm of fire—was beyond salvation. Wooldridge still hoped to see Holmes and Mrs. Cubitt coming out of the building and was prepared to use his pistols to protect them if he had to. But he saw nothing except smoke and flames pouring out of every window.

Wooldridge walked around to the front of the building, on Dearborn, but here too the flames were so intense, and the smoke so thick, that he held out little hope that anyone could escape. After waiting anxiously for another fifteen minutes, he watched in horror as the brick walls of the hall collapsed, dooming anyone who may have been inside.

His only hope now was that Holmes and Mrs. Cubitt, if she was with him, had somehow gotten out of the hall unnoticed and had returned to the black maria. But as he neared the wagon, he saw only the driver, sitting where he had left him, and Wooldridge felt his heart sink at the thought that Sherlock Holmes, the world's greatest detective, had died in some Chicago hellhole.

Chapter Thirty-nine

ʃ ʔ

"This Is a Thing I Must Do Myself"

FROM THE NARRATIVE OF DR. JOHN WATSON:

When Sherlock Holmes announced his plan to set the Sons of Hibernia Hall afire, I put the obvious question to him: "How shall we escape without being seen by the mob outside?"

"I am counting on smoke and confusion to be our confederates," said Holmes. "There is also the elemental fact that heat rises."

"Ah, I see what you're gettin' at," said Rafferty. "When the fire goes up, we go down."

"Precisely. I noticed several cellar windows which should be large enough for us to escape through. The fire will rise if we set it on the ground floor and that should afford us enough time to get out through the cellar."

"Let us pray those windows are very large," said Rafferty, patting his ample stomach, "or I will go down with the building."

"We shall not let that happen on any account," Holmes said. "Indeed we will go out the back door if necessary, though I fear gunmen may still have it in their sights. We must hope that Mr. Wooldridge will still be on the scene and in a position to help if we do come under fire."

Everything now went according to plan, or so it seemed, and I began to think that all of us might survive the night after all. We found two old kerosene lanterns, both nearly full of fuel, in a small closet. Next, we slipped down the back steps toward the vestibule where the man shot in the head by Rafferty still lay in a pool of blood, part of his battering ram beside him. Wooldridge's rifle appeared to have cleared out the crowd outside, although as Holmes had noted it was entirely possible men were still hiding nearby. However, no one shot at us as we crept past the corpse and through the vestibule into the central hallway. There, we stacked up wooden chairs and other pieces of furniture, doused the pile with kerosene and ignited it.

The pile exploded into flames, and we waited to make sure it was burning fiercely before we went toward the cellar. We had saved a small amount of fuel in one lamp and took it along to provide illumination.

"You must remember that Coughlin and that other man — Banion is it? — are hiding somewhere down there," Elsie Cubitt reminded us.

"But neither of them is armed, as I understand it," said Holmes, "and if they attempt to give us any trouble, I am sure we shall be able to handle it."

As we reached the vestibule, gunfire broke out again, and much of it appeared to be coming from somewhere very close. A bullet slammed into the corpse, hitting his chest with such force that his entire body shook.

"Get down and stay back," said Rafferty, who had been the first of us in the vestibule.

We took cover in the hallway, fire roaring behind us while bullets barred the path ahead. It was clear we could not stay where we were, for the fire was growing hotter and larger by the second.

Then the gunfire seemed to die down again, and Rafferty said, "Better a bullet than burnin', I guess. Let's get to the basement while we can."

With Rafferty still in the lead, we went in single file through the vestibule, again stepping over the corpse, and reached the cellar without further incident. The cellar, which proved to be extremely damp and moldy, was built up of rough limestone walls subdivided into several storage rooms and bins. The windows Holmes had noticed were on the north side, facing Twenty-first Street, and we saw that they were indeed sufficiently large to allow for an escape. Unfortunately, we also saw that behind their panes of frosted glass the windows were heavily barred — something Holmes could not have noticed from outside.

The optimism I had felt moments earlier quickly dissolved, for it seemed fate had in the end decided not to favor us after all. While Thomas stood guard with his shotgun, Rafferty and Holmes went over to examine the bars. Rafferty gave them a pull but even his exceptional strength could not budge them.

"Ah, these are beauties, they are," he said, "and a man would need a very good hacksaw or even a stick of dynamite to get them out."

"Perhaps a few gunshots might dislodge them," I offered.

"'Twould be a waste of ammunition, doctor. The bars are heavy forged steel by the look of them. Besides, if we start blastin' away, whoever's left out there will come around and start shootin' back. No, we'll have to find another way out."

"And quickly," said Holmes, who drew our attention to the basement steps. Smoke was already creeping down from the rear vestibule, sucked into the basement by an air current Holmes had not anticipated.

As if to render our situation even more desperate, gunfire resumed outside the back door. Almost at the same instant, we heard a great rumble and crash inside the coal bin behind us, as though the contents had suddenly shifted.

"Rats," Rafferty said, spinning around and staring at the bin's door, "but I'm guessin' they're of the human variety."

"It must be Coughlin and Banion trying to get away," said Elsie Cubitt, who stopped when she realized what she had just said.

"Of course," said Holmes. "How stupid can we be! A coal bin has a small door to the outside to receive deliveries. It is our best chance of escape."

The basement was already filling with smoke when we reached the old wooden door to the bin. Rafferty yanked it open just in time for us to see the posterior of a very large man—Coughlin himself, I was later to learn—squeeze through the loading door and disappear into the darkness beyond. The exertions of Coughlin and Banion had presumably knocked loose a large amount of the coal, which lay three-feet deep in the bin like a rough black carpet.

Holmes clambered up on the pile ahead of everyone else and said, "I shall go first."

We all knew, of course, that the first person through the coal door would be in the greatest jeopardy from snipers or other members of the mob who remained outside. We also knew Holmes would be unwilling to debate the point.

"Just be careful," Rafferty said. "I don't think Mrs. Cubitt would like to lose you now after all that has happened."

Then, to the surprise of us all, Elsie Cubitt put her arms around Holmes's neck, stood on her tiptoes and kissed him on the lips. "Godspeed," she said to Holmes, who looked more shocked—and dare I say, frightened?—than I had ever seen him before.

"I shall be careful," he murmured as he turned to look out the small door, which Coughlin had not bothered to close in his haste to escape. "I see no one outside but a shed a few feet away is on fire. You must all follow me out as quickly as you can and then keep moving."

Rafferty and I gave Holmes a boost, shoving him out through the door head first. Mrs. Cubitt went next, followed by Thomas. Rafferty and I brought up the rear.

To our great relief, the yard behind the hall was empty, no doubt because the heavy smoke pouring from the hall had driven everyone away. We found that all was now darkness and confusion in the alley, for the fire, as Holmes had predicted, was being pushed rapidly ahead by the wind.

"Follow me," Holmes said. "I know a safe place."

We crossed Twenty-first Street without being challenged, went east to State Street and then turned north just as a stream of fire engines coming down from the Loop passed us by at full tilt. It took us but ten minutes to reach a large black police wagon discreetly parked in a side street just off State. It was the same vehicle, we soon learned, in which Holmes and Wooldridge had ridden to the Levee district. The driver greeted us and we went at once into the wagon to await Wooldridge's return.[1]

However, we had hardly taken seats inside the wagon when Holmes said he must leave "to take care of one final matter."

Rafferty, as usual, was the first to grasp what Holmes meant. "You are goin' after the woman, I suppose—the one who calls herself Mary Mortimer," he said. "I've spent a good deal of time wonderin' about her. I even have a crazy idea as to her real identity."

"Your idea will undoubtedly prove correct, Mr. Rafferty," Holmes replied rather cryptically. "I am certain that she is the grand orchestrator of this entire affair, and I shall not rest until she is brought to justice"—here he paused, before adding ominously—"in one way or another."

"Ah, so you must know where she is," Rafferty noted. "Gettin' away has been her strong suit in the past."

"Not this time," Holmes replied.

Rafferty nodded and said, "I don't imagine you'd allow Wash and me, or Doctor Watson, to come along."

"No. This is a thing I must do myself."

I now felt compelled to speak up, for I suddenly realized who Mary Mortimer must be. "Holmes, I strongly advise—"

"My dear Watson, I have made up my mind," he broke in, "and you will not change it. Now, when Detective Wooldridge returns—as I pray he will shortly—he will answer the many questions I am sure all of you have."

Elsie Cubitt, who had listened with mounting alarm to the conversation, said, "But why must you go off alone, Mr. Holmes, to this final confrontation you have in mind? At least let me accompany you, since I have suffered as much as anyone in this affair and would also like to see justice done."

"You have indeed suffered, Elsie, and far too much," Holmes replied tenderly. "But our adversary was after me all along—you were just a means to a larger end—and so I am the one who must see this terrible affair to a conclusion. And I will return. You may count upon that."

Just as Holmes was about to step out of the wagon, I heard approaching footsteps and then a clipped, familiar voice ask our driver, "Hey, Paulie, have you seen any sign of—"

"I imagine you are looking for me, Mr. Wooldridge," said Holmes, poking his head out the wagon door. "Why don't you come inside? There are some people here I would like you to meet."

After making quick introductions—only I had met Wooldridge before—Holmes stepped back outside and said, "Ah, I see a hansom coming down the street and I must take it. Are you still at the Sherman House, Watson?"

"Yes," I said, wondering why, if Holmes knew my hotel, he had not contacted me there earlier.

"Then I will see all of you there before the night is done."

Without another word, he slipped away into the darkness.

"Now where's he going?" asked Wooldridge. "Man never sits still, does he."

"He's goin' to settle business once and for all," said Rafferty as Wooldridge rapped on the roof, a signal for the driver to move out, "but he tells us that you can explain how the two of you found your way to Hibernia Hall tonight."

Rafferty, I noted, seemed slightly taken aback by Wooldridge, whose physical size was hardly in proportion to the magnitude of his exploits. I supposed that Rafferty had expected to find a big bruiser of the type common to police departments. Wooldridge, however, looked more like a punctilious little accountant. Yet his aggressive features—a long narrow nose, well-defined cheekbones, a pugnacious jaw, a bristling gray mustache waxed to a fine sheen and flinty gray eyes—suggested that he was indeed the formidable figure Chicago's criminals had come to fear. His speech was as sharp as his features, for his words came out so quickly that he seemed to communicate in a kind of verbal shorthand.

"Tell you what I can," he began in response to Rafferty's request. "Holmes'll have to fill you in on most things. Called me Tuesday night and told me craziest story you ever heard. Kidnapping, murder, drugs, big to-do in New York, train ride in coffin, escape in Pennsylvania, etcetera. Finally ended up in Chicago looking for lady here. Told me coppers in Chicago were bought and paid for—no news there—and I'm only one who could help him. Of course, said he could count on me. It's well-known Clifton Wooldridge is incorruptible."

"So I have heard," said Rafferty, who appeared to enjoy the little man's refreshing lack of modesty. "How did you track down Mrs. Cubitt?"

"Wasn't too hard. First, had to 'disappear' for a while, so nobody'd know I was helping Holmes. Made up cover story about leaving town"—I now knew why Rafferty and I had been unable to reach Wooldridge—"and set to work. Holmes figured lady'd been taken from train station in coffin. So we did some nosing around. One thing led to another. Upshot is, by yesterday afternoon we'd tracked her down to Sons of Hibernia Hall."

"Yet you didn't attempt your rescue until after dark," I noted. "I am surprised that Holmes did not try something earlier."

"He would have all right," said Wooldridge. "Trouble was, hall being guarded like Fort Knox. Didn't see how we could sneak in in broad daylight. Drove Holmes crazy not doing anything but told him it'd be suicide if we tried. So we waited until nightfall. Holmes had something else to do anyway."

"What was that?" I asked.

"Broke into Mortimer woman's apartment down on South Michigan."

"Did he now," said Rafferty. "Tell us more about the lady if you would."

Wooldridge readily agreed and provided a brief sketch of Mary Mortimer's activities in Chicago. When he described her appearance, all of us except Elsie Cubitt felt a chill of recognition.

"I don't like to say such a thing, but I hope Mr. Holmes knows what he's doing," said Thomas in his usual grave, considered way. "She's a mighty dangerous woman, that one."

"As dangerous as they come," I agreed.

After Rafferty and I had explained something of Mary Mortimer's background to Elsie Cubitt, Wooldridge continued. "Holmes got back from burgling about half past nine. Went over plans and set up watch outside hall just after ten. Brought along rifle—part of Holmes's plan—and found a good spot in alley up on roof. Holmes watched front but lots of men hanging around—must have been meeting at hall—so we kept waiting."

It occurred to me now that Holmes and Wooldridge must have arrived not long after Elsie Cubitt's escape, as word of the reward spread and men began to search for her.

Wooldridge said, "By eleven place was clearing out and Holmes came around to join me. Talked for a while to make sure we had plans worked out. Don't know how we missed you three"—he was referring to Rafferty, Thomas and myself. "Must have slipped by while we were talking on roof. Holmes was getting ready to go inside hall when we heard first shot. Pretty soon all hell broke loose. Screaming, more gunfire and then mob of cadets poured into alley. Started yelling, 'Hand her over, hand her over.' Well, Holmes, he just went crazy. Said he was going in no matter what. So I cleared away cadets with my rifle and Holmes went racing across to hall. Rest you know."

It was nearly two in the morning by the time the police wagon delivered us, unceremoniously, to the front door of the Sherman House. We thanked Wooldridge profusely and promised to let him know at once when we heard from Holmes. I obtained additional rooms for Rafferty and Thomas, as well as Elsie Cubitt. Then, at once weary beyond measure and filled with nervous apprehension, we waited for the return of Sherlock Holmes.

Chapter Forty

§ ₹

"There Will Be No Court"

The run-down establishment known as Murran's Livery was about two miles south of the Loop, on Clark Street, and lay all but marooned amid a wide swath of railroad tracks belonging to no fewer than nine different lines. The tracks, which seemed to swoop and curl in all directions like great steel chains binding the flat Chicago earth, were busy around the clock, for the railroads stopped for neither time nor darkness. A steady stream of freights, their locomotives throbbing in the heavy summer air, rumbled past the old livery stable, and now and then a fast passenger train—one of the limiteds from the east, perhaps—came clipping by in a blur of light and sound.

Before the railroads swallowed up almost every square foot of land around it, the livery had been a booming business, serving the warehouses and industries clustered along the busy south branch of the Chicago River. The river—its course only recently reversed by the greatest public works project in the city's history—looped to the east here, and its turbid yet surprisingly deep waters reached almost to the stable's back door. How the stable had managed to survive so long was a matter of considerable speculation, the consensus being that the owner, who presumably had friends in high places, must be demanding a king's ransom from the railroads for his little piece of property.[1]

The stable itself was a long, listing wooden shed that had last seen paint in the days of U. S. Grant's presidency. Despite its advanced state of disrepair, it still catered to a few discreet customers. Among them was a woman who paid exceedingly well to have her horse and buggy kept ready for use at a moment's notice, day or night.

Even so, the young stable hand assigned to the night shift was more than a little surprised when, just after two in the morning, he was shaken awake. He looked up from his bed of straw to see a tall, slender woman in a bonnet staring down at him. She had already lit the lantern that dangled from a rafter overhead and in that soft light the boy thought she looked as beautiful as an angel. Her first words, however, were decidedly down-to-earth.

"I shall be needing my buggy," the woman said without any preliminaries, handing the boy a five-dollar gold piece. "See to it at once."

"Yes, ma'am," the boy said, scrambling to his feet. "Must be an emergency, I guess."

The woman—who wore a plain high-buttoned dress to go with her gray bonnet—said, "Yes, it is something like that. Be quick, boy, and there will be another five dollars for you."

As that was more money than the boy had ever seen in his life, he went to work at a furious pace, promising the woman he would have her big chestnut harnessed to the buggy and ready to go "in no time." He became so preoccupied with this potentially lucrative work that he failed to notice the lanky man who stepped out from the shadows at the rear of the stable and came up behind him.

"You may go now," said Sherlock Holmes, giving the boy such a start that he felt his heart skip a beat. "The lady will not be needing her horse and buggy tonight."

Mary Mortimer was as stunned as the boy by Holmes's sudden appearance. "You!" she said, staring at Holmes as though he had just materialized out of Aladdin's lamp.

The boy spun around and saw that the man who had caught him unawares was not only very tall, with a hawk nose and riveting eyes, but also held a pistol in his right hand. "I'm supposed—" the boy began, still thinking of the payment he had been promised.

Holmes put a ten-dollar gold piece in the boy's hand and said, "Leave us now, lad, and do not come back here tonight. Do you understand?"

The boy nodded in agreement as it dawned on him what was about to happen. He gave Holmes a salacious wink and said, "The hay's nice and soft." Then he raced off into the night with his new fortune.

Holmes stepped up into the lantern's light and said to the woman, "It seems we were destined to meet one last time, Mrs. Mortimer, although I imagine this is not exactly the sort of rendezvous you had in mind. I might also note that the wig does not really become you."

"It is merely a temporary convenience," she said calmly, having already regained the composure that was but one of her many remarkable features.

Holmes had first encountered her in 1894, in the doomed village of Hinckley in the bleak Minnesota pineries, where she operated a brothel and was allied—to what extent, Holmes could never be entirely certain—with the mad arsonist known as the Red Demon. Going then by the name of Mary Robinson, she had somehow escaped the conflagration which brought that terrible affair to an end. A detective named Thomas Mortimer had been a key figure in the affair of the Red Demon. Holmes assumed that Mary Robinson, or whoever she really was, had taken Mortimer's name as a subtle way of signaling Holmes—and drawing him into her trap—since she never did anything without purpose.[2]

Nearly five years later, in the spring of 1899, she had surfaced again during Holmes's investigation into the rune stone mystery. She had by then acquired a husband and a new name—Mrs. Mary Comstock—and presided over a sprawling bonanza farm on the vast prairies surrounding the Red River of the North. Again, she had been at the center of a bold criminal enterprise and again she had escaped from Holmes's grasp at the last minute.[3]

And now, Holmes knew, it was she who was behind the incredible affair that had brought him halfway around the world and to the brink of death and ruin.

"Using the name of Mrs. Mortimer was, as always, an elegant touch," Holmes remarked. "It brought back many memories of Hinckley and the Red Demon."

"They were pleasant memories, I trust," she said. "I can think of one occasion in particular when we had a most interesting time together. Perhaps we could do so again, for we are all alone, are we not?"

As she spoke in her sensuous contralto, she looked, Holmes thought, as beautiful as ever, despite the wig that hid her long auburn hair and the dowdy dress she had selected as her traveling garb. Her glittering violet eyes, haughty face and still youthful figure all bespoke great vitality, even though she was now well past her fiftieth year. And she still wore the Jicky perfume that was virtually her trademark.[4]

Mary Mortimer's treachery, however, had made Holmes immune to her allure and he said coldly, "You have nothing I want, Mrs. Mortimer. Besides, I do not imagine you were planning to stay in Chicago for long. Indeed, I suspect you intended to leave tonight, drive your buggy to some nearby city and then take a train to whatever your new destination might be. In that way, anyone watching the depots in Chicago would not know of your departure. It is an approach which worked well for you in the past."

"Yes, it did," she said, with a tinge of regret, "but I can see now that I was foolish to try my luck for a third time."

"It was one of your few mistakes," Holmes said. "Your plan was on the whole quite brilliant. The use of the dancing men code, the actor and the prostitute you hired as impersonators in England, the forged letters, the body conveniently left in my hotel room in Liverpool, the clues strewn about so ably by Mme. DuBois, not to mention the great charade in New York City, complete with an assassin imported from Chicago—it was all a truly grand production. Purchasing the services of Tammany Hall was an especially clever and effective touch. I did not know your influence was so extensive."

"Your role in capturing the Tammany Hall man in London made it very easy to secure the cooperation I needed in New York. A number of the leading politicians of that city were happy to cooperate with me, for the right price, as were certain newspaper reporters. That is the wonderful thing about this country, Mr. Holmes. Money will buy anything."

"Did it buy Mme. DuBois's services as well or was her loyalty to you more of a family affair?"

"Ah, you have been busy, Mr. Holmes. Yes, Aunt Ethel, as we call her, was willing to work for free to avenge the death of her dear nephew Abe. Her long theatrical experience was of great help, of course. Too bad, isn't it, that she's now lost her other nephew as well. She is quite distraught."

"You, on the other hand, seem to have taken Jake's death in stride," Holmes remarked, adding, "even though he was your lover."

"I have found that men are always easy to get over," she replied. "They need so much more than any woman can give that there is no point in hanging on to them for too long. They simply become a problem after awhile."

The woman, Holmes had understood since their first meeting in Hinckley, was the rarest of nature's creations, a beautiful monster, and so he was not surprised by her coldheartedness. He was, however, curious as to why she had devoted so much time and such vast resources to his ruination.

"Apparently I was your biggest problem of all, Mrs. Mortimer, for you must have spent a small fortune to seek revenge upon me," Holmes noted. "Was it really worth it? And why undertake such a scheme in the first place when I was no longer a threat to you?"

"I like a challenge," she said, as though this was an entirely satisfactory explanation. "Besides, it was Jake who was thirsting for your blood, and Elsie Cubitt's. He held the two of you responsible for Abe's death, but he was not sure how best to take his vengeance. I merely helped him carry out his plan."

Holmes knew this to be a lie, even if Jake Slaney was a more accomplished schemer than his brother. No, the entire case—with its subtlety, mocking humor and quiet viciousness—bore Mary Mortimer's imprint as clearly as the royal seal on a proclamation.

Feeling a rising sense of anger, Holmes said, "And did you also help him with his plan to violate Mrs. Cubitt in the most degrading way imaginable at Hibernia Hall?"

"I knew nothing about that," Mary Mortimer insisted.

"I do not believe you," Holmes shot back. "I only wonder how you, as a woman, could countenance such cruelty. But then, the deaths of hundreds in Hinckley did not seem to bother you, either."

"I do not concern myself with events for which I bear no responsibility," she said. "The world is a cruel place. I wish it were not so, but wishing in the end is of little use, as I am sure you would agree."

"Tell me," Holmes now asked, "how was your great

scheme of revenge to end? I am told you sent out invitations to a supposed wedding at the Everleigh Club at which Mrs. Cubitt and myself were to be the bride and groom. I imagine, however, that the nuptials would never have occurred. Was there to have been an argument between the lovers, and then perhaps a murder and suicide? The newspapers, I am sure, would have delighted in such a lurid tale."

"I am sure they would have," she acknowledged, "and I only regret that certain people failed me. Otherwise, we would not be having this conversation, would we?"

Holmes had not expected her to show remorse, for he doubted she had a conscience of any kind. Nor did he anticipate any sort of confession. Still, one question gnawed at him and he hoped she might answer it at last. The question, however, had nothing to do with the elaborate details of her scheme, which in any event might take months to sort out.

That she had somehow linked up with Jake Slaney, probably not long after fleeing Minnesota in the wake of the rune stone affair, was obvious. So too was the fact that she had been his lover—sex, to her, had always been a means of conquest and control, as Holmes was well aware. And while Holmes was still uncertain as to the real identities of all the players in her production, he was confident that such matters could be sorted out in due time.

No, what ate at Holmes was how a monster like Mary Mortimer had come to be. How had a woman possessed of both great beauty and great intelligence—two assets rarely combined in the same person, in Holmes's experience—come to move through the world with such pure malevolence?

Choosing his words carefully in hopes of appealing to her vanity, Holmes said, "I have often stated that you are the most remarkable woman I have ever met, and I cannot help but wonder how you came upon your particular set of talents. It is rare to find a man with the craft, cunning and ruthlessness you possess, but it is doubly rare to find such criminal genius in a woman. Did you perhaps have a teacher when you were young?"

Mary Mortimer looked at Holmes with a kind of joyful malevolence and said, "One of the biggest troubles with men is that they always want explanations. I find them to be of little value myself, but as you have asked, I will give you one. My given name, if you must know, is Mary Kershaw and I grew up in Bates County, Missouri, near the Kansas border, during the time of the great troubles there. Do you have any idea what the state of Missouri was like during the War Between the States?"

"No," Holmes admitted.

"When the war broke out, Missouri was a border state, which meant that neither the Union nor Confederacy really controlled it. The whole state was at war with itself, overrun by gangs for whom killing, burning, looting and raping were all in a day's work. I saw my parents killed and our house burned to the ground by Bloody Bill Anderson, the most vicious of all the partisans. I saw terrors which you cannot even imagine. And so I learned at a very young age, Mr. Holmes, that power is the only thing in the world that matters and I was determined to take my fair share of it. That, I believe, is all you need to know."[5]

"I should like to know much more," Holmes said.

"As would I," she replied, then suddenly changed the subject. "I have been wondering, by the way, how you found me here, and I must conclude that you have been in my apartment."

"I have," Holmes acknowledged. "In addition to the monthly payments you made to this stable, I found other documents which I believe will prove quite incriminating."

"Then perhaps we had better proceed immediately to court," she said coolly, "although I have heard disturbing rumors that even justice itself can be purchased in Chicago."

"There will be no court," Holmes replied. "You see, the documents I discovered in your apartment suggest that, unknown to your partners, you have been taking far more than your share of money from the Everleigh Club. I have heard rumors, to use your phrase, that Mr. Coughlin and Mr. Kenna are not the sort of gentlemen who will take this news well."

"So you will have them do the dirty work you are afraid to do," she said defiantly, walking toward Holmes. "Come on, why don't you use that gun of yours? Or are you afraid?"

"I will do what I must," Holmes said, taking a step back, "and—"

Before he could continue she reached up and pulled him toward her, kissing him with such force that he almost tumbled over backward. As she did so, he felt her hand come up toward his chest and he grabbed it just in time to wrench away the derringer she had pulled out from somewhere inside her dress.

Holmes shoved her so hard that she fell to the ground. He bent down to pick up the small, single-shot pistol—a .41 caliber Colt that, fired at close range, would have killed him in an instant.[6]

"What do you intend to do now?" she asked, staring up at Holmes with undisguised hatred.

"I intend to take you to a secure place. Come morning, Mr. Kenna and Mr. Coughlin will be made aware of your embezzlements. After that, I intend to drop you off at Mr. Coughlin's saloon. I am sure he will be pleased to hear what you have to say, even though I know you despise explanations."

She rose to her feet and said, "You will have to shoot me first, and I do not believe that you are up to it."

"True, but I will bind your wrists and take you back by force if necessary," Holmes said, reaching for her arm. But she twisted away and, using a stick she had picked off the dirt floor, poked viciously at Holmes's left eye. Holmes felt a searing stab of pain and buckled to his knees, and when he looked up, Mary Mortimer was holding his pistol.

"You have been careless, Mr. Holmes," she said. "It will cost you your life."

Holmes stared at the barrel of the revolver and then looked up into Mary Mortimer's fierce violet eyes. He said, "Would you really shoot a man in cold blood?"

"Yes," she replied, and pulled the trigger.

Nothing happened. She pulled the trigger several more times with the same result.

"You were right," Holmes said, advancing toward her. "I could not shoot a woman—even you. That is why I took the precaution of emptying my revolver, in the event you might try to use it against me. You are finished, Mrs. Mortimer, and you will now come with me or I shall be compelled to use brute force."

"I think not," she said as Holmes tried to grab her by the wrist. But she managed to break free and ran out the stable door, hoping she could lose Holmes in the darkness and noise of the surrounding rail yards.

Directly beside the stable were the low, steep banks of the Chicago River. As Mrs. Mortimer ran out, she became temporarily disoriented in the darkness and stepped too close to the embankment. She suddenly lost her footing and tumbled down the almost vertical slope into the river.

There had been many inches of rain in Chicago in recent weeks, causing the normally sluggish river to have a much stronger current than usual. Weighed down by her heavy dress and unable to see anything beyond the inky waters, Mrs. Mortimer struggled to find something to hold on to. But the banks were nothing but slippery mud and loose stone, and she felt herself drift away from shore just as Holmes called out her name.

She struggled for some minutes in the dark filth of the river, but swimming was one skill she had never mastered. She cried out once and heard Holmes's voice calling back. But he already seemed far off. Then, after a final struggle, she went under and disappeared into the turbid, swollen river, swept away with all the other detritus of the city, toward the cleansing waters of the Mississippi.

Epilogue

❦ ❧

"I Do"

In the days and weeks following the death of Mary Robinson, as Holmes preferred to call her, many details of her vast scheme emerged, especially after Elsie Cubitt told her story to the press. While recovering in Chicago— where Holmes, Rafferty and I stayed for several days with her—Mrs. Cubitt gave to the *Tribune* and several other dailies a vivid account of her two-week-long nightmare. The tale made headlines in Chicago, New York, London and even in Rafferty's hometown of St. Paul.

All of us—including, I was pleased to note, Inspector Hargreave and Detective Bissen—were hailed as heroes, as was Elsie Cubitt herself. So intense was public interest in the story that three publishers made book offers to Mrs. Cubitt, but she rejected them all, since achieving notoriety had never been her goal. Instead, she consented to the interviews because she wished to put to rest any lingering suspicions that Holmes himself had been involved in her abduction.

The police in New York and Chicago, as well as at Scotland Yard in London, quickly realized the error of their ways once Mrs. Cubitt's story became public. Suddenly under intense reportorial scrutiny, authorities in all three cities claimed that they had never really believed

Holmes could be a criminal and in fact had been working all along to free Mrs. Cubitt. Chief of Police Devery in New York was particularly shameless in this regard, telling reporters that he and Hargreave had deliberately misled the Slaney gang by pretending to believe that Holmes was the real kidnapper.

Hargreave, with whom we visited before returning to England, found this about-face to be richly comic and for a time considered telling the "real story" to New York's eager press. But in the end he decided it would not be worth the trouble.

Rafferty, a policeman himself for several years in St. Paul, was also amused by these official explanations. With his usual good-hearted cynicism, he told me, "The nice thing about coppers, doctor, is they're even better liars than criminals. In this case, however, I'm not sure anyone could digest all the mighty whoppers bein' told without gaggin'."

Anxious to get back on the good side of public opinion, the police in both England and America finally began doing the work they should have done all along. Scotland Yard quickly learned more about Lily Young, the actress and sometime prostitute found murdered in Holmes's hotel room in Liverpool. The Yard discovered, among other things, that a man looking very much like Belgian Jack had been seen with Miss Young at several locations in Norfolk not long before Mrs. Cubitt's abduction. Belgian Jack was later spotted in Liverpool and it was therefore concluded that he, presumably with Little Pete's assistance, had murdered the unfortunate Miss Young.

Scotland Yard was also able to establish that Jake Slaney, traveling under an assumed name, had arrived in England in early June and taken up residence at a small hotel in London only a few miles from our flat on Baker Street. Among his visitors at the hotel, it was learned, was

Mme. DuBois, who had been the first of the gang to arrive in England. Through dogged detective work, the Yard traced Jake Slaney's movements and found out that he, too, had been in Norfolk when Elsie Cubitt was kidnapped.

Perhaps the best news of all to come out of England was that Mrs. Cubitt's dramatic rescue and the press inquiries which followed proved fatal to the career of Deputy Chief Inspector David Butler. The insufferable fellow was roundly criticized for his cavalier treatment of Holmes and was soon vanquished to an obscure post in Scotland Yard's records section, from which he has yet to emerge. Inspector Martin of the Norwich constabulary fared much better — and deservedly so — receiving a commendation for his work.

Meanwhile, the New York police were able to verify where and when the Slaney gang, including by then the assassin Billy Wainwright, had stayed in that city. Perhaps the police's most intriguing discovery, of great interest to me, was that I was to be Wainwright's first target at St. Paul's Chapel. The assassin had told an underworld associate, who later talked to the police, that his assignment was to shoot me "if possible." Inspector Hargreave was to be the next target. My death, the conspirators believed, would serve as further evidence of Holmes's demented state of mind, since it was he who had supposedly hired Wainwright. The police, however, never succeeded in tracking down the ten thousand dollars stolen from my bag at Grant's Tomb, and the money presumably found its way into the coffers of Tammany Hall as partial payment for its services on Mary Robinson's behalf.

Inspector Wilson Hargreave was not involved in any of these later investigations, for in early August he tendered his resignation and took a job with the Pinkertons. In a letter to Holmes, Hargreave said that the famed private detectives were "at least moderately honest" and paid more than the City of New York as well. Detective

Bissen, meanwhile, received a promotion after his work was cited in the *World*, which was as quick to proclaim Holmes's innocence as it had been to declare his guilt.

The newspapers in New York proved less effective, however, when it came to digging out the story of Tammany Hall's involvement with the Slaney gang and Mrs. Robinson. Not even the *Times*, which had done so much to bring down Boss Tweed nearly thirty years earlier, could untangle Tammany's role in the affair, and Boss Crocker was never prosecuted.

In Chicago, the investigation also moved forward with considerable speed following Mrs. Cubitt's deliverance, although one principal—Bathhouse John Coughlin— received virtually no scrutiny and was never charged with a crime. As Wooldridge later explained to us, "Bathhouse is still untouchable in this town and will be until the money runs out."

Spurred on by the newspapers, the police in Chicago did, however, have the good sense to put Wooldridge in charge of the case. It took him little more than twenty-four hours to discover, among other things, that Mme. Simone DuBois was in fact Ethel McBride, née Slaney, and that she was an aunt of the two dead brothers. Perhaps not surprisingly, she turned out to be an actress, leading Holmes to observe dryly that we had "nearly been done in by a gang of thespians."

Having made her home in California, Mrs. McBride was a regular on the theatrical circuits in the West and South, but only very rarely stopped in Chicago. Elsie Cubitt recalled, as a very young child, seeing a certain "Aunt Ethel" once or twice at the Slaney house, but she did not remember her well enough to identify her years later in her role as Mme. DuBois.

Mrs. McBride was arrested at a train station in St. Louis, Missouri, a few days after Elsie Cubitt's rescue and was brought back to Chicago, where she eventually was charged with kidnapping, accessory to murder and a variety of other offenses. Holmes and I interviewed her at some length in the Cook County jail, but she proved to be remarkably elusive—"a champion liar," as Holmes put it—and we learned nothing of value from her.

She was arraigned in court the day before we left Chicago, and according to the newspapers gave such a stellar performance when asked to enter a plea that the judge, in one correspondent's words, "dropped her bail to a mere $500 out of sheer gratitude for having witnessed such an astonishing example of the theatrical arts." Other observers, however, were of the opinion that the judge, a known associate of Hinky Dink Kenna, had been bribed in the standard Chicago manner. Mrs. McBride duly posted her bail and, to no one's surprise, failed to appear in court some months later for her trial. As I write these words, she remains at large somewhere in the wilds of the American West.

The other conspirators, including the man who played Sherlock Holmes, did not fare nearly so well. Detective Wooldridge quickly established that Holmes's stand-in was an actor named Charles Swain, who was probably hired on Mrs. McBride's recommendation. Swain came to his role with impeccable credentials, for in 1895 he had starred as Holmes in an unauthorized version of a second-rate play called *Under the Clock*. His performance was sufficiently convincing, I later learned, to earn plaudits from newspapers in Chicago, St. Louis and Baltimore. However, a more astringent New York reviewer found Swain to be "an overcured ham."[1]

Charles Swain's acting career ended abruptly the day after Mrs. Cubitt's release when his body—weighted with two bullets in the head—washed up on the shores of Lake Michigan in Chicago. By a certain coincidence, his corpse was found not far from the Potomac Apartments, where Mary Robinson had made her home. The lake soon gave up two more bodies with similar wounds. The victims were readily identified as Peter (Little Pete) O'Riley and John (Belgian Jack) Flannery, both well-known criminal figures from the Levee. It was assumed that all three had been executed by other members of the gang for allowing Holmes to escape from the *Pennsylvania Limited*.

Curiously, the body of Mary Robinson was the last to be found, for it was not until three weeks after her fall into the Chicago River that her decomposed remains were found in a side channel near the city's stockyards. Holmes and I were back in England by this time and could not view the body. She was identified primarily by her clothes, since her features were horribly distorted by so many days in the water.

This rather tenuous identification left Holmes wondering aloud whether Mrs. Robinson had "engineered yet another last-minute escape." I thought this highly unlikely, as I am sure did Holmes himself. Still, enough of a doubt remained to leave Holmes uneasy for months to come. Equally disconcerting was the fact that Chicago police detectives, even under Wooldridge's peerless direction, had no success in unlocking the mystery of Mrs. Robinson's past—or, at least that portion of it preceding our first contact with her in Hinckley in 1894.

In a letter to Holmes after months of fruitless digging, Wooldridge wrote that, "Mary Robinson is a regular phantom. No one seems to know where she was born, what her real name is or how she occupied herself before you first met her in Minnesota. I have my doubts we will ever know."

Holmes had by this time already made an attempt of his own to trace her history. Before leaving Chicago, he sent a telegram to the clerk of court in Bates County, Missouri, asking for information about a girl named Mary Kershaw, possibly born in the county sometime in the late 1840s.

The reply, which came back a day later, was as follows: DEAR MR. HOLMES: HAVE INSPECTED ALL APPROPRIATE RECORDS AND WISH TO INFORM YOU NO CHILD BY NAME OF MARY KERSHAW BORN IN THIS COUNTY, IN 1840S OR ANY OTHER TIME. NOR DO I KNOW OF ANYONE BY THAT NAME WHO WAS EVER A RESIDENT OF THIS COUNTY. YOURS TRULY, G. HARGENS, CLERK OF COURT.

"Are you surprised?" I asked Holmes after he had shown me the message.

"No," he said. "Indeed, I suppose she has now gotten her final revenge in a way, for I shall always be left to wonder who she really was and how she came upon her extraordinary villainy."

As for Elsie Cubitt herself—surely the most remarkable woman of all in this affair—the ending of the story must be accounted at once triumphant and bittersweet. Her triumph, of course, lay in her ability to survive an ordeal that few other women—or men, for that matter—could have endured with such grace, courage and continual presence of mind. But the one man whose heart she hoped to win proved, in the end, unready to accept the gift she offered—perhaps to his own lasting regret.

In the days immediately following her release, however, all of us took joy in the fact that she had won back her freedom despite the vicious and cunning forces arrayed against her. So it was that on Tuesday night, July 23, we sat down in the dining room of the Sherman House to salute Mrs. Cubitt and to say our farewells. Mrs. Cubitt, Holmes and I were to begin our long return trip to England in the morning, while Rafferty and Thomas intended to catch a late-night express to St. Paul. Wooldridge also joined us, and the six of us spent much of the dinner discussing the singular case which had brought us together.

Mrs. Cubitt provided a riveting account of her abduction in England and all that followed, and in the process she answered many of our questions about how she had finally managed to make her escape. Then Holmes took the floor to tell his tale from the time of his kidnapping to his arrival at the Sons of Hibernia Hall. He, too, cleared up several questions, including one question which had nagged at me for days.

Said Holmes, "Dr. Watson has been wondering why I did not attempt to contact him immediately after my escape at Horseshoe Curve. Believe me, it is something I very much wished to do. However, I concluded that it would not be wise for two reasons. First, I could not be certain where he was, and, second, I learned from reading the Altoona newspaper that both he and I had become not merely criminal suspects but criminal fugitives in the eyes of the law. I therefore thought it best to remain undercover until I reached Chicago and could get in touch with Detective Wooldridge."

"Fact is, neither of us knew you were in Chicago, Dr. Watson," said Wooldridge. "Didn't know Mr. Rafferty and Mr. Thomas were here either. So busy tracking down Mrs. Cubitt didn't have time to think about anything else. Too bad, I guess, but worked out in end."

"Indeed it did," I said. "By the way, Holmes, I must ask, did you deliberately leave behind the cufflink and matchbox we found in the tunnel beneath St. Paul's?"

Holmes's answer came as a surprise: "I honestly do not know, though I think it quite likely. I was knocked almost senseless by the blow I received to the head and have only a vague memory of being carried through the tunnel on a man's shoulders, presumably those of the late Belgian Jack Flannery. It is possible I was able to slip the matchbox out of his pocket and loosen my other cufflink as well.

However, I admit it's possible the clues were left behind by my kidnappers to draw you to Chicago."

Thomas now weighed in with a question which had also been on my mind. "I understand what Mrs. Robinson and Jack Slaney were up to," he said, "but I don't see how they thought they could pin the blame on you for Mrs. Cubitt's kidnapping. I'll grant they paid off the police in New York and Chicago, but could they have bribed Scotland Yard as well? From what you've told us, Mr. Holmes, it's pretty obvious you and Dr. Watson couldn't have done many of the things you were accused of doing, especially in England."

Holmes replied, "As usual, you have made an excellent point, Mr. Thomas. I do not believe Deputy Chief Inspector Butler or anyone else at the Yard was bribed. However, if Butler and the Yard had conducted a competent investigation from the start, they certainly would have discovered that I could not have kidnapped Mrs. Cubitt. For example, on the day I was supposedly escorting Mrs. Cubitt—or, as it turned out, her impersonator—on a train to London, Watson and I were in fact investigating her disappearance at Ridling Thorpe Manor. Numerous witnesses, including Butler himself, could testify to this fact. I am capable of many things, but I have not yet mastered the art of being in two places at once! Still, our adversaries sowed so much confusion and doubt that the Yard, which had reason to think poorly of me as it was, seized on the opportunity to make me a suspect, despite obvious evidence to the contrary."

The next question came from Rafferty: "What about that crazy weddin' invitation? Was that just another way of makin' sure we'd all troop to Chicago and walk into a trap?"

Holmes smiled and said, "If nothing else, the invitation demonstrates that Mrs. Robinson possessed a macabre sense of humor to go with her unbridled malevolence. But you're right, Mr. Rafferty, in thinking that the intent of the invitation was to draw all the principals here. We now know that an invitation was in fact delivered to Watson's hotel in New York after he had left to stay with Hargreave. However, I believe Watson, fast-moving fellow that he is, arrived more quickly in Chicago than Mrs. Robinson and the others had anticipated, although we may never know whether that was actually the case."

"Well, I am simply happy that all of you did arrive," said Elsie Cubitt, who despite her terrible ordeal looked radiant in a long blue dress with a white choker collar. I also noticed that she wore silver earrings which, like Holmes's cufflinks, bore a tiny image of Ridling Thorpe Manor. She added, surveying the table with her sparkling eyes, "I could not have survived much longer without all of you."

"Ah, but the fact that you did survive is a testament to your courage and tenacity," said Holmes, who now raised his glass of port and said, "I propose a toast to Mrs. Elsie Cubitt, the bravest woman I have ever known."

As there was universal agreement with this sentiment, we all took turns joining in, until Rafferty—with his uncanny flair for the mischievous—said, "Speakin' of bravery, Mr. Holmes, I'm wonderin' if you and this lovely lady have plans together. Are we perhaps to see a real marriage one day? 'Twould be an event I'd travel around the world and back to see, if I had to, and that's a fact!"

Mrs. Cubitt responded to this thinly veiled suggestion with a coy smile. Holmes, on the other hand, looked as flustered as a man who had gone out for a walk through the heart of London but had somehow forgotten his pants.

"Really, Mr. Rafferty, I do not think that is an appropriate question," he said. "I have no plans. That is to say, I have certainly not—"

"Don't dig too deep a hole for yourself, Mr. Holmes," Rafferty said with a broad grin, "or you just might fall into it. Well, we'll let nature take its course, though I must say the two of you would make a fine couple. Don't you agree, Wash?"

"Couldn't be better," Thomas said.

"How about you, Dr. Watson?"

"I think I shall leave that to Holmes and Mrs. Cubitt to decide," I said diplomatically, though in truth I found it hard to countenance the idea of Holmes ever getting married, even to a woman as exceptional as Elsie Cubitt.

I now turned the conversation to other topics—for which, I believe, Holmes was eternally grateful—and the dinner went on merrily until almost ten o'clock, when Rafferty and Thomas left to catch their train after many farewells. Before leaving, Rafferty promised to deliver a complete report of our adventures to James J. Hill, who had done his utmost to help us. Wooldridge soon departed as well, and I followed suit, leaving Holmes and Mrs. Cubitt to themselves. What they talked about I do not know, and come morning, as we set off for New York and then England, he had nothing to say about any "plans" he and Mrs. Cubitt may have made.

Our return to England proved to be something of a second ordeal. Photographers and newspaper reporters gathered to give us a sendoff in Chicago and there were members of the local press at every stop, including Altoona, where Holmes, after escaping the throng, quietly arranged to make restitution for the various acts of thievery he had committed following his escape from the *Pennsylvania Limited*.

Upon arriving in New York, we were all but besieged by a small army of newspaper reporters and finally had to be escorted to our hotel by a phalanx of policemen. We then had a reunion with Hargreave and Bissen and introduced these two stalwarts to Mrs. Cubitt. They were, of course, charmed, and we later enjoyed a delightful dinner in a private room at Louis Sherry's Restaurant during which Hargreave regaled us with many phenomenal tales about Tammany Hall. He also apologized profusely to Holmes for being duped into "spying" on him at Chief Devery's request. Holmes told the inspector that he understood completely and that he only wished he could have "such a courageous and capable spy" working with him on every investigation.[2]

We stayed only one night in New York before boarding the Cunard Line's *Lucania*, again with the press in full attendance, for our return to England. The voyage was smooth and for me, at least, uneventful. Holmes and Mrs. Cubitt spent a great many hours together—indeed, I felt very much like a large, old and very squeaky third wheel—but I did at one point manage to speak to her alone. She confided to me that although she loved Holmes greatly, she did not think his feelings toward her would ever blossom beyond those of deep friendship.

"He is too much the solitary figure," she told me, a certain wistfulness evident in her bright and knowing eyes. "I do not believe he would ever marry, for he is a man who has been wed all his life to ideas and nothing else. Still, I shall always cherish his friendship, and yours, Dr. Watson."

"You are right about Holmes," I said. "He is quite different from other men." Indeed, I could not help but think how different he was, for how many men were there in the world who could fail to fall hopelessly in love with a woman like Elsie Cubitt?

It was August 4 by the time we reached London, again amid much hoopla in the press. But other news soon pushed us—to our great relief—off the front pages, and on August 6 we said goodbye to Elsie Cubitt at St. Pancras Station. She cried softly and gave Holmes another kiss before boarding a train back to her home in Norfolk.

"I hope you realize what you have done," I said to Holmes—perhaps impertinently—as we watched her train depart.

"I do," said Holmes, who never brought up the subject again.

However, he continues to correspond with Mrs. Cubitt and to meet with her at least once a month, and who can say what the future may bring for two souls at once so different and yet so much alike?

Notes

PROLOGUE

1. Although Sherlock Holmes did not believe in fairies, the man who introduced him to the world, Sir Arthur Conan Doyle, did. In 1916 Doyle became a convert to spiritualism and it led him to defend a number of hoaxes, including what became known as the Cottingley fairies. The hoax began in 1917 when two English girls—one fifteen, the other eleven and both from the village of Cottingley in Yorkshire—made photographs of themselves with tiny figures that the girls claimed were fairies. Doyle heard about the pictures in 1920 and, ignoring evidence such as the supposed fairies' taste for the latest in Parisian fashions, came to their defense, writing a favorable article for *Strand Magazine* in December of that year. Later, he dashed off a book entitled *The Coming of the Fairies.* "He was," writes one biographer, "well and truly suckered." Only in old age did the girls finally admit that they had faked the pictures. For a good account of this unfortunate episode, see Martin Booth, *The Doctor and the Detective: A Biography of Sir Arthur Conan Doyle* (New York: Thomas Dunne Books, 2000), 320–25.

2. Holmes's breaking of the code and his capture of Abe Slaney are related by Watson in one of his most famous tales, "The Adventure of the Dancing Men."

3. St. Paul's Chapel, on Broadway between Fulton and Vesey streets, dates to 1766 and is the oldest church building in Man-

hattan. Modeled on one of London's most famous churches — St. Martin-in the-Fields (1721–26) — St. Paul's was built as a "chapel-of-ease" for parishioners of Trinity Church who lived too far away to attend services there. It remains a part of Trinity Church to this day. George Washington worshiped at St. Paul's on April 30, 1789, after his inauguration as the first president of the United States. Both houses of Congress also attended the services that day, and Washington frequently worshiped at the chapel during the next two years, when New York City served as the nation's capital. The chapel acquired a special place in the hearts of New Yorkers after terrorists brought down the twin towers of the World Trade Center and several nearby buildings on September 11, 2001. Located only a few blocks from the twin towers, St. Paul's miraculously survived the attack without so much as a broken window, although its graveyard was covered with six inches of ash. After an inspection revealed the chapel to be structurally sound, it quickly became a haven for rescue workers as well as the site of many memorial services. For handsome photographs of the chapel and a brief account of its history, see Roger Kennedy, *American Churches* (New York: Stewart, Tabori & Chang, 1982), 116–17.

4. The post office, built in 1875, was a massive granite pile at Broadway and Park Row, designed in the then-fashionable French Second Empire style. Its architect was Alfred Mullett, who in the same year designed the even more grandiose Executive Office Building in Washington, D.C. Both buildings were widely reviled in the press (no less a critic than Henry Adams called the Washington building "Mr. Mullett's architectural infant asylum"), which may help explain why Mullett committed suicide in 1890. The post office was torn down in 1939 and its site is now part of the green expanse of city hall park. For a good photograph of the post office in all of its overwrought glory, see Mary Black, *Old New York in Early Photographs* (New York: Dover, 1976), 43. At thirty stories and 319 feet, the twin-towered Park Row Building, at 15 Park Row, was the world's tallest office structure when it opened in 1899. Its reign atop the New York skyline lasted until only 1908 when the 612-foot Singer Tower opened a few blocks to the south on Broadway. The Park Row Building still stands today. For more on the building, see Sarah

Bradford Landau and Carl W. Condit, *Rise of the New York Sky-scraper, 1865–1913* (New Haven: Yale University Press, 1996), 252–56.

5. Watson's account of Holmes's duel with Professor Moriarty in April 1891 at Reichenbach Falls is recounted in "The Final Problem." Holmes thereafter began what is known as the "Great Hiatus," wandering the world for three years to elude Moriarty's henchmen. He finally turned up again in London in April 1894, a joyous homecoming related by Watson in "The Adventure of the Empty House."

6. The New York *World,* founded in 1860, was acquired by Joseph Pulitzer in 1883 and within four years its Sunday edition had the largest circulation of any American newspaper. By 1900 the *World* was in hot competition with William Randolph Hearst's *New York Journal.* Both papers published a version of a popular cartoon known as "Yellow Kid." The cartoon inspired a name—yellow journalism—that is still used to describe an emphasis on highly sensational news stories.

CHAPTER ONE

1. Dr. John Watson's narrative of the case I have titled *The Disappearance of Sherlock Holmes* constitutes one of the more intriguing chapters in the Sherlockian legacy. Known to scholars simply as the "Cubitt Manuscript," the narrative—now with Watson's other papers at the British Museum in London—is disjointed and incomplete. However, it offers invaluable insight into Watson's thinking during what must have been an extraordinarily difficult time for him. The form of the manuscript, which is handwritten in some sections and typed in others, leaves little doubt that Watson labored over it for many years. It is not known why Watson never saw fit to complete the narrative, but it may well be that Holmes—concerned about the highly personal nature of the case—vetoed the idea of publication. I have edited the narrative to avoid repetition and to fill in a few missing details, but it is presented here largely as Watson wrote it. To fill in the rest of the story, I have built a narrative based on contemporaneous newspaper accounts, excerpts from various personal docu-

ments left behind by Shadwell Rafferty, and the unpublished memoirs of Detective Clifton Wooldridge (at the Chicago Historical Society). Of course, the thoughts I attribute to Sherlock Holmes, Elsie Cubitt and other characters fall into the realm of fictional reconstruction.

2. The "affair of the Napoleons," as Watson calls it, involved the mysterious destruction of busts of Napoleon Bonaparte by someone in London. The case, one of Holmes's most famous, was first published as "The Adventure of the Six Napoleons" in *Collier's* magazine in April 1904. Henry H. Holmes, who went by several other names, is believed to have murdered scores of women in Chicago in the early 1890s, luring them to a grotesque mansion—complete with torture chambers—he maintained on the city's South Side. He was finally hanged in Philadelphia in 1896 for another murder. Holmes's monograph on serial killers referred to by Watson would be a pioneering work in the history of criminology. Unfortunately, no trace of the monograph has ever been found and it's not clear whether Holmes ever completed it.

3. As Holmes notes here, Watson had not published "The Adventure of the Dancing Men" as of July 1900. The story, in fact, did not appear until December 1903, in *Collier's* and *Strand* magazines.

4. Holmes read the London *Daily Telegraph* faithfully because of the extensive coverage it usually gave to strange and sensational crimes. Princetown Prison (often referred to as Dartmoor because of its location on the famous moors of that name) was built in 1809 and is still in use today. It is located less than ten miles from the port of Plymouth, where Abe Slaney went after his escape. Dartmoor, of course, is also the setting for *The Hound of the Baskervilles*, one of Holmes's greatest adventures.

5. Watson's reference to the "German Ocean" reflects a term for the North Sea that was commonly used in England before the First World War.

6. Inspector Martin's first name was not mentioned in "The Adventure of the Dancing Men," an oversight that Watson corrected in this account.

7. Holmes's familiarity with Eban Patrick, Elsie Cubitt's fa-

ther, suggests that the great detective must have done some re-
search following the conclusion of the "The Adventure of the
Dancing Men." Patrick's first name was not mentioned in that
tale, although Watson did quote Abe Slaney as saying that
Patrick was "the boss of the Joint" and "a clever man."

8. I have been unable to find any record of a Smythe's Inn in
the village of North Walsham, which leads me to believe that
Watson, for some reason, used a fictitious name for the establishment.

CHAPTER TWO

1. Holmes talked often about Moriarty's dark genius. In "The
Adventure of the Empty House," for example, Holmes told Watson, "A criminal strain ran in his (Moriarty's) blood, which, instead of being modified, was increased and rendered infinitely
more dangerous by his extraordinary mental powers."

CHAPTER THREE

1. For an account of Holmes's and Watson's adventures during the "Hinckley fire," which occurred in Minnesota in 1894, see
Larry Millett, *Sherlock Holmes and the Red Demon* (New York:
Viking, 1996). The Good Sword of Winfarthing, enshrined in a
village of that name in southern Norfolk, is a medieval relic said
to possess the power to locate stolen property and, perhaps more
importantly, enable women to rid themselves of unwanted husbands.

2. A sovereign, or pound, was worth about five American dollars in 1900—no small amount at that time.

3. The market cross Watson refers to here is a pavilionlike
structure in the center of North Walsham. It was renovated in
1899, when the clock was installed. For a photograph of the
structure, see Neil R. Storey, *Norfolk: A Photographic History, 1860–
1960* (Phoenix Mill, England: Sutton Publishing, 1996), 82.

4. Watson's journal has a lengthy account of the theft of the
Chesterfield ruby, said to be one of the largest in the world. However, Watson never "wrote up" the case, perhaps because Holmes

suspected the thief was a high-ranking member of the English government. The gem was stolen in March 1900 as it was being transported from the vault of a London bank to a special exhibit at the British Museum. The theft occurred despite the presence of two guards assigned by Scotland Yard. Holmes's critical remarks about the Yard's investigation may be found in the April 16, 1900, edition of the *Daily Telegraph*.

5. The Church Army was an evangelical organization that held open-air religious meetings throughout England. The army's itinerant preachers typically traveled in specially equipped horse-drawn vans. There is a photograph of one of these vans in Storey, *Norfolk*, 21.

CHAPTER FOUR

1. Watson, who over the years described many aspects of Holmes's appearance, never mentions that he had "a peculiar way of holding his head." However, Watson did note in *A Study in Scarlet* that Holmes's hands "were invariably blotted with ink and stained with chemicals."

CHAPTER FIVE

1. Although Irene Adler appears in only one of Watson's stories, "A Scandal in Bohemia," her relationship with Holmes has long been a fertile source of scholarly discussion and debate. Watson's reference here to Holmes's "long and rather mysterious entanglement" with Adler is intriguing, but there is nothing in the doctor's journals—or in any other known document—that expands upon this statement. As a result, the exact nature of Holmes's relationship with Adler, a New Jersey–born opera singer who is believed to have died in about 1890, may never be known.

2. The Midland and Great Northern Joint Railway, created in 1893 by consolidating a number of smaller lines, offered train service from London to various communities in Norfolk. The line apparently did not enjoy a good reputation, since its initials were sometimes said to stand for "Muddle and Go Nowhere." After further consolidations, the line was closed in 1959.

3. The iron train shed at St. Pancras Station, completed in 1868, was for many years the widest structural span in the world, covering 245 feet in a single great arch. The shed is still used today.

4. The St. Pancras Hotel, designed by Sir George Gilbert Scott, opened in 1876 and remains one of London's most impressive Victorian buildings.

5. Cunard Lines launched the *Campania* and its sister ship, the *Lucania,* in 1893, and for a time they were considered the finest liners afloat. Holmes and Watson were very familiar with the *Campania,* having made at least three crossings of the North Atlantic aboard the liner in the 1890s.

Chapter Seven

1. Mycroft Holmes, Sherlock's older and equally brilliant brother, held an important post in the British government, which is why he would have been a logical candidate to intercede on Sherlock's behalf. Unfortunately, Mycroft's exact position with the government is unknown, despite much digging by Sherlockian scholars. Mycroft appears in only two of Watson's stories — "The Greek Interpreter" and "The Adventure of the Bruce-Partington Plans."

2. A man named Stamford did indeed introduce Watson to Holmes, in March of 1881. However, Stamford's first name is unknown, since Watson neglected to mention it in *A Study in Scarlet,* the novel that describes the doctor's first encounter with Holmes. The Trials Hotel, at 56-62 Castle Street in Liverpool, remains in operation today and is only about two blocks from what is probably the city's most famous modern attraction — the Cavern Club, where the Beatles got their start.

3. The 704-foot-long, 17,000-ton *Oceania* was the biggest ship in the world when it was launched by the White Star Line in 1899. However, it was soon outshone by larger, more luxurious liners (among them the White Star's *Titanic* in 1912) and ended its days ignominiously in 1914 when it ran aground in the Shetland Islands.

4. The 535-foot-long *St. Paul* was an 11,000-ton liner built for the American Steamship Company in 1895. Its sister ship, suitably

called the *St. Louis,* was launched in the same year. The ships, capable of speeds reaching nineteen knots, were the fastest American-built liners of their time. The *St. Paul* earned a small footnote in history on November 15, 1899, when one of its passengers—Guglielmo Marconi, the inventor of wireless telegraphy—published the first-ever newspaper at sea, which he called the *Transatlantic Times.* Marconi used his wireless set to receive the latest news from a telegraph station in England and had his newspaper out by the time the *St. Paul* docked at Southampton, England.

5. Albert Dock, a gigantic complex of wharves and warehouses built in an impressively severe style between 1841 and 1848, has today succumbed to the seemingly inevitable fate of nineteenth-century industrial architecture—it is a tourist attraction. Museums, shops, restaurants and offices now occupy the buildings that once served a thriving world trade.

6. Lanier (first name unknown) was the *Daily Telegraph*'s crime reporter and apparently Holmes's closest contact among London newspapermen. Watson first mentioned Lanier in connection with the rune stone case of 1899. See Larry Millett, *Sherlock Holmes and the Rune Stone Mystery* (New York: Viking, 1999), 110.

7. The North Western Hotel opened in 1871 next to Liverpool's main train station on Lime Street. It was designed by Alfred Waterhouse, one of England's premier Victorian-era architects, in a style that can only be described as overpowering. The hotel later fell on hard times and was acquired in 1999 by John Moores University, which renovated the structure and turned it into a residence hall.

8. George Square lies in the heart of Glasgow and is surrounded by some of the city's major public buildings, including the post office, the Bank of England and the City Chambers. "Under Scott" refers to one of the square's other monumental attractions—a statue of Sir Walter Scott mounted atop a 70-foot-high Doric column.

CHAPTER EIGHT

1. Although Marconi transmitted radio signals over significant distances in the 1890s, his system did not come into common

use aboard ships until the early years of the twentieth century. The key moment came in December 1901, when Marconi succeeded in sending a signal across the Atlantic, from Newfoundland to England. Before this decisive demonstration, some scientists believed that radio signals could only be transmitted a distance of 100 to 200 miles because of the curvature of the earth.

2. Sidney Edward Paget (1860–1908) was the foremost illustrator of Sherlock Holmes. Beginning in 1891 with drawings for "A Scandal in Bohemia" in *Strand Magazine*, Paget produced a total of 357 illustrations for Sherlockian tales. His image of Holmes was modeled on his brother, Walter Paget. For more on Paget, see Arthur Conan Doyle, *The Annotated Sherlock Holmes*, ed. William S. Baring-Gould (New York: Clarkson N. Potter, 1967; Wings Books, 1992), 33–36.

CHAPTER NINE

1. Holmes's "little investigation" on behalf of Lord Salisbury is another of those tantalizing tidbits Watson so often dropped into his stories without further explanation. I was unable to find any other mention of such an investigation among Watson's papers, but the matter must clearly have been of great import since it appears to have originated at the highest level of English government. Lord Salisbury was Robert Arthur Talbot Gascoyne-Cecil (1830–1903), the arch conservative prime minister of England from 1895 to 1902. For a good brief sketch of Salisbury—a brilliant, strange and difficult man—see Barbara Tuchman, *The Proud Tower* (New York: Macmillan, 1966; Bantam Books, 1967), 4–12.

2. Holmes's comments here are a restatement of his famous observation to Watson recorded in *The Sign of Four:* "How often have I said to you that when you have eliminated the impossible, whatever remains, however improbable, must be the truth?"

3. What Watson refers to here as the "customs office" was actually called the Barge Office—a large towered building that stood along the outer wall of the Battery at the lower tip of Manhattan. Although an immigrant receiving station had been opened in 1892 on Ellis Island, it burned to the ground in June 1897. While new facilities were being constructed on the island, immigrants

were received at the Barge Office. Ellis Island reopened on December 17, 1900. For historical information on the Gansevoort pier, see Ann L. Buttenwieser, *Manhattan Water-Bound*, 2nd ed. (Syracuse, N.Y.: Syracuse University Press, 1999), 85–102.

4. Little is known about Inspector Wilson Hargreave beyond the slim information provided here by Watson, whose first reference to Hargreave came in "The Adventure of the Dancing Men." Even less is known about the "notorious Tammany Hall embezzler" cited by Watson, since there is no other mention of the case in any of Watson's stories, journals or correspondence. Moreover, Tammany Hall produced so many crooks during its long history in New York that the embezzler could have been almost any high-ranking member of the organization.

5. The old New York police headquarters building, constructed in the 1860s, was at 300 Mulberry Street, between Houston and Bleecker streets. In 1909 the police moved to new headquarters at 240 Centre Street, not far from city hall.

6. Now the Albert Apartments, the Hotel Albert, at East Eleventh Street and University Place, was built in 1883. Its architect was Henry J. Hardenbergh, designer of some of Manhattan's most splendid buildings, including the Dakota Apartments (1884) and the Plaza Hotel (1907).

7. The 300-room Astor House, originally known as the Park House, was constructed in 1836 to the designs of architect Isaiah Rogers. It was built for John Jacob Astor, the fur baron and real estate tycoon, on the site of his mansion (he built a new and larger one elsewhere, of course) and for many years was considered Manhattan's most splendid hotel. Statesmen and celebrities from around the world stayed at the hotel, and president-elect Abraham Lincoln delivered an impromptu speech in one of its many public rooms in February 1861. By 1900, however, the Astor House was a fading dowager—long since supplanted by newer, grander and better equipped hotels to the north in midtown—and it finally closed its doors for good in 1913. The south half of the old hotel was demolished in 1914, and the remainder came down in 1927. Office buildings now occupy the site. For photographs, see Black, *Old New York*, 38; Edward B. Watson, *New York Then and Now* (New York: Dover, 1976), 6–7; and Nathan Silver, *Lost New York* (Boston: Houghton Mifflin, 1967), 68.

8. The case Holmes refers to here is described in Larry Millett, *Sherlock Holmes and the Secret Alliance* (New York: Viking, 2001).

9. For an account of the various corruption scandals that plagued the New York Police Department in the nineteenth century (and the twentieth), see James Lardner and Thomas Reppetto, *NYPD: A City and Its Police* (New York: Henry Holt, 2000).

CHAPTER TEN

1. Holmes often talked about the value of maintaining an open and unfettered mind when considering a problem. In "The Cardboard Box," a story dating from 1893, Holmes tells Watson that he approached the investigation "with an absolutely blank mind, which is always an advantage."

CHAPTER ELEVEN

1. The Western Union Building, at the northwest corner of Broadway and Dey Street, was among the tallest buildings in New York when it opened in 1875, although it was only ten stories high. Designed by George B. Post, the building featured a tall mansard roof topped by the usual tower. A huge operators room occupied the entire eighth floor, which was encircled by an elaborate iron balcony. Although it looked purely decorative, the balcony was used to carry the numerous telegraph wires that fed into and out of the operators room. One of the first skyscraper fires in the history of New York City damaged the building's upper floors in 1890. These floors were rebuilt in 1891 as part of a project that included construction of another building for the company next door. Both buildings have been demolished. For more information and photographs, see Landau and Condit, *New York Skyscraper,* 78–83.

CHAPTER TWELVE

1. Rafferty's saloon, known simply as "Shad's," was located in the Ryan Hotel at Sixth and Robert streets in downtown St. Paul. It was in operation from about 1888 to 1920, when Rafferty apparently sold it. Both the saloon and hotel are long gone. For a fuller

description of the establishment, see Larry Millett, *Sherlock Holmes and the Ice Palace Murders* (New York: Viking, 1998), 86–91.

CHAPTER THIRTEEN

1. Gay Street is a short, crooked little lane, between Christopher Street and Waverly Place, in what is known today as the West Village. The street is lined with three-story, Federal-style townhouses, dating from the 1820s to about the 1860s. Any one of them might have been the house Watson refers to here.

2. The 14,000-ton *Saxonia* was launched by Cunard Lines in 1899 and plied the Liverpool-to-Boston run for a decade. The liner, built in Glasgow, was rather slow (fifteen knots top speed) for its time but nonetheless remained in service until 1925, when it was scrapped.

3. The fourteen-story Hotel Manhattan, another deluxe design by architect Henry Hardenbergh, opened in 1896 and was located just a block west of Grand Central Station. For a historic photograph of the hotel, see Jeff Hirsh, *Manhattan Hotels, 1880–1920* (Dover, N.H.: Arcadia Publishing, 1997), 27. For a detailed discussion of Manhattan's magnificent turn-of-the-century hotels, see Robert A. M. Stern, Gregory Gilmartin and John Massengale, *New York 1900: Metropolitan Architecture and Urbanism, 1890–1915* (New York: Rizzoli, 1983), 252–79.

4. The "Mr. Hess" referred to here was Jacob Hess, one of four members of a board that oversaw the New York Police Department in 1900. However, a law enacted that year finally abolished the board and created a single police commissioner—a system still in use today. See Lardner and Reppetto, *NYPD*, 155.

5. Named for the intersection of the five streets a few blocks northeast of New York City Hall, Five Points was for much of the nineteenth century the city's most wretched slum and a haven of gang activity. Under pressure from reformers such as Jacob Riis, the city in the 1880s cleared out many of the old tenements in Five Points and replaced them with what is now known as Columbus Park. Today, much of the old Five Points area lies within Chinatown.

6. For more information on the houses along "Vanderbilt

Row," as well as photographs, see Stern, Gilmartin and Massengale, *New York 1900*, 309–14.

7. The Astor mansion was actually a double house, built for Caroline Astor and her son, Col. John Jacob Astor IV, and completed in 1895. It was designed in a sumptuous French chateau style by Richard Morris Hunt, perhaps most famous today as the architect of Biltmore (1887–95), George Washington Vanderbilt's fabulous North Carolina estate. The Astor residence, like most of the mansions once found along Fifth Avenue, is gone. A synagogue, Temple Emanu-el (1927–29), now occupies the site. For more on the Astor double house, see Stern, Gilmartin and Massengale, *New York 1900*, 316–21.

8. Caroline Webster Schermerhorn Astor (1830–1908) was married to one of John Jacob's descendants, William Astor, and was for many years the queen of New York high society. Her husband, who died in 1892, was not especially fond of the social scene, so Mrs. Astor hired a man named Ward McAllister to act as her social arbiter. McAllister made sure that guests at Mrs. Astor's monthly balls were only of the very best sort, once telling a reporter that "there are only about four hundred people in fashionable New York Society." Conveniently, this also happened to be the number of guests Mrs. Astor's ballroom could accommodate. Thus was born the famous "Four Hundred," New York's most exclusive crowd. One chronicler of New York said of Mrs. Astor that she "lacked beauty and brains, wore a black wig because her hair was falling out, but rose to undisputed leadership in society because she had $50,000,000 and the personality of a Prussian drill sergeant." See Edward Robb Ellis, *The Epic of New York City* (New York: Old Town Books, 1966), 413.

9. Holmes by 1900 seems to have acquired a hearty dislike of the large and fractious Astor clan, no doubt because of his experiences a year earlier when he became entangled in an Astor family feud. The case, which Watson never wrote down in any detail, involved a dispute between John Jacob Astor IV and his cousin, William Waldorf Astor, over the Waldorf-Astoria Hotel (actually two hotels, owned separately by the cousins but operated jointly after the two temporarily patched up their differences). Holmes was hired by John Jacob Astor IV for a princely fee and came to

New York in late September 1899. But he soon quarreled with Astor and left New York to assist Shadwell Rafferty with an investigation in Minneapolis. What little Watson wrote about the Astor case can be found in Millett, *Secret Alliance*.

CHAPTER FOURTEEN

1. Orange Street is in Brooklyn, in the neighborhood directly across from Lower Manhattan known as Brooklyn Heights. The three-block-long street is just south of the approaches to the Brooklyn Bridge. Perhaps the street's most famous building is Plymouth Church of the Pilgrims (originally Plymouth Congregational Church), which was built in 1849. Despite its austere appearance, Plymouth was for many years one of the nation's most influential churches, most notably under the leadership of its great abolitionist preacher, Henry Ward Beecher, who was pastor from 1847 until his death in 1887.

CHAPTER FIFTEEN

1. Union Square, along Broadway between East Fourteenth and East Seventeenth streets, appeared in city plans—as Union Place—as early as 1807 but was not developed into a public park until the 1830s. By 1850, it was surrounded by fashionable houses and hotels. Later, as Manhattan's wealthy classes migrated north, theaters and restaurants filled in the neighborhood, along with retail stores. However, some of these businesses had already begun to move away by 1900. *King's Handbook of New York*, which Watson mentions, noted in 1893 that Union Square was "a favored place for large outdoor mass meetings." Rebuilt several times, most recently in 1986, Union Square is today a National Historic Landmark. The equestrian statue of George Washington, which dates to 1856, was sculpted by Henry Kirke Brown and J. Q. A. Ward. Architect Richard Upjohn designed the pedestal. There were a number of other sculptures in the park, including one of Lafayette by Frederic Auguste Bartholdi, best known as the creator of the Statue of Liberty.

2. The "tall, craggy building" Watson mentions here is almost certainly the Dakota Apartments at 1 West 72nd Street. Built in

1884, the Dakota was New York's first luxury apartment house and remains a prestigious address to this day. The Dakota has a large courtyard that perfectly fits the description given by Watson.

3. Watson's mention here of Holmes's fondness for "motor cars" is fascinating, since the detective was not otherwise known to be especially interested in automobiles. In 1900, automobiles were still a relative rarity in New York City, although they were growing in popularity every year. The first automobile in the city appeared in 1895 and was owned by the financier James B. ("Diamond Jim") Brady. Four years later, the city recorded its first fatal automobile accident. Many more were to follow. See Lardner and Reppetto, *NYPD*, 152.

4. Grant's Tomb (officially the General Grant National Memorial) opened in 1897, twelve years after the death of its principal occupant, Ulysses S. Grant. Some 90,000 people worldwide contributed $600,000 toward construction of the tomb, designed by architect John H. Duncan, who won a competition for the project. The tomb, North America's largest mausoleum, was refurbished at a cost of $1.8 million in 1997 and now attracts about 100,000 visitors annually. It is operated by the National Park Service. For more on the tomb's provenance, see Stern, Gilmartin and Massengale, *New York 1900*, 121–23. Watson's reference to being "of some service to" President William McKinley "only recently in Minneapolis" concerns events of October 1899 described in Millett, *Secret Alliance*.

5. Julia Dent Grant died in 1902 and now lies next to her husband in the sarcophagus mentioned by Watson.

6. The injured guard Watson encountered in the tomb was almost certainly not a soldier, but was probably either a moonlighting New York policeman or a private guard hired by the Grant Monument Association, which maintained the tomb until it was transferred to the National Park Service in 1959.

7. The "new automatic" referred to here was undoubtedly the Colt model 1900 automatic pistol. The .38 caliber weapon, with a six-inch barrel, held seven shots in its magazine. It was manufactured between 1900 and 1903, when Colt introduced an improved model.

8. The "large buildings" Watson saw were presumably St. Luke's Hospital (1892–96), on 113th Street and, next to it, the wonderfully named Home for Old Men and Aged Couples

(1897). The hospital, although much modified, remains standing today. The "ruins" Watson cites were in fact the early phases of the Cathedral Church of St. John the Divine, begun in 1892 and still under construction. It should also be noted that Ninth Avenue is today called Columbus Avenue. For more on the development of the Morningside Heights area of Manhattan, see Stern, Gilmartin and Massengale, *New York 1900*, 396–419.

9. "Suicide Curve," also known as "Angels Curve," was one of the wonders of turn-of-the-century Manhattan. The curve's sixty-foot-high trestle was necessary to maintain the grade of the elevated line as it went from the island's western ridges across the Harlem valley. The Ninth (Columbus) Avenue elevated line was the first in New York (and the world, for that matter). Construction began in Lower Manhattan in 1867 and four years later the line reached Sixty-first Street. By 1881 the line extended all the way to 155th Street at the northern tip of the island. Three other major elevated lines—on Second, Third and Sixth avenues—were also built during the period in Manhattan, and the entire system, including connections, was essentially complete by 1891. The opening of Manhattan's first subway line in 1904 gradually doomed the els. The Ninth Avenue line closed for good in 1940 and the tracks were torn down a year later. For an account of a ride on the Ninth Avenue el in 1881, see Clifton Hood, *722 Miles: The Building of the Subways and How They Transformed New York* (New York: Simon & Schuster, 1993), 51–53. For a large-scale photograph of "Suicide Curve," see Black, *Old New York*, 202. There is also a good account of the els in Edwin G. Burrows and Mike Wallace, *Gotham: A History of New York City to 1898* (New York: Oxford University Press, 1999), 1053–58.

10. There was an elevated station at 110th Street for many years, but old photographs suggest that it was not built until sometime after Watson's visit to the area in 1900.

CHAPTER SIXTEEN

1. The Planter's Hotel was for many years a downtown St. Louis institution. Founded in the early nineteenth century, the hotel by 1900 was in its third home—a large building at Fourth

and Pine streets built in 1894. Both the hotel and the building are now gone.

2. For more on Rafferty's friend Majesty Burke see Millett, *Secret Alliance*, 21–24.

CHAPTER SEVENTEEN

1. Many of the stations on the Ninth Avenue el were in a curious Swiss chalet style, apparently for no other reason than that the draftsman employed by the line's chief engineer hailed from Switzerland. Despite their rather odd appearance, the stations were nicely fitted out with mahogany paneling and leather seats. For a picture of one of these stations, see Elizabeth McCausland, *New York in the Thirties as Photographed by Berenice Abbott* (New York: Dover, 1973), pl. 39.

2. As Watson points out here, the Ninth Avenue el was still using small steam locomotives in 1900, despite the noise, stink and soot they produced. The locomotives ended their service in 1903 when the entire line was finally electrified.

3. Richard Croker (1841–1922) was an Irish-born pugilist, gang leader and politician who in 1886 became the boss of Tammany Hall in New York City and held power for fifteen years amid the usual carnival of corruption. During his storied career, he was accused of at least one murder but got off, in part because of the convenient fact that he happened to be serving as the city's coroner at the time. One contemporary described Croker as a man with "a strong frame, a deep chest, a short neck and a pair of hard fists. . . . He speaks in monosyllables and commands a vocabulary that appears to be limited to about three hundred words." Nonetheless, he was considered to be among Tammany Hall's most brilliant leaders. He fled the city in 1894 during a corruption investigation but returned in 1897 to resume his position of leadership. He was finally ousted from power in 1901 and thereafter retired to Ireland, where he raised horses and donated some of his ill-gotten gains to philanthropic causes. For a good account of Croker's career, see Oliver E. Allen, *The Tiger: The Rise and Fall of Tammany Hall* (Reading, Mass.: Addison-Wesley, 1993), 170–205.

CHAPTER EIGHTEEN

1. The Creedmoor rifle was made between about 1873 and 1890 and is regarded as one of the finest rifles ever produced by the Remington Arms Company. Only a few hundred of the Creedmoors were made and can command prices of over $6,000 today. The weapon took its name from a rifle range maintained by the National Rifle Association near the village of Creedmoor, on Long Island about fifteen miles from New York City. For a brief account of the Creedmoor range in the late nineteenth century, see James D. McCabe, Jr., *New York by Gaslight* (Philadelphia: Hubbard Brothers, 1882; New York: Crown Publishers, 1984), 527–29.

2. There are brief mentions of Harry Varnell, a well-known Chicago gambling boss in the late nineteenth century, in Herbert Asbury, *Gem of the Prairie: An Informal History of the Chicago Underworld* (New York: Alfred A. Knopf, 1940; DeKalb, Ill.: Northern Illinois University Press, 1986), 145–46, 159–60.

CHAPTER NINETEEN

1. The Battle of Maiwand, at which Watson fought and was wounded, occurred on July 27, 1880, in southern Afghanistan. The British forces were defeated, with heavy losses, and forced to retreat to their base in Kandahar. Watson was saved from death by an orderly who managed to bring him back to the British lines on a packhorse.

CHAPTER TWENTY-ONE

1. The "sunburst ornament" (known as a "glory") that Watson notes here is one of the most famous features of St. Paul's Chapel. It was designed, as was the chapel's entire altar, by Pierre Charles L'Enfant, best known as the man who created the plan of Washington, D.C. There is a photograph of the glory in Kennedy, *American Churches*, 116.

2. Richard Montgomery (1736–75) was an Irish-born soldier who immigrated to America in 1773 after years of service in the British military. In 1775, as the Revolution began, he was ap-

pointed a general of the Continental Army. He was killed on December 31, 1775, while leading an attack on Quebec as part of an unsuccessful effort to dislodge British forces from Canada.

3. William Devery was one of those wonderfully colorful characters that New York City has always produced in abundance. A longtime policeman, he was discredited during one of the city's periodic corruption investigations in 1895. It appeared that his career was over, but he was mysteriously rehabilitated three years later and suddenly found himself chief of police. Known for his commanding presence and irascible temperament, Devery once fined a policeman a month's pay for "not hittin' nobody" after he was accused of recklessly firing his pistol. Devery left the police in 1901 after the election of a "reform" mayor and became a successful businessman whose enterprises included co-ownership of the city's first American League baseball franchise—a team that was to become known as the New York Yankees. For more on Devery and his times, see Lardner and Reppetto, *NYPD*.

CHAPTER TWENTY-TWO

1. For a picture of the Potomac Apartments, once located at Michigan Avenue and Thirtieth Street, see Larry A. Viskochil, *Chicago at the Turn of the Century in Photographs: 122 Historic Views from the Collections of the Chicago Historical Society* (New York: Dover, 1984), pl. 107.

2. Mike (Hinky Dink) Kenna and Bathhouse John Coughlin were indeed quite a pair of scoundrels, although Kenna appears to have been the brains of the outfit. It was Kenna, elected to the city council in 1897, who is said to have established the standard rate (fifty cents) for buying a vote in Chicago at the time. Called Hinky Dink because of his small stature, Kenna tended to operate in the shadows while the flamboyant Coughlin kept up public appearances. Coughlin was famous not only for his wild attire but also for his love of publicity. Perhaps the most amazing thing about Kenna and Coughlin is that both managed to die at home of old age (Coughlin in 1938, Kenna some years later)—no mean feat for Chicago gangsters of the period. For more on the duo, see Asbury, *Gem of the Prairie*, 276–80.

3. For a brief sketch of the Everleigh sisters and a detailed description of their famous brothel, said to have cost $200,000 to furnish, see Asbury, *Gem of the Prairie,* 247–55.

CHAPTER TWENTY-THREE

1. The "Selkirk" Watson refers to here was an English sailor named Alexander Selkirk who was at the center of one of the greatest sea yarns of all time. In 1704, after arguing with the captain of the privateer on which he served, the stubborn Selkirk was put ashore, at his own request, on the remote, uninhabited island of Juan Fernandez, located hundreds of miles off the coast of Chile. Another ship finally rescued Selkirk five years later. Selkirk's story, much embellished, became the basis of Daniel Defoe's classic novel, *Robinson Crusoe,* published in 1719. For a full account of Selkirk's saga, see Diana Souhami, *Selkirk's Island: The True and Strange Adventures of the Real Robinson Crusoe* (New York: Harcourt, 2001).

CHAPTER TWENTY-FOUR

1. The *Pennsylvania Limited* was introduced in 1881 and remained the Pennsylvania Railroad's elite New York to Chicago train until 1902, when the faster *Pennsylvania Special* (which later evolved into the legendary *Broadway Limited*) was introduced. The huge Exchange Street station in Jersey City opened in 1892 and was a combination ferry terminal and rail station. Rail travelers in and out of Manhattan used the station until 1910, when the first Pennsylvania Station was completed in Manhattan, a massive project that, among other things, involved building a tunnel under the Hudson River. For more on the Exchange Street station, see Carl Condit, *The Port of New York: A History of the Rail and Terminal System from the Beginnings to Pennsylvania Station* (Chicago: University of Chicago Press, 1980), 152–68. So-called Atlantic-type locomotives were developed in 1888 and featured four large drive wheels and six smaller wheels (four in front and two in back) in a 4-4-2 arrangement. Atlantic locomotives were especially popular for fast passenger trains and some models built in

the early twentieth century were designed to run at well over 100 miles an hour.

2. The book by Dr. Franz Hartmann that Holmes had read was titled *Buried Alive* and was published in Boston in 1895. It contained a collection of lurid—and largely apocryphal—stories about people who suffered the misfortune stated in its title. For more on Hartmann and the fear of premature burial, see Jan Bondeson, *Buried Alive: The Terrifying History of Our Most Primal Fear* (New York: W. W. Norton, 2001).

3. Little is known about the "bizarre affair of Lord Huntington's blue toes" other than that Watson briefly mentioned the case in a journal entry from October 12, 1898. In the entry, Watson states that "Holmes has come upon a most ingenious solution to the case that began with Lord Huntington's blue toes. Phenobarbital, Holmes believes, played a key role in the business, and he is now conducting chemical tests in hopes of confirming his hypothesis."

CHAPTER TWENTY-FIVE

1. Tammany Hall grew out of the Tammany Society, founded in New York City during the Revolutionary War. Its name supposedly came from Tamanend, a sachem (chief) of the Delaware Indians in the late seventeenth century, and Indian names were incorporated into many of Tammany's operations. Its headquarters, for example, were known as the wigwam. Over the next twenty-five years, the organization evolved into an immensely powerful, and notoriously corrupt, political machine that dominated New York City politics for much of the nineteenth century and well into the twentieth as well. For more information, see Allen, *The Tiger.*

CHAPTER TWENTY-SIX

1. The bridge Elsie Cubitt saw under construction was the so-called Rockville Bridge, just north of Harrisburg, Pennsylvania. It replaced an iron bridge built on the site in 1877. The new bridge, with forty-eight identical masonry arches spanning a total

of 3,830 feet, opened in 1902 and remains to this day the longest stone arch railroad bridge in the world. For a dramatic photograph of the bridge, see David Plowden, *Bridges: The Spans of North America* (New York: W. W. Norton, 1974), 26–27.

CHAPTER TWENTY-SEVEN

1. The Brooklyn Heights neighborhood, with its proximity to Manhattan and its superb views across the East River, began developing as a middle-class residential district in the 1820s and today remains one of New York City's most desirable places to live. Joralemon Street is near the southern edge of Brooklyn Heights and is a main east-west thoroughfare. A number of the oldest homes in Brooklyn Heights, dating to the 1830s, are located along Joralemon.

2. Henry Street runs in a north-south direction more or less down the middle of Brooklyn Heights and terminates at the approaches to the Brooklyn Bridge.

3. The Brooklyn Bridge, which opened in 1883, remains one of New York City's great icons. With a main span of nearly 1,600 feet, it was at that time by far the longest suspension bridge in the world. It held that honor until 1903, when the Williamsburg Bridge (longer by a mere four feet) opened less than two miles to the north across the East River. All manner of trains and trolleys crossed the Brooklyn Bridge at various times. Cable cars were the first to be used, but they proved inadequate and trains pulled by steam locomotives were later substituted, especially for late-night runs. In 1898, new tracks were added to the bridge to accommodate electric trolleys. At the same time, el trains were thrown into the mix, running on the cable car tracks for much of the day (although the cable cars continued to be used during rush hours until about 1908). The "small trains" Watson refers to here were presumably the el trains that operated all night. For good historic photographs of the bridge and its many kinds of rail transport, see Mary J. Shapiro, *A Picture History of the Brooklyn Bridge* (New York: Dover, 1983).

4. Beach's pneumatic subway was formally unveiled on February 26, 1870, and instantly became a huge sensation. Over

400,000 people rode the subway during its first year of operation. Some sources suggest that the cost was a quarter, not five cents, as Hargreave told Watson. In either case, the subway was an unqualified success, at least in terms of ridership. Beach himself was a fascinating character. Born in 1826 in Massachusetts, he was the son of Moses Yale Beach, founder of the New York *Sun*. At the age of twenty, in 1846, Alfred borrowed money to buy a small, newly created journal called *Scientific American*. Beach went on to edit the magazine for fifty years, until his death in 1896. He was also a classic Yankee tinkerer, with a number of inventions to his credit, including a typewriter for the blind. There are many accounts of Beach and his subway. One of the best is in Hood, *722 Miles*, 42–48.

5. "The Western Tornado" apparently took its name from the fact that it was manufactured in Indiana, which to a New Yorker would qualify as the West. The fifty-ton fan, which could produce 100,000 cubic feet of air a minute, was so massive that a special train was required to bring it to New York City.

6. William Marcy Tweed (1823–78), head of the notorious Tweed Ring, which systematically looted New York City's treasury in the late 1860s and early 1870s, was finally ousted from power in 1871 following a series of investigations. This cleared the way for Beach to obtain a charter from the state to expand his subway. However, various obstacles—both technological and financial—finally doomed the project. The subway was shut down in 1874 and the tunnel was eventually sealed and forgotten. It wasn't formally "rediscovered" until 1912 when construction workers digging a new subway accidentally ran into it.

7. For an excellent account of the domed *World* Building, which at the time of its completion in 1890 was New York City's foremost skyscraper, see Landau and Condit, *New York Skyscraper*, 197–201. Joseph Pulitzer's private office was on the second level of the dome, enabling him literally to look down on all of his competitors along Newspaper Row. The *World* itself died in 1931 but the building stood until 1955, when it was razed to make way for wider approaches to the Brooklyn Bridge.

8. For a good photograph of the Devlin Store, long since demolished, see Black, *Old New York*, 52.

9. Hargreave's recollections of the furnishings in the subway's waiting room are accurate, right down to the goldfish tank. Other accoutrements included a grandfather's clock and a fountain. See Hood, *722 Miles*, 46.

CHAPTER TWENTY-EIGHT

1. Horseshoe Curve, now a national historic landmark, is still used today by Conrail freight trains. A visitor center, complete with a small funicular railway leading up to the top of the curve, was completed in 1992. The curve continues to attract rail fans from around the world. For a complete history of the curve, see Dan Cupper, *Horseshoe Heritage: The Story of a Great Railroad Landmark* (Halifax, Penn.: Withers Publishing, 1992).

2. Although freight trains almost always required a helper engine to ascend and descend the curve's 1.8 percent grade (steep by railroad standards), this was not always the case with lighter passenger trains. However, old photographs suggest that some passenger trains did indeed employ two engines around the curve, and I have assumed this was the case with the *Pennsylvania Limited*.

3. The tunnel referred to here is known as the Allegheny Tunnel and was built by the Pennsylvania Railroad in 1854 at Gallitzin, about four miles west of Horseshoe Curve. At the time, it was the longest railroad tunnel in the world. The 3,600-foot tunnel is at an elevation of 2,167 feet—the highest point along the line. A second tunnel was completed next to the Allegheny Tunnel in 1904. The twin tunnels remain in use today.

4. There appear to have been four sets of tracks at Horseshoe Curve in 1900, reflecting the heavy use it received as the Pennsylvania Railroad's main route over the Allegheny Mountains. Although the curve still sees plenty of train traffic, the level had dropped sufficiently over the years to permit the removal of one set of tracks in 1981.

5. In 1900 the standard spacing between sets of railroad tracks was generally about eleven feet. Given the dimensions of railroad cars of that era, this would have left somewhere in the neighborhood of four to five feet between passing cars—a hazardous leap, to be sure, but not beyond the realm of possibility.

Today, the minimum distance between tracks is usually thirteen to fourteen feet.

CHAPTER TWENTY-NINE

1. The Chelsea neighborhood in Manhattan is bounded roughly by Fourteenth and Twenty-eighth streets, and Tenth and Seventh avenues, although it originally extended all the way west to the Hudson River. The neighborhood long had a Bohemian reputation but in recent years has undergone steady gentrification of its many handsome townhouses. One of the neighborhood's most famous natives was Clement Moore (1779–1863), grandson of the man who named the neighborhood and today most famous as the author of the poem "A Visit from St. Nicholas" (also known as "The Night Before Christmas").

2. Watson served in Afghanistan in 1880 as an assistant surgeon for the Fifth Northumberland Fusiliers during what was known as the Second Afghan War. He suffered a bullet wound (either in the shoulder or the leg, depending on which version of the story is to be believed) at the Battle of Maiwand. Watson often spoke, not always fondly, of his experiences in Afghanistan.

3. There were three ferry stations along the Hudson River in Manhattan that transported passengers to the Pennsylvania Railroad's station in Jersey City. The Twenty-third Street station was the farthest north. The others were in Lower Manhattan at Desbrosses Street and Cortlandt Street. See Condit, *Port of New York*, 153, for more details.

CHAPTER THIRTY

1. The city of Altoona was founded by the Pennsylvania Railroad in 1849 and contained huge locomotive shops. It was therefore one of the main hubs along the New York to Chicago route. The station mentioned here was a rather grim-looking affair built around 1890.

2. According to an 1897 Pennsylvania Railroad schedule, the *Western Express* made the run from Altoona to Chicago in about eighteen hours and twenty-five minutes. The *Pennsylvania Limited*

went the same distance—with the same number of stops (at Johnstown, Pittsburgh and Fort Wayne)—in fifteen hours and ten minutes.

CHAPTER THIRTY-ONE

1. The first Sherman House, at Clark and Randolph streets, was built in 1845 and named after its owner, Francis C. Sherman, who later became a mayor of Chicago. A new hotel building was erected on the same site in 1861 but was destroyed in the Chicago Fire ten years later. The third Sherman House, where Watson stayed, opened in 1872 and was designed by prominent Chicago architect William Boyington. It was a seven-story affair, vaguely French Second Empire in style, and it survived until 1910, when it was replaced by yet a fourth hotel building of the same name. This last Sherman House closed in 1973. The State of Illinois Building now occupies the site. For photographs of the various Sherman Houses, see David Lowe, *Lost Chicago* (Boston: Houghton Mifflin, 1978), 114–15. The Chicago Loop takes its name from the elevated tracks that circle around the heart of downtown and remain one of the city's most distinctive features. The Loop was completed in 1897 by Chicago's magnificently devious "traction king," Charles Tyson Yerkes (1837–1905), in an atmosphere of bribery and corruption that was exceedingly ripe even by Chicago's exalted standards. According to one calculation, a particularly difficult 4,000-foot section of the Loop cost Yerkes twice as much in bribes as it did in actual construction costs. For more details, see David M. Young, *Chicago Transit: An Illustrated History* (DeKalb, Ill.: Northern Illinois University Press, 1998), 59–62.

2. Chicago had six major railroad stations serving intercity passengers in 1900: La Salle Street Station, Dearborn (or Polk) Street Station, Chicago and Northwestern Station, Grand Central Station, Illinois Central Station and Union Station, where Watson arrived from New York. There were also smaller stations for local commuters. No other city in America could boast of so many stations.

3. The Hotel St. Benedict Flats, at Wabash and Chicago av-

enues, dates from 1882 and appears to have been more of an apartment building than a hotel, despite its name. It was built as a series of "French flats" (essentially, one-story apartments) but may have had some transient rooms. It's curious that Rafferty would have stayed there, although it's worth noting that the St. Benedict was designed by James J. Egan, who was also architect of the Ryan Hotel, where Rafferty lived in St. Paul. That connection may explain why Rafferty chose to stay at the St. Benedict rather than one of Chicago's numerous downtown hotels. For a photograph of the building, which at last report was still extant, see *AIA Guide to Chicago,* ed. Alice Sinkevitch (New York: Harcourt Brace, 1993), 125.

4. The *Chicago Tribune,* founded in 1847, was indeed a "respected paper," as Watson noted. Under the distinguished editorship of Joseph Medill (1823–99), the *Tribune* had by the turn of the century become one of the nation's leading newspapers, noted for its thorough coverage of events and its rock-ribbed Republicanism.

5. The area known as "Bed Bug Row" was located at the northern edge of the Levee, near West Nineteenth and Federal streets. Today, the area lies near the heart of Chicago's Chinatown. See Asbury, *Gem of the Prairie,* 264.

Chapter Thirty-two

1. Joseph Pyle's 1894 trip to London is described in Millett, *Red Demon,* 2–13.

2. For more on Hill's fishing lodge, which he generally visited at least once a year, see Albro Martin, *James J. Hill and the Opening of the Northwest* (New York: Oxford University Press, 1976; St. Paul: Minnesota Historical Society Press, 1991), 531, 588.

3. The Chicago Civic Federation was formed in 1894 at the behest of William T. Stead, an Englishman who had come to Chicago for the World's Fair only to be astounded by the city's blatant corruption and immorality. He soon published a book, *If Christ Came to Chicago!,* that aroused a good deal of public indignation over this sorry state of affairs. The federation took on, with limited success, the city's flourishing vice trade but was

never able to turn Chicago into "the model city of the world"—the goal Stead had outlined in his messianic book. Stead himself lived his ideals. He went down on the *Titanic* in 1912, and was last seen, according to one historian, "loading women and children into lifeboats." For more on Stead and the federation, see Donald L. Miller, *City of the Century: The Epic of Chicago and the Making of America* (New York: Simon & Schuster, 1996), 533–39.

4. Great Yarmouth is a popular seaside resort in Norfolk, located about twenty miles southeast of North Walsham. It would thus have been within easy reach of Elsie Cubitt's home at Ridling Thorpe Manor.

5. Harrison Street is in the southern part of the Chicago Loop and was for many years the location of the large police station where Clifton Wooldridge was based.

6. The revolver Elsie Cubitt found was probably a Colt New Pocket Double Action revolver. This weapon, which came with barrels anywhere from two and a half to six inches long, was manufactured between 1893 and 1905 and was the first in a long line of similar revolvers made by Colt.

CHAPTER THIRTY-THREE

1. The city hall building Watson refers to here was a grandiose, Renaissance-inspired pile that took twelve years to build, finally opening in 1885 at a cost of five million dollars. Critics questioned the cost, but its defenders argued that it was expensive only because it had been built for the ages. As it turned out, however, the "ages" in a dynamic city like Chicago proved to be very short, and the building—designed by the prolific James J. Egan—was demolished in 1908. See Lowe, *Lost Chicago*, 8.

2. The 1,600-foot Washington Street tunnel, built in 1869, was one of two tunnels under the Chicago River in the Loop. The other, finished in 1871, was at La Salle Street. The tunnels were built because heavy boat traffic on the river often blocked bridges, which all had to be lift or swing structures of some kind because of the city's extremely flat terrain and the river's low banks. Both tunnels were lowered in about 1906 when the river was deepened to improve navigation, but flooding problems

eventually forced them to close. See Libby Hill, *The Chicago River: A Natural and Unnatural History* (Chicago: Lake Claremont Press, 2000), 93–95.

3. Union Station, at Canal and Adams streets, was built in 1871 and was already overcrowded by 1900. It was replaced in 1923 by a much larger station, which still stands.

4. The "Graceland" mentioned by Rafferty is Graceland Cemetery on North Clark Street in Chicago. Founded in 1860, the cemetery contains the graves of many of Chicago's most illustrious citizens as well as tombs designed by some of its finest architects.

CHAPTER THIRTY-FOUR

1. In 1899 Coughlin wrote a poem called "Dear Midnight of Love" that—no doubt because of his political influence—was set to music and became a popular song. The chorus was as follows: "Dear Midnight of Love, why did we meet? Dear Midnight of Love, your face is so sweet. Pure as angels above, surely again we will speak; loving only as doves, Dear Midnight of Love." Coughlin's talents obviously did not lie in the realm of poetry. For more details, see Asbury, *Gem of the Prairies*, 280.

CHAPTER THIRTY-FIVE

1. Rafferty's pocket rifle—basically a long-barreled pistol with a detachable stock—was a customized version of the New Model Pocket Rifle No. 40, first manufactured in about 1896 by the Stevens Arms Company of Chicopee Falls, Massachusetts. His pistol was probably a Smith & Wesson—the handgun he seems to have preferred above all others. Rafferty was a great collector of weaponry and left behind over a hundred pistols, shotguns and rifles at his death in 1928, according to records at the Ramsey County Probate Court in St. Paul.

2. The "Alley El" was built by the Chicago and South Side Rapid Transit Company, beginning in 1892, to serve the huge crowds anticipated for the 1893 World's Fair. As Rafferty states, much of the elevated line ended up running through alleys be-

cause the cost of obtaining street rights was prohibitively expensive under state law, which required the consent of affected property owners. Such consent could be had but only for a steep price, as builders of the Loop el later discovered. To get around this obstacle, the Chicago and South Side simply bought its own alleys and built much of its line along them. See Young, *Chicago Transit*, 57.

3. Holmes's and Watson's earlier tour of the Levee is described in Millett, *Ice Palace Murders*, 4–5.

CHAPTER THIRTY-SIX

1. John R. Tanner (1844–1901) served as governor of Illinois from 1897 to 1901, dying just four months after he left office. A longtime Republican Party stalwart who later became state party chairman, Tanner won the 1896 gubernatorial election in a landslide over the incumbent, Democrat John Altgeld (1847–1902). Altgeld had incurred public wrath for pardoning three of the men convicted in connection with the 1886 Haymarket Riot in Chicago and for protesting the use of federal troops to break the 1894 strike against the Pullman Company in Chicago. James J. Hill was not yet a big player on the Chicago railroad scene in 1900 but was soon to be. In 1901, after a struggle with another rail tycoon, Edward H. Harriman, Hill acquired the Chicago, Burlington and Quincy Railroad to add to his Great Northern and Northern Pacific. However, he was forced to operate the Burlington as an independent line as a result of a 1904 anti-trust decision by the U.S. Supreme Court.

CHAPTER THIRTY-SEVEN

1. Rafferty served with the famous First Minnesota Regiment of Volunteers, which fought at numerous Civil War battles, including First Bull Run, Antietam and, most notably, Gettysburg, where he received the Medal of Honor. For more on Rafferty's military service, see Millett, *Ice Palace Murders*, 155–57. See also Richard Moe, *The Last Full Measure: The Life and Death of the First Minnesota Volunteers* (New York: Henry Holt, 1993; St. Paul: Minnesota Historical Society Press, 2000).

2. The fire Holmes refers to here is, of course, the great fire of October 8–10, 1871. There's still debate about how the fire started, but there's no question where it began. The flash point was about a mile southwest of downtown in a barn behind Patrick O'Leary's home on DeKoven Street (a site that, fittingly, is now home to the Chicago Fire Academy). Abetted by tinder-dry conditions and sixty-mile-an-hour winds, the blaze quickly spread through the heart of what was then a largely wood-built city of 300,000 people. The fire consumed virtually everything in its path, including most of the central business district, before finally burning itself out against the shores of Lake Michigan. All told, the fire claimed at least 250 lives, left another 100,000 people homeless and destroyed nearly $200 million worth of property (including over 17,000 buildings). What is not so well-known is that at the same time, a far larger and deadlier fire 150 miles to the north blazed through the Wisconsin logging community of Pestigo, near Green Bay. That fire killed an estimated 1,100 people, or about half the population of Pestigo, making it the most lethal forest fire in American history. Much of the timber that fed the flames was owned by Chicago lumbermen. For a brief, nicely illustrated account of the Chicago Fire, see Harold M. Mayer and Richard C. Wade, *Chicago: Growth of a Metropolis* (Chicago: University of Chicago Press, 1969), 103–16.

CHAPTER THIRTY-EIGHT

1. French Em's and Van Bever's were two of among six or seven brothels that occupied the same block as the Everleigh Club. Some sources estimate that there were as many as 1,000 brothels and 5,000 prostitutes in the Levee district around the turn of the century, producing $60 million a year in revenues. Wooldridge, who knew the Levee as well as anyone, once described its blatantly libidinous milieu this way: "Here at all hours of the day and night women could be seen at the doors and windows, frequently half-clad, making an exhibition of themselves and using vulgar and obscene language." Quoted in Miller, *City of the Century,* 508.

2. Wooldridge's skills at self-promotion were as legendary as his detective work. When not busy dressing in exotic disguises or

capturing various crooks, Wooldridge found time to write at least two potboiling books: *The Devil and the Grafter* and the marvelously titled *Hands Up! In the World of Crime: or 12 Years a Detective*. Not a man to be excessively burdened by modesty, Wooldridge wrote of himself in *The Devil and the Grafter* that "no braver, more honest or efficient police officer ever wore a star or carried a club." For more on Wooldridge's exploits, see Asbury, *Gem of the Prairie*, 124–29.

3. The Levee district did in fact gradually fade away in the early years of the twentieth century in response to increased public and official opposition to its open vice trade. The Everleigh Club, for example, was finally shut down in 1911 by Mayor Carter Harrison Jr. The mayor, who does not appear to have been a doe-eyed idealist, said he decided to close the famous resort "because of its infamy, the audacious advertising of it, and as a solemn warning that the (Levee) district had to be at least half-way decent." However, establishments that were presumably "half-way decent" continued to operate for many more years. For more on the battle to shut down the Levee, see Asbury, *Gem of the Prairie*, 281–311.

CHAPTER THIRTY-NINE

1. The intersection of Dearborn and Twenty-first streets, where Hibernia Hall was located, no longer exists. Both streets were vacated in this area to make way for the Raymond M. Hilliard Center, a large housing complex completed in 1966 that includes four towers in a parklike setting.

CHAPTER FORTY

1. Chicago owes its existence to the peculiar geography of the little river that bears its name. The earliest explorers of the area discovered, as Native Americans had long known, that only a very short portage (and in wet weather, no portage at all) separated the Chicago River—which originally flowed to Lake Michigan— from the Des Plaines River. The Des Plaines in turn led into the Illinois River and then down to the Mississippi River, creating an invaluable connection to the heart of the continent. The first exploitation of this natural link occurred in 1836 with the construc-

tion of the Indiana and Michigan Canal, which eliminated the seasonal portage. This work also intermittently switched the river's flow. But it was not until 1900, with the completion of the much deeper and larger Chicago Sanitary and Ship Canal—the largest earth-moving project in the nation's history up to that time—that the flow was permanently reversed. The new canal, which cost the then-astounding sum of $33 million, was designed not only for navigation but to keep Chicago from choking on its own filth, since the pumping of sewage into Lake Michigan had endangered the city's water supply. With the new canal, Chicago, which had grown from 300,000 people in 1870 to a population of almost 1.7 million in 1900, was literally able to flush its toilets to the Mississippi. There is a detailed description of the canal project in Hill, *Chicago River*, 123–35. It should also be noted that the eastern loop of the river described here was eliminated in 1929 when the river was straightened to free up badly needed land.

2. For a description of Holmes's first meeting with Mary Robinson, see Millett, *Red Demon*, 89–106.

3. Holmes's reintroduction to Mary Robinson—then going by the name of Mary Comstock—can be found in Millett, *Rune Stone Mystery*, 69–78.

4. Jicky perfume, made by the French firm of Guerlain, was introduced in 1889. Its use of synthetic oils made it one of the first perfumes to be considered "modern" by today's standards.

5. There is a good overview of the gruesome guerilla war in Missouri, as well as a brief account of "Bloody Bill" Anderson's depredations, in James M. McPherson, *Battle Cry of Freedom: The Civil War Era* (New York: Oxford University Press, 1988), 783–88.

6. The weapon carried by Mrs. Robinson must have been a Colt Third Model Derringer, introduced in about 1870 and in production for more than forty years thereafter. It had a two-and-a-half-inch barrel and was a very popular weapon in its time.

EPILOGUE

1. *Under the Clock,* a spoof written by Charles Brookfield and Seymour Hicks, is the earliest known play to feature the characters of Sherlock Holmes and Dr. John Watson. It opened on

November 25, 1893, in London, six years after the publication of *A Study in Scarlet,* the tale in which Holmes and Watson were introduced to the world by Sir Arthur Conan Doyle.

2. Louis Sherry opened his first Manhattan restaurant in 1890 in a mansion at Fifth Avenue and Thirty-seventh Street. In 1898 he moved his elegant establishment seven blocks up the avenue to Forty-fourth Street and into a new twelve-story building designed by the prominent architectural firm of McKim, Mead and White. The so-called Patriarchs, a group of twenty-five society nabobs picked from among Mrs. Caroline Astor's 400, dined at the restaurant. One of the most lavishly absurd dinners in New York City's history occurred at Louis Sherry's in 1903, when a Chicago millionaire treated thirty-six guests, all mounted on horseback, to an elaborate meal. A champagne bucket, it was said, hung over each horse's neck, and the final tab came to $50,000. For more on the restaurant, see Stern, Gilmartin and Massengale, *New York 1900,* 223–24.

AUTHOR'S NOTE

As with my four previous adventures featuring Sherlock Holmes, this book threads a fictional plot through a background fabric of fact. However, unlike my earlier tales—all set in Minnesota—*The Disappearance of Sherlock Holmes* is not based on any specific historic event, such as the Hinckley forest fire or the discovery of the Kensington rune stone.

Even so, I have done my best to insert Holmes, Watson and my cast of characters into realistic settings, whether in North Walsham, Liverpool, New York, Altoona or Chicago. This means that, wherever possible, I've put the characters on real ships and trains, in real buildings and on real streets to lend an air of authenticity to their adventures.

Thus, there truly was a huge liner called the *Oceania*, Manhattan did indeed have an elevated train running along Ninth Avenue with a "suicide curve" at 110th Street and an infamous brothel known as the Everleigh Club really did exist in Chicago's Levee district (also a genuine historic place). Alfred Beach's secret subway beneath Broadway, bizarre as it sounds, was also very real, although the extension to St. Paul's Chapel is pure fantasy on my part.

At least two important locales in this book are fictional, however. Ridling Thorpe Manor, of course, was invented by Sir Arthur Conan Doyle and briefly described in "The Adventure of the Dancing Men." I've tried to remain faithful to his description for the purposes of my tale. Another noteworthy fictional site in this book is the Sons of Hibernia Hall, which nonetheless is modeled on the sort of fraternal halls commonly found in American cities around 1900.

Many of the real places, buildings, trains and ships described in this book—the Manhattan els, the *Pennsylvania Limited*, the Levee district—are long gone, victims of time and progress. But much also remains from the world I've depicted here. Visitors today can still visit the Trials Hotel in Liverpool or look at the lovely little townhouses on Gay Street in Greenwich Village or watch freight trains (complete with helper engines) labor around Horseshoe Curve in the Pennsylvania mountains.

This book also mixes real and fictional characters. Among the genuine historic figures in this book are, in no particular order, James J. Hill, Joseph Pyle, Caroline Astor, William Devery, Bathhouse John Coughlin, John Tanner and Clifton Wooldridge. In general, I've tried to depict these characters as I think they might have been, but I make no great claims to historical accuracy.

Three other important characters—Elsie Cubitt, Abe Slaney and Wilson Hargreave—come, in name at least, from the pages of "The Adventure of the Dancing Men." Of these characters, only Slaney is somewhat developed in Doyle's tale but is dead by the time my story begins. On the other hand, Elsie Cubitt and Inspector Hargreave are given large new roles to play in *The Disappearance of Sherlock Holmes*, and I can only hope that Sir Arthur would approve.